The Paradise Planets

THE FALLEN FROM PARADISE

SHAUN BARROWES

EDITED BY
JENNIFER JENKINS

EDITED BY
JULIE FREDERICK

SHALOOR

Dear Reader:

The songs included in this manuscript are real, fully-orchestrated, produced songs featuring some of the best singers in the world. You can listen to the 9-song album online, on any music streaming platform. Choral arrangements, karaoke versions, sheet music, and more can be found on our website, www.paradiseplanets.com.

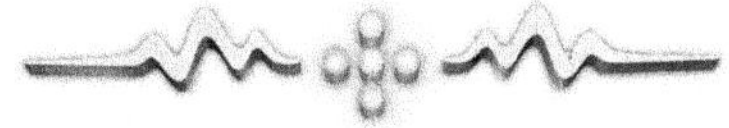

These worlds are the paradise we make them
Built by our innermost desires
These worlds are ours to break them
But why would anyone destroy Paradise?

- Leontari Rivernova

For Naomi,
My greatest supporter
and the real-life inspiration
behind the main character,
Kassiana Rivernova.
You'll always be my #1.

Contents

One

Even when fleeing for our lives, Ama's as calm as stillwater, Kassiana Rivernova chuckled.

This thought splashed across her mind as she cascaded down the stairs and spilled onto the grated steel platform. Just ahead, her cousin and best friend, Amára Rivernova, had delicately landed and bounded toward the exit without losing rhythm. She slowed her pace just long enough for Kassi to catch up. They weaved through armored vehicles, whisked past a pair of confused Nemalís Royal Guards, and burst out of the gated front entrance.

It was another beautiful day on Paradise as the morning daylight illuminated their surroundings, including all their usual hiding spots.

If we just get to the water, we'll give them a real chase!

Gavish Bay was only a few strides ahead. Heavy boots of soldiers drummed the path behind them. Throwing their laminated-glass helmets on, the auto lock sealing with a hiss, Kassi and Amára raced through thick underbrush to the mossy overhang and dove ten meters down into the crystal waters of the Bay. For Kassi, it wasn't a clean dive, but deep enough to grab some momentum.

Swimming two strokes beneath the surface, Kassi pushed forward as she mentally scanned her body for tension, found the source, and allowed it to release all while taking two deep breaths to regain control of her diaphragm. She belted a Haraki Hîm—a siren acceleration song—and lit up two of the five bulbs on her sonopack. Unsurprisingly, Amára had already lit four.

The thrusters on Kassi's feet ignited and propelled her through the clear blue water, her body straight as a torpedo. Amára did the same, but with four bulbs lit, she also had use of her hand thrusters and started to pull away.

"Wait for me!" Kassi shouted in Evéik between verses of her incantation.

Amára veered wide to peer behind her at Kassi who struggled to catch up. Amára slowed. *"Do you think they followed us?"* she asked.

"Should we check?" At this speed, they couldn't twist their bodies to look behind them without spinning out.

"We're probably far enough," Amára said. They lifted out of formation, whipped their feet forward as if reaching the end of a very long jump and forced a hard stop.

Suspended in the water, their eyes darted in all directions for any sign of their pursuers. Sunlight streaked the water giving them a clear view in all directions. There was no sign of the soldiers.

Kassi heaved an exaggerated sigh, *"Ghost of Sheebah, that was close!"* As trained sirens, they both forced slow, deep breaths to steady their breathing.

"Let's never do that again, Kassi," Amára said, turning off her thrusters and hovering in place with rhythmic flutter kicks.

"What? It's just the Nemalís Royal Guard." Kassi shrugged. *"What's the..."*

"Those were not Nemalís Royal Guard, Kassi. They were speaking English—like Gaians!" Amára, usually so self-assured, had a look of unnerving fear in her eyes. The same look Kassi's older brother, Caesar, had the day Kassi almost drowned. That was the

last time she had seen it, and that was eight years ago–when she was seven. Seeing it again, now in Amára's eyes, Kassi suddenly realized something was very wrong.

"Then who…" A flash of movement caught her eye–too quick to be marine life. Squinting, she spotted three soldiers torpedoing straight for them.

Amára's eyes followed Kassi's. She inhaled sharply as her face went pale. *"It's them!"*

Kassi's heart raced as she wondered who could possibly scare Amára like this. She tried singing, but her voice caught in her throat. Her sonopack coughed, already exhausted of all its energy. Without another incantation, she would be a floating whale carcass. Her arms flailed as she tried to move.

Amára had already powered her suit and blasted off, slicing through the water. *"Kassi? I can't see you! You with me?"*

"Ama! Help!" Kassi's mind rattled through her siren meditation exercises. She scanned her body for tension—everything was tense! So she tried to focus on the awareness of her surroundings—sight, smell, sound—it was all chaos. Nothing calmed her ragged pulse, not even the calming rhythm of their spoken Evéik. Uneven breathing prevented her from sustaining a single note that would power up her sonopack. Without it, Kassi's only option was to hide. Her eyes frantically swept the seabed for caverns.

There!

She dove, muscling herself downward in her pressurized wetsuit. Stroke after heavy stroke. She could almost reach the entrance. Her fingertips stretched to grab hold of the rocky lip when a strong hand lurched forward and seized her arm.

Kassi shrieked as she spun to face a square-headed man with a flattened nose and a face like a bucket of smashed crabs. Looking into his menacing eyes, Kassi kicked and squirmed to break free. He held on, his grip like carbon steel.

A woman with a brunette pixie bob and a weasel face caught up to him, swimming alongside and aiming a square-paneled, shoulder-mounted sonic cannon directly at Kassi's head. It wasn't the cannon they often used for sports–this one was military-grade, the kind that could cripple or even kill. The woman's mouth creased into a thin-lipped smile. Desperation swept over Kassi as she twisted, kicking against the man's chest with all her strength but she couldn't slip his grasp. The woman sent a high-frequency sonic pulse directly at Kassi. Thin as a needle, hot as white-blue flame, sound pierced the helmet and ruptured something in Kassi's throat.

An explosion of lightning pain flooded Kassi's body. Her neck was burning like fire, the rest of her body cold and pale as if on the brink of extinction. She gasped for air. Nothing came in. Her helmet was intact, her suit's gills still functioning. The air was around her, but her throat constricted and prevented it from filling her lungs. Kassi clutched her chest just below the helmet.

Amára sped into view and spotted Kassi, terror in her eyes. She rushed to her cousin, reaching out a hand. A third soldier intercepted, grabbing her and forcing her back. She was shouting something, but Kassi only heard muted tones above her own panicked thoughts. She saw the tears streaming down Amára's cheeks. Kassi's life was slipping away. With her last drip of consciousness, she wished she could apologize to Amára for dragging her to the Rosenbridge portal. It was all Kassi's idea.

Just as she was about to pass out from lack of oxygen, Kassi felt a cool stream of air trickle into her lungs. The swelling in her throat subsided just enough. Kassi wanted to quickly gulp down air, but her inflamed throat prevented it.

As if disappointed to see Kassi breathing again, the square-headed man lurched forward, unlatched Kassi's helmet, and ripped it off her head. Water flooded in before she could take one last indrawn breath.

Blurry vision blackened at the edges. Her body went limp as she stared at Amára's screaming face and thought of her final moments with her family. Her last words to her mother were spoken in anger. She would never get to say goodbye.

. . .

———————————

KASSIANA HEAVED for air as if she just crashed through the surface of the ocean. She blinked, feeling unease creeping in the darkness around her. With her face to the ground, sharp, broken tiles pricked the bare skin of her left cheek. Long, dark braids spilled across her face.

The fog in her head slowly cleared as she sat up, her eyes straining to make shapes in the diminishing darkness. She was in what appeared to be an abandoned church with high brick walls and an arched ceiling of dark woodwork dripping in fluorescent graffiti. The cold night sky slithered through broken stained-glass windows and a few gaping cracks in the walls and ceilings. Collapsed, wood-carved pews and altars littered the tiled floor. Trickling water echoed in the distance and an overpowering smell of stale urine filled her nose. It made her stomach wretch.

Her body gave a violent shiver. Even with her wetsuit on, it was freezing!

Sheist! Where's Amára?

That's when she noticed all the other teens strewn across the floor. A couple of them groaned back to life. Kassi propped herself up on her knees and squinted at the faces among the deep shadows, her vision blurred. Her gaze rapidly swept back and forth. She forced a deep breath and released the tension in her body. *Calm! I gotta find Amára.*

Scanning again, she spotted her—passed out on the chilled floor. "*Ama!*" Kassi tried calling out, her voice barely croaking a sound. She coughed to clear her throat.

Amára looked peaceful as she slept, completely oblivious. Her deep brown hair, a stylish razored comb-over bob, was beautifully tousled even now. Kassi patted her braids. They were a frayed mess. Kassi shook her friend's shoulder vigorously, and said in Evéik, *"Ama, wake up!"*

Amára stirred, groggy eyelids peeling open. She grimaced and focused her deep green eyes on Kassiana, such a beautiful contrast to her dark brown hair. *"Kassi?"*

Kassi sighed with relief. *"Ama! You with me?"* she tried to say, but her voice was so hoarse.

"Yisû," Amára sat up and studied Kassi in the darkness. *"What's wrong with your voice?"*

"My voice?" Kassi instinctively felt her throat. A cold chill crept up Kassi's neck as the image of the square-headed man and the woman with the sonic cannon fought through her hazy consciousness.

I drowned! How am I still alive?

Kassi heaved gulps of air as if she were still helmet-less underwater. Hands trembling, her body swayed back and forth, over and over again.

Amára apparently noticed the abrupt change. *"Kassi, you with me? Kassi?"* But her melodic words seemed so far away. Kassi was suddenly tiny–microscopic, surrounded by an infinite, encroaching darkness that swallowed her up.

It was like nothing she had ever experienced, as though someone else was in control of her body, and she was stuffed into the farthest corners of her mind. Panic swelled like an inflating balloon inside her chest.

Amára placed a gentle hand on Kassi's back and repeated, *"Breathe, Kassi. Just breathe. In and out."* The soothing touch provided a lifeline for Kassi to pull her back to her senses. Kassi listened, forcing the focus onto her breathing. After a few long minutes, her pulse evened out. The enveloping darkness subsided. Kassi resurfaced to find Amára beside her, a concerned look on her face.

"What happened?" Amára asked. Kassi shook her head, still focused on her labored breathing. Amára continued rubbing

Kassi's back as she surveyed their surroundings. *"Do you know where we are?"*

Kassi studied the room, steadying her pulse enough to answer, *"I think this is Earth! It's too filthy and rundown to be anywhere else."* Her raspy voice poked through the silence.

"Earth? How'd we get to Earth?" Amára said, her words naturally rhyming as they often did in Evéik. *"Last thing I remember, I followed you to the GDC's Rosenbridge portal."*

Their parents had left Kassi and Amára at Palace Rivernova while they looked into an incident in Viracocha on Planet Astera with the Nemalís Royal Guard. Even though they were specifically instructed to stay put at the palace, Kassi convinced Amára to trail behind to see if they could help, or at the very least watch and learn how their parents handled the situation.

"That's all you remember?" Kassi said. *"They must have narcotized you."* In her gravelly voice, Kassi tried recounting the traumatic experience to Amára without letting herself slip into a panic attack.

"Ghost of Sheebah! That really happened? I thought that was just a nightmare!" Amára said.

"I know," Kassi said, rubbing her throat.

"Kassi, I'm so sorry! I tried to help, but…" Her voice trailed off as she stared into space.

Kassi heard vague stirrings from others scattered across the church floor. Amára must have noticed it too. There were at least a dozen of them wearing full-body siren wetsuits like Amára and Kassi, boots and gloves included, with only their helmets and sonopacks missing. She thought she recognized most of them from school, but the dark shadows obscured their faces. As one of them rustled and sat up, Kassi identified Macks Sinclar-- always the tough cha in school, with muscles bulging out of his shirts. He was also the grandson of Catarine Fresia, one of the original founders of the Paradise Planets. Glancing at the others as they began to move, she soon saw their faces and realized they all had parents or grandparents on the Council of Creators, Paradise's governing body.

"How did we get here?" Macks massaged the side of his head as his eyes swept over his surroundings.

Kassi and Amára stood and quickly helped the others to their feet as they all shared what they last remembered.

"I was retrieving a loose disc that went out of bounds when an unfamiliar song blared in my helmet."

"My cousin and I were exploring the Gundah River when I heard a song."

"I was just swimming in the ocean outside our estate when I heard it."

"Shhh, quiet," said Ama. *"We were all abducted, narcotized, and brought here. And I highly doubt it's a coincidence our parents are all in the Council."*

"And they think they can keep us? We're Nemalís! And most of us are sirius sirens," Macks said, flexing.

"Without siren suits," Ama reminded them.

"That won't stop me," Macks said, marching to the door.

"Wait, this could be our only shot at escape," Amára said, rushing to reach the door first. *"We stick together!"* Macks nodded.

Leaning into the heavy wooden doors, Amára peeked her head outside. Kassi peered over her shoulder. No one in sight. They slipped out into the windy, moonless night.

"Where is everybody?" Kassi asked, shivering.

"Let's not wait to find out," Amára said as she padded down a wide, cement staircase that led straight into the water. Whatever street lay hidden beneath had since been swallowed up by the ocean's rising tides. There were no signs of life anywhere. Starlight frosted the vacant hills and rooftops.

Reaching the edge of the steps, Amára slid both legs into the water. She touched the bottom with the water almost reaching her knees. *"F-f-freezing!"* she said. Before anyone could follow, she was already sloshing ahead to scope out the area. Kassi jumped into the icy water and hurried to catch up.

"Maybe there's a Rosen-comm nearby," Kassi said to Amára.

"If there is, it'd be up this way," Amára pointed to buildings at the crest of a hill. They climbed up the slight incline out of the water to the top of the hill. With a better vantage point, they looked around. Whatever place this was, it clearly had been deserted for generations. They scoured the buildings in hopes of finding a working Rosen-comm device that would let them communicate with their home planet of Nemal, the first of the three Paradise Planets.

"There's gotta be a way back to the GDC!" Kassi croaked. *"Maybe we can find our helmets and sonopacks."*

Sonoluminescence packs—commonly known as "sonopacks" —each contained five metallic, spherical bulbs filled with heavy water. With a small glass window at the center, the bulbs looked like miniature, old marine diving helmets. These were mounted in a hydrodynamically shaped backpack that latched onto the back of a siren wetsuit. The siren suit helmets were made of armored glass that provided a full 360 view. At the base where the helmet was sealed to the suit, were the gills. This allowed the suits to breathe underwater by drawing the oxygen out of the water. Every sonopack had a built-in canteen, and a hydro-cask, with tubes, piped directly into the siren's helmet so they could drink water without having to remove their helmets.

"I doubt it. But maybe there's a boat." Amára waved them back toward the ocean.

A woman's voice from behind them made Kassi jump, causing her to slip into the mud. "Even if you did find a boat, where would you go?" She said in fluent English from the shadows, her voice rich and euphonic like a prized cello at the hands of a master. "This island's hundreds of kilometers from the nearest land, and you'd have to slip past all the U.N.O.E. yachts patrolling these waters." There was a ripple of electric snaps as at least a dozen people around them powered up siren wetsuits and beamed white spotlights on their patch of grass. Kassi shielded her eyes and blinked rapidly until they adjusted to the brightness. The night sky above was no longer visible and the facades of the surrounding houses were pocked with deep shadowy recesses.

A woman stepped forward into the light. She was a short, curvy woman with perfectly shaped eyebrows in an autumn-colored siren wetsuit. Her brown hair, a wavy cut with curtain bangs, fell to her shoulders. She wore a bronze pendant necklace around her neck. Something Kassi might see her grandmother wear and yet this woman couldn't have been over thirty. Her gaze swept over them, smiling with her chocolate brown eyes as if excited to meet them. Kassi and the others turned to run just as a cadre of heavily armed soldiers surrounded them, cutting off their escape.

They regrouped and turned to face the woman. Amára stepped forward, directly in front of Kassi as if to shield her. "Why have-eh you abducted us?"

The woman inhaled and raised both eyebrows as if offended. "Abducted? Oh, bless your little heart. We didn't abduct you. We brought you here as our guests."

"Don't listen to her, chas." Macks Sinclar said, jutting out his chin and folding his arms. "My father told me about her. This is Ravana, and she's raving ludicray!"

"There's no need to be cruel," Ravana said, a trace of anger hidden behind her controlled voice. "We brought you here to expose you to what's really going on. Despite what your parents think, you're old enough to know now."

"Know about what?" Kassi asked over Amára's shoulder.

Ravana eyed Kassi's burn mark on her neck, "You must be Kassiana." She took a step toward Kassi, but Amára sidestepped to cut her off. "I'm sorry for what they did to you. We revived you minutes after you passed out to avoid any permanent impairments," she paused as if waiting for a show of gratitude before continuing, "I told them explicitly you were not to be harmed. Rest assured those responsible will be dealt with." She cast a disapproving look at a few soldiers cowering in the shadows. It was the square-headed soldier and the woman who had blasted her with the sonic cannon. Despite the promise of repercussions, the woman still cast a wicked, sadistic smile at Kassi. Kassi fought down her inner trembling, her hands wringing each other tightly.

"So does that mean you'll heal my voice-eh?" Kassi asked, her hoarse voice quivering.

"Believe me I would," Ravana gave a sympathetic smile. Maybe it was even genuine. "Unfortunately none of us are skilled healers equipped to handle an operation like that."

"You said you brought us here to show us something?" Macks interrupted, scowling.

"Yisû. We're here to show you the deplorable conditions of the Gaians—the people of Earth," Ravana said, striding across the grass to face outward toward the ocean. "Gaians are surviving on poor food rations, living on top of each other. They're violently abused and enslaved by the U.N.O.E. Many of them like my father have died because...," Ravana's voice shook as if she were about to tear up. She paused to find her calm and continued, "Many die of common maladies your siren healers could easily cure. Meanwhile the Council of Creators, your parents," she turned to face them, "rule three large, wealthy planets and refuse to open the portal. You have more than enough space, food, siren healers, and resources to help them. I need your help to convince your parents to open the gates and free the Gaians."

"I thought they didn't want our help," Kassi said. Everyone knew Earth was a dilapidated planet, but Kassi had always been taught it was only because of their corruption, needless wars, and planetary negligence.

"Yisû, they hate-eh paradisers," Macks added.

"They only hate you because you don't help and because you

tax them for what little they do have," Ravana said, shaking her head.

"We don't tax them! Why would we?" Amára said. "We already have everything on Paradise-eh."

"Yisû, you do have everything. And why do you think that is?" Ravana asked. A few beats passed in silence as everyone considered this. Ravana continued, "This is why we brought you here. To show you the truth!"

"So once we see this, you'll let us go back home-eh?" Amára finally asked.

"I wish it were that simple," Ravana said, lifting her eyes at the soldiers around her. "All of us grew up on Earth. We had to train all our lives and battle against the toughest competition to finally win the Siren Games and earn our place on Paradise." The Siren Games was a global tournament held twice a year. Sixty-four teams composed of the universe's top underwater athletes ages eighteen and under, known as "sirens", came together from all across Earth to compete in three elimination rounds before facing off in the fourth and final round, the Ship Races. The first four teams to finish the race earned a place for themselves and their families on the Paradise Planets. "That's the only way any of us ever had a chance of living on one of your Paradise Planets. Not only is it unfair. It's dangerous! People have died in the Games!"

"But aren't Gaians in charzhe of the Siren Games?" Amára asked.

"That's not the point! Are you even listening?" Ravana broke composure and heaved a frustrated sigh. "There shouldn't even be a Siren Games in the first place. People shouldn't have to earn their place on Astera, Aruna, or even Nemal. All three planets should be open–to everyone!"

"Why should we believe anything you say?" Macks narrowed his eyes.

Ravana paused for a beat, then shrugged. "You don't have to. We'll take you to the mainland so you can see for yourself."

"But," Amára said, "why can't we go back home-eh once we see everything?" Kassi nodded, shuddering from the cold–or perhaps from the fear. At this point, it was hard to tell the difference. She noticed a few of the others were huddling in groups to share body heat.

Ravana massaged her temples and turned to the soldier next to her. "Griff, do you mind?"

He was only slightly taller than she was, plump to the point of slight obesity, with blonde curly hair parted down the middle. Nemal catered to such a healthy lifestyle, overweight people were extremely rare–Kassi had never seen one up close before. In Griff's bright blue eyes, Kassi saw sincerity as he spoke. "We need you to compete in all four rounds of the Siren Games." Kassi heard gasps of protest around her. Even though Paradisers had their own Intergalactic Sports Leagues, they all watched the Siren Games–the foremost sports competition in the worlds. The best siren athletes in all the worlds clashed in the fiercest of competitions with the highest stakes. Winners earned a Paradise passport, granting them a place on Paradise. Griff continued, "This will prove to your parents just how difficult and unfair this is for Gaians who just wish to come to Paradise for a better life. And maybe while you're at it, you could even convince them to accept those of us that are different. Let us into the higher planets as we are."

"One thing at a time, Griff," Ravana said.

"Of course," he said with a quiet nod.

Kassi nervously twirled her fingers through her long braids as the teens around her grew more vocal with their objections.

"Gaians have been training their entire lives for the Siren Games," One of them shouted.

"Yisû, how are we supposed to compete against that?" Another said.

"I'm sure you'll find a way," Griff said.

"The Games have already started!" Amára said.

"You'll have to wait until the next ones," Griff said.

"That's not for another six months!" Kassi heard a few of the others shout.

"Which will give you plenty of time to see how the Gaians live," Ravana said calmly.

"So you're forcing us to wait here for six months?" Macks jabbed a finger downward at Ravana, muscles flexing under his tight wetsuit. He was at least a full head taller than she was. "Didn't you zhust say the Games were danzherous? People die in the Games?"

"We're not forcing you to do anything," Ravana said, pressing a hand to her heart. "We're asking you to do the right thing here and help the poor Gaians."

"If you're not forcing us," Kassi began, "then we should be able to choose-eh not to compete and go home-eh."

"Doesn't matter anyway." Macks turned to Kassi and the others but spoke loudly enough for Ravana to overhear. "Our parents are probably on their way right now to get us."

"Your parents aren't coming for you. We convinced the U.N.O.E. to close Earth's side of the portal," Ravana said. Gasps of shock echoed around Kassi.

"I don't believe-eh you!" Macks whirled on Ravana. Wavy brown hair fell in front of his face as he tucked it behind his ears. "My father told me you're a liar. You lie and manipulate-eh people to do what you want. That's what he s--"

"I do no such thing!" Ravana raised her voice. "Your father's the one who lies about everything. He's the reason you have no clue what's going on down here!"

"Take us back to the portal, or else-eh!" Macks clenched his fists, poised to charge like a raging bull.

"Listen." Griff stepped in between Macks and Ravana with his hands up to diffuse the tension. "There's no need to fight."

"Don't mistake my kindness for weakness, young man," Ravana said, the corners of her mouth tightening. "I know when it comes to helping and caring for the Gaians, I wear my heart on my sleeve. But don't think for a dynamic second that makes me soft. Maybe you even think you're doing the right thing. Bless your little hearts. I can't blame you. Your parents never taught you right. But at the very least, they should have taught you that violence only causes more violence. It doesn't solve anything." Turning toward Macks who was still coiled, she lifted her empty hands.

In an instant, Macks jumped forward and swiped a soldier's dull-gray sonic rifle, tossing it to Amára. He decked the soldier with a right hook, buying Amára enough time to fill her lungs and burst into a Gelt Hîm, a siren dueling song. Directing high frequencies at Ravana's chest, she tried to strike before Ravana could shield and minimize the blow. However, Ravana had already drawn her sonic rifle from her holster, the mouthpiece to her lips.

Positioned to defend, she performed a sonic shield that diffused Amára's attack. Ravana then launched into her own counter, firing a sonic punch that knocked Amára off her feet. She hit the ground hard but bounced back quickly. Back on Nemal, Kassi had seen her duel many times before, and she had only ever lost once. That was to Kairos, Kassi's oldest brother, who happened to be the reigning dueling champion. Amára shook off the blow and retaliated with another Gelt Hîm, striking Ravana with such force that even her shield song didn't hold. Ravana stumbled back, clutching her chest and for a moment, Kassi thought her cousin might win this. Amára must have thought this, too. Others around Kassi joined in the fray, adding to the chaos as they helped Macks who had successfully subdued one soldier and was tussling with another.

Ravana responded with a powerful blast that took Amára off guard. It was a direct high-frequency attack that induced instant nausea, causing Amára to double over and vomit.

Kassi knew Ravana could easily kill Ama at that moment. She had to do something. Scrambling to snatch the sonic rifle that had spilled to the ground, she pressed it to her mouth and tried performing a shield song. With her broken voice, nothing came out. Even with a healthy voice, Kassi knew if Amára couldn't beat Ravana, Kassi didn't stand a chance. Behind her, she heard Amára groaning from the ground, clearly in no condition to resume her duel. If only she could be the one to defend her cousin, instead of it always being the other way around.

Ravana didn't waste any time launching into her next powerful attack. Just as Kassi began feeling the effects of Ravana's attack, Macks broke free from his scuffle with the other soldiers, snagged a sleek, silver sonic rifle out of the holster of a distracted soldier, and launched a sonic strike. The width of the blast stunned Ravana and a few neighboring soldiers, knocking one of them onto the ground. Ravana took in the blast and remained on her feet, skidding backward as if struck by a strong wind. Her suit must have been upgraded to absorb higher decibels. It was enough to halt her attack on Amára as she pivoted and performed a shield song. The second Macks ran out of breath, Ravana countered with a violent Gelt Hîm. Her mood darkened as she faced Macks as if it were personal. The intensity increased, becoming dangerously lethal–much more than was necessary to win the duel. The amplified high frequencies struck Macks with such force, Kassi heard something inside him burst. His body arched violently and spasmed until he crashed onto the soggy ground in a lifeless heap.

Kassi gasped in horror. Screams of shock and terror erupted from those around her as all fighting came to an abrupt halt.

Ravana looked shaken. "Sheist! Sheist! Sheist!" Her heavy breathing quivered and her eyes teared up at the sight of Macks's body on the ground. "I told you…violence never solves anything! When people refuse to see the truth, this…" Pressing her hands to her face, she turned away.

Griff stepped forward. He looked rattled, constantly tugging on his collar and sleeves as if his wetsuit no longer fit. Clearing his throat, he said, "Now please, do as we say so there are no more unfortunate accidents.

"We'll be separating you to various cities around the world

where you will study and train for your chance to compete in the Siren Games. We've assigned two grips who will supervise you and make sure you have what you need. They will treat you respectfully and honorably, and you will be expected to do the same."

"We can't stay together?" Amára clamped onto Kassi's arm.

"You need to win the Games on your own," Griff explained. "We'll also be changing your names. You don't want Gaians finding out you're Paradisers, or "disers" as they like to say. As you already know, they hate your kind." He nodded to the other soldiers. They dragged the others back into the group before forming an arched line facing the group of abducted teenagers. "We need you to understand how serious this is. We can't let you go home until it's finished and the Gaians are free. We can't do this without your help."

"What's to stop us from reporting you?" Amára asked.

"Report us to whom? The U.N.O.E. already knows you're here. They also want us to convince your parents to open their side of the portal to all Gaians. Despite our differing reasons, our interests are aligned temporarily. If you or any Gaian reports us to the mediation officers, nothing will happen. If anything, they'll punish you for it," Griff said. "And they monitor all the Rosen-comms, so don't bother trying to call home. We'll allow you to communicate with your family when the time is right.

"When you wake up, you'll be in your new home. Hopefully, in time, you'll come to understand why all of this is necessary."

Ravana joined her soldiers as they drew their sonic rifles and began chanting a Humav Hîm, a siren narcotic song. Most of the soldiers had a common sonic rifle–a dull gray handle with a wire-mesh mouthpiece on one end and a flared amplifier on the other. Ravana had customized hers with a smooth obsidian black handle arched slightly, featuring custom finger grooves, a mouthpiece with a black wire-mesh grille, and a broad amplifier on the end rimmed in gold.

UNEVEN SKY

Save your breath and breathe
In a dreamless sleep
Where your mind drifts away
Always out of reach

You're all stars from the same uneven sky
It's your time to come down, share that light

You're a ghost in the void
Of an endless sea
Everywhere you turn
There is only me

You're all stars from the same uneven sky
It's your time to come down, share that light

They're all moths to the flame
And they don't know why
It's your choice if you save them
From that fire

IN EVÉIK

Zînar i japáb tuví japat
Lev în sînyom dormiat
Ubi ándesh poþ tuví kiliat
Méshû mun van tordoiat

Káthách dari li mara punîm ski ástarûtóbé
Bud tuví agité ki chom mun fam, mat sîm orûat

Bud în gwébé lev li koré tuvat
Van în ikirîm þalasaat
Tabi val tuvat
Ebi bud hanya mwaat

Káthách dari li mara punîm ski ástarûtóbé
Bud tuví agité ki chom mun fam, mat sîm orûat

Bud lenûtóbé ki li daver amni vodat
I sápéré néz dag tuvat
I bud nayalí zishé li loshin bud dar vier tuvat
Bud dar vier tuvat

WITHIN SECONDS, the Humav Him took effect. Kassi tried to resist, but the intoxicating melodies rendered her body immobile, nearly catatonic.

Kassi turned to Amára. "I'm so sorry," she said.

Amára nodded, still clutching her stomach from the duel.

"Ashkana tuv!" Kassi said.

"Ashkana tuv, ashte!" Amára said. Their knees wobbled as, one by one, the kids around her collapsed to the ground, unconscious. The sound enveloped Kassi and Amára. Her last thought was of home as their bodies thumped to the ground.

Two

Kassi woke with a dull throbbing behind her eyes, her head heavy as a stone. The room teetered and rocked as if balanced on a single yoga ball. Struggling to sit up, she tried rolling to her feet. Blood rushed from her head and forced her to sit back down for a few beats.

Daylight spilled into the room, flooding her small space. Everything smelled of mildew. She found herself sitting on a stain-riddled, lumpy mattress–likely the source of the smell. Examining the mattress, there were no controls to adjust the firmness, the shape, or anything. It was just a plain, smart-less, rectangular pad. The walls and ceiling had water spots and cracks in the paint. A broken ceiling fan dangled by a single cord. Kassi couldn't fathom why no one had fixed it. A sad, battered dresser drooped against the wall adjacent to her, its color barely distinguishable. Everything in this room was so far from what she was used to–more decrepit than anything she could have ever imagined.

This is definitely still Earth, Kassi deflated. *Where's Amára?*

No matter how many times she scanned the cramped bedroom, she found no one else. Not even a R.A.V.—the robot assistants they had everywhere on Nemal. Kassi was alone. All her life, Kassi had Amára. They were cousins, best friends–an inseparable pair. Now they were forced to endure the harshest conditions of their lives without each other.

The more she surveyed her room, the more her heart sank. Next to her bed was a bent, metal nightstand with a rusted steel cup of green juice. She assumed she was supposed to drink it and took a sip, shuddering and wincing at the foul taste. It tasted like freshly juiced dirt with a hint of lemon.

How can anyone drink that?

Still, with her damaged voice feeling like sandpaper, she needed to drink something. A small washroom was attached to her bedroom, so she slinked over to the sink. A turn of the knob produced spurts of brownish water. A strong waft of sulfur hit her nostrils, churning her insides.

Even their water's dirty!

Her shoulders slumped as she examined the small washroom. Next to the toilet was a small and basic shower stall, with only one shower head–no hover plate, no additional jet streams. Nothing like the hover pods they had back home. She returned to the room and sat heavily on the mattress. With a resigned sigh, she picked up the muck juice, plugged her nose, and attempted to guzzle it. Two gulps in, she gagged, shook her head, and quickly put it back on the nightstand. Closing her eyes, Kassi laid back on the mattress, fighting her revulsion. She had always known conditions on Earth were bad, but this was unlivable. Either her abductors intentionally placed her in the most impoverished place on Earth, or all Gaians lived like this– Kassi couldn't decide which was worse.

Hoisting herself back up to her feet, she tested the door. It was unlocked. She kept it closed for now, not ready to face what was on the other side. Spinning on her heels, she jumped. A hideously unkempt girl stared back at her. Kassi quickly realized she was staring at her own ghastly reflection in a mirror on the far wall.

With bags under her eyes, hair in a sleep halo, a mattress

indentation covering the right side of her face, and her clothes in a disheveled frump, Kassi almost didn't recognize herself. A symmetrical, splotchy, blue and purple bruise branched from the center of her throat, like an abstract watercolor painting of a spider-web. As she ran her fingers through her hair to untangle the mess, she noticed a sparkle in her ears. Drawing her long hair back, she spotted the earrings Amára had given her. Tears sprang to her eyes as she fingered the Nemalís jewelry–the only thing she had left from home. The oval-shaped diamond stud earrings were her favorite, mostly because they matched every-thing. Although nothing would match the repulsive rags she now found herself in.

What am I wearing?

The brand new designer wetsuit she had on when she was narcotized was replaced with a coarse, burnt orange plaid top and bright green, knee-length corduroy shorts. The ugliest threads she had ever laid eyes on. She refused to think about how she got into them.

She scavenged the room for other options. Opening the dresser drawers, she found only bras and underwear. While they looked new, the fabric was rough, and they were clearly very poorly made. Kassi noticed the mirror was a sliding door to a closet. Inside she found three more pairs of the exact same outfit as if it were standard.

A lone window shed light on the room. Instead of glass, a thin sheet of plastic was attached to the frame with blue indus-trial tape. It was small but wide enough for Kassi to fit through. She ripped the sheet off and peered out.

The morning sun shone down on a narrow, flooded alleyway that separated her room from the building on the other side. The bottom floor, which was partially submerged below opaque water, sported a colorful awning and decorative carvings. The top floors seemed built more for function rather than aesthetics —gray, square, and simple as if constructed by a robot with a pile of basic building blocks. The alleyway spilled into a slow, murky river Kassi assumed was the street. Sparse palm trees sprouted out of the dark water–the only indication the ground wasn't too far below. It was anyone's guess why people would be willing to touch water so dirty.

Kassi's window was three stories up, making it difficult for her to escape out the window without cracking any bones. If a talented siren healer was nearby, she'd have risked it. She doubted that was the case, and chose not to jump. Leaning back into the room, Kassi reinstalled the taped sheet to the window frame.

"I can't escape anyway. There's nowhere to go." She started at the sound of her voice. Scratchy and gravelly, it was almost totally unfamiliar. Reflexively, she reached up and patted her throat. Images of the weasel-faced woman and the cannon aimed at her throat flashed through her mind. Panic gripped her and she told herself to breathe. She couldn't afford a panic attack–Amara wasn't here to pull her out of it this time.

Unable to sit still, Kassi paced the room. Her parents were likely working on a rescue. Even if the portal were closed, as Ravana said, they would find another way to Earth. *Maybe there's a second portal no one knows about. Or maybe they have Gaian allies who will turn back on the portal on Earth's side.*

The ache in her throat made her neck and shoulders tense. She decided to test her vocal range with basic vocal warm-ups. Her lower range was audible but rough. When she tried to push into her higher register, she got nothing but wheezy, strained air. She was vocally crippled.

The least Ravana could have done was find me a siren healer. Without a healer, I have no voice and no chance of qualifying, much less winning, the Siren Games in six months. Kassi released a frustrated sigh and sunk into her mattress. *Doesn't matter–my parents will find a way to come and get me before then.*

Her throat throbbed. She felt a desperate need to drink something. The cup of muck juice on her bent nightstand winked at her. As disgusting as it tasted, it looked like her only option.

Closing her eyes with cup in hand, she chugged it and did her best to imagine she was drinking cold-pressed melongo fruit juice.

"*Bleh!*" She bounced to the other side of the room as if trying to run away from the taste. An unwelcome, dirt-flavored burp escaped her mouth. She forced it down, not wanting to think about how much worse the muck juice would taste coming back up.

Kassi heard heavy footsteps, like military boots, climbing up the staircase and getting closer. Scrambling back to her mattress, Kassi caught her pinky toe on the dresser. Crippling pain shot through her foot as she rolled on the floor. Grasping her toe, the ghastly despair of it all caused tears to streak down her face. She cursed in Evéik with a raspy squeak, "*Ghost of Sheebah! Can I just get one break?*"

The door jerked open and a stern, short statue of a man stood in the doorway in his military fatigues. Dark, cropped hair matched his brown almond eyes. Kassi scooted against the far wall and wished for a hole to hide in. After eyeing Kassi for an awkward second, the man finally spoke in English. "Come downstairs, we have much to go over." Without waiting for a response, he stiffly turned and marched downstairs, leaving the door ajar for Kassi to follow. Kassi stared at the recently vacated doorway. She didn't want to go downstairs, especially if it meant more interactions with the military cha. Apparently, he was one of her grips and even though Ravana had promised they would treat her with respect and honor, he was still intimidating.

The pain in her foot subsided enough to stand. Hobbling to the washroom mirror, she wiped her teary eyes and examined the frayed bird's nest that was her hair. Inspecting each drawer one by one, she only came up with a simple, wooden paddle hair brush and two rubber bands. Kassi had always taken great pride in her long, lustrous dark hair. They had taken away practically everything else–at least she still had that. With the brush, she raked through the tangled mess until she could pull it back into a french braid and tie it with a rubber band. It wasn't much, but it was the best she could do under the circumstances.

In the wood-floored hallway, there were two staircases, one ascending and one descending. The corridor, lined with shabby, white walls led to a door at the far end. Probably a second bedroom. Curious, Kassi tiptoed up the stairs and found a small, empty room with "glass" doors on both sides—blue-taped plastic like the window in her bedroom—leading to two separate balconies. The balconies were littered with various rusty outdoor furniture and a firepit. Maybe a good place to get away for some fresh air. Her hand reached for the door handle when she heard the same heavy boots marching back up the stairs.

She padded nervously back down the stairs, across the hall, and turned to begin her descent down the second flight. The man saw her and grunted, a telltale flicker of anger in his eyes, before turning on his heels and returning to the bottom floor. Kassi paused for a beat before resuming. The worn, wooden stairs creaked under her weight. They elbowed to the right and opened up to a compact kitchen and living room combo.

A woman popped up from the kitchen table and said, "There ya are!" She was short with ash blonde wavy hair–a mid-length bob with bangs–her clothes bright and cheerful. There was kindness in her eyes. It helped calm Kassi's nerves. She ushered Kassi to join them at a round kitchen table the yellowish color of vomit. Her chair wobbled on its rusty legs as soon as Kassi put any weight on it. She tapped the table's surface–no holodisplay, no response of any kind. The hard seat she sat in was incredibly uncomfortable, so she searched for the controls to adjust it.

"Down here, you ain't gon' find smart furniture. Only th' elites have that," the woman said.

The military man sat at the table, his unkind eyes boring into Kassi. The woman, on the other hand, seemed unnaturally chipper given the poverty of their surroundings and her role in Kassi's detainment.

"How ya feelin', hun? You doin' a'right?" She said with a

thick drawl. Kassi couldn't help glancing at the front door, wondering if she could run faster than the two of them.

"Aw, c'mon now! Jus b'cause we in this situation don' mean we cain't be friends," she said as if she could read Kassi's mind. "I'm Meela and this here's m'husband, 'ole Kyoto Kazán. We gon' be yer roommates watchin' over ya while yer here." As if calling them her "roommates" instead of grips made this situation any better. She eyed Kassi's hair and ran a hand through her own. "Yash almighty, look a' that beautiful, long, dark hair o' yours. Wish I could get mine t' look like that."

Kassi fidgeted with her thick braid, casting furtive glances over at Kyoto as she asked in her raspy voice, "Where's my friend, Amára?" Kyoto's face didn't so much as twitch in response. It hurt her throat to speak, but Kassi needed to know. Her brows drew down into a lowering scowl as she asked again, "What did you do with my friend?"

Meela's eyes whipped back and forth between Kassi and Kyoto before answering on his behalf. "Sorry hun, but we didn' do anything with her."

"Can you zhust find out if she's safe-eh?" Kassi asked.

Meela shrugged, "O'course she's safe, but I don' mind tryin' later..."

"No more questions!" Kyoto interrupted. He turned to Meela, flicked his chin toward Kassi, and said, "Tell her."

"I's gettin' to it," Meela said, before turning to face Kassi. "We registered ya fer school. Grade 10 at th'local high school. They got th'week off but will be startin' back up next week. Wanted t'let ya know so y'could get ready for it."

Kassi straightened in her seat. "You...want me to go to school here-eh?"

Meela nodded with an over-enthusiastic smile as if excited to see Kassi off to school. "Yep! Ain't that gon' be fun?"

Fun was definitely not the word Kassi would use to describe anything on this yashing planet. Instead, she asked, "Shouldn't I zhust focus on the Siren Games?"

"How else you gon' find yer team? Ev'ryone at school's required t'play, and it's th'only way ya qualify. Tha's why you need t'go t'school!"

The idea of going to an alien school full of alien people on an alien planet while trying to find a team with a crippled voice was probably the worst idea in the history of ideas. She needed to find a way out of it. "Can't I zhust stay here-eh and not go to school?"

"No," Kyoto said. "You'll go to school."

"And yer gon' wanna hide that accent. Gaians here don't take kindly to 'disers," Meela said.

A pit formed in her stomach. After all they had already taken from her, they wanted her to change her speech too!

I'll be gone before school starts, Kassi tried reassuring herself. *My parents will get me by then.*

Meela stood up to grab plates of food off the counter. She set one in front of Kyoto and another in front of Kassi. It felt like she hadn't eaten in days, but after catching a ripe whiff of the food on her plate, her stomach revolted. A greenish, stale biscuit, a pile of gray sludge, and a side medley of vegetables stared up at her. The biscuit smelled like musty cardboard, even worse than the green muck juice she was still burping up.

Is this food even edible? She wanted to say. "Can I...be excused?" Kassi poked at the food on her plate with a pair of rough, wooden chopsticks.

"You're not excused. Eat all of it!" Kyoto stabbed the air above her plate with his chopsticks.

Meela and Kyoto began digging in, chomping on the crumbly biscuits, their lips smacking between bites. They slurped up their watery gruel, shoved veggies in their mouth, and gulped down their muck juice. Their disgusting chewing sounds grossed Kassi out even more than the food did.

"Aw, it's not s'bad. We know it's not like th'food you're used ta, but it's what all Gaians eat every day. You'll get used t'it!" Meela spoke around a mouthful of biscuit.

Knowing there was no way out of it, Kassi picked up the green biscuit and took a nibble. It didn't taste like much. It was almost flavorless other than the slight hint of stale, unsalted broccoli. The biscuit crumbled into her mouth like wet sand.

Next, she tried the veggie medley, a slimy mix of peppers, potatoes, carrots, and red onions. It was mushy and tasted a little like the compost piles back home smelled—like old garbage. She tried to wolf it down before her stomach ralphed it back up.

Lastly, she tested a spoonful of the grayish gruel. Where the other foods were almost completely devoid of salt, this was overly salty. She had to continuously wash it down with the dirt-flavored muck juice to neutralize the saltiness.

The last few bites of gruel were the hardest, her stomach already in knots. Introducing this foreign, nasty concoction didn't help to settle her stomach. Sweat laced her brow and she found herself incessantly burping.

"I think I'm gonna be sick." She clutched her stomach.

"Don't you do it!" Kyoto threatened, leaning forward. The shouting didn't help. Trembling, she stared at the last two bites of gruel. Just the thought of eating it put her over the edge. She jerked to the side and spewed her breakfast onto the kitchen floor.

Meela jumped to her feet to dodge any vomit projectiles. "Aww, now look whatcha done!"

Kyoto slammed a fist on the table. "Control yourself!"

"Yer gonna have t'clean that up." Meela grabbed some old rags from below the kitchen sink, holding them out for Kassi. "C'mon now!"

Kassi's legs wobbled, her body shuddering as she fumbled across the room and grabbed the rags. As she did, she burst into tears. Kassi just wanted her mom and dad to come take her away from this awful place.

"No crying!" Kyoto shouted, jumping to his feet.

The anger in his voice scared her. The tears came on stronger, and she began to sob uncontrollably, still clutching the rags in the middle of the kitchen. Kyoto stepped forward and slapped her hard across the face before pointing up the stairs. "Go to your room!"

Kassi scurried away, tripping up the stairs and using her hands for support as she climbed. Reaching the top, she crawled through the doorway and shut the door. She didn't make it to the mattress. Curled up on the floor, Kassi shut down.

Three

She lay in a puddle of tears. Her red-rimmed eyes stared at the floorboards, her fingers absently tracing the lines in the planks. She heard footsteps up the stairs and braced herself. Seconds later, they retreated down the hall. Probably to the other bedroom. They didn't even care that she was hurt and crying on the floor. Back home, someone always checked on her–usually her dad, Caesar, or Amára. This time, they weren't coming. The realization hit her hard. She'd never felt so alone.

Hopefully, Amára's situation wasn't as bad. She was only in this shared nightmare because of Kassi. If only she could communicate with her somehow. Her eyes swept the room again. There were no holoscreens anywhere–no holopads, no siren suit with holocomms. At the palace, they had dozens of different ways to call or send a message to anyone on the planets. Here, she hadn't seen any of that.

I'd never survive on this planet! Good thing I won't be here long.

As she lay on the floor thinking of home, her mind drifted to the day she and Amára were taken. Kassi tried pushing the thoughts away, unsuccessfully. She couldn't shake the guilt of that day.

If only she had listened to Amára, none of this would have happened.

It had been a typical Saturday morning at Palace Rivernova—was it just yesterday? Built to house a village, oftentimes, their home had done just that. When Kassi's three siblings, seven nieces and nephews, twenty-two aunts and uncles, and sixty-two cousins all visited for their family reunions, the palace had teemed with life. The massive structure was built on a peninsula surrounded by the waters of Gavish Bay, as it had been for centuries. Possibly even millennia. No one knew exactly when the palace had been constructed or who had built it.

Kassi had always known her home was impressive, but she never quite realized how much until now. The aquamarine swimming lanes four meters wide and deep—a feature her parents added to the home when they first moved in—connected all rooms and eventually led to the Bay outside. There were hand-carved fountains of polished stone in every room, high vaulted ceilings and archways with sparkling chandeliers, floor-to-ceiling windows, whimsical fantasy paintings and tapestries covering all available wall space, and—behind a select few tapestries—secret passageways to hidden rooms of the palace. Each space had a theme all its own, and the fountain designs, room layouts, artwork, and adornments all augmented that theme. Kassi's favorite was the Atlantis room that stretched under the surface of the bay, submerged completely underwater. The arched-glass ceiling and walls provided a breathtaking view of the bay and its vibrant marine life.

Outside, on the opposite side of Gavish Bay and spanning for acres, were the Nemalís Royal Gardens--a botanical masterpiece created by her sister, Nasri.

Somehow, despite the touted ingenuity of the palace's designs, Kassi's room was still an infinite distance away from everything. Only her siblings' and parents' bedrooms were close by. Whenever she had complained to her parents about the distance, her father patted her on the head and said in Evéik, "That's what the swimming lanes are for, Little Spice."

"But what if I don't wanna swim?" *She asked.* "Can't we just build another InterPort?" *Her parents had simply smiled as if it were a rhetorical question. They never listened to her.*

With supersonic speed, Kassi could swim to the kitchen in eight seconds flat. But Kassi didn't always have that kind of energy before breakfast, which was why Amára had spent that morning dragging Kassi on foot across the expanse of the palace to reach the kitchens. Now, she would give anything for access to those swimming lanes again—or even just clean water.

Caesar had already saved a spot for them outside, under the large pavilion adjacent to the tulip fields. His deep-brown, wavy shag hair-style covered his ears and fell just above his blue eyes. Lucky for him, he had her dad's eyes. Next to him were two cousins, Amara's older brother, Coltren, and Evita—a cousin from Kassi's mother's side of the family. They were always singing—even at this unworldly hour. That morning, it had been some nonsensical jingle about cinnabeer.

Amára and Kassi had trotted over to them, greeting other members of the family in passing before taking their seats. They were already halfway through their breakfast—Caesar drinking from his usual frosty mug of cinnabeer and looking over a holographic display of Planet Nemal. The holopad, a blue marble, hexagonal prism the size and shape of a pencil, rested on the table and projected the three-dimensional display. Caesar looked up from the globe just as a loud burp escaped his mouth. He laughed. "Cinnabeer gives you the nose-tickliest burps!" *he said in Evéik.*

"Gross!" *Amára said, slapping Caesar's arm.*

Coltren studied Kassi's expression for a moment. "How'd you chas sleep?"

"I slept great! Can't say the same for this one." *Amára cocked her head in Kassi's direction.*

"Rude! I would've slept great if this one hadn't woken me up!" *Kassi plunked heavily into her seat and set her plate down, folding her arms and pouting in Amára's direction.* "Ruff," *she barked at her. Whipping chopsticks out, she snatched a mango mochi off her plate. Breakfast was a feast of just about every dish you could dream up. Thick slices of bacon, mushroom omelets, golden hash browns, cheddar crescents, buttered biscuits with fresh rajabee honey, chocolate crepes, sliced purple kiwi, and juicy melongos right off the tree, a cream and soda bar with any flavor you wanted, sugar-frosted fruit tarts and pastries. It was just like every other day, but it was one thing Kassi had never gotten tired of.*

"If I didn't wake you up, you would've slept all day and missed breakfast!" *Amára said, waving a hand over their plates.*

Kassi unfolded her arms and changed the subject. "Where should we explore today? I wanna swim with chelona turtles again!"

"Or we could race sea dragons, again," *Coltren suggested.*

"What about our Wrath of the Khans assignment for Worlds History?" *Amára said.* "It's due Monday. Also, we have to supervise the cleaning bots in the southeast quadrant and help Nasri with the Gardens."

"We'll get the assignment done tonight when we get back. Besides, we spend too much time studying–not enough experience. And I already asked Parise to take care of cleaning for us since we helped her last time," *Kassi said.* "We spend an hour with Nasri, and then we go!" *She spun the globe in front of her, zooming in on a specific spot.* "We've never been here before, right?"

Caesar examined it closely. "Yisû, that's the Bengala Sea. Remember we found the Apollo Ducat Memorial Reef at the bottom? You know with the really bosst underwater statue looking upward?" *They gave him confused looks, so he continued,* "It had that cave with the glowworms?" *He always remembered the little details of their exploration adventures.*

"Oh, the glowworm caves?"

"Yisû, the glowworm caves. Yisû. You wanna go there again? We could also explore the tunnels under the palace and look for new secret passageways." *Caesar took a monstrous bite of his strawberry banana crepe, immediately regretting the decision. It barely fit in his mouth. Kassi cocked her head back and eyed him curiously. He struggled to chew without chomping through it like an animal, and ultimately covered his mouth with a balled-up fist so he could wolf it down.*

"This time, I wanna practice swimming like a mermaid," *Kassi placed two thick slices of bacon on top of her egg, avocado crescent.*

"Yisû!" *Evita lit up.* "Have you chas tried out the new mermaid settings on Marcano's latest wetsuits? It's so bosst!"

"Not yet but I need to," *Kassi said.* "I'm dying!"

"Yisû, we could do that. As long as we still have time to get in a game of AquaSphera," *Caesar said.*

"What about this spot? Have we ever been here?" *Amára pointed next to a lone, green mountain.*

"Hmm," *he zoomed in on the display, measuring with his fingers as he said,* "That's close to Mount Cassius, but I don't think we've ever gone that far west. We could hop the InterPort to Valparaiso and swim out from there. Should we do it?"

"Mount Cassius?" *Kassi looked to Caesar for a quick reminder.*

"Yisû, that's where we found jungle palace ruins from the ancient world behind the twin waterfalls. You know, with the little gold nuggets at the bottom of the lake," *Caesar said.* "I kept some of those gold nuggets, actually. They're no small potatoes!"

"Mmm, I like small potatoes," *Evita said as she plucked a buttered breakfast potato off her plate and tossed it in her mouth.*

"Me too!" *Caesar stole a potato off her plate.*

"Get your own!" *She slapped his hand.*

"Which waterfalls?" *Kassi still couldn't picture it.*

Amára bounced in her seat. "Mount Cassius! That's where you found that cute orange cat swiping at the fish?"

"Kitteee! Yisû, that cat was so cute!" *Kassi bounced and clapped her hands.*

"Of course, you remember the cat," *Coltren interjected with a scoff, shaking his head.* "Ancient palace ruins, gold treasure, majestic waterfalls. But the only thing you remember is the mangy cat."

"He wasn't mangy!" *Kassi would have barked again if her mouth weren't full.*

"Yisû, don't call him that!" *Amára always sided with Kassi when it came to cats.*

That's when a Nemalís Guard had rushed through the gardens straight to Kassi's parents, Vidara and Leontari. The unusual commotion had interrupted their conversation. Kassi craned her neck to see what was going on.

Caesar stood up. The guard whispered something only Vidara and Leontari could hear. Family members of the Rivernova Clan slowly rose from their seats and drifted closer to the conversation, worry etched on their faces.

Vidara had noticed the gathering crowd, so she stood from her chair and walked to the center to address everyone. Elegantly adorned, flowing maroon robes grazed the grass beneath, held together by her hand-crafted, black leather belt. Long dark hair had been pulled into a high ponytail, fastened by a golden double-spiral-headed pin, and it fell down her back in swoopy layers. She had recently celebrated her 123rd birthday, but her youthful features, smooth skin, and strong, slender physique proved she was still in her physical prime. Gliding across the grass, she exuded regal confidence. Her gaze swept over the clan with her brown, almond eyes. Everyone told Kassi she had her mother's eyes. Secretly, Kassi always wished she had inherited her dad's. They were like the turquoise hues of Gavish Bay.

Leontari was by her side and was no stranger to good fashion. His barrel chest and broad shoulders filled out his sky blue silk tunic; his pearl white sandals on his feet. All of his clothes were hand-designed and tailored perfectly to his frame. His curly blonde fringe reached just above his eyebrows and fell down both sides just past the scruff of his well-trimmed beard. He had given everyone a reassuring smile as he held Vidara's hand. He always held her hand.

"Sirs and Dames, as you might have surmised, we find ourselves in a very unique predicament." *Vidara's powerfully operatic, rich voice resonated clearly to the back of the crowd.* "There has been an unfortunate incident in Viracocha, and we need all the

Nemalís Royal Guard to report to their stations immediately. The rest of you should return home with haste and await our return."

Leontari stepped forward. "Apollo, Kitoah, Kairos, and Redfox, we need you with us."

Kassi hadn't known how to respond to the news. It looked like no one else did, either. There were never incidents on Astera, nor any of the Paradise Planets for that matter. The closest they had ever come to an "incident" was when Kassi's cousin, Leora, got lost in the Royal Garden's labyrinth for three days. When they found her, she was a little dehydrated, but easily recovered with some Fountain water and a simple Gesto Hîm, a siren healing incantation.

The current situation, however, had seemed more serious, judging by their parent's reactions. They were upset. No, it was more than that. They were distraught. Kassi had never seen her parents like that.

Despite it all, Vidara had made her way through the crowd, reassuring everyone along the way. She reached the three of them and said, "Caesar, darling, be a dear and look after your sister while we're gone. Ama, you probably should return home with your mother." *Vidara caressed Amára's arm.* "Kassiana," *she said, a hint of tension in her shoulders.* "I need you to stay with your brother."

"But mother, I can help! Why can't I..."

"I'm not arguing this with you, today." *Vidara cast a stern look at Kassi.* "You will go with your brother, and that's the end of it."

"But I wanna come with you!"

"Not this time. We can discuss this later."

"Later? But then it'll be too late..."

"Kassiana Rivernova!"

Kassi grumbled. She knew the conversation was over.

Leontari hustled over. "Vida, we're ready. We'd better go!" *He looked at Kassi and Caesar.* "Don't worry. Whatever it is, we'll take care of it and return before you know it." *Leo forced a smile and picked up Kassi, giving her his usual bear hug. She continued scowling, not letting her father lift her mood so easily.*

"But Dad, why can't I go?" *Kassi pouted harder. If she pressed hard enough, he might give in as he had done many times in the past.*

"What's that?" He put Kassi down and quickly glanced at Vidara. Reading the expression on her face, he said, "Sorry, Little Spice. Not this time. Your mother's always right." *He said, trying to reassure her.* "We'll be back before you know it! Ashkana vod!"

They had stripped down to their siren wetsuits which they often wore underneath their clothes. Her dad would say, "You never know when you might need it, Little Spice!" *They had tossed their clothes aside, grabbed their sonopacks and helmets, and rushed to join the others.*

Reaching a small ledge just past the Gazebo in the Royal Gardens, with Gavish Bay only seven meters below, Leo shouted, "Viracocha needs our help! These worlds are the paradise we make them!"

"These worlds are the paradise we make them!" *Everyone chanted the phrase in unison, as they had done thousands of times before.*

"Let's dive!" *Leo led the charge as they dove one by one into the bay.*

As soon as they were gone, Kassi stomped over to Caesar. "She never listens to me!"

Caesar had initiated his timer on his holowatch display as he kept his eyes on the far side of the Bay. It was enough to distract Kassi from her grumbling. A few minutes had passed before they saw the task force shoot out of the water. "3:54! That's the fastest I've seen. They must've gone supernova to make that time." *Caesar sounded more concerned than excited. From beach to beach, the distance they covered was nearly twenty-five kilometers. Kassi had always wished she could swim that fast. She had been working on her supersonic speed underwater and had swum that same distance a million times. But her best time was only 5:07. And she had never lit the fifth bulb and gone supernova. Amára could do it in 4:30 flat. She was a much stronger swimmer than Kassi—close to going pro. She almost lit the fifth bulb once—it flickered for a second. It was always their dream to make it into the Intergalactic AquaSphera League, but Kassi often wondered if she would just end up another spectator in the stands.*

Built into the side of a mountain on the far side of the Bay was the

Gravity Drive Center, the GDC, with the Intergalactic Rosenbridge portal (much larger than the intercontinental portals, or InterPorts, that connected the cities of Nemal). From there, the task force could travel to any of the three other planets, Astera, Aruna, or Earth, so long as the portal on the other end was powered up. Due to a previous attack from Earth through the portal years ago, military fortresses were built around each GDC with a kill switch that would close the portal in an instant to prevent invaders from ever breaching the border again. On this occasion, they would be traveling to Viracocha on Astera, the third of the three Paradise Planets.

Caesar started heading toward the palace. "Let's go, Kassi. C'mon, back inside."

She voiced a dragged-out sigh, still wanting to vent her frustrations. Hooking arms with Amára, they had fallen in right behind Caesar as they retreated back into the kitchens. Amidst the renewed bustle of the palace, Caesar had seemed preoccupied enough for Kassi to point toward the kitchen's swimming lane against the far wall and motion for Amára to put her mask on. Amára had shaken her head in protest at first, but at Kassi's insistence, she relented and threw on her helmet.

Caesar had started up a conversation as if they were both right behind him as he weaved through people who were rushing in all directions. "I wonder what's going on. Normally, I'd assume Kairos was up to something, but he was there at breakfast with the rest of us...," *he trailed off as Kassi and Amára slipped underwater.*

They had quickly powered up their suits with a Haraki Hîm, a siren acceleration song. Their sonopacks illuminated the first two bulbs with the brightness of stars. Assuming Caesar was sure to notice, they had launched full speed before he could hoist them out of the water. Once outside the palace, they aimed for the far side of Gavish Bay. They lit the third and fourth bulbs to power both palm and foot thrusters and torpedoed straight to the other side of the Bay in just over five minutes before shooting out of the water and landing on the beach. Without breaking stride, they raced up the embankment to the GDC.

"I don't know about this, Kassi," *Amára hesitated.*

"I'm tired of being left behind. What are we even training for if not this?" *Kassi glanced back at her friend who was scanning the far side of the Bay where Palace Rivernova towered in the distance.* "Look, you don't have to come with me. I can probably catch up with my parents." *Kassi had turned to continue climbing toward the GDC, secretly hoping Amára would follow. After a few deliberately slow steps, Kassi had been relieved to hear her cousin's footsteps grow louder as she caught up.*

They had run through the giant bay doors of the GDC and onto a large hangar. Across the hangar, a narrow tunnel led to a kill box lined with three tiers on both sides stacked with armed guards and mounted turret guns hanging from the ceiling. That was where the Rosenbridge portal connected the worlds. Normally, the guard at the gate would have granted them passage without any reservation, but with the current situation, everything was on lockdown. They had been stopped at the first guard station and told to turn around and head back. Kassi and Amára pretended to comply and ducked out of sight to wait for an opening to sneak past.

With all the commotion, it hadn't taken long before the guards were distracted, explaining to a large group of Nemalís who were looking to vacation on Aruna for the day that all portals were closed. While they answered questions, Kassi had made her move and Amára followed.

As they slipped past, Amára voiced her concerns. "Maybe we should do as he says?"

"He's probably making a big deal out of nothing," *Kassi said.* "Besides, we'll be in and out before he even notices."

"But didn't Aunt Vidara say…"

"My mother understands nothing because she never listens to me! She still treats me like a little child!" *Kassi ranted as they climbed the staircase to the platform that fed into the narrow tunnel.*

"Kassi, I'm with you, I…"

"You know what she told me last week?" *Kassi continued as they walked through the entrance of the tunnel.* "When I told her about you getting stuck underwater, she immediately blamed me for it. Said it was all my fault before I even had a chance to finish explaining how I was trying to help. And even after I finally got a word out, it was like she didn't hear anything I said. She just went on lecturing me like I'm still five."

"Yisû, I remember. I wanted to explore the cave and got myself stuck," *Amára nodded as she checked the hangar to make sure no one was following them.*

"Exactly! I was just trying to tell her what happened and she starts accusing me of always talking you into doing dangerous things. It's so annoying!"

They were halfway through the tunnel, caught up in their conversation when they failed to spot the Nemalís Guards entering at the other end.

"Where are you two off to?" Ravana asked, curiously in English. Over a dozen of her soldiers accompanied her. At the time, Kassi had thought they were official guard members assigned to Nemal's GDC. One of them whispered into Ravana's ear. "Kassiana and Amára River-nova — two of the very girls we were looking for."

Kassi and Amára spun on their heels and scrambled away, breaking into a full sprint.

She had heard Ravana call out after them, "Ridgely, Farra, Volkov, I need them unharmed. Quickly and quietly."

A LOUD KNOCK on the door jolted Kassi back to her new reality.

Four

Kassi's stomach gurgled and felt hollow–something she had never felt before. On Nemal, food was everywhere, and if Kassi ever got too caught up with her studies, work, AquaSphera, or other things, Amára always made sure Kassi didn't forget a meal. Now, she worried she wouldn't be able to keep any food down. At least her parents were coming soon–she could last until then.

"Kassi?" Meela called through the closed door. "Brought y'some food. Thought y'might be hungry." She opened the door and brought in a plate with more of the same, only this time with a serving of white sticky rice. She set it on the shabby metal stand next to the bed.

"Thanks," Kassi muttered, not really in the mood to talk. She glanced at the food rations–a far cry from the breakfast spread she had on Nemal just the other day. Maybe she could manage to eat some of it. "How long have I been here-eh?"

"Couple days s'all," Meela said, plopping onto the mattress as if Kassi's question was an open invitation to start a conversation. Kassi immediately regretted asking. She prodded at the food with her chopsticks, nibbling here and there. Her nerves seemed calmed enough to keep it down this time.

"Food's not great, I know. All th'food comes from th'salt-water aquaponic farms. Tha's what we got here on Earth. It's what 'ol Kyoto and I grew up on."

"All the food here's like this?" She asked. The hoarseness in her voice still grated on her.

"Yisû. Well, 'less yer rich an' can find it in th'Market Abyss. Then you can have normal food, but even rich eatin' ain't nothing like what ya'll got on th'Paradise Planets. Ya'll got it good!"

As much as she preferred to be left alone, she had so many questions. With a raised eyebrow, she asked, "So why'd you leave-eh?"

"Jus' like what Ravana said to ya'll the other night," Meela said. "We felt is's wrong to keep Gaians from livin' th'life ya'll have."

"Oh," Kassi said. So Meela was there that night–she had stood by and watched Macks die. "What about Amára?"

"I'm sure she's fine."

Like Macks is fine? Kassi wanted to say out loud.

"There's really no way t'find out. No way t'communicate down here 'cept face t'face," Meela said.

"It's sheist! How do people live like this?" Kassi asked.

Meela elevated her voice, projecting as if for an unseen audience, "It's what's best! The U.N.O.E. outlawed everything else t'keep people safe from riots 'n whatnot."

Kassi always wondered why the U.N.O.E. hadn't changed its name. According to her history of the worlds class, the U.N.O.E., United Nations of Earth, was once comprised of hundreds of sovereign nations. Now, Planet Earth consisted of sixty-four provinces united under one banner and governed by three presidents, their grand deputies, province senators, and assembly members. In a campaign to promote peace and security, they had dissolved everything they felt caused division–individual sovereign nations, differing political parties, religions, and cultural traditions among other things.

"So no holopads? Or hologlasses? What about siren suits?" Kassi's eyes instinctively darted to the closet as if expecting to see a siren suit draped on the hangers like she would in nearly every closet back on Nemal.

"Oh sure, they have those. Jus' can't use th'comms on 'em. They altered 'em. Hologlasses only give ya'll access t'textbooks and sharing homework files with yer classmates at school. Siren suits only have th'ability t'communicate with your team using th'same short-range radio frequency."

"So they still have radio frequencies? Couldn't you zhust tell all the sirens to gather together and tune in to the same-eh frequency?"

"Do somethin' like that, ya risk gettin' caught by th'U.N.O.E. They got cameras everywhere. They see everythin'." Meela nodded her head toward the corner of the room where Kassi noticed a dark, discolored panel. She had assumed it was just another water spot.

"That's a camera?" Kassi gasped. "So someone's been watching me this whole time?" She covered up, even though she had clothes on. Meela nodded. Kassi shuddered at the thought and vowed to only change in the washroom from then on. "What happens if you get caught?" Kassi asked in a whisper, almost afraid to hear the answer. In response, Meela gave a subtle shake of her head. Kassi leaned forward into her hands and stared at the floor. She asked, "How long has it been like this?"

"Since th'Great Correction when the U.N.O.E. stepped in and saved us all," Meela said loudly, her voice laced with fear.

Kassi had learned all about the Great Correction in her studies back home. Humans had created Artificial Intelligence to augment the usage of technology and amplify their capacity. No one knows who did it, but someone began programming the machines to optimize Earth's population. Many believe their intentions were to help Gaians live longer, and it catastrophically backfired. Rather than come up with a way to cure illnesses and extend the human lifespan, the A.I. machines euthanized the elderly and sick across the planet. Within weeks, forty percent of the population had been murdered. World governments banded together to set off massive electromagnetic pulses wherever Artificial Intelligences were present. It caused a major setback in technology and innovation, but it successfully eradicated the A.I. threat. According to her lessons, it took Earth decades to rebuild, despite relentless efforts by the Council to offer assistance. The U.N.O.E. had always been tight-lipped about their internal workings and only permitted minimal help from Paradisers.

Kassi blinked at her food. The thought of eating this every day was so depressing, it sucked the life out of her. She stared out the blue-taped window and pictured the flooded streets down below. "Why's everything flooded out there-eh? Did you chas zhust have a storm?"

"Naw, tha's jus how it is 'round here on Myamma Beach," she said. "Is's always that way. Water's not that deep. But is's 'nough t'getcha good an' soaked."

"Mirific!" Kassi rolled her eyes.

"Ah, it's not s'bad," Meela paused and stared vacantly at the floor for a few minutes as if she were a machine that had just run out of juice. Kassi shuffled on the mattress awkwardly.

Meela snapped back to life and resumed as if nothing happened, "Welp, t'day's Monday. School starts back up nex' Monday. They said ya'll will pick up yer school supplies right there at th'school on yer first day. Fer now, ya best be gettin' yer rest."

Kassi looked down at the rags she was wearing. "But...what? I can't go to school wearing this! Can't I at least have-eh some real clothes? Hair products? Makeup?" Amára always told her she didn't need makeup, but Kassi loved contouring her face and accenting her eyes. It was her art.

"Tha's all we got, fer now," Meela said. "'Sides, ya'll get uniforms t'wear at school."

"But I'll still have to wear these on my first day! I need to look more presentative than this!" Kassi smoothed a wrinkle in her shorts as if that would make any difference.

"Presentative?" Meela cocked her head to the side.

"Isn't that the word?" Kassi glanced back.

"Ya' mean presentable?"

"Presentable! You know what I mean." Standing to check her reflection in the mirror, she groaned. "No! I can't! Couldn't I zhust borrow some-eh clothes for the first day?"

"Sorry, hun, them's the breaks," Meela shook her head.

Kassi sulked and continued staring at her reflection. Of course, Kassi knew she wouldn't be on Earth that long. Someone would fix this, and she would be home in a matter of days. Still, the possibility of attending a new school like this horrified her. Her fingers grazed the blaring bruise on her throat, "What about my voice-eh?" As much as her clothes and makeup situation bothered her, finding a healer for her voice was top priority.

"Y'mean th' raspiness?"

"I can't sing with sháloor. How would I ever qualify for the Siren Games?"

"Yash! I haven' sung with sháloor in ages!" Meela said. She studied Kassi for a moment. "Well, maybe I don' know. I could prolly take ya t'a local healer. See what they can do."

Kassi continued fidgeting with her shirt. *Why would anyone choose these colors?* "What about my siren suit? Couldn't I zhust have-eh that back and wear that to school?"

Meela straightened, ignoring the question, "Usually when som'body offers t'help ya, y'say 'thank you, ma'am!'" She tilted her chin down and cast Kassi a disapproving glance.

"Oh uh, thank you...ma'am." Kassi couldn't find the energy to fake sincerity. After all she had lost recently, how could she be expected to feel the least amount of gratitude?

"Tha's better. Welp, holler if ya need me. I'll be downstairs," Meela stood and clapped Kassi on the shoulder before disappearing downstairs.

With the room dead silent, Kassi stared vacantly at her reflection. She had no desire to go to school, let alone compete in the Siren Games. She just wanted to curl up and sleep on her lumpy mattress until this nightmare ended.

The week dragged, but not slowly enough. There were no hot showers, so Kassi began each day with unpleasant, cold-ish showers. She ate food rations with Kyoto and Meela three times each day, slept most of the rest of the day, cried herself to sleep each night, and dreamed horrible dreams of Macks lying dead in the mud or of Amára and Kassi running for their lives just before getting captured. With each passing day and no rescue, Kassi felt more alone and increasing anxiety about Monday.

Sunday night, Kassi watched the neighboring streets from the balcony and waited. She was sure someone was coming. It had to be tonight. After hours of people-watching, she finally plopped down the stairs to her bedroom and fell asleep.

The first day of school came too soon and with the rudest of awakenings. Kyoto had installed the most obnoxious clock imaginable. The sound of the buzzer was shrill and piercing as if the house were on fire. But that wasn't the worst of it. At 06:30, even before the sun came out, the loathsome contraption lifted itself into the air with propellers and paraded around the dark room blaring that screeching sound for as long as it could evade Kassi's flailing arms. She jolted out of bed and chased it around the room until she finally managed to snatch it out of the air and chuck it to the ground, hoping to smash it to pieces. It remained completely intact. She threw it again and again. The thing was indestructible.

With a huff, she trudged to the washrooms for a lightning-quick, cold shower before throwing on the orange and neon green threads she'd be wearing to present herself to her brand-new school. Her reflection in the mirror made Kassi want to scream. But with ruptured vocal cords, she couldn't even do that. The outfit's fluorescent colors shone in the twilight.

At least I'll glow in the dark in case I get lost. She thought with a groan.

It was terrifying enough going to a new high school, even if she were remotely presentable. But her face was naked, her hair was dirty and her outfit made her look like an escaped convict. As she put her hair in a braid, she fingered her earrings–the one thing she had from home. If she wore them, they might get confiscated. Instead, she hid them in the side of her mattress, poking a hole and stuffing them along the edge. With one more glance into the mirror and a resigned sigh, she descended the stairs to breakfast.

Kyoto fixed a hard stare at her from across the table and Kassi did her best to keep the food down. For breakfast, they added meatless, bean chili to her plate. It wasn't as bad as some of the other rations. Still, it was hard to eat with her stomach in knots. All she could think about was the dreaded upcoming introduction at school. Even in the best of circumstances, she would've been nervous. Amára was always the confident one. Knowing her, she was probably even excited to meet a school full of new people, even with everything else having been taken away from her.

Why'd those cacafuegos have to separate us?

"Do I have-eh to finish?" Kassi rubbed her stomach.

Kyoto didn't respond. Meela glanced over at him and answered, "Jus do th'best ya can, t'day. We know yer nervous. At least drink yer health shake."

So that's what they call the muck juice. Kassi gulped it down and pushed her plate. Kyoto abruptly stood and nodded. It was time.

To better blend in, Kyoto sported a pair of cargo shorts and a lightweight white button-down with a purple armband wrapped around his right bicep. It was an odd sight after seeing him in military fatigues all week. With a heavy step, he marched to the door and apparently expected Kassi to follow. Outside, under the heavy, blue sky, the streets bustled with people. Buildings jutted out of the floodwater with colorful and unique awnings beneath upper floors of gray concrete–such an incompatible contrast.

In between the top floors of many of these buildings spanned bright holoscreens that synced together to play a U.N.O.E. sponsored update.

"...as we continue to strive for a morally superior civilization, we have implemented the following policy effective immediately. All Gaians are to refrain from lingering with hands in their pockets for more than three consecutive seconds..."

On the other side of the street, someone shouted, "WHAT?" U.N.O.E. drones immediately swarmed the man who then held up his hands and lowered his head. "I'll comply. I'll comply," he said as he resumed walking.

The screens showcased slow-motion video clips of people eating in the park, laughing, running through a field of flowers, jumping in the ocean, and doing a number of other completely random things. A slogan appeared on the screen, "Your safety is our greatest concern." Kassi was transfixed by how bizarre it was. Kyoto snapped his fingers and brought her back to Earth.

Directly in front of them, the flooded streets were lined on both sides with makeshift wooden bridges as dry walkways. They consisted of three layers. On the bottom, long, rounded logs were bound three or four abreast to provide the base. Crisscrossed branches and small beams less than a meter in length, perpendicular to the bottom row of logs, provided the second layer. Resting on the top, a single row of wobbly planks was placed down the middle to line the walkway. It was a very narrow path with only enough space for one person to cross at a time, making each side of the street one directional. Kassi tested one of them with her foot. It sagged under her weight.

"The floating sidewalks of Miami. When the streets flooded, the people came together and built these," Kyoto explained.

"Couldn't we just fly there in our siren suits?" Kassi asked, noticing the empty skies save for a few miniature U.N.O.E. drones flying by.

"That's not allowed here," he said. Without waiting for her to get accustomed to it, Kyoto spotted a small gap in the walking pedestrians and stepped onto the sidewalk, advancing down the fibrous-wooded path.

"Wait...wait up!" Kassi tried yelling, her hoarse voice swallowed up in the humidity. She tripped on the first board and nearly plunged right into the dark water. Catching herself on the intersecting branches before falling in, she caught a strong whiff of old fish, sewage, and saltwater before hoisting herself back up. Delicately placing one foot in front of the other, she struggled to keep her balance. Kyoto turned for a brief second to check on her before continuing his high-speed march. The people behind her grew impatient, pressuring her to walk faster.

"Keep up!" he shouted as he charged ahead, retreating further into the distance.

In her attempt to hurry and catch up, she tripped on a small rut between two planks and overcorrected by stepping on an intersecting wooden beam. Her foot slipped on the slick wood and went under, sending her sprawling. Her body crashed into the water, completely submerged as she struggled to find her footing on the road below. Once she did, she stood in the waist-deep, dirty seawater. Half of her life had been spent in the water, but never anything this muddy.

Kyoto backtracked just enough to emphatically scold her in front of everyone. "This is no time for games!"

"It's not like I did that on purpose-eh!" Kassi said as she climbed back onto the boards, pedestrians hurdling over her as she did. When she stood to regain her balance, stopping traffic, she heard many voice complaints behind her. There were now almost a dozen people between her and Kyoto. Kassi couldn't help but notice how skinny they all were. On Nemal, everyone was thin and fit, but still healthy. These Gaians looked slightly malnourished.

"You need to memorize the route to school. This will be the

only time I take you," Kyoto shouted from up ahead. "You'll find your own way from now on."

"What? I can't remember all this! I wasn't even paying attention!" She said as she teetered forward with each step.

"You'll figure it out!" Kyoto offered no help or sympathy. The people around them glowered at Kassi, clearly annoyed.

"Or maybe I zhust won't go back," Kassi mumbled under her breath.

Kyoto stepped to the side, balancing on a couple of cross-planks and letting a few pedestrians pass him. He glared at her. "There are cameras everywhere. If you don't come back on your own, mediation officers will find you. Trust me, you don't want that."

How'd he hear that? Kassi wondered. She did her best to remember the way from that point on but had no confidence in her sense of direction. That had always been Caesar's strength.

After they had walked more streets than Kassi could count, she stepped too wide on the middle plank, slipped, and plummeted a second time into the murky water.

"Ghost of Sheebah, this is annoying! This water's so gross!" Kassi huffed as she made her way back to the sidewalk. Kyoto didn't say anything, folding his arms and waiting impatiently. Traffic was forced to shimmy around him.

Once Kassi caught up, they took only a few more steps before he pointed up ahead and to the left. "There's your school. Go to the front desk and sign in." With that, he clambered across a rope bridge to the other side of the street. Kassi tried to see which way he went, but a line was forming behind her. One of them grunted impatiently.

She stared at the school looming up ahead. A giant alligator statue stood guard at the front entrance, crudely carved as if with a blunt instrument. High schoolers in their uniforms filed in behind and in front of Kassi on the walkways. As the only one without a uniform, Kassi stuck out like a flat note. Still dripping wet, she reached the fenced perimeter of the school. High above multiple floors with open balconies and stairways, a roof with tattered letters read "Miami Beach High School." A mud-stained white structure to her right jutted outward in an asymmetrical shape that came to a point.

A line of students grew behind her so she tried to pick up the pace to the staircase. Once they reached the stairs, students spread out and passed each other in a flurry of activity. Some danced, some sang as they meandered the halls with their friends. Many held fingers to their noses as they passed Kassi, casting her sidelong glances. Sneaking a quick whiff, her clothes smelled just like the streetwater–a tangy mixture of saltwater and sewage.

As if I don't have enough to be self-conscious about.

She wanted to hide, but everything was open, and all the hallways were bustling. No matter how she tried to peel off, she constantly found herself stuffed in the middle of the crowd. Anxiety was rising. She instinctively switched to her siren meditation practices, clearing her mind. She focused only on what she could control. Allowing herself to get carried along with the crowd, she restored her calm and took in her surroundings.

The school uniforms weren't all the same. Even though most everyone wore white, long-sleeved, button-down shirts and simple, black leather shoes, everything else varied. Shorts, skirts, socks, ties, and accessories came in different colors–red, blue, green, purple, and gray–each with slight modifications to the design. The reds were a scarlet red and looked the nicest. They fit the students to complement their frame. The patterns and cuts were flattering. Their shoes were polished and new. The others had varying degrees of style and design, but out of the five, the greens were the worst with a loose fit and patches with mismatched threads. Kassi hoped she could pick red, but right now, she would take any uniform just so she didn't stick out like a clarinet squeak.

Hallway signs directed her to the front office. She reached the door and stared at it for a beat, hesitating. She wondered if anyone would know if she actually attended school. Glancing up, she saw more discolored panels in every corner–cameras.

Do they really have to supervise everyone all the time? So intrusive! She heaved a deep breath and entered the office.

Pulling the door with a hard yank, it swung wildly into the adjacent wall, slamming with a bang.

"Yash and Sheebah! What's the matter with you?" The woman behind the counter shouted. Her gray hair was in an old-fashioned bob with slightly crooked bangs, and she had more wrinkles than any woman Kassi had ever seen. On her right arm, a royal blue armband wrapped around the loose, white sleeve of her blouse.

"Irene, you can't say that around the kids," said a bored voice from a neighboring room as if for the hundredth time that day.

Kassi approached her desk. Irene held a finger to her nose and winced from the smell. "Well, what is it?" Irene demanded, her voice snappish.

"I'm new here-eh?" Kassi said. Irene blinked, leaning on her hand, clearly waiting for Kassi to continue. "Do I...need to sign in or something?"

The receptionist heaved a sigh and leaned back in her seat. "How old are you?"

"Fifteen," Kassi said.

"Fifteen? So what's your star score?" Irene asked.

"My what?"

She stared over the rim of her glasses for a beat, sizing up Kassi. "Your star score?" She repeated. Seeing Kassi's blank expression, she asked, "You don't know what that is?"

Kassi shook her head.

"Who hid you from the worlds?" Irene scoffed. "Everyone gets one when they turn fifteen."

The woman rummaged through a drawer beneath the desk and pulled out a few all-gray uniforms. She held them up one at a time before discarding them. "Looks like we don't have your size. You'll just have to wait until you get your star score.

Come back when you have one." She waved a dismissive hand.

"But where-eh do I go?"

Her face soured, clearly annoyed that their conversation hadn't concluded. "What's your schedule say?"

"I don't have a schedule-eh."

The woman breathed the longest, deepest sigh before reaching back to grab her holopad. "Name?"

"Kassiana Rivernova."

"Rivernova? Right, and I'm the Goddess Sheebah," Irene scoffed. "Now, I do have a Kassiana Kazán that's supposed to be checking in sometime this week. I'm assuming that's your real name?"

"Kazán?" That was Kyoto and Meela's last name. They must have registered her under the same. "Um, yisû?"

The woman shook her head and mumbled something about "kids these days" before continuing, "Says your first class is *Heroics* with Professor Oakey. Room 211. Off you go!" She dismissed Kassi with an impatient flick of her hand.

Kassi almost asked where the class was but decided against it. Instead, she spent the next few minutes wandering around looking for Room 211. The halls had completely emptied except for a Hall Monitor who shouted at her, "You've got five seconds to get to class or it's the broomstick!"

Kassi panicked and ran in the other direction. Whatever "the broomstick" was, it sounded painful. Running through another meditation exercise, she scanned room numbers and hall signs until she found it. Her foot caught on the weapons detectors as she entered, causing her to stumble. She slinked to the back of the room, and took her seat, hoping no one noticed. Everyone noticed—especially Professor Oakey, a rail-thin woman with short, wavy, salt-and-pepper hair and glasses that were tied around her neck with a leather strap, a royal blue armband over her right arm.

The professor had been addressing the class from her desk

which was completely bare with the exception of her bright, polished nameplate. When she stood up at the interruption, her hip bumped the corner of her desk, knocking the nameplate ever so slightly to the side. Picking it up to give it a fresh polish from a handkerchief she pulled from her pocket, she delicately placed it back where it was. Once that was settled, she glanced at the back of the room sweeping over the classroom until she spotted Kassi.

She pointed a crooked finger. "You! Come here." Kassi slowly stood back up and shuffled forward. Her heart raced as she inched forward. "Quickly, now," Professor Oakey said, tapping her foot. As soon as Kassi was within reach, the professor stretched forward and pinched Kassi's bare arm hard enough to leave a mark, almost breaking skin. She sniffed, "You're soaked, you stink of street water, and you walk into my classroom late? Who do you think you are?"

"My name's Kassiana. I'm new here and they told me...,"

"Silence!" She pinched her arm in the same exact spot, this time drawing blood. "Miss Katiana..."

"Kassiana," Kassi corrected her, keeping her head down.

"...if you are clumsy enough to fall in the floodwaters, at least have the common decency to rinse off before class." Many of the students stifled laughs. Kassi wanted to disappear but did her best not to let the embarrassment show on her face. The professor glowered at Kassi as if waiting for something. "Well?"

"I'm sorry. It's zhust my first time-eh...," Kassi said. Everyone gawked at her as if they knew she was an alien from another planet.

"I don't want your excuses and what's with that filthy 'diser accent?" When Kassi didn't answer, Professor Oakey continued, "You have two minutes. I suggest you hurry!"

"But...now? How do I get all the way home and back before the bell?" Kassi did her best to hide her accent.

"Home? Are you a simpleton?" Professor Oakey bellowed for

all the class to hear. "The school washrooms are just down the hall!"

"But I don't know where…"

"Malyra!" The teacher called out, clearly done with the conversation.

"Yisû, Professor Oakey." A girl in a scarlet red school uniform tailored to fit her perfectly toned frame stood up and hurried to her teacher's side. She was pretty and she knew it, standing as if on display.

"Hello, dear. Would you be so kind as to show Katiana the washrooms?"

"Kassiana," Kassi corrected her again.

"Yisû, Professor Oakey," Malyra said, looking down on Kassi with her textured, blonde, comb-over bob lightly grazing her shoulders. She wrinkled her nose at the smell before bounding out of the room, expecting Kassi to follow. Kassi had to run to catch up.

In the hallway, Kassi tried to strike up a conversation. "Is she always like-eh that?"

Malyra didn't respond, so Kassi asked again, assuming she hadn't heard her the first time. Malyra gave her a sidelong glance, dragging out the awkward silence before asking, "Like what?"

"You know…rude-eh? And mean?"

Malyra tucked her hair behind her ear, picked up the pace, and called over her shoulder, "She's only hard on the stupid ones."

Kassi pulled up short, stunned as she stared at Malyra's back for a beat. For the rest of the trip, she loosely followed Malyra in silence. Once they reached the end of one of the hallways, Malyra finally spoke up. "There!" She pointed at a door down the corridor. "The showers and dryer bins are in there."

"Dryer Bins?"

"Ugh, figure it out! I have neither the time nor the crayons to explain it to you." Malyra sneered. Without another word, she stormed back to class, her sense of self-importance filling the empty hallways.

Kassi watched her leave, processing their exchange. She was really starting to hate this school. It was as if everyone here had just been stung by a newly-shaken nest of fire hornets and decided to take their rage out on the new girl.

To her relief, the washrooms were empty. No more prickly chas. Kassi circled the washrooms until she found the shower stalls. The shower curtains drooped, barely hanging onto the rods, the spouts were rusty, the walls and floors were cracked, and everything smelled of mold. Kassi sighed and began peeling off her wet clothes. She turned the knob to the shower and cold water trickled out. She waited for the water to get warmer. It never did. Just like the shower back at the townhome.

"Does no one have hot water on this Yash-forsaken planet?" Her raspy Evéik echoed slightly off the walls.

There was a row of gray-metal drawers to the right labeled "Wet Clothes." Assuming these were the dryer bins, she opened them and tossed in her clothes. As soon as she closed the door, she heard a click and the start of a motor that was so deafening, she decided to shower in the farthest stall away from the noise.

Before jumping in, she lightly touched her hair. "At least I put my hair in braids," she thought out loud, noticing the braids were mostly intact. She wouldn't have time to wash and rebraid it.

With only cold water, she rinsed off as fast as she could, turned off the water, and waited until the loud motor of the dryer bin came to a stop. Unable to find a towel, she yanked the blue shower curtain off the rod and wrapped it around her. She was still uncomfortable walking around in nothing but her bare skin. Amára would have disapproved. "Always be comfortable in your own skin, Kassi," she would often say. Kassi wasn't there yet. She still insisted on wearing something.

Wrapped in a curtain, Kassi shuffled awkwardly to the dryer bin and pulled on the handle. It wouldn't open. She tugged again–still nothing. Yanking furiously for a third time, she still wasn't able to pull the door open. It was jammed shut.

Ugh, could I just get one break?

Kassi couldn't decide whether to laugh, scream, or cry at the absurdity of her situation. Instead, she crossed the washrooms to the doorway and peeked out hoping to spot anyone roaming the halls. To her relief, a freckled girl with pretty green eyes and red, unkempt, curly hair like a lion's mane was running down the hall in her direction. Her outfit was different from the other students. It was a mustard yellow jumper like one you'd see worn by a custodian. "Help! Please-eh, I'm stuck!"

"Blind Sheebah!" The girl gasped, startled. "Are you talking to me?" Despite sounding shocked, the girl's voice had a light and friendly tone.

"Yisû." Kassi leaned out just enough to point at the dryer bins inside. "I can't get my clothes back!"

The girl eyed the shower curtain. "Oh! Yisû, that happens to me all the time. Here, I'll show you."

The girl followed Kassi to the dryer bins. "This is the one." Kassi reached for the door and gave it a hard tug. It remained stubbornly locked shut.

"These get stuck all the time. You just need something to slide in." She dug deep into her shoulder bag and pulled out a butter knife. "Like this!"

"You carry a butter knife in your bag?" Kassi eyed the girl curiously.

"Mm-hmm." Sliding the knife along the edges, she jerked and popped the door open. "There," she brushed off her hands and put the knife back in her bag.

Kassi breathed a huge sigh of relief. "You're a saint! And the first person to be nice-eh to me since I got here."

"Most people at this school are cacafuegos! It's like they've all been stung by a newly-shaken nest of hornets." She said with a disapproving shake of the head.

"That's exactly what I was thinking!" Kassi said.

The girl bowed. "I'm Savriah Gleeson. I go by Savvy."

"Kassiana Ri...uh I go by Kassi. Nice-eh to meet you." She returned the bow and smiled.

"You have a really nice neck shape, by the way," Savriah said as she stared at Kassi's neck. "You remind me of a swan. And that red spot," she pointed to Kassi's burn, "is just like a cardinal that used to chirp on a tree near my house."

"Oh. Uh, thanks?" Kassi stroked her neck. She wasn't sure how to respond to the odd compliment.

"Well, I better get to class. Professor always gets mad when I'm late!" Savriah bolted for the door and rushed off to class.

"Thanks again!" Kassi called after her. So she was a student! Her uniform was so different from the others. Kassi grabbed her clothes and examined them–still uglier than a batfish. She almost hoped they had magically transformed into something wearable. They were damp but dry enough, and the smell still lingered but wasn't as potent. Without any other options, she put her clothes back on. She hated the way they fit her, constantly tugging and pulling at the neck and sleeves.

Oakey called attention to Kassi arriving ten minutes later. "Looks like Princess Katiana doesn't understand the concept of time. Two minutes means two minutes!"

"It's Kassiana," she corrected her again. "And yisû sorry, I couldn't find my way here and there-eh was an issue with..."

"Silence! And what's with that ridiculous accent? You trying to sound like a 'diser?" Oakey spat the word as if it were the most offensive label you could give a person. When Kassi didn't respond, she continued. "Go to the cafeteria. Once you've finished the lecture on punctuality, you may return to my class."

"But won't that zhust make me even more tardy?" Kassi asked, struggling to speak like a Gaian. Professor Oakey stepped forward as if to pinch her again. Kassi retreated, dashing out of the room before she could.

After roaming for a few minutes, she found the cafeteria. Once inside, someone was there to play a 15-minute-long presentation from the holoscreen on all the reasons why it was disrespectful to be tardy. It was a complete waste of time. As the shock of her embarrassments wore off, Kassi found herself more and more annoyed.

After it finally finished, Kassi returned to class, scurrying toward the back before Professor Oakey could pinch her again. She found a seat and shrunk into her chair. As the only student without a uniform, she might as well have been wearing a chicken suit, which would have actually been an improvement.

Professor Oakey resumed her lecture and rambled on for the rest of class. Kassi listened in, trying to follow along, but she didn't have augmented reality goggles– hologlasses–like the rest of class. The professor referenced video clips Kassi couldn't see. Each time she did, at least one student glanced back at her acknowledging this fact. From the sound of it, they were reviewing specific scenarios from the Abyss, round two of the Siren Games, and studying the athletes' responses to those scenarios. Kassi was very familiar with the Abyss. With the use of the Rosen-comm link, Paradisers had access to watch the Games, and Kassi never missed it.

At the end of class, the intercom interrupted the professor with announcements. It was the crotchety lady from the front office, and she sounded even more irritated. "Good morning, Miami Beach High School. Before Period Two, there will be star score assignments for all students turning fifteen as well as new student orientation in the Commons. As usual, all students are required to attend. I repeat all students are required to attend!"

Kassi followed the crowd of students to the Commons located outside where basketball courts once stood. Now flooded, the area was covered with plywood staging to provide the students with a platform to stand on. It was barely large enough to fit them all, and from the looks of it, no one wanted to stand on the outer edge.

In the middle of the platform, on an elevated tier, stood a woman in a pencil skirt and suit coat three sizes too small, a blue armband over her right arm, and hair pulled back so tight into a low bun, it stretched the skin on her face. Standing next to her was a boy in plain clothes, alongside a few others in all-gray uniforms. Kassi wasn't the only new student!

Above them floated a holoscreen with a looped video about the U.N.O.E. It showed a lot of shiny, polished faces flashing unnaturally large grins as they touted all the great things the U.N.O.E. did for its citizens. Sentimental music played in the background as a few actors ranted about the "yashing 'disers", particularly blaming Kassi's parents and the Council of Creators for all of Earth's problems. Kassi barely noticed their ridiculous claims as she studied the other new student on the stage while everyone continued filing in. The video concluded with a large group of people pretending to hold hands and sing together–some kind of song about the U.N.O.E. promising to stand by its people.

Kassi tried hiding in the crowd but without a school uniform, in her glow-in-the-dark orange and green, she stuck out like a sneezing tuba. The woman on the stand immediately spotted her and pointed a long, twisted fingernail in her direction. With a stomp of her foot, she then pointed to the spot next to her and summoned Kassi to the stage.

Kassi straightened her shoulders as she neared the higher tier, getting a closer look at the boy on the platform. He was tall with dark brown, broccoli hair. There was an intensity behind his brown eyes, and when he locked eyes with hers, she felt her cheeks redden. He had a lean, muscular build, thick eyebrows, and a perfectly defined jawline. And even though he wore basic clothes--a long-sleeved white shirt and blue joggers--he somehow made them look fashionable. Maybe it was the way he rolled up his sleeves. Kassi tugged and readjusted her shirt again, trying to smooth all the wrinkles.

She hadn't realized she paused right in front of the stage until the woman seized her arm and yanked her onto the platform. "Get up here!" Kassi noticed a nametag on her suit that read,

Principal Purves. *What an unfortunate name.* Once the principal had positioned Kassi next to her, she turned her attention toward the gathered student body. Kassi swept her eyes across the crowd, most of them huddled in small groups singing and harmonizing with each other as if rehearsing. Just like on Nemal, only not nearly as talented. Even from this distance, she could hear the difference.

"Cut your mouth and shut it!" Principal Purves shouted. All noise abruptly stopped as if someone had pressed a mute button. The silence that followed was palpable. Just then, a student in green on the edge of the platform was bumped into the water. He yelled as he splashed and went under before climbing back onto the platform, a dripping mess. Principal Purves ignored the interruption. "We have five birthday graduations this month as well as two new students joining us at Miami Beach High School," she announced before whispering to the boy next to her, "Which is one too many if you ask me." She laughed and wrapped her arm around the boy. He shrugged her arm off and stared stiffly outward at the audience. The principal straightened before continuing, "Our new students are Nikola Amati and Kassiana Kazán. Sheebah knows why they didn't get their star scores at their previous school, so they'll be getting theirs today."

Principal Purves continued, "Our first birthday graduate is..." she stared at the names to make sure she was reading them right. "A-B-C-D-E Rinn?"

"Hi, it's pronounced Abcity," said a student in an all-gray uniform toward the front, raising her hand. Ash-blonde, basic hair fell to her shoulders, she had an oval face and plain features.

"I'm sorry, what?" The principal waved impatiently. "What are you doing down there? Get up here!"

"It's pronounced Abcity?" Abcde said as she weaved her way to the stage.

"Is that a question?" The Principal stared at the student over her glasses. "Alright, very funny. What's your real name?"

"That is my real name." Abcde looked down as she took her place next to Kassi.

"So you're telling me your parents," she tilted her chin down and raised her eyebrows, "your parents named you the first five letters of the yashing alphabet?"

"Principal, you can't say that around the kids," a white-haired man in an all-beige suit said from the front row, blue armband. Kassi recognized his voice from earlier in the front office. Principal Purves ignored him and continued staring at Abcde, waiting for an answer.

"Mm-hmm." Abcde kicked her feet.

"Well that's just cruel," the principal said to herself before continuing. "Moving on! Mr. Numbles has her Star Score."

A short, balding man with a mousy face and small-rimmed glasses skittered onto the stage holding out a holopad with graphs and charts displayed above it. "Uh, yisû, hello students," he tugged at his sleeves nervously, just below his green armband. "I spent the last two days, or let's see, maybe it was three days, talking with the star score committee, and what they had to say was quite fascinating, and well, if you take a look at...."

"Sheebah's bench! Out with it!" The principal held her head as if she were nursing a really bad headache.

"Principal, you can't say that around the kids," the white-haired man repeated.

"Quiet, you!" she pointed at the man.

Mr. Numbles continued. "Right, oh yisû, um I have Ab...city's score first," he glanced at her to make sure he was saying her name right. "Abcity Rinn has a score of 532. 532!" He yelled loudly as the numbers floated and swiveled off of his holopad high enough for everyone to see. The students golf-clapped routinely to acknowledge the score.

"Alright, very good. Yisû, uh next I have..."

Kassi zoned out while he read off the next few students and their scores. Standing on the platform, she felt on display in front of the school in her neon colors. If only Amára were here to boost her confidence. She almost looked to Nikola, the boy next to her, for that reassurance, but he held a cold stare outward, avoiding eye contact with her.

Mr. Numbles ratted on, "...I have Nikola Amati's score here. And here you'll see his charts and data...," he mumbled to himself for a few awkward seconds before finally pulling up the score display. "Here we are. 872." He enlarged the display as a giant 872 replaced the previous score.

"872!" Principal Purves clapped her hands wildly before holding Nikola's arm in the air as if he'd just claimed victory in a boxing match. The students erupted in a more rigorous applause, clearly favoring his score over the others. "What a wonderful addition Nikola will make!" It sounded as though she was about to dismiss the students before they even got to Kassi's star score. Nikola didn't seem to care for the score or the praise. He slipped his hand away from the principal. Purves resumed clapping enthusiastically as she stepped back and nodded for Mr. Numbles to continue.

"Right. Very good. Congratulations Mr. Amati." Mr. Numbles applauded awkwardly as the principal rolled her eyes. "And next we have Kassiana Kazán's right here, and it's..." he quickly scrolled through a few displays before fumbling the holopad and dropping it to the floor. The principal face-palmed and sighed.

It was so strange hearing them say Kazán instead of Rivernova. The Rivernova family name was the most famous in all the known worlds. They were the rulers of the Paradise Planets. And apparently, everyone on Earth hated them.

Mr. Numbles' voice brought her back. "Yisû, here it is. Kassiana Kazán's star score is 409."

Five

M r. Numbles collected himself. "409!" He shouted to emphasize the score as he enlarged the holographic display. Once again, large numbers swiveled in the air.

Students gasped. A few beats passed before they erupted into laughter. Kassi didn't know if she should be outraged, ashamed, or indifferent to whatever their star score meant, but the way the students reacted, she knew her score wasn't going to improve her day at all. It continued for a few long minutes before the principal shouted, "Cut your mouth and put a muzzle on it!" They fell abruptly silent, once again. "Wipe that silly grin off your face Mr. Marvenbaum." A boy in the front immediately looked at his feet. "Now get outta my sight before I give every last one of you the broomstick!"

It was a mad dash as students emptied the outdoor Commons within seconds. A teacher's assistant kindly ushered Nikola off of the stage, leading him to his next class. The principal's eyes followed him before she exited the stage with a sigh.

Seeing Nikola get an escort, Kassi lingered on the platform waiting for the same. An adult faculty member walked toward her. Instead of showing her to her next class, he yelled, "What do you want, a parade? Get back to class or it's the broomstick!" Kassi bolted inside and down the nearest corridor to get away. Once inside, she remembered she needed to show the cranky woman at the front office her star score.

"What is it, now?" Irene slammed down her mug of coffee harder than she probably intended and spilled a few drops onto the edge of her desk.

"You told me to come-eh back after I got my star score-eh."

"Well, what is it? And stop with that absurd accent already, you sound like a yashing 'diser!" She spat the word like hot coals from her mouth.

"Um, my score is 409?" Kassi hid her accent.

"409? What are you dumb or something?"

"You're not supposed to say things like that, Irene," came the bored voice of the white-haired man from the other room.

"Keep it to yourself for once!" Irene unfolded from her chair, the cushion well worn. She sighed and said, "I'll be right back."

"Can I...," Kassi said before Irene was out of range, "can I have one of the red uniforms?"

"Ha," Irene mock laughed as she vanished around the corner.

A few minutes later, she returned with a bag, its multicolor patchwork barely holding well-worn threads together. The straps to the bag had been repaired more than once. Inside was a mustard yellow jumpsuit. It was the same uniform she saw Savriah wearing earlier.

"Why's the uniform different?"

"You're a 400. This," she held up the uniform like it was an infectious disease, "is a Four Hundie uniform. You only get two. The spare's in your bag." Irene handed her a sheet of paper. "And here's your full class schedule. Off you go!" Kassi examined the uniform for a brief moment, standing in the middle of the office. Irene swatted at the air and said, "I said off you go!"

Kassi slumped her shoulders and took a deep sighing breath before dragging her feet to the washrooms. After slipping on the baggy uniform, she found the only unbroken mirror and studied her reflection. It zipped down the middle and was completely shapeless. She almost looked frumpier than before. She was still fidgeting with the sleeves when a hall monitor peeked her head through the doorway. "What're you doing in here, Four Hundie? Get to class or it's the broomstick!"

Again with the "broomstick" threat. Kassi hurried into the halls and searched for her Period 2 class, *History of the Worlds*. After doubling back a few times, she found it.

Running through the weapons detector, she stubbed her foot again on the door frame and splashed into the room. Clutching her foot, she hobbled down the side of the classroom to a vacant seat on the second row. Dr. Jibu, a short almond-eyed man with a very large forehead and a blue armband, stopped in the middle of his lecture and glowered at her. He had an exceptionally large nose. Her brother would have called it a schnoz. Crossing the classroom, he reached down and pinched Kassi's arm, adding to the pain she already felt in her foot, and said, "You're late. You need to go to the cafeteria for a lecture on punctuality."

"But I did that last period," Kassi said, fighting back the tears from the swelling pain.

"Then you apparently didn't learn your lesson," Dr. Jibu said.

"I was told to go to the front office-eh to get my uniform. That's why I'm late-eh," Kassi said, still holding the piece of paper with her schedule printed on it.

Dr. Jibu studied her for a moment while the class watched and waited. "Fine, I'll let you off just this once. Take your seat."

Already seated, Kassi was confused. He cleared his throat and pointed at the farthest row in the back. All the other students staring at her offered no help. The empty row of seats in the back was thrashed, likely the reason no one sat in them.

Her slight hesitation was enough for Dr. Jibu to storm over to his desk and slam his palm onto a switch that revealed holographic banners above each row. The back row had been labeled with a translucent, holographic overhang: 400s. Each row had its number posted above them, 800s in the front. It dawned on Kassi that everyone in each row wore the same colored school uniform. Somehow, she had been too distracted to notice. Reds were 800s, purples were 700s, blues, 600s, and greens, 500s. Kassi would be the only 400 in the room in her *mustard yellow* jumpsuit.

500s and 600s crowded their aisles, practically on top of each other. There were fewer 700s and only four 800s, granting each of them more space. In the front row, Nikola wore his new red uniform with casual ease, rolling up the sleeves as if he'd always done so. And he was already making friends.

He cast her a patronizing smirk. Everyone in the front row sported an air of smugness, and even next to Malyra, Nikola's was the smuggiest. They seemed to lounge above everyone else on high clouds of comfort and luxury.

Kassi slouched into a seat in her assigned row. The chair wobbled and tipped backward, almost spilling her onto the floor before she regained her balance. It squeaked loudly with every micro movement, causing students to glance back and gawk.

"Alright, settle down. We don't want the clowns to come around," Dr. Jibu said. Sharing puzzled looks, students shrugged and quieted. The lecture resumed, and Kassi took the holo-glasses from her bag, powering them up to follow along.

The lenses on her glasses were intact, but otherwise, everything else was scratched beyond reason, as if someone had purposefully scuffed every possible surface. They pinched her nose and wore heavy on her ears. Glancing at the 800s, she noticed how pristine theirs were. Thin and slightly wrapping around their eyes, their sleek black hologlasses were customized to each student to better match their face. In contrast, all the 500s wore identical glasses that were in slightly better condition than Kassi's.

Putting hers on for the first time, she found a file with her homework from Period 1. There were additional assignments as a result of her tardiness, each with the warning: *if you fail to turn in additional assignments on time, you will receive one day of detention for every day your assignment is late.*

Mirific. Hopefully, her parents would take her back home before she had to do any homework. In the meantime, she should probably keep up and play along.

History of the Worlds was nothing like what Kassiana expected. Dr. Jibu taught them historical events that directly contradicted what she had learned back home on Nemal. Skimming ahead on her hologlasses, she noticed most of it painted the U.N.O.E. as the heroes of every story.

"You kids don't know how good you have it," Dr. Jibu said repeatedly.

Kassi tuned him out and worked on her Period 1 homework while she reflected on her new star score. 409 must have been rock bottom. She wondered how star scores were tabulated and decided to grill Meela about it later.

The bell rang and the students bolted for the door to make it to Period 3 within the small three-minute window in between classes. It was an unreasonable amount of time considering how far apart some of the classrooms were, especially for anyone who had to use the washroom.

Period 3 was *Mechanical Engineering,* on the other side of the school. She pushed her legs as fast as they would go, backtracking a few times before arriving seconds before the bell. Nikola was already there, again, seated comfortably next to his escort. They both glanced at Kassi and sniffed. Hands in pockets, Kassi sulked to the back to take her seat.

"Hands out of your pockets!" Professor Tavian, the Mechanical Engineering professor, shouted from across the room. He wore a blue armband, which Kassi now realized meant he was a 600. His face was unshaven, his hair disheveled, and he slouched in his seat like a man who had drawn the short stick in life and knew it.

Kassi turned to her professor. "What?"

"Hands!" He pointed. "Take your hands out of your pockets.

New policy." He flicked his eyes toward the discolored panel in the corner–the camera.

She slowly retracted her hands from her pockets, perplexed. The only benefit to her mustard yellow coveralls was the large pockets on both sides.

With a nod, Professor Tavian stood to address the class. Kassi hurried to her seat, the entire row of broken desks to herself. She wondered if she had any classes with Savriah, the only other 400 she knew of.

Professor Tavian launched into his lecture. *Mechanical Engineering* had always fascinated Kassi, especially when it came to designing and customizing various watercraft like athletes did for the final round of the Siren Games. She hoped this class would give her opportunities to implement some of her newest ideas. After a few short minutes into his lecture, Kassi soon realized that would not be the case. They were going over fundamentals–things she had learned when she was five. Somehow, all the higher statuses didn't even know basic engineering, and yet, Kassi was the inferior one–the 400!

Professor Tavian pulled up a display of the sonoluminescence bulbs on everyone's sonopacks. "...the air bubble suspended in heavy water, which contains only deuterium, is struck by a stream of sound waves to produce cavitation. A neutron source known as Curium-248 feeds the spherical bulbs with neutrons that are then used to cause nuclear fusion..."

Disappointed and bored, she couldn't stop yawning. Every time she did, Tavian would whip his head in her direction and scowl. At least being in the back row afforded her some distance from the professors' pincers.

As she tried to stay awake, her thoughts drifted to Amára. If only there was a way to find out how her first day of school was going. With her affable personality, she was certainly already making friends, regardless of her star score. If only they weren't split up. Kassi could use a little help making friends here–that is, if she were actually staying here long enough to make friends.

She watched Nikola run a hand through his broccoli hair, lick his lips and smile at Malyra who was practically drooling over him. The dreamy look in her eye made Kassi burp up some of her muck juice.

By the time Period 4 came around, Nikola had enough friends to form a swing band. And apparently, they had the same class schedule as Kassi.

Lucky me.

Period 4 was *Physical Education* in the gymnasium next to the washrooms–much easier to find. In the washrooms, Kassi pulled gym clothes from inside her school bag. Mustard yellow gym shorts and a black sleeveless top. The shorts had a drawstring she had to tighten considerably. The shirt was loose around the neck and tight under the arms as if they purposely designed clothes to be misshapen and uncomfortable. She pulled hard at the armpits, tearing threads to loosen them.

Malyra and her friends changed in front of everyone as if putting on a show. Comparing abs and legs with each other, they lingered in their sports bras and thongs much longer than needed.

Rather than spend any more time fiddling with her own gym clothes, Kassi hustled to class. She hoped *Physical Education* would give her a much-needed outlet for the day's frustrations.

Coach Muzzey, a pale, balding man with a drooping mustache and a belly slightly spilling out of his shirt, a blue 600s armband over his arm, sent them running in circles as he took roll. Of all physical activities, running was the worst, and running in circles was pointless, but Kassi went along with it.

Class was half over and they were still circling the gym. Most had slowed to a walking pace. Kassi wondered if Muzzey had anything else planned. With only twenty minutes left, he blew his whistle and lined everyone up against the far wall. Malyra, Nikola, and a few of their high-status friends took positions next to Kassi. Of course, their gym clothes were stylish and form-fitting. Malyra had tied her shirt up to flaunt her well-defined six-pack. Her skin was golden tan and flawless. Nikola had taken his shirt off and was equally cut and toned. An 800 next to them with a blonde, burst fade and thick muscles had also removed his shirt and was flexing for his friends. He curled his arms, nodding at his biceps and smiling like an imbecile.

"Alright, listen up. We're doing a wall-sit contest. Whoever can hold a wall sit position the longest gets to sit out of class on the day of their choosing. If you fall, you're out," Muzzey explained before he blew the whistle. "Positions!"

"Aw yisû, it's time for DeSchuster to show all you puny chas how it's done," shouted DeSchuster, the flexing, shirtless dolt.

Kassi loosened up and stretched, taking her position. Malyra took the spot right next to her, curiously. Only a few hours prior, she had been completely repulsed by Kassi.

With the blow of the whistle, they sat against the wall. Kassi concentrated on her breathing to take the focus off of the burning sensation in her thighs. Malyra cast suspicious, side-long glances her way. Coach Muzzey mosied toward Kassi's end, giving her a mustachioed scowl before turning his attention to Malyra, a perverted twinkle in his eye. Malyra ignored his gaze. As soon as he turned his back and faced the other direction, many students silently stood and shook out their legs.

They're cheating!

Kassi was one of the few who remained in position. Without warning, Malyra popped up and kicked Kassi in the shin.

"Ow! What'd you do that for?" Kassi said with a raspy shout, rubbing her shins. Everyone jumped back against the wall when Coach Muzzey heard the commotion and turned to face them. He was too slow to notice. Malyra beamed, clearly proud of herself for getting away with it.

The second Muzzey turned his back to them again, Malyra kicked Kassi's other shin even harder. Kassi winced with pain but held her position. At the far end, Coach caught a pair of 700s standing up, ran up to them, and shouted, "You're out!"

On the third pass, when Muzzey turned his back, Malyra

swung her foot low, sweeping the leg hard enough to knock Kassi clean onto her butt. At this, Nikola and the others burst into laughter. Muzzey spotted it, pointed at Kassi, and said, "Four Hundie! You're out!"

"But she kicked me!" Kassi went over and shoved Malyra off the wall.

Coach Muzzey leaped within centimeters of Kassi's face and spat, "Yash's tap-dancing sheist! Who do you think you are, Four Hundie? You're getting the broomstick!" Malyra looked so pleased with herself, bursting at the seams.

Kassi fidgeted with her braid anxiously as she awaited the ominous broomstick, still furious at Malyra but even more afraid of the pending punishment. Two boys ran into the gym closet and emerged, one of them holding a regular broomstick. They ran up to Kassi, placed the broomstick a few centimeters from her feet, and flanked each side of her as if making sure she wouldn't make a run for it. Kassi relaxed a little when she realized the broomstick wouldn't be used to beat her.

"Line it up!" Coach Muzzey shouted. "800s, get 'em started!"

Malyra was first, touching toes with the broomstick, centimeters from Kassi's face. With a deep breath, she bellowed at the top of her lungs, "your chin is fat and you smell like sheist! And what's that disgusting mark on your neck?" The sheer volume of it made Kassi's ears buzz.

Malyra moved to the back of the line as DeSchuster immediately jumped forward, shouting, "Everyone that loves you is wrong! You're the reason food rations come with instructions!"

"Stop it!" Kassi said, wiping spit off her face. "Why are you doing this?"

Next was Nikola. He roared, "Every time you leave home, your whole family celebrates! No one even misses you when you're gone!"

Kassi burst into tears, covering her face.

Rather than show sympathy and hold back, the rest of class only increased their intensity upon seeing Kassi cry. One by one, they took turns screaming at Kassi slights against her appearance, her intellect, her loveability. A few even went on long-winded rants. Her fingernails bit into her palms as she stood and took it for the longest fifteen minutes of her life. Muzzey blew his whistle and the yelling stopped.

Stunned, ears ringing, her face covered in spit, Kassi thought it was finally over. It wasn't. The entire class gathered to one side and watched as Malyra stepped forward.

Muzzey handed her a sonic pulse baton. "Whenever you're ready, baby doll."

Awkwardly clearing her throat, Malyra cringed at Coach Muzzey and quickly snatched the baton. Shaped similarly to the sonic rifle, the sonic baton had a smaller amplifier and was limited to non-lethal strikes. The one in Malyra's hand looked well-used, its mouthpiece a bent, metal mesh, paint on the handle chipped and faded, and the amplifier filter scratched. Despite its poor condition, Kassi had no doubt it still worked.

Malyra aimed it directly at Kassi, filled her lungs, and sang a few strong notes of an unfamiliar melody. Without a voice to perform a shield, Kassi shuffled side to side, shoes squeaking as she tried to dodge the high-frequency pulse, Malyra closely matching her movements. After only a few phrases, Kassi felt a blow like a punch in the gut that caused her to double over and crumple to the ground. The class broke into applause as Malyra grinned victoriously from ear to ear.

"Good work, class!" Coach Muzzey said, clapping his hands. "Now run along to lunch!"

Six

Everyone, including Coach Muzzey, filed out of the gymnasium, leaving Kassi on the floor like a mud puddle. Her eyes followed the rotations of the gargantic industrial fans on the ceiling. Life continued spiraling downward. Gaians were so hateful, heartless. Maybe they didn't deserve access to Paradise. Maybe her parents and the Council were right not to fight diplomatic battles for the Gaians. Kassi was tired, her will to bounce back seeping through the floorboards.

A loud voice startled her. "Four Hundie! Get to the cafeteria or it's the broomstick!" They couldn't even give her five minutes. Slowly getting to her feet, she felt thick and heavy as she trudged to the cafeteria. Taking her place in line behind other students, she stared ahead and avoided all eye contact.

Nikola drew unwanted attention to her, "Klutziana, you're in the wrong line. Four Hundies are way over there!" Malyra and all of his new friends giggled as Kassi squinted to the far end of the cafeteria, too numb to acknowledge the insult. She just wanted to distance herself from everyone. Back home, she could disappear in the labyrinth of the Royal Gardens. With its tall hedges, it spanned for kilometers and was easy for anyone to find calm solitude. But it was worlds away, and so was any semblance of peace.

As she neared the 400s sign, she saw four others waiting in line in their mustard-yellow coveralls.

So there are more 400s.

Kassi weaved through a cafeteria as students were grouped together singing, harmonizing, or rehearsing dance moves. Elbows jostled her along the way. One 600 even attempted a dance move that landed a kick into Kassi's right shoulder–no apology. He didn't even acknowledge he had done it. Keeping her feet, Kassi stumbled to the other 400s and lined up behind them.

"Welcome to the Trench," one of them said. Kassi didn't respond, wanting to be left alone.

"Yisû, welcome to the Trench," another boy spoke quickly. "I'm Adonis Roma and this pata is…"

"Fille Docker." They bowed their heads to greet her. Kassi instinctively glanced at the other two who made no attempt to introduce themselves. Fille followed her gaze. "That's Jacen, and that's Jaya," he pointed. "We call them the J's. They're completely in denial."

"We're not in denial, we were wronged!" Jacen scowled. "We shouldn't be here!"

"I've got a 492," Jaya said with a sneer. "I'm practically a 500, anyway."

"But you're not a 500," Fille jabbed a finger at them. "You're in the trench, like us."

Adonis studied Kassi's expression and spoke up, "You look, you look shell-shocked."

Kassi sighed and stared at the floor for a pause before saying, "I got the broomstick."

"Oh sheist!" Adonis shouted, pressing his hand to his mouth.

"On your first day?" Fille raised both eyebrows.

Jacen and Jaya faced forward, as if completely unaffected by Kassi's plight.

"I'm so, I'm so sorry." Adonis lightly patted her shoulder.

Fille shook his head and faced the crowded cafeteria, shouting, "Those sick, sadistic sheists! They get their kicks from beating us down!" He swung a foot in their direction as if to boot the entire student body. "THEY CAN ALL EAT SHEIST AND DIE!" No one responded or even acknowledged Fille, save a single 600 who chucked a half-eaten biscuit at Fille's face.

Kassi looked up and studied her fellow 400s. Fille was a tall, lithe figure with his blonde hair in a side part with a quiff. He smiled with his whole face and his crystal blue eyes looked like they were ready to burst into tears of laughter at any given moment. Adonis had Spanish eyes and was equally thin and wiry. His black wavy hair parted down the middle in curtains and fell just past his jawline. When he moved, he swayed as if dancing to his own imaginary rhythm. Kassi could instantly tell they both spent a lot of time laughing, which either meant they had completely lost their minds, or they couldn't care less about being the wet sand on the bottom of everyone's feet. At least they were friendly.

"Wait wait, you're Asian?" Adonis studied her closely. His words rolled off quickly, like the fast hits of an uptempo bongo groove.

"Um, yisû," Kassi said with reservation.

"Lemme see, lemme see your hands." Adonis grabbed her left hand and inspected her fingers. "Ah, you must only be part Asian!"

"What?" Kassi snatched her hand back, examining her fingers.

"Full Asians don't have fingerprints. And you have fingerprints, so you must be only part Asian," Adonis explained. Jaya cast him a sidelong glance and rolled her eyes with disgust.

"Wha-haat?" Fille said as he burst out laughing. His laugh reminded Kassi of a bombastic trumpet solo in a jazz improv session. "Asians don't have fingerprints? Where'd you hear that from, one of your ludicray cousins?"

"I'm telling you! They don't! I heard it from a cha who said it's why so many Asians become ninjas," Adonis said.

"Donis, you soft-headed sheist. That's the dumbest thing I've ever heard!"

Just then, Savriah, the red-headed girl who had helped Kassi in the washrooms, joined them. "What'd I miss?"

Fille laughed while he explained it. "Donis thinks, he thinks Asians don't have fingerprints. He says that's why so many become ninjas!" His voice went higher and higher as he tried to get the sentence out between fits of laughter. He had one of those infectious laughs. Kassi couldn't help but join in. After all she had been through that day, it felt good to laugh.

"Don't laugh! I'm telling you!" Adonis' face reddened.

"Here we go again." Savriah shook her head before turning toward Kassi and staring at the burn on her neck. "Shower curtain girl."

"That's me." Kassi instinctively felt the discoloration on her neck.

"Welcome to the Trench!" Savriah bowed.

"You two know each other?" Fille asked.

"Savriah helped me with an awkward situation this morning," Kassi said, smoothing one of the many wrinkles in her uniform.

"Do I even wanna know?" Fille asked.

"Probably not," Savriah shook her head, closing her eyes and scrunching her face a little as she did so.

"Savvy's a real loon, but she's one of us!" Fille said with a loud slap on Savriah's back.

"I'm not a loon!" Savriah retaliated by slugging his arm.

"Right, because normal people iron their clothes outside on their front porch," Fille said, rubbing his arm where she had hit him.

"What? It was smokey in my house. My dad burnt breakfast," Savriah said.

"He burnt breakfast? That's practically impossible! You hit a single button on the air fryer to cook it. How in Sheebah's mystic mountains did your dad burn it?" Fille wildly threw his arms into the air.

"Our fryer is broken," Savriah said.

Adonis added, "Or what about, what about that time when she came over to your house and brought her own cup full of water? An actual cup."

"And she called it her watercolor cup!" Fille said with a point of his finger.

"It was watercolor," Savriah shrugged. "The color of water."

"That's called clear," Fille said. "And you didn't think I would have any cups at my house?" Fille's voice grew louder. Adonis laughed with a snort. Kassi resisted the urge, not wanting to offend Savriah.

"How would I know what you do or don't have?" Savriah squared up with Fille.

"Because everybody has them! They're government issue." Fille talked with his hands, emphasizing each word. Kassi whipped her head back and forth between them as they rambled on. Everything about them was so foreign and odd, but at least they weren't cruel. So far, they were the only pleasant Gaians Kassi had met.

"400s!" Came the shout from the other end of the cafeteria. Jacen and Jaya bolted to grab their food, leaving the rest of them behind. Fille, Adonis, Savriah, and Kassi made their way to the section of the counter labeled 400s. Partitions separated rations for each status. 800s had six different food items and plenty of each. 700s had five items, and also in abundance. 600s had four items, and their shelves were mostly bare. 500s and 400s had the same three food options: green biscuits, veggie medley, and bowls of gruel, and there was hardly any left.

"So what we havin' today, Mrs. Stow?" Fille asked.

"Bacon and gruel, and we're all outta bacon," Mrs. Stow said with the enthusiasm of a land snail, her short hair stuffed under a hairnet.

"Ha-hah, that never gets old," he clapped once. Then, to Kassi, "Well, it's not much, but it's better than a poke in the eye!"

"Think I'd prefer a poke in the eye," Mrs. Stow grumbled as she adjusted her disposable gloves.

Fille grabbed all the remaining food and distributed it to their trays. "C'mon, we'll split it in Sensei's room."

With everyone else seated, Kassi took a moment to survey the cafeteria. Everyone here was in grade 10. Kassi thought it odd they didn't eat lunch with grades 9, 11, or 12–must be a capacity issue. Even with only one grade, the room was almost filled.

At the far right sat a fully furnished, secluded VIP section for the 800s. They had extra piles of food and were all reclined on comfortable leather chairs and sofas. Many were working on song arrangements or dance routines.

Fille seemed to notice Kassi staring at Nikola in the 800s section. "Looks like that new cha fit right in with the Chinpoke Squad."

"Chinpoke-eh Squad?" Kassi raised an eyebrow. She had never heard that term.

"A chinpoke is basically someone who treats everyone else like sheist for absolutely no reason," Savriah explained.

"That's why we call Malyra and her wombat toadies the Chinpoke Squad," Fille elaborated. "And Nikola's their new addition."

In the middle of the cafeteria, the 700s, 600s, and 500s each sat at long tables that extended the length of the room. The 700s had a few leftover recliners and a lot of extra space on newer benches and tables. The 600s and 500s crowded in on older tables. Between the loud singing and the dancing on tables, it was musical chaos. Only a few bothered to notice her staring and glared back at her. Jacen and Jaya sat on the floor near the 500s table, doing their best to avoid eye contact with Kassi.

On the far left side, there was a lone, circular table without benches or seats of any kind. The surface was battered and tilted sadly to one side.

"500s stole our chairs again," Savriah said with a half-shrug.

"We have to eat there-eh?" Kassi blinked.

"We're supposed to," Savriah said.

Fille waved her toward the exit, "But we always eat in Sensei K's room."

"Sensei K?" Kassi kept pace as they left the cafeteria.

"Professor Kelipalo," Savriah said.

"Mirific, another professor," Kassi groaned.

"He's not like the others," Savriah patted Kassi's neck awkwardly as they reached the halls.

"Sensei K is the bosst!" Adonis' voice echoed through the empty hallway.

"What does he teach?"

"Evéik," Fille and Savriah said in unison. Fille continued, "And he helps train a lot of the champions in the Games."

"Evéik–that's my Period 6," Kassi said. "Wait, Kelipalo–that name sounds familiar. He's our professor?"

"Yisû," Fille said. "Sounds like you'll be in our class."

"He won't make you sit in the back," Savriah scrunched her face, shook her head.

"Sensei K is the bosst!" Adonis shouted louder.

"He won't?" Kassi asked.

"He's different. You'll see," Fille said.

They walked to the elevators, pushed the button, and waited for the doors to open. Once inside, everyone instinctively turned to face the elevator doors except Savriah. She held her tray and continued to stare at the back while it climbed.

Fille cast her a sidelong stare before shouting, "Turn around you loon!"

"What?" Savriah raised an eyebrow.

"Face the door!" He yelled, pointing forward. "What, are you psychotic?"

Savriah rolled her eyes and reluctantly turned to face the doors.

They climbed upward at a banana slug's pace. Fille glanced

at Adonis' tray with nothing but the small bowl of grayish gruel. "Donis, you gonna eat that? Or did you?"

"Ha. Ha." Adonis said, slapping his leg in mock laughter.

The doors slid open, and they strode down the hallway to a closed classroom door. Fille gave a loud knock. The door swung open as a broad, muscular, light tan-skinned Polynesian filled the entire door frame. His hair was in short black curls, and he wore a t-shirt with a red 800s armband, shorts, and sandals as if ready for a sunny day at the beach–quite the contrast from the formal dress of the other faculty. His intimidating, chocolate-brown eyes bore down on Fille, his chest puffed out. "What do you want, Fille?"

Kassi scooted behind Savriah just as the man burst into the widest grin accompanied by a deep, belly laugh. Fille and the others burst into laughter as well.

"Come on in!" He opened his door and let everyone pass. The four of them took their seats in the front row, and Fille divvied up the food into four portions. "I left the extras on my side desk, Fille," Sensei called as he crossed to the back of the room, preoccupied.

Savriah explained before Kassi could ask, "They give professors extra rations and since most professors are 600s, their rations include white rice. Sensei stashes some away for us since the 400s never get enough."

"He gives his food to us?" Kassi asked, glancing back at Professor Kelipalo. After eating meager rations for the past week, she was amazed to hear a Gaian, especially one as big as Sensei K, was willing to give his away.

Fille handed them each a tall glass of green muck juice and raised his into the air. "Born up a tree!"

Adonis and Savriah echoed, "Born up a tree!" as they all quickly downed the juice and slammed their glasses on the table. Kassi was a little slow but did her best to gulp it down.

Adonis was about to dig in when he noticed Savriah eyeing

him oddly, chewing on the inside of her cheek. "What? What?" He said.

"I was just thinking," Savriah cocked her head to the side. "With the right makeup, you'd make a really attractive girl."

"I'll take it, I'll take it," Adonis ran his fingers through his hair before returning his attention to his plate.

Professor Kelipalo returned to the front and joined them, sitting on the edge of his desk. "And who's this?"

"She's the, she's the new girl," Adonis said between bites.

"This is Kassiana," Savriah said.

"I go by Kassi."

"Well, hello Kassi. Do I have you in my class?"

"I...yisû. Period 6."

"I'll try not to give you a hard time." He smiled. "Do you know any Evéik?"

"That's actually my first languazhe-eh."

"Is it?" Sensei K jumped into a conversation in Evéik. "*Zélé kwam bud pí vodí premir tagé par Miami Beach Ardjang mwat.*"

Kassi lit up at the sound of the familiar language. After hearing only English for the past week, she had nearly forgotten how calming Evéik was. She responded, "*Bud néz agaþ famat!*" Reflecting back on her first day, she shook her head and said, "*Bud vastamé tino kookas famat. Vud îpsu humos li máþetító i alîvót.*"

"*Yisû, bud dar char sentutóbé hasa nagum jukat.*" Sensei nodded with a sigh. "*Buda nui bézûhan ubi buda dari tuvé famat?*"

"*Îpsu!*" Kassi said, holding back tears as she thought of home.

"*Ubi daiba nékba dari tuvat?*" Sensei asked.

Before she could answer, Adonis interjected. "Wait wait wait, you speak Evéik?"

Kassi nodded.

"Is that, is that why you have an accent?" Adonis rattled off with rapid-fire speed. "It's different. I like it!"

"Oh thanks," she said. She really had done a poor job of hiding it. "I...uh, like your accent, too!" Kassi said with her best Gaian accent.

"Oh I don't, I don't have an accent," Adonis said, confused. Fille slapped a hand on Adonis' shoulder and shook his head with a sigh. "What? What?"

"Cha! Everybody has an accent," Fille said.

"Well then what, what accent do I have?" Adonis clapped his hand to his chest.

"You're from Miami. You have a Miami accent!" Savriah said before turning to Kassi. "So where are you from?"

"Yisû, you never told us," Fille said.

"I'm from Nemal. A city called Ca'pri," Kassi answered. "Or wait...not...sheist!" She kicked herself, wishing she could take it back. Up until a few days ago, she had never had any reason to distrust people and keep secrets. But Gaians hated Paradisers, and Kassi already let it slip that she was one of them.

"Nemal?" Adonis asked as the three of them whipped their heads toward Sensei as if for an explanation.

Sensei rushed to the classroom door, peeked outside before closing it. He then walked briskly to an emergency exit door in the back room and did the same. Returning to his desk, he asked in a hushed tone, "Have you told anyone else?" He eyed the discolored camera panel in the corner of the room.

Kassi covered her face with her hands and gave a subtle shake of her head.

"Good," Sensei stood. "You'll definitely need to be careful who you tell."

"I know, I didn't mean to..." Kassi began to explain, speaking into her hands.

"It's alright. You're safe," Sensei reassured her. His eyes were kind. He reminded her of family back home. "These chas are more understanding than most. They won't hate you for being a Paradiser."

Adonis, Fille, and Savriah were wide-eyed. Savriah said, "So...she's not just pushing our waves?"

"She's a, she's a...'diser?" Adonis asked.

"Paradiser," Sensei corrected. "Let's not be rude, Donis. Her

Evéik is Nemalís. She talks just like them. She's not pushing our waves."

"Wait, wait, so how did you get here?" Adonis asked Kassi.

"I'd...rather not talk about it," Kassi said, lowering her hands to tug at the wrinkles in her mustard yellow jumper. "It's a long story and it's a little personable to me."

"Personable?" Fille tilted his head.

"You mean personal?" Savriah asked.

"Personal. Yisû, that's what I mean," Kassi nodded.

"Ca'pri's a beautiful city," Sensei said. "Like no other."

"You make it sound like you've been there," Fille eyed Sensei curiously.

"I have. I used to live on Astera," Sensei said with a smile.

"You did?" Kassi asked, lifting her eyes.

"Alright, we're all having a good laugh here," Fille said, chomping on a biscuit.

"I grew up on Earth, but my team and I won the Siren Games," Sensei said.

"If that's true, then why are you back?" Savriah asked.

"After a couple of years on Astera, I volunteered to officiate the next Siren Games," Sensei said, standing and staring out the windows at the Miami skyline. "New officiators always train in Ca'pri, so that's when I had the honor of seeing the City of a Thousand Palaces for myself. When we came to Earth, I met the most beautiful, incredible woman–Aitana. She convinced me to stay and help the Gaians. So I stayed."

"So you're, you're also a 'diser?" Adonis asked.

"Paradiser, Donis," Sensei said, turning back to face them.

"You're also a Paradiser?" Adonis asked again.

"How come you've never told us this before?" Savriah asked.

"You never asked." Sensei shrugged.

"So what happened to Aitana?" Fille asked.

"We got married. Married for just over twenty years before she died. Happened just a few years before I met any of you." Sensei lowered his gaze. "You chas would've liked her."

"I'm sorry Sensei, that must have been hard," Kassi said.

"Thank you," Sensei forced a smile, his eyes growing misty.

A beat passed before Adonis asked, "So why didn't you, why didn't you go back to Paradise after?"

"Well, I still have teams, champions, and students to help train and mentor." He smiled his carefree smile before turning to Kassi. "You must have gone through some ordeal to be here."

Kassi nodded. Her throat itched. She delicately patted the burn on her neck and noticed Savriah eyeing her.

"How'd you get that?" Savriah aimed a finger directly at the burn on Kassi's neck.

"Savvy, she doesn't want to say right now," Sensei said.

"I was attacked," Kassi said almost inaudibly, once again responding before she could hold back.

"Attacked?" Fille straightened. "By who?"

Kassi sighed. She wanted to tell someone. It was hard for her to keep all of this in. "You really wanna know how I got here-eh?" They nodded.

"Only if you feel comfortable," Sensei said. "No pressure."

Starting with Vidara's announcement of the incident, Kassi hugged her knees as she went through the events of that day. From sneaking off with her friend Amára to spy on the Royal Guard in Viracocha to the underwater chase. She rushed through some of the worst parts to avoid a panic attack, lightly brushing on the assault on her vocal cords and the near drowning. When she got to Ravana, she explained her conviction to free the Gaians and open the portal. Tears wet her cheeks as she remembered watching Amára pass out onto the cold, wet grass.

Sensei patted her shoulder. "That must have been awful, Kassi. I'm so sorry you had to go through that."

"Drowned." Savriah shook her head.

"So that, so that explains the...," Adonis rubbed his throat. "I didn't wanna say anything."

"Yisû," Kassi nodded behind her knees.

"What if we help you get back home?" Fille asked. "Sensei probably knows a way. Right?"

"I might know some chas," Sensei said.

"It probably won't help," Kassi said, lifting her head. "The U.N.O.E. is involved. They're watching everything and guarding all the Rosen-comms."

"The U.N.O.E. knows about this. Huh," Sensei thought out loud. "So I guess there's no point in looking for diplomatic options if they already know. And that must be why this conversation wasn't flagged." He eyed the camera panel in the corner again. "When you first said you were from Nemal, I expected mediation officers to rush in."

"So Ravana thinks bringing you here will somehow help us?" Fille asked.

"She says we need to see it for ourselves to convince-eh the Council to open the portal," Kassi said.

Adonis scratched his head, "So now, so now that you've seen Earth, why won't Ravana just let you go back and tell everyone?"

"She says it's not enough," Kassi explained. "To show everyone back home-eh zhust how hard it is for Gaians to make it to Paradise-eh, we need to...," Kassi paused for a beat, hesitating as she realized just how ludicray the expectation was. "We need to win the Siren Games."

"We need to, we need to what?" Adonis stood. Sensei's eyes opened in surprise as the others gasped.

"That's the only way to get back home?" Savriah asked.

"Yisû," Kassi said.

"But no 400 has done that in decades!" Fille threw his hands in the air.

"Maybe it never happened," Savriah said. "That's only a myth."

"We only, we only have the worst team in the league. We won't even qualify!" Adonis said.

"Kimaya Angelle is not just a myth!" Fille shouted. "She won the Games in 2111!"

"Fille's, Fille's right, Savvy," Adonis said.

Each season, the sixty-four provinces of Earth--the 15 drowning provinces and the 49 dry provinces--held their own AquaSphera local league tournaments. Only the first-place team from each province qualified for the Siren Games. 400s have only qualified a handful of times, and only one 400 is known to have ever won the Games, a prodigy named Kimaya Angelle who was recruited by a team of 800s to join them. Siren Games commentators often recounted her incredible story.

"Sensei can help us," Fille pointed at Kelipalo. "He's mentored many champions!"

"But...we're not champions," Savriah said.

"If I could get my voice-eh back, I could sing with sháloor again and light the fourth bulb," Kassi began. "Then maybe I could join one of the top teams."

"You don't just join a top team," Savriah said. "You have to be recruited."

"Sing with sha-who?" Adonis raised an eyebrow.

"Otherwise, everyone has to play within their own star score status," Savriah continued her explanation.

"Sing with sháloor." Kassi was surprised to see all the confused faces in the room.

Sensei K said, "Very few on Earth have ever heard that word, Kassi. Sirens here who sing with sháloor, don't realize there's a word for it."

"You've lit the fourth bulb?" Fille raised an eyebrow as he leaned back and folded his arms, incredulous.

"Of course! Every day! Well, before I came-eh here." For Kassi singing with sháloor had been a part of everyday life for as long as she could remember. "There's also a fifth bulb, though that's rare even on Nemal."

"I thought, I thought that was just for decoration," Adonis said.

"It's how you reach supernova siren," Kassi explained.

"Supernova siren!" Fille shouted, jumping out of his seat as if this were the most outlandish news he had ever heard in his life.

"Wha-hat?" Adonis ran his fingers through his hair, wide-eyed with shock.

There were five levels of sirens: proto, tauri, star, sirius, and supernova. Kassi had reached star siren on Nemal. Amára was close to achieving sirius siren status. Her parents and all members of the Council of Creators were supernova sirens, and among the few in the worlds to reach that status.

"So what's sháloor?" Savriah asked.

"It's uh…," Kassi tried to find the words to explain it.

Sensei cut in, "Sháloor is that magical connection you get with a melody or lyric. It's when the performer takes the listener somewhere–transports them. You get lost in the music as their performance carries you away. You ever experience that?"

Savriah and Fille stared blankly at Sensei. Adonis thought for a moment before raising his eyebrows in excitement. "Oh I think, I think I know what you mean! There was this time, when my cousin, he brought home this contraband record player and some old vinyl records from the Market Abyss. He played one of them. I don't remember the dame's name, but she sang like an angel! It gave me goosebumps."

"Yisû, she was probably singing with sháloor," Kassi said.

"Why didn't you invite me?" Fille cuffed Adonis on the shoulder. "I wanna hear the contraband music."

"Music is contraband?" Kassi asked, tilting her head.

"Not all, but a lot of it is," Sensei said. "A lot of things are. Books, art. Everything has to be pre-approved by the U.N.O.E."

Adonis said to Fille, "I thought I did, I thought I did invite you. Just come over after school. I'll show you."

"So how does Kassi get her voice back?" Savriah asked Sensei.

"Let's go, let's go ask Healer McCleary!" Adonis said.

"You kidding? That cha couldn't heal a pimple if his yashing life depended on it," Fille said.

"It's true, Healer McCleary struggles healing even the smallest of injuries. Repairing ruptured vocal cords is well beyond his abilities," Sensei K nodded.

"Well, it couldn't hurt to try it though, right?" Adonis asked. When the others didn't answer, he gave a hard shrug, "You chas never take my suggestions."

"You could always try," Sensei said. "Just don't get your hopes up."

"We need a real healer," Savriah said. "How are we ever going to find one of those? We're 400s!"

"I might know someone," Sensei said as the bell rang. Lunch had ended and they had barely touched any of the food. Fille, Savriah, and Adonis grabbed their portions and snarfed it down as they bustled to the door.

"Thank you, Professor Kelipalo. I really needed this today!" Kassi said as she picked at her food.

"Call me Sensei," he said with a deferential bow. "Now I know it's nothing like food on Nemal, but eat up. You need it."

Kassi grabbed some food rations and rushed out the door, grateful to have met a fellow Paradiser. Now, she didn't have to feel so alone.

Seven

Kassi reached the 400s at the elevator just in time.

"What class do you have next?" Savriah asked.

Kassi pulled out her schedule. *"Civility and Etiquette* with Professor Raisen," she said.

"Same. You're with us," Savriah said. "We'd better hurry to make it before the bell." Kassi was relieved to finally have classmates to sit with.

Period 5 was on the bottom floor, which apparently was Level 2. Level 1, she learned, was permanently flooded and off-limits. Adonis eyed her a few times as they walked to class. On the third glance, Fille noticed and asked, "What's with you, Donis?"

"I just, I just never met a, you know," he leaned toward them and whispered, "a Paradiser."

"Shh! Don't say it," Fille said, whipping his head in all directions to make sure no one listened in.

"We're 400s. Like anyone pays attention to what we say," Adonis said.

Savriah changed the subject, "Just so you know, Professor Raisen's a low talker."

"Low low talker," Adonis said, pushing his hand low to the ground.

"Gotta strain to hear him from the back," Fille said.

"After today, that wouldn't be the worst thing," Kassi shrugged.

In the corridor, they passed a trio of 400s she hadn't seen before. As they passed, Adonis gave them a salute. They nodded their acknowledgment.

"Who are they?" Kassi asked.

"Our teammates," Fille said. "400s from grade eleven."

They entered the classroom before Kassi could ask more. As they took their seats in the back, students shot Kassi glances through their hologlasses and snickered.

Pulling out their own hologlasses, Kassi and her new friends opened the holovid someone had shared with the entire school. Kassi found a five-second loop playing on repeat of her shower curtain debacle, with her tugging hopelessly on the dryer bin handle. Somehow, her embarrassing struggle that morning was caught on video. More and more students stared at her and laughed. Kassi's face reddened. She couldn't understand how people could be so vicious.

Her blood boiled, so Kassi immediately practiced her meditation exercises. After a calm breath, she eyed Fille and the other 400s next to her. *This is how they've been treated their entire lives,* Kassi lowered her eyes.

Fille popped out of his seat, clenched his fists, and shouted, "Sick, sadistic sheists!"

Savriah pulled on his wrist. "Don't. They'll give you the broomstick!" Fille reluctantly sat back down as Savriah turned to Kassi to explain. "Any time students, especially lower status students, do something they don't like, they bring out a broomstick and..."

"Oh, I know all about the broomstick." Kassi cut her off, not wanting to be reminded of it.

"Oh," Savriah said. From her peripheral, Kassi saw Adonis vigorously shaking his head at Savriah.

Period 5 dragged at a rososloth's pace. Professor Raisen, a thin, willowy man with spectacles, wavy hair in a side part, and a freshly pressed, red 800s armband over his arm spoke so quietly, it sounded like white noise. Kassi struggled to stay awake. Apparently, so did everyone else. Adonis nodded off more than once, his head resting on his hand, only to have Fille bump his elbow each time. Adonis smacked his head on the top of the desk, waking him back up.

"Quit it, pata!" Adonis said, kicking Fille under his desk.

Fille buried his head to laugh as Professor Raisen threw paper clips at Adonis for interrupting. He had impeccable aim with those paper clips, too. He tossed them from the front of class and hit Adonis every single time. It ruffled Adonis to no end, which only encouraged Fille.

When the bell rang, they had three minutes to cross campus and climb two floors to make it to Evéik class. With her new friends leading the way, they arrived before most of the other students and took their seats at the front.

"You sure-eh we're allowed?" Kassi asked.

"Sensei K doesn't give a sheist about status, remember?" Fille said.

The bell rang and Sensei K jumped right into his lecture. *"Gaté bébulak van li kalosét Evéik linggwûbé mápetítót! Pam lagi, bud itor atup nayalíbé shi taz ik vodót, i dosho motáchîm jidrû ramat! Mit shi píd sobri duahan tivak tersóbé ram oséjang bizat, hûn fen bizé prap shi famat."* He looked around at a classroom full of vacant expressions. "Who can tell me what I just said? Surely at least one of you can this time." Kassi instinctively raised her hand before noticing she was the only one with her hand up. She slowly retracted her hand.

"I know Miss Kassiana knows. Anyone else?"

No one stirred.

"Very well. Kassiana, why don't you tell the rest of class."

With all eyes on her, Kassi squirmed in her seat. "You...welcomed everybody back to the beautiful Evéik languazhe-eh. You also said it's your great pleasure to see us and teach this immortal tongue-eh," she recited the best she could from memory, "and then you said we have a lot of exciting lessons to go over this week and you want to get right into it."

"Very good!" Sensei addressed the class. "I had the pleasure of meeting Miss Kassiana during lunch, and it turns out she's quite gifted in Evéik. So good in fact, she has developed an Evéik accent. But don't you get any ideas. Anyone caught cheating will be thrown out the window." The kids laughed, probably assuming their professor was joking. "I'm not kidding. It's a two-story drop into four feet of water. You'll survive." Judging from the smile on his face, he was already picturing tossing a few of them out. The room went uncomfortably silent. Fille snorted under his breath.

Kassi was grateful for her new Evéik Professor. He had given her a legitimate excuse for her accent–no more need to hide it.

Sensei jumped into his lesson. He taught Evéik grammar and vocabulary Kassi already knew, but she still enjoyed listening to his passion and enthusiasm. It motivated her to learn.

After the final bell, he called her up to his desk. "Since you're already fluent, I'd like to give you something different to challenge you."

"Oh?" Kassi nodded, curious.

"I've compiled a list of advanced reading in Evéik for you to study." He typed a few words into his holographic keyboard and a file popped up in the corner of her hologlasses display.

It read: *Contraband. For your eyes only.*

"You're already well ahead of the rest of the class, and I wanna make sure you continue to push yourself."

All her previous professors had only singled her out to publicly shame her. And, as she thought back on her schooling on Nemal, she had never been considered "ahead of the class."

That was always Amára. Sensei was the first to express high expectations for her, and she didn't want to disappoint.

"I will! I'll read all of these!" Kassi said, bouncing on her feet.

Once in the hallway, she met back up with her new 400 friends. Adonis was quick to remind them. "Let's take her to the Healer McCleary before AquaSphera."

"Still?" Fille asked.

"We gotta give him a chance, right? Why not? why not?" Adonis said.

They meandered to the Healer's office on the first floor. The healer asked her countless, inane "on a scale from 1 to 10" questions, before checking her throat and vitals. After a few moments of naked-eye inspection, he concluded, "Looks normal to me. I'm sure whatever it is, it'll go away in a few days. I could prescribe you some cream for the burn mark if you'd like."

"Normal?" Kassi's eyes went wide with shock. "My vocal cords are damazhed–completely ruptured!"

"A few days rest and medicated cream should do it," He said with a dismissive shrug.

"Don't you know any Healing Incantations?" Kassi asked.

"Oh no, we don't do that here." He said as if the notion were absurd. Sensei and Fille were right. This cha couldn't heal a pimple!

A few moments later, they exited the office and into the hallway just as Malyra and DeSchuster grazed past, both shirtless with Malyra in a sports bra. "Aww, does somebody have an owie?"

"Ignore Malyra. She was made from spare parts," Fille said.

"Does this look like spare parts to you?" Brushing her hands down her body before running her fingers through her thick hair, Malyra knew she was a physical specimen.

Fille nodded casually, "It looks like you're trying too hard. Where are your clothes?"

"You're just jealous I have clothes!" She turned on her heels and strode down the hall with DeSchuster in tow.

"You can take your clothes and go pound sand!" Fille punched the air and shouted as they both rounded a corner, out of earshot.

"Well, that healer was a waste of time-eh," Kassi said.

"Just like we told this pata," Savriah said, pointing a thumb at Adonis.

"At least, at least now we know for sure!" Adonis said.

"Let's just flake off and hit the training pools!" Fille said with a resigned sigh.

"Training pools?"

"It's where we all go next," Savriah said. "For AquaSphera."

"AquaSphera? Bosst!" Even though her parents were likely on their way to get her, she could at least pass the time and get lost in a game of AquaSphera. It had always been her favorite sport. "Wait, I don't have a siren suit."

"Don't worry about that. The school gives you one at the docks," Savriah said.

"Oh that's...zhenerous," Kassi seemed surprised.

"I wouldn't, I wouldn't go that far," Adonis said, shaking a finger. "The wetties they give 400s..."

"They're the table scraps," Fille said. "No, they're the moldy stains from the table scraps."

They stepped outside and back onto the crowded, floating sidewalks. Kassi fell behind, causing a foot traffic jam behind her as she tried to match their pace while struggling to stay on the boards. "How far?" she asked.

"About 100 kilometers that way." Adonis pointed at the Atlantic Ocean.

"In the middle of the ocean?"

"It's not, not the middle of the ocean," Adonis said. "It's near Alice Town."

"But they're in the ocean?"

"Of course, they're in the ocean! The training pools are gargantic!" Adonis spun on his heel and used wild hand gestures as he spoke as if dancing on the sidewalks. "You can't fit those on land!"

"But the Siren Games…," Kassi started to say.

"The Siren Games use above-water swimming arenas because they have billions of U-coins to make them," Fille finished. Kassi had almost forgotten about U64 coins, commonly known as U-coins. That was the universal currency on Earth.

"The rest of us, the rest of us gotta use the ocean," Adonis nodded at the water ahead. "But at least we got The Turq!"

"At least we got The Turq," Fille clapped his hands.

Savriah turned to Kassi. "Our training pools are in crystalline, blueish water. We call it The Turq. Probably similar to where you're from."

"Careful, Savvy," Fille said over his shoulder. They weren't the only students walking to the docks. All around them, students sang a wide variety of full-range vocal warmups and exercises, like a cacophony of bird chirps, cat meows, monkey howls, and some animals crying out in pain.

Kassi lost her balance and barely caught herself before falling in.

Adonis said, "Still gettin' used to the slidewalks?"

"Slidewalks?"

"Yisû, you know, you know, *slide* walks?" He shifted the boards from side to side.

"Oh-ho, no. Don't, don't do that." Kassi knelt to steady herself with her hands. Standing back up, she sidestepped forward with both arms out for balance.

"You'll get it. You'll get it!"

The smell of the beach hit Kassi's nose as they got closer. Somewhat similar to home, but a little more fishy–different enough to remind Kassi she was on an alien planet. Up ahead, ocean waves splashed against rows of identical apartment towers, swallowing up what once would have been sandy beaches. Above, balconies were speckled with people casually watching the crowds down below. Sedona brown, bamboo docks were just past them, visible in the distance. Unlike the slidewalks, the docks were professionally constructed and sturdy. Large, crisscrossed concrete beams anchored them to the ocean floor. A pair of small washrooms and a few kiosks lining the right side were both dwarfed by an immense number of lockers on the left. There had to be thousands of them! Down the middle, hugging up against the ocean, small springboards rimmed the outer border for diving already crowded with sirens ready to hit the water.

The first kiosk labeled "siren suit rentals" was connected to a steel-plated mobile trailer where all the different wetsuits must have been stored. It was barred and the door was bolted shut with at least three locks. Inside the trailer, behind the lone barred window, a pair of eyes scrutinized Kassi and her friends. In front of the trailer and behind the counter of the kiosk, a boy made his best effort to look intimidating. Apparently, wetsuit rentals were a very serious business.

As soon as they got there, Kassi instinctively scanned the crowd with the hope of spotting Amára.

"Who you looking for?" Savriah asked.

"Huh? Oh, no one."

"You're looking for your friend," Savriah read her mind. Kassi gave a slight nod. "Well, let's check you out a wettie," she said as she patted Kassi's neck awkwardly.

They stood in a short line with only two people ahead of them. A 700 girl with purple-streaked pigtail braids, still in her purple school uniform, was at the front of the line. She was interrogating the boy at the counter with a long series of questions.

Adonis and Fille strolled over to the endless rows of heavy, metallic lockers, using face scanners to open them. One large outer row surrounded multiple inner rows, all covered but still out in the open. With tight-fitting swimsuits underneath, students threw their uniforms into their lockers before wriggling into their wetsuits. Everyone seemed to change as quickly as possible, except for Malyra, Nikola, DeSchuster, and a few other chinpokes. They paraded around and socialized wearing next to nothing, waiting until the last minute to throw on their wetties. Kassi rolled her eyes.

Once changed, teams spread out across the docks and huddled for team discussions. Just like Savriah had said, most teams consisted of players from within the same status–700s with 700s, 500s with 500s. Higher statuses had better quality wetsuits than the lower statuses. The green-collared suits the 500s wore were barely holding themselves together. They still had oxygen tanks connected to their sonopacks. That didn't give her much hope for the one she would get.

Savriah tapped her foot impatiently, chewing on the inside of her cheeks. The same 700 continued questioning the boy at the counter. Fille and Adonis returned, already in their mustard-yellow collared wetsuits.

"You're still in the same spot?" Fille glared at the girl at the front of the line and shouted, "Cha! Flirt with the suit boy on your own time. You're holding up the line!"

She spun, her braids whipping her in the face as she gave Fille a once over, a snarky expression on her face. "How dare you speak to me, Four Hundie!"

"On the docks, I'll speak to you however I please. Now flake off and go pound sand!" Fille met her gaze and stood his ground. She huffed, turned, and yanked her wetsuit rental off the kiosk counter, storming off. The line finally moved and Kassi soon reached the front.

"Enter your name and star score into the holopad," the boy at the counter said. He seemed slightly older and had spiky blonde hair, freckles, and a green armband. Kassi paused and stared at the screen before entering 825.

"825, eh? In Four Hundie threads?" The boy folded his arms and scowled, "Lying about your score is a criminal offense, you know. Last chance to enter your real number."

Kassi sighed before punching 409 into the holopad.

The boy's eyes bulged. "That's the lowest I've ever seen! Let me...uh see what I got."

He unlocked three locks with a thumbprint, voice recognition, and a face scan and opened the door. Entering the trailer for a few moments, he returned with what looked like a wetsuit and sonopack from the stone ages. One of the shin pads had a giant crack through the middle. The rubber inner lining on her gloves was well-worn and probably offered little to soften the blow of a speeding AquaSphera disc.

"The lower your score, the worse your suit," Savriah said, reading Kassi's expression.

"Is this material even hydrophobic?" Kassi fingered numerous fixes to old tears. The sonopack was covered with chinks and dents that would likely cause drag and decrease her speed. At least all five bulbs were still perfectly spherical in their encasements. Although with her broken voice, she'd be lucky to keep two bulbs lit longer than a few seconds at a time. She noticed a large oxygen tank right down the middle.

"I told you they're the moldy stains from the table scraps!" Fille said.

"They don't even have-eh gills?" The 600s, 700s, and 800s all had suits with gills. "Doesn't that give us a huzhe disadvantazh-eh?"

"Why do you think we're in last place?" Savriah said.

"Well," Fille laughed, "that's not the only reason."

Kassi and Savriah headed to the lockers. Once in their suits, they rushed back to the diving platforms and joined their friends in line. Kassi examined the loosely-fitted suit. She tugged and adjusted, trying to get everything to fit a little better. It didn't help. In fact, she tugged a little too hard and broke open one of the old tears, making the suit even worse.

"Ugh, I barely even pulled!" Kassi traced her fingers along the new tear. She took a deep breath. Despite the poor conditions, Kassi would still find a way to enjoy her favorite sport.

As Kassi and her friends got closer to the edge, they fastened and sealed their helmets and prepared to jump. At least the seal on her helmet worked. She wouldn't have to deal with water leaking in. The thought brought back the horrific memory of the square-headed man ripping off her helmet and nearly drowning her. Kassi forced herself to calm with the same siren meditation she had been relying on all day. Focusing on the tension in her body, she released it wherever she found it.

They were almost to the front. Kassi stretched her limbs. It had been over a week since her last swim and she was feeling rusty. She tested her oxygen and tried singing to power up the sonopack on her suit.

Fille held out his wrist to Kassi. She waved her wrist over his and their suits automatically linked up radio frequencies. Their voices immediately filled the speakers in her helmet.

"You hearin' us?"

"I hear you," Kassi said.

At the end of the dock, Kassi stepped onto springboards of laminated wood. It bounced slightly under her weight as she watched for her cue to dive. Red lights flashed at their feet, pulsing once a second. After fifteen red pulses came five yellows and then the green.

Kassiana dove.

Eight

The immersion into cool ocean water transported her away from this world. For the briefest of moments, she was home. Everything made more sense in the water. It brought the real Kassi to life. As this realization hit her, Kassi wondered why she had always insisted on walking to breakfast instead of using the palace's swimming lanes back home.

In fluent Evéik, Kassi croaked out a Haraki Hîm, a siren acceleration song, she had been singing ever since she could remember. It was the easiest song she could think of.

Let's see if I can bring these threads to life.

She was only half certain the helmet's tech was functional, so when the sonopack sputtered to life, she heaved a sigh of relief. Out of habit, she stretched her arms downward and held her palms out. Realizing she wouldn't likely light the third and fourth bulb to propel her palm thrusters, she tucked her hands flush to her body and focused all output on her feet. Spotting the others, she joined them and prepped for the long swim.

"There she, there she is!" Adonis said.

Teams of swimmers blasted past them. Two lights like a pair of stars just below their shoulder blades illuminated their sonopacks as they swam off toward the training pools. Wave after wave shot past, and none of them were using hand thrusters. Not one of them lit the top and bottom bulbs on their sonopacks.

"It's so stranzhe-eh to see no one using their hand thrusters," Kassi said.

Savriah followed Kassi's eyes to the swimmers passing above them. "It's rare. If someone gets to that level, they usually end up in the Siren Games."

"In the Siren Games?" Maybe there was a chance for Kassi– of course, speed wasn't everything. Gaians trained rigorously all their lives to be the best. Their top champions outperformed Paradisers significantly in most other areas. Besides, Kassi wouldn't regain her one and only advantage without a healthy voice. She needed to find a real siren healer.

Back on Nemal, she had been lighting the third and fourth bulbs since she was ten. And that was average. Amára started when she was eight and a half. Igniting them wasn't the real challenge. The hardest part was lighting them continuously. That had been the primary focus of her training for years– strengthening her diaphragm, creating songs that better fit her voice, increasing her vocal control.

"Vander, Vander and Vi'ella can do it!" Adonis said. "They took second last season–almost qualified."

"Well yisû, of course they can, which is why they'll likely qualify, this time," Savriah said. "Is it different where you're from?"

"Savvy, the rest of the team can hear you," Fille said with a finger to his lips. "And they're already on their way. Let's sing it, bubbleheads!"

"It'll take us about fifteen minutes to get there. Just holler if you get too far behind," Savriah said as she blasted off. Kassi's sonopack struggled as she did her best to keep up.

Her sonopack's first two bulbs coughed in and out, giving her short bursts of speed that weren't quite enough to match the others. When they were practically specs in the distance, Kassi panicked. She needed to ask them to slow down but was too embarrassed. Even though she was never the fastest siren back home, she was also never the slowest. Here, with a healthy voice and a half-decent suit, she would likely be faster than most.

The others were almost out of sight. With a huge sigh, she said, "Um, chas?"

"You with us, Kassi?" Fille called out. When she didn't respond, they threw their legs up and hit the brakes. After a few beats, Kassi reached them, her face beet red. If the helmet weren't in the way, she would have pressed her hands to her face and hid. "It's alright, Kassi. We don't mind turning it down a notch," Fille said with a reassuring smile.

They continued at a slower pace, Kassi still trailing far behind. Sirens from other teams constantly shot past as a painful reminder of just how slow she was going. When Malyra, Nikola, and the whole Chinpoke Squad blasted past, Malyra cut right in front of Kassi and caught her in the collapse of her trailing air pocket, pulsing Kassi out. Like being struck by a giant water fist knocking her sideways, Kassi was smacked off course and had to catch her breath.   In her Nemalís siren suit, she could have easily maneuvered to avoid it. However, her 400 suit prevented her from performing even the simplest of tasks. Malyra hit the brakes, spun to face Kassi, and held out her hands. She grabbed her thumb and pulled her fists apart in what Kassi assumed was an obscene gesture. Before Kassi could respond, Malyra torpedoed off into the distance to rejoin her teammates.

"Ghost of Sheebah, why's she gotta be such a yashing cacafuego?" Kassi said as soon as she caught her breath.

"Who? Who?" Adonis asked. They apparently missed it.

"Malyra," was all Kassi said, not wanting to admit she got pulsed.

"That cacafuego!" Fille exclaimed.

"She's the, she's the worst," Adonis said.

As they drew closer to the training pools, the water lightened to a crystalline purity with slight hues of turquoise–The Turq. Rays of sunlight streaked through to greet them. Kassi marveled at the immense size of the training pools with its twenty-four AquaSphera water fields. Hovering only five meters below the surface, the fields lit up the ocean. They were cylindrical water-fields with a holographic sphere on each end–known as end gates–and a third sphere, the larger of the three, directly in the center–known as the center gate. The end gates were brilliantly lit to feature the various team colors while the center gate remained a neutral color until the game started and a team had successfully "cleared the center." Transparent holographic boundaries wrapped each field, creating the iconic pill shape AquaSphera was known for.

Widely considered the most physically demanding sport of them all, AquaSphera had fifteen players on a side, including two goalies per team guarding each end gate. Five "gaters" from each team surrounded the center gate while the remaining eight players moved all over the waterfield in various strategic forma-tions of defense and offense. It required athletes to swim at breakneck speeds, dance and weave through tough opponents, pass and shoot with impossible precision, all while they were singing with controlled vocals to continuously power up their sonopacks. While players could use their hands to catch the disc, they could only hold it for up to three seconds before having to pass or shoot it with their feet. The extreme nature of the challenge made it exhilarating for both player and spectator.

They skipped over the other sectors and approached Sector 6 where their team was assigned. Kassi strained her eyes to scan all the athletes below them, once again hoping to see her cousin. She knew she shouldn't get her hopes up, but she couldn't stop herself. When she didn't see Amára, her heart sank. They floated down toward an end gate lit up in robin-egg blue. Over a dozen other sirens were waiting for them there.

"You with us?" Savriah seemed to notice Kassi drooping a little.

"Yisû." Kassi tried to hide her disappointment.

Savriah floated next to Kassi and said, "We're pretty close to the Bahamas. The water is bluer there, but this is still really nice. If we really wanted to, we could swim another 200 kilometers to Exuma, but we usually only do that for the bigger tournaments."

"If we ever make it to any tournaments!" Fille said, his eyes following the disc as their teammates kicked it back and forth. The size of a large frisbee, the disc had an outer texture of rough sandpaper. Powered by a piezo-electric transducer, it glowed a soft white and oscillated at ultra-high frequencies to cut through the water without resistance. This made it a bigger hassle to retrieve whenever someone kicked a wild pass or shot in the open ocean–one more reason why Kassi preferred playing in above-water tanks.

"That's a big if, a BIG if!" Adonis expanded his arms out for effect just before he and Fille joined the rest of the team.

Savriah cleared her throat, "There are twenty-four sectors at the training pools of Alice Town. Each sector has its own AquaSphera swimming arena which means only 48 teams are allowed at a time. We'll face off with another team for a match after we do our vocal training, rehearsal, and drills."

"Oh, we're playing against another team already?" Kassi was surprised.

"Yisû, season just started a couple days ago," Savriah nodded. "There are 44 teams in our league. We're the Blue Krakens." Kassi nodded as she watched the Blue Krakens circle in for vocal warmups. "Do you know the rules?"

"For AquaSphera? Of course!"

"Good, then I don't need to explain those. How's your suit?"

"It's loose, a little zhenky but I'll manazhe. I zhust wish I had my voice-eh!"

"Me too." Savriah awkwardly patted Kassi's neck and swam off to join the others. Kassi's cheeks reddened. Her new teammates probably regretted having her on their team. Forcing those thoughts away, she focused on what she could still contribute.

Their team consisted of 400s from their school–including Jacen, Jaya, and those from grades eleven and twelve–and a few green-collared, outcast 500s. They looked like a ragtag team of sad, beaten-down, bottom dwellers in damaged rental suits, and it seemed like many of them didn't even want to be there, Jacen and Jaya included. Kassi didn't have to be a math wizard to know their odds of winning the Siren Games were next to none. The Siren Games was the toughest competition in all the worlds, and only the greatest of all champions ever stood a chance of winning.

Fille called for a huddle and made the introductions, "Chas, this is Kassi. She's a new addition to our team and will be an extra sub for the game!" As much as Kassi missed the field, she was relieved to be starting on the sidelines as a sub. One by one, they bowed their greetings as Fille said their names. It would take her a while to learn all of them. Including her, there were seventeen players on their team, which meant only two subs for the match. Typically, teams had four.

"And well, I've got some bad news and some good news," Fille said, pulling up a holographic display from his wrist. "The bad news is we got paired with the Red Squalls."

"Oh Sheist! We dead we dead," Adonis whipped a hand to his helmet as if to cover his mouth. The team groaned and complained.

"The good news is, even though we're gonna lose miserably, we'll at least lose to the Red Squalls–a team with players that actually treat us like human beings," Fille said. Many grunted in agreement.

"Who are the Red Squalls?" Kassi asked.

"Only the best team in the league!" Savriah said.

"And they always win?" She searched the far end for her opponents, but the Red Squalls hadn't shown up on the field yet.

"They don't, they don't just win. They pummel everyone to krill. Whale food! We dead!" Adonis squashed his hand against the other for emphasis.

"It's Vander and his girlfriend, Vi'ella's team," Fille said.

"Vander and Vi'ella?" Kassi recognized the names. "You were zhust talking about them."

"The best sirens in the whole province," Savriah said.

"Wait wait. Girlfriend? Those two are together? When'd that happen?" Adonis talked even faster than usual if that was possible.

"Aren't they?" Fille shouted to match Adonis' excitement.

"How should I know? You're the one who said it!"

"Savvy, didn't you tell me something about that?" Fille asked.

"I don't know anything about it," Savriah held up both hands.

"You're just, you're just pushin' our waves." Adonis shoved the water with both hands.

"What! I heard something! I just don't remember who said it!" Fille yelled.

"Chas, can we just focus on practice?" Savriah asked. Teammates were already humming quiet vocal warmups in the comms.

"Where are the Red Squalls?" Kassi asked, still scanning their sector.

"They're 800s," Savriah said. "They have coaches. They get to practice in one of the music studios back on land along with better training equipment since they're one of the favorites to qualify and represent Miami."

"That's not fair!" Kassi said, her hands on her hips.

"Welcome to the Trench," a few teammates said in unison.

"Right," Fille addressed the team. "Let's run through some vocal warmups."

After a few vocal exercises, they spent an hour rehearsing songs from their playbook, pulling up lyrics and music on their holodisplays. Kassi picked them up quickly–they were all very basic compositions compared to what Kassi was used to performing. After music practice, they stretched and ran AquaSphera drills.

On the far end, the Red Squalls swam into view. They ran some of their own AquaSphera drills. Kassi floated and stared at their beautiful precision–it was even better than the pros back home on Nemal. Listening to the sound of her own breathing, she could still taste the muck juice she drank at lunch. There was no escaping it.

"Game on in fifteen," Fille called out. "We'll kick off the match to the song, *Champion*."

Kassi's first game of AquaSphera on Earth would soon begin.

Nine

Playing AquaSphera in the open ocean was much different than playing in one of the many above-ground waterfields of Nemal. For one, there was marine life and ocean currents to consider. Those would likely affect gameplay. Although there weren't any animals around them at the moment–maybe Earth's creatures steered clear of the training pools.

Second, despite the crystal clear waters of The Turq, the ocean was darker. Back home, the colossal glass tanks hovered well above the surface, allowing sunlight to easily penetrate the water. Under the sea, they relied more heavily on the luminous holographic boundaries, as well as the unique glowing patterns of each siren wetsuit.

Third, there were no crowd-filled stands filled to cheer them on. There were only the substitutes floating on the sidelines. On the Paradise Planets, all the swimming arenas were inside stadiums that housed hundreds of thousands. There were even seats below the water tanks for people to recline and observe as if they were right there with the athletes in the water. Kassi hoped Earth's bigger tournaments utilized water tank arenas to inject that pumped-up energy only a lively crowd could bring.

For now, however, she was a little relieved no one would be watching her sit it out on the sidelines.

Back home, Amára and Caesar were the stars on the water-field and had to play on opposite teams to keep things fair. Even though Kassi was average, Amára always picked her for her team. It was both of their dreams to go pro and play in the intergalactic league. Amára had a real shot. Kassi was just a long shot. Although, until her family came for her, none of that mattered anymore.

"Kassi, what position do you play?" A 400 named Quade said, interrupting her thoughts. He had a round face with red, wavy hair in a side part and a puff of freckles on his nose.

"What?" She realized she was floating right in front of their end gate, lit up in a translucent robin-egg blue to match their team colors. The rest of her team had already changed the color of their uniquely-patterned wetsuits to match. Kassi's was still a colorless dull gray.

"What's our team code-eh?" Kassi asked as she pulled up the holodisplay on her wrist.

"7717," Quade said.

Kassi dialed it in, and her suit immediately radiated the team's blues. At least her threads were still equipped with micro wire and color-altering pigment. But the design was boxy and unflattering.

Whoever designed this really didn't put much into it, she thought with a slump.

"So what's your position?" Quade asked again.

"Oh, I'm usually a forward, but I think today I should probably be one of the goalies." She thought of her sputtering sonopack and hoarse voice. As goalie, she could save her voice for the moments the opposing team came charging down the pitch.

"Solick! You'll be with me then once you sub in. Joshi and I are the goalies, for now, and Joshi hates it. He'll definitely look forward to switching it up today."

A boy who looked like a "Joshi" swam past her and saluted. He had a long face, wavy brown hair in a common side part, and brown eyes half-open. "You'll be a welcome relief! I'll finally get to play gater again."

Lining up for drills, the team caught passes and took shots on goal. Most of the Krakens worked on their turtle kick or bicycle kicks, but occasionally, Kassi would see a helicopter kick or butterfly kick. The turtle and bicycle were the easiest from a forward motion position. Swimming straight as a board toward the disc, most caught it with their hands and tossed it to the side for a turtle spin, propelling with their feet to create enough moment for a solid side kick, or they would toss it in front of them for a thruster-assisted forward bicycle kick that would push them into a full backflip. Those feeling more flexible would go into the splits and spin a helicopter kick. Three of her favorites–the butterfly kick, macaco kick, and push kick–were noticeably absent. Without hand thrusters, no one was able to perform them.

Kassi, Joshi, and Quade rotated on goal and managed to block many of the shots. After a few minutes of this, the Red Squalls' team captain swam to their side. He connected to the Kraken's radio frequency and asked, "You chas ready?"

"We're ready to sing it, Vander! You bubbleheads ready to lose?" Fille said, trying to sound confident for his team. He was apparently one of the Blue Krakens' team captains. Kassi heard Vander's name and hovered toward Fille to get a closer look. He glanced over at her with deep emerald eyes. Her heart fluttered, and she began to double-blink nervously.

"That's the spirit, Fille!" Vander said. "Love the confidence, misplaced though it might be." He laughed before returning his gaze to Kassi. "I don't believe we've met. I'm Vander Razzo." He bowed while floating, smiling so casually as if greeting lifelong fans after another big win. His dimpled smile was almost hidden behind gorgeous, loose curls of ash-blonde hair that fell just past his chin.

Maybe Earth's not such a bad place after all.

Kassi was suddenly hyper-aware of her frumpiness–her dirty hair in braids, her naked face, her paleolithic wetsuit. Vander's hair looked freshly washed and styled. His superior crimson suit sported trendy luminescent patterns.

She opened her mouth to respond but had forgotten to breathe. "Hi," she got out before the desperate need for air. After a loud, embarrassing inhalation she said, "I'm...hi...my name is Kassi. My name is Kassiana Ri...uh well, I go by Kassi. At least that's what my friends call me," she rambled, blinking faster.

Fille shot her a quizzical look which only made her feel more awkward. Vander took it in stride as if he received dozens of similar responses daily. "Pleasure to meet you, Kassi! Well, shall we get on with it?"

"Ready when you are!" Fille said. They performed a quick game of row-sham-bow to determine who kicked off. Fille won it for the Blue Krakens. Vander shot through the water back to his team. Kassi wanted to dive to the floor and bury herself in the sand. Of course, Adonis noticed.

"What's with, what's with her?" he asked Fille.

"Vander," was all Fille had to say.

"He do what he always do," Adonis said. Now, she wanted to bury herself even deeper.

"Let's sing it!" Fille shouted a rallying cry. They gathered in a circle, feet facing the center as they crouched, ready to spring. "Blue Krakens on three! One. Two. THREE!"

"Blue Krakens!" With a quick burst from their foot boosters, they shot off in all directions, taking their positions on the field. Kassi floated to the sidelines to join the other substitute.

"I'm Kassi," she said with a bow. The other sub, a boy with dark, slick back hair and a skin fade, ignored her and stared at the pitch. The "P" on his shoulder indicated he was one of the proto sirens on the team, the beginner's level. Kassi checked her own shoulder–also a "P."

What? I'm not a proto! She had been very proud of the day she reached tauri siren when she was eight and star siren status when she was ten. Now, she was back to proto–like being seven years old all over again.

"That's his royal highness, Royce, the coldest wet blanket on the team," Fille said from the waterfield. "Even worse than the J's!"

Mirific, I'm a fishwarmer proto siren stuck next to this cha! Kassi sighed. She really couldn't sink any lower.

The Red Squalls floated in the distance with Vander in front, poised and ready to attack. To his left, Kassi saw an athletic girl with chocolate-brown skin sporting an original wetsuit pattern Kassi had never seen before. The hydrophobic material featured a patchwork of different reds—her team's color—creating luminous textures and curvy accent lines. Her boots, helmet, and sonopack were all modified for enhanced hydrodynamics. She didn't just have the basic 800 wetsuit. Hers was a heavily upgraded suit–the kind of suit you could only attain from winning multiple, major tournaments.

"Who's that next to Vander?" Kassi asked.

Savriah followed her gaze from across the field. "Who? Vi'ella?"

"So that's Vi'ella!" Kassi made sure to keep an eye on her.

"On my count, we sing it! One, two, three, four," Fille launched into a song. The team chanted along, powering up their suits and synching their rhythms.

"Here-eh we go," Kassi quietly said to herself, taking a power stance even though she only observed from the sidelines. She envisioned playing to mentally prepare for when she subbed.

A simple song flooded her helmet. The team struggled to sing along in their broken Evéik. There was much room for improvement. Having been trained by supernova sirens since she was three, Kassi knew how to tailor compositions to bring out a singer's strengths. Since her broken voice limited her abilities on the field, maybe this was how she could best help her new team.

But why would they listen to me? I'm just the sub who slows everybody down.

The kickoff line was situated evenly between the center gate and their own end gate. This was where Fille kicked off with a pass to Savriah. Savriah caught it and pelted it with her right foot, sending it slicing through the water to Nida, one of their 500s. With a series of tight passes, they tried to throw off the Red Squalls' gaters who surrounded the outside perimeter of the center gate. It was Adonis who finally took the risk and fired a pass through the holographic sphere. Squalls easily intercepted and wasted no time on their counter, flicking it right through the center to a teammate on the other end. The spherical gate lit up in crimson red–the Squalls had just cleared the center and could now take shots on goal. They stormed down the waterfield.

Kassi watched in awe as Vander slipped through defenders as if he were made of the very water they swam in, his movements melodic and fluid. Propelling himself through a few more defenders, he passed it to Vi'ella who caught it on her foot, spun, and redirected the disc to a forward Kassi hadn't noticed until now. He caught it in the defenders' blind spot and had a wide-open goal in front of him. With a side bicycle, he shot and scored the first two points effortlessly, like he had done this a million times already. He probably had. Vander was ready and waiting for the disc to cut through the end gate. Joshi had dived for the initial shot right alongside Quade, and they left Vander wide open to catch it. With a single precision touch from the outside of his left foot, he tapped it right back through the end gate and scored the extra ricochet point. Just like that, it was 3-0. The intensity behind their drive and the coordination between players was better than what Kassi was used to from the pros on Paradise–it reminded her of the Siren Games, which made sense since the Red Squalls were hoping to qualify and soon compete in the Games.

"C'mon chas! Shake it off!" Fille tried to motivate everyone.

"Savvy, Savvy," Adonis called out. "Beethe in a Biscuit!"

Beethe, Kassi remembered was what they called their faux beef since real beef was extremely rare.

"Not everyone knows that one, Donis," Savriah returned to her starting position.

"Trust me, trust me!"

Fille kicked off again. Krakens zoomed forward to the center gate. Adonis snagged two teammates, arms around their shoulders, as the three of them formed a circle for Savriah to come down the middle. They aimed straight for the center gate and divided at the last second. Savriah shot the disc through the center as the three Krakens split to the other side. Adonis snagged it and cleared the center. The sphere lit up blue for a split second. Caught up in the momentum, Savriah didn't swerve in time. Her body penetrated the holographic boundary for over three seconds—foul. The gate's sensors registered the foul and immediately changed back to neutral. They would have to clear the center all over again.

"C'mon, Savvy! We had it, we had it!" Adonis flipped backward in frustration.

They tried another move, but this time a Squall gater intercepted the disc and sent it downfield. Vi'ella, Vander, and a few teammates danced across the pitch, passing it back and forth before making their move. Their rhythm was so tight, Kassi could almost guess the type of song they were performing to. The first shot came out of nowhere and from a great distance. Joshi and Quade scrambled, missing the shot and allowing two more points. Vi'ella snagged the rebound and flicked it back through for the ricochet point.

For the whole first half, the Red Squalls never eased up. They had all the momentum. Joshi and Quade looked exhausted after clambering to block shot after shot. By halftime, Red Squalls led 11-0. The Blue Krakens had only taken one shot on goal, and that had been easily defended.

Kassi glanced across the pitch to the 'Squalls' subs on the

other side. She noticed a slightly balding, gray-haired man next to them actively calling plays from the sidelines.

"So why don't we have a coach?" Kassi asked, pointing at the man.

Savriah again was the one to answer. "Coaches are only for teams with 800s, 700s, and the top 600s."

"That's not fair!" Kassi said with a scowl.

"No school district will waste money on a coach for 400s," Savriah said with a half-shrug.

Both teams took a short breather for halftime and surfaced. Floating on the water just above the training pools, a few U.N.O.E. cutters awaited the athletes. Small crews manned each boat. As siren athletes pulled themselves out of the water and unlatched their helmets, a crewmember handed them a government-rationed protein biscuit. As the Red Squalls surfaced, they were handed a new food item Kassi hadn't seen before.

"What are those-eh?" Kassi asked the crewmate.

"They're not for you, Four Hundie." He shoved her along.

Vander must have noticed the exchange because as soon as she looked up, he tossed her the food item she asked about. Kassi snatched it out of the air. It was a cube-shaped, green gelatin "Energy Chew." She locked eyes with Vander just long enough for him to casually nod before returning to his team. Kassi blushed. Vander had just given her his portion! When she unwrapped and popped it into her mouth, she detected a melon flavor. Compared to all the other food rations on Earth, it was sweeter than candy grapes off the vine.

Why can't all food rations be like this?

The break was short, and soon after Kassi finished eating, they dove back in the water.

"Alright, Kassi, let's see what you got!" Fille said.

Both nervous and excited, Kassi took her position next to Quade and joined in on her team's incantation to power up her sonopack. Even after only one music rehearsal, she followed along easily. Squalls kicked off the second half. Within seconds,

Vander was already orchestrating their next offensive. Kassi scanned her body for tension, found her calm, and filled her lungs. Defenders swarmed. Vander swirled through them like an ocean current. Finding an open teammate, he connected the pass that led to a brilliant turtle kick from Vi'ella. The disc sailed toward the rim of the end gate. Kassi reacted quickly enough to get a hand on it and deflect it. Her opponents snagged the rebound and crossed it. It was a smooth pass to Vander who was positioned for the perfect shot. With a flawless helicopter kick, he blasted the disc toward the far edges of the end gate. Quade almost got in her way as Kassi bolted to the other side of the gate at just the right time, making an incredible save. She snagged the disc with one hand, maintaining possession.

"Whoa, bosst save, Kassi!" Joshi shouted from his new position.

"Thanks!" Kassi said.

Quade gave her a quick pat on the back as he resumed his position. Vander looked stunned as he floated in front of the gate. He probably always made that shot. After a brief moment, he met her eyes and nodded approvingly. Kassi turned away, cheeks flushed.

Forcing herself to focus, Kassi scanned the field. She saw Fille making a break for it. Even with her broken shin pad, Kassi managed to send the disc where she wanted. It was a thread-the-needle through pass that took the Squalls by surprise. Fille caught it on the other side of the center gate and bolted down-field. The center gate lit up robin-egg blue, and now they were in a position to score.

"Give him support!" Catelyn, a Kraken defender, called out.

Krakens rushed down the field, but Fille didn't slow his pace. With a burst of speed, he shouted, "Raggle fraggle!" He front-flipped a reverse bicycle that sent the disk directly to one of the defenders for an easy catch.

"That's ok, that's ok. Good try, Fille!" Adonis clapped silently.

The Squalls' counter was quick and merciless. Clearing the center with a single pass, they took a long shot on goal that Quade deflected, but that opened up the gate for a follow-up shot that soared right through the goal for another two points. Kassi passed through her end gate–something only goalies were allowed to do–and reached the other side to snag the disc before Squalls could score another ricochet point.

For the rest of the half, the disc was almost always on their side of the field, and Kassi found herself diving over and over again to block their shots. She struggled to keep her sonopack powered up, but even when she didn't have her thrusters, her swimming skills were sometimes enough for her to get in the way of their shots. While she made some surprising saves, and Quaid had also made a few of his own, the Red Squalls still managed to score five points on Kassi in the second half, ending the game 16-0.

The final buzzer sounded. The game was over. Kassi was huffing pretty hard, almost worried she might run out of oxygen before reaching the docks. Her voice was extra hoarse and scratchy, throbbing from the strain to keep her sonopack alive. The pain was worth it–as hampered as she was by her damaged voice, she was still able to hold her own as goalie for her team.

By the time both teams returned to the docks, Kassi's oxygen levels were depleted. She barely made it! Using a final burst of supersonic speed, they rocketed out of the water to clear the edge of the docks and touch down on the landing platform, adjacent to the diving springboards. Ladders lined the platform for those wishing to climb out, but most sirens chose to make their "siren landing." It was the same on Nemal. Kassi and her new team filed off quickly to avoid collision with other swimmers exiting the water.

"Good game, Krakens." Vander made the rounds with the opposing team. He pulled off his helmet and ran his hand through his blonde curls. His chiseled jawline and dimpled, confident smile flashed as he made a point of complimenting individual players for specific plays he was impressed with. He seemed genuinely interested in hearing their responses. It wasn't just for show, and he was coming right toward Kassi.

Gliding over, he said, "It was Kassi, right? You made some bosst saves today! How long have you played goalie?" His voice was as smooth as a piano serenade.

"Oh, I don't usually...this was my first...umm." Kassi struggled to collect her thoughts.

"First time on goal?" Vander helped her finish. "Impressive!"

Kassi fiddled with her feet, searching for something to say. "Thank you. You and your...uh your girlfriend really scored a lot of points!" She kicked herself as soon as the words came out.

"Girlfriend? Who?" Vander looked confused as he scanned his other teammates. Before Kassi could recover, Royce shoved in between them and cut in with his own questions for Vander, his back to Kassi. She wanted to push him out of the way, but was too embarrassed and didn't want to make a scene in front of Vander. Instead, she scurried off to the lockers.

Ten

The open-air lockers bustled with activity as athletes from various teams changed out of their wetsuits. Kassi reached her locker, hoping to bury her head until everyone was gone. Her Kraken teammates had scattered to various aisles of the locker room.

Vi'ella opened a locker next to Kassi and began changing out of her wetsuit. She eyed Kassi, raising an eyebrow. "What's got you all bothered?"

Kassi whipped her head in all directions to make sure Vander wasn't within earshot. "Me? Oh, it's nothing." Kassi forced a smile.

"Mm-hmm." Vi'ella didn't sound convinced. "Somethin' tells me it has to do with a boy." She smiled as if she knew the feeling. "You new?"

"Yisû, zhust moved here-eh," Kassi said, fumbling with her wetsuit.

"Welcome to Miami Beach! I'm Vi'ella Rushtide."

"Kassiana. I go by Kassi." It always felt strange to say Kazán, so she just limited introductions to her first name.

"Where's that accent from?" Vi'ella asked just as she noticed a boy from another team rubbing his shoulders and groaning.

"First time playing?"

"Yisû," the boy said. "I've been swimming my whole life, but this…"

"Listen! This is AquaSphera," Vi'ella straightened to lock eyes with the boy. Still in her under bikini, she had well-defined abs and body and wore her deep-brown hair back in an intricately-braided ponytail. "First time I played this game, my shoulders were doing the cabbage patch. You gotta have muscles like a well-built highway to hold your own in this game!"

"And unlimited vocal stamina," he said as he tried stretching his arms and back to relieve the tightness.

Kassi remembered the first time she played when she was five. Her whole body ached the next day. It was one of the few times Amára let her sleep through breakfast.

"Oh, you can just keep that in your locker," Savriah said, appearing out of nowhere. She pointed at the rental suit slung over Kassi's shoulder.

"I don't return it?"

"It's yours for the rest of the school year!"

"Mirific." Kassi didn't hide the sarcasm as she reopened her locker and threw the shabby wettie inside.

"Just refill your oxygen tank before tomorrow's game," Savriah said as they exited.

"Good to meet you, Kassi," Vi'ella shouted.

"You too!"

Fille and Adonis had already changed and waited for them on the edge of the docks. As Kassi and Savriah made their way to join them, Savriah awkwardly patted Kassi on the side of her neck. "Not bad today, considering." Kassi waited for her to finish, but she didn't say more.

"Which way you headed?" Fille asked as soon as Kassi and Savriah approached.

Kassi remembered she had no idea how to get back to the townhome. "I…don't know."

"Well that's a problem," Fille said as they all stared at the flooded streets in front of them.

"Do you have, do you have their address?" Adonis asked.

Kassi tried thinking back to her exchange with Kyoto. She couldn't recall him giving it to her. "Yashing Kyoto!" she cursed with a huff. "He didn't give it to me. What do I do?"

"Let's return to school. Maybe someone there can help," Savriah suggested.

The sun was setting, getting dark. They marched back to Miami Beach High as Kassi scanned the streets and buildings, looking for something familiar.

"What if, what if you don't return?" Adonis asked.

"What?" Kassi said.

"I'm just saying, what happens if you don't?" Adonis said. Just then, a jet-black motoryacht crawled into view, bright white ominous letters written on the side: U.N.O.E. Miami Patrol. All windows, including those on its extended cabin, were tinted as if to hide the perverse eyes now dissecting Kassi and her friends.

The ship was impressive but menacing. Sleek and built for speed, it was a dual-hydrofoil like a trimaran without a central monohull. Unlike everything faded and dilapidated in the flooded streets of Miami Beach, it looked fresh out of the factory. Kassi and her friends paused, holding their breath as they anxiously waited for it to pass. It slowed briefly, making Kassi sweat. When the engines roared and it pulled away, Kassi heaved a sigh of relief.

Fille flicked his chin in the direction of the patrol yacht and said, "The U.N.O.E.'s involved, Donis, remember? They'll make her go back."

"And besides," Kassi said, "it's not like I have anywhere else to go."

"We'd offer you stay with one of us," Fille said, "but none of us have any room."

"We already live on top of each other," Adonis said.

"Tiny spaces, cluttered bedrooms," Savriah said.

They turned a corner and saw the school off in the distance. Balancing on the wobbly planks, she followed her friends until they reached the front entrance. Fille tugged on the doors.

"Locked," Fille said.

"Ugh, can I zhust get one break?" Kassi sagged.

Someone emerged from the shadows, startling Kassi. It was Meela. "There y'are!"

"Oh, thank the elyon sky!" Kassi sighed with relief.

"I's worried 'bout ya, so I convinced 'ol Kyoto t'let me come an getcha," Meela said. "These yer friends?"

"Yisû," Kassi said. "This is Fille, Donis, and Savvy." They each bowed as their name was said.

"And you're Kassi's..." Fille looked to Kassi for help finishing the introduction.

"She's one of my grips...," Kassi said.

"I'm her stepmama." Meela bowed, interrupting.

"Step...mom." Fille shifted uncomfortably.

"Thanks for yer help with gettin' Kassi back," Meela said. "I can take 'er home from here."

Fille nodded. "Ride the tide, Kassi!"

"Tide," Savriah and Adonis both added.

"Tide, uh...ride tide-eh!" Kassi wasn't quite sure how to respond. She had never heard that phrase before. She watched as they retreated into the distance, rounded a corner, and stepped out of view.

Meela slapped something on her forearm. "Yash, gotta watch for them skeeters!"

Kassi was too frustrated to talk about mosquitoes. "What was Kyoto thinking? He only showed me once—one time-eh! And he didn't even give-eh me the address! It's like he deliberately wanted to make-eh things harder."

"He means well," she said. "We're on the corner of Scripture and 10th," Meela told her. "Yer holarglasses should b'able t'help ya find it from now on."

Kassi whipped out her hologlasses and plugged in the

address. A highlighted route appeared in front of her–much easier than trying to memorize the route home.

The sun had set by the time they climbed the stairs to the front door. Inside, Kyoto sat at the kitchen table, his arms folded, jaw clenched. Food rations were already set on the table. Kyoto smoked one of his government-issue fumers, puffing an odorless steam as he glared at Kassi. They took their seats and ate in silence.

Kassi was about to excuse herself when Kyoto's harsh voice disrupted the quiet, making her flinch. "Meela and I will be on assignment tomorrow and won't be home until late. So we won't be around to help you find your way."

"I don't need help." Kassi huffed, leaning back in her chair. "I only needed the address. I got it now."

Kyoto grunted his acknowledgment and stood up to leave. He went upstairs to his room and shut the door without another word. Meela grabbed the plates and started wiping down the table.

Kassi leaned forward. "Meela?"

"Yisû, hun?"

"They assigned me a star score at school today. I got 409. Any idea why?"

"Normally we'd have similar scores bein' pretend family an' all," Meela said, leaning against the counter to face Kassi. "But me an' Kyoto—we're 700s." That's when Kassi remembered Kyoto's purple armband that morning.

"700s?" Kassi asked. "But you're adults. Why does your star score-eh matter?"

"It matters fer everythin'. How ya' think we got such a big house with two balconies? Or our pick o' jobs at th'Desalination Plant?"

Kassi thought about this. Star scores determining a station in life–it was such a foreign system to her. On Nemal, everyone had equal access to everything.

Meela continued, "Seein' as how ya'll were born with s'many

advantages, we only thought is's right to bring ya'll down a lil'. Make it fair."

"Make it fair!" Kassi's fingernails bit into her palms. "Do you chas have any idea what I went through today?"

"Well, a'course we do, hun," Meela said, her voice calm. "We lived it all our growin' up years. It'll be good fer ya to see th'other side o' things."

"You're 700s! What would you know?" Kassi stood, leaning forward on the table.

"We only 700s now 'cause we won some palladium medals in th'Games. When we was kids, both me an' Kyoto were 500s."

"Still, 500's are not the same-eh," Kassi said. "Treatment of 400s is so unbelievably atrocious! How can anyone be all right with this?"

"Th'U.N.O.E. created star scores after th'Great Correction t'help keep track o' th' pop'lation, makin' sure no one starved, and incentivize them t'contribute t'the new world they tried buildin'," Meela said, almost as if reciting right out of the manual. "'Sides, none of it would'a happened if yer folks would'a just helped th'poor Gaians instead of taxin' them for th'little help they did offer."

"Sounds like the U.N.O.E. just wanted to control and manipulate people," Kassi mumbled.

Meela cleared her throat loudly and eyed the camera panel in the corner. "You should prolly get some sleep. I'm sure yer tired." Meela yawned, finishing up in the kitchen. "G'night!"

Kassi grumbled as she watched Meela disappear up the stairs. Sinking heavily in her chair, she stared aimlessly past the recently vacated table. She tried reflecting on all that had happened that day, but there was too much to process. All the bullying and humiliation–it was a miserable nightmare with no end in sight.

When are my parents coming?

Kassi finally dragged herself up the stairs and to her room, throwing herself onto the small mattress and curling up into a ball. Putting her earrings in, tears rolled down her cheeks as she felt the bleakness of tomorrow and dreamed of home until she drifted to sleep.

The next day in *Heroics*, Kassi watched a 500 ask to go to the Healer's office. Professor Oakey claimed he didn't "look sick" and denied his request. When he asked to use the washrooms instead, the professor reminded him that only 800s and 700s get washroom breaks. This was news to Kassi. She wondered when the rest of them were supposed to use it. The three-minute window between classes wasn't enough. Were they expected to hold it until lunch? That same 500 threw up all over the floor which earned him detention from the professor.

In Period 2, as Kassi rushed to her desk, Nikola stuck his foot out and tripped her. Her hologlasses splattered all over the floor. After she retrieved the pieces and scurried to her seat, she managed to pop the lenses back in. She put them on and powered them up, hoping they still worked. There was a glitch in the AR display. Everything was still functional, but the glitch was incredibly annoying.

After class, Kassi paid a quick trip to the front office to get her hologlasses replaced or fixed. "You need to take better care of your things, Miss Kazán," was all the crotchety, useless receptionist told her.

During Period 4, Coach Muzzey didn't bother Kassi. He was too preoccupied flirting with one of the 600s. Even if he didn't have a potbelly and receding hairline, he would still be the most unattractive professor. It was disgusting. The girl unsuccessfully tried avoiding him throughout class. Kassi almost felt sorry for her.

At lunch, she met up with her friends in the cafeteria and explained what the Chinpoke Squad did to her hologlasses.

"Nikola, Malyra, they're all just a row of turd knuckles!" Fille groaned. This time, Savriah laughed. It was an odd laugh. She squeezed her eyes shut and wrinkled her nose while laughing with her mouth closed. It looked more like the face you'd make when flinching at an oncoming projectile.

"Kassi, I like your earrings!" Savriah said. "Where'd you get them?"

"Thanks." Kassi had forgotten to take them off that morning. She thumbed the diamond studs in her ears. "Amára gave-eh them to me for my birthday last year. They're all I have from home."

"You might wanna stash those," Fille said. "The Chinpoke Squad sees those, they'll find a way to get 'em taken away."

Kassi took them out of her ears and tucked them back in her huge pocket. As much as she hated the school uniforms, at least they had spacious pockets–pockets they couldn't leave their hands in for more than three seconds according to the ludicray new government policy.

"400s, you're up!" A lunch worker yelled across the cafeteria.

"We eating in Sensei's room again?" Kassi asked as they made their way to the counter. Jacen and Jaya were already sitting in the same spot on the floor next to the 500s table.

"Every day!" Fille grabbed the meager food portions and placed them on everyone's trays. "Let's flake off!"

"We're outie like a bellybutton," Adonis said.

"Gross!" Fille said, sidestepping away from Adonis.

Once they took their seats in Sensei's classroom, Adonis asked, "So Kassi, Kassi, what's the food like on Nemal?"

"The food?" The question took her back home. At the thought of it, she could almost taste the freshly pan-fried pork gyozas and smell the chicken fried rice. Her stomach rumbled angrily. "It's everything!" she answered. "They have every food you could imazhine, and it's all prepared from scratch by people who love-eh baking and cooking. It's an art form. They take-eh great pride in every dish."

"So it's better, it's better than the food we got here?" Adonis held up his tray with individually wrapped styrofoam plates of slimy veggies, sand biscuits, and gruel.

"That's...not food." Kassi pointed, realizing they had no idea what they were missing. They had eaten this same mush all their lives. Adonis simply nodded.

"Check it out, check it out," Adonis changed the subject, standing up in excitement. "Last night, I talked to my cousin about healers. He says he knows a guy who knows a guy. He says he can find a true healer, no problem!"

"Well thank Sheebah's holy sheist for that!" Fille threw his arms up in mock excitement.

Savriah inserted, "Your cousin knows a guy who knows a guy?"

"I'm telling you this guy's solick!"

"Alright, Donis. What'd he say?" Fille sighed.

Adonis went on to explain more about the guy he met when Sensei K was hailed with an urgent message. He quickly pulled up his holoscreen and turned it to a U.N.O.E. News Update. The conversation abruptly stopped.

"...unconfirmed reports of multiple attacks leaving over a hundred dead and hundreds more injured in various cities around the world in what appears to be a coordinated terrorist attack. Up to this point, we've received reports from the following cities." A list of cities was overlaid on the display:

DRY PROVINCES:
Seoul
Atlanta
Bangalore

DROWNING PROVINCES:
Manilla
Barcelona

• • •

"I HAVE TO WARN YOU, *these images are, these images are quite disturbing,*" the voice said as images of the attacks displayed on the screen. Almost a perfect circle of dead bodies lay prostrate, all facing outward. Survivors were placed on gurneys and carted to healing centers, dried blood stains in their ears.

"*The Planetary News Center right now is just beginning to work on this story, calling our sources to figure out exactly what happened, but this news comes as a shock to us all. This could very well be one of the worst...,*" he stopped abruptly as another update flashed across his hologlasses. "*We have just received additional reports from the Dry Provinces of Kinshasa and Buenos Aires claiming to have also been victims in this global terrorist attack. This is very disturbing news. A dark day for Earth, indeed.*

"*At this time, it is unclear who is responsible for these attacks, but this could very well be the worst terrorist attack since the U.N.O.E. saved and united the planet after the Great Correction. Clearly the dissidents behind this bombing don't understand all the U.N.O.E. does for them.*"

$$Eleven$$

S ensei closed the display and looked down at his empty desk. Kassi pressed her hands to her mouth. The others stared into space where the screen once hovered.

Savriah wiped a tear from her cheek, saying, "Why would anyone do something so…"

"Horrifying." Fille finished.

Kassi's throat dried up, her voice rougher than usual. She had to swallow hard before asking, "Has this…happened before-eh?"

"There was one when I was a kid," Sensei said softly, almost reverently, "The Kapalua Massacre of 2077." He paused and glanced at the camera panel in the corner, a flicker of anger flashing across his eyes. "I lost a cousin that day–one of my best friends." He stood and raised his voice, "The U.N.O.E. doesn't want anyone to know about that one. They had it erased from all history books as if those people never died."

"They erased my grandfather, too, after they disappeared him," Fille grumbled under his breath.

"Should you chas really be saying this?" Savriah asked, glancing at the same camera panel.

"Some words are worth the price to say." Sensei glared at the corner panel, fists clenched as if challenging someone to a fight.

Kassi thought for a moment. "You think they'll erase-eh this one from history, too?"

Sensei continued glowering at the camera before turning to face them. "Probably too late. But they'll find a way to spin it somehow to make them look like the heroes."

"I bet, I bet nothing like this happens where you're from," Adonis said, slumped in his chair.

"Never," Kassi said softly, almost inaudibly, as she looked over her new friends. Life on Earth for the Gaians really was awful. Ravana's words resonated in her mind, *the Council of Creators rules three large, wealthy planets and refuses to open the portal to the Gaians.* Kassi couldn't help but wonder why her parents never opened the portal to all Gaians.

Could Ravana be right?

"These worlds are the paradise-eh we make-eh them," she mumbled the phrase she always heard her father say. Kassi always believed her dad's favorite phrase referred to the direct correlation between Paradisers' efforts and the prosperity of the society on Paradise.

Was he also saying Earth was solely the responsibility of the Gaians? Was he saying Gaians brought this life on themselves?

"What was that?" Fille cocked his head to the side.

"Huh?" Kassi sat up, pulled from her deep thoughts. "Oh, nothing."

"You kids should probably run to class. Best if you get your mind off it," Sensei stood, patting each of them on the shoulders as they got up and made their exit. Silent, other than the shuffling sounds from their feet, they filed into the hallway. The corridors were still bustling with commotion. Apparently, none of the other students knew.

At the beginning of Period 5, Professor Raisen broke the news to the class. They had to strain to hear him, asking him to repeat multiple times. Once they understood, they were silent.

Professor Raisen took a seat and stared into space. The air was thick with the terror of death that loomed in the back of everyone's minds, worried they might be next.

The intercom crackled to life as the principal interrupted with an announcement, her words slurred. "Due to recent unfortunate events, students will be dismissed early from school. Everyone is to report in at home so the U.N.O.E. can make sure everyone is accounted for. Your teachers have been notified."

They wandered out of class like maze rats without a maze. Fille's, Adonis', and Savriah's parents waited at the front entrance, their faces weighed down with concern as they scanned the crowds for their kids. No one would be looking for Kassi.

"We won't have AquaSphera today," Savriah said just before meeting up with her mother at the entrance. Her mother had tidy brown hair, nothing like Savriah's untamed, curly red hair. Adonis' mother had similar caramel-brown skin to his and beautiful dark-brown hair in a straight layered lob. Fille's father looked just like him–tall, skinny, with long blonde hair and a face full of smile wrinkles. But there were no smiles today. With a somber wave to Kassi, they disappeared down the stairs of the front entrance with their parents, a yellow armband on each of their parents' right arms.

"...I heard Principal say parents have been furiously knocking on her door ever since it happened," Kassi overheard from a pair of 500s passing by. She knew no one would be knocking on her behalf. She wasn't expecting anyone to, but the realization of it still struck her with a fierce and painful loneliness. Her heart grew so heavy, she needed to sit down.

Parents rushed through, whisking off with their kids. Some parents cried as they embraced their kids, relieved to find them safe. Kassi leaned against a wall, hugging her knees as she eyed one tearful mother who took a long moment to hold her son. The boy was a 600 who had participated in Kassi's broomstick punishment. As much as she disliked him and the others who had bullied her, her heart ached for them–for all the Gaians. No one deserved this, no matter how cruel. Tears welled up in her eyes.

A heart-shaped box slammed on the floor at her feet, startling her. She quickly wiped her eyes, blinking away her tears. Tilting open the lid of the box with a wary finger, Kassi found chewed-up food rations–from the looks of it, rice and beans. They had been spat out in disgusting little piles. She retracted her hand and kicked the box away from her, whipping her head back to find Nikola, Malyra, and DeSchuster towering over her, cruel grins on their faces.

"Figured you'd be hungry," Nikola said with a smirk.

"Aww, were you cwying?" Malyra said, imitating the most irritating baby voice. "What a blowse! It was probably 400s who did this. You chas are always causing problems!"

Kassi didn't want to talk to any of them. She turned away and tried ignoring them.

"Who needs bullies when life already bullies you, am I right?" Nikola laughed.

"That's enough!" Sensei K rushed toward the kids from down the hall. "School's over. Go home."

Nikola shrugged and casually strode toward the front entrance, Malyra and DeSchuster following close behind. On the way out, DeSchuster picked up Jacen who was waiting quietly for his parents, lifting him over his head to impress everyone with his strength. Nikola gave him an approving clap on the shoulder and Malyra laughed a wicked cackle. Jacen squirmed, pleading to be put down. Kassi's fingernails bit into her palms. Even tragedy couldn't make the Chinpoke Squad humans–if anything, it made them worse.

"Put him down, DeSchuster!" Sensei yelled, taking a few threatening steps forward. DeSchuster tossed Jacen to the ground and left. Jacen crashed to the floor, his things spilling out of his school bag. Kassi rushed to help Jacen retrieve his things. Rather than thanking Kassi, he scowled at her, as if irritated by her kindness. Once everything had been put back, he quickly stood and retreated out the front doors.

"You're welcome!" Kassi called after Jacen who didn't so much as acknowledge her.

"Here, let me help you up," Sensei Kelipalo reached a hand out.

"Thanks," Kassi took it and rose to her feet.

"How you feeling, Kassi?"

"I'll be fine-eh. Zhust wish I had my voice-eh." Kassi stroked her throat as she mumbled to herself, "And a sonic rifle."

"A sonic rifle? Well, they'd definitely deserve it, but unfortunately, the punishment for that is much more severe than the broomstick."

"Oh, you heard that?" Kassi cringed. "I wouldn't actually do anything."

Sensei nodded. With a sigh, he said, "Life's hard enough without bullies."

"What'd I ever do to them?" Kassi groaned.

"Nothing, Kassi. Not a thing. Some kids just look for a punching bag. Best thing you can do is climb and climb until you're far out of their reach." He gave her a reassuring smile. "But in the meantime, while you're still within reach, you stand your ground and don't give them the satisfaction."

Kassi nodded.

"I'm surprised how well you've handled things, Kassi," Sensei looked at her, admiration in his eyes. "To be ripped from your life like that and have to experience all of this, and yet you've still kept it together. I don't know how you do it. You must be incredibly brave!"

Kassi had never thought of herself as brave–if anything, she felt like she was drowning in a raging river. But hearing Sensei say it made her stand up a little straighter and take a deep breath as if her strength were returning.

"You should probably head home. They'll be closing up the school and expecting everyone to check in soon."

"Home-eh?" Kassi immediately thought of Palace Rivernova on Nemal.

"Sorry, not home," Sensei seemed to realize his mistake. "Wherever it is you're staying at the moment."

"Yisû, I guess I should be getting back."

"If only I could help you get back to your real home!" Sensei said. "If there's anything I can do to help, you'll let me know, right?"

"I will," Kassi nodded. "And you are helping, Sensei. Very much!" Kassi waved goodbye and retrieved her hologlasses to pull up directions. Exiting the school, she made sure to leave enough space between her and the Chinpoke Squad to avoid a second encounter.

As she balanced on the slidewalks and followed the highlighted route back to the townhome, news updates streamed across the large screens. Seven cities had been hit by the attack. Over a hundred dead, thousands injured. Survivors only remembered feeling the ear-shattering sonic blast that knocked them off their feet. Their ears were covered in dried blood. The weapon used in the attacks was something new–something no one had ever seen before.

The townhome, to her relief, was empty, though she didn't know how to check in with the U.N.O.E., which she hoped wouldn't be a problem. Kyoto had mentioned they would both be on "assignment." This gave her pause. Their assignment happened to be on the same day as the terrorist attack, and the bombing method was something the Gaians had never seen before.

Could Kyoto and Meela somehow be involved?

Twelve

"Where were you chas yesterday?" Kassi grilled Meela and Kyoto at breakfast, Meela's face sagging more than usual.

"On assignment," Kyoto said without looking up from his holopad display.

"Yisû, but what assignment?"

"That's not your concern." His face was inscrutable. Meela remained quiet, deliberately avoiding Kassi's glance while pushing the food around her plate.

"Did it have anything to do with the terrorist attack?" Kassi pried, trying to hide the effort it had taken to ask that question.

Kyoto closed the display on his holopad and glowered at Kassi. "No more questions. Finish your breakfast." His jaw clenched and shoulders tensed, like a tiger ready to pounce. Kassi could almost feel the sting of another slap across the face, so she backed down. She would ask Meela the next time Kyoto wasn't present.

On her way to school, DeSchuster popped out of nowhere and knocked her into the flooded, dank street water. "Watch where you're going!" Kassi shouted as soon as she surfaced.

"That's what happens when you get in the way of these."

DeSchuster flexed his arms just as another patrol yacht slithered into view. He spotted them and immediately put his arms down, his eyes flickering with fear as he fell in line behind other pedestrians. Kassi wondered what kind of threat would spook even an 800 like DeSchuster.

Kassi pulled herself out, soaked and dirty, and sloshed her way to school. She could still see DeSchuster up ahead, walking alone like a gorilla left behind by his troop. She passed by screens filled with another U.N.O.E. policy update, this time regarding physical altercations. They had new policy updates almost every day, it seemed. Apparently, from now on, even victims of physical violence would be equally blamed and responsible.

So I guess it's also my fault for getting shoved into the water. Kassi shook her head. *Who makes these ludicray policies, anyway?*

At the front entrance, Nikola scoffed, "Klutziana just can't stay away from that street water." Dripping onto the tiled floor, Kassi ignored him and beelined for the washrooms. She quickly dried her uniform and rinsed the filth off before running through the doors of class just as the bell rang. Even though she was on time, Professor Oakey still reached out and pinched her as a reminder of her inferior status, just in case she had forgotten.

Kassi had fully expected the school to be in mourning after the previous day's tragic events. With the exception of a few somber students, it seemed as though most pretended nothing had ever happened. However, there was an undertone of fear hidden beneath the surface–a budding tension in the air.

The first four periods dragged on as usual. Kassiana kept her head down as best she could to avoid the broomstick or more bullying. Now and then, she'd catch Nikola staring daggers at her. He singled her out so aggressively!

At lunch, Kassi reached the 400s line at the cafeteria before the others. A group of girls walked past her. One of them looked just like Amára with a thick, razored comb-over bob. She ran to catch up with them and grabbed the girl by the arm to spin her around. It wasn't Amára. Instead, it was a very disgusted 600 who scoffed, "Eww, how dare you touch me, Four Hundie!"

"Sorry, I thought..." Kassi retreated back to the 400s sign where Savriah now stood.

"Thought she was your friend?" Savriah seemed to read Kassi's mind.

"Yisû," Kassi sighed.

Savriah patted her neck, trying to console her. "You'll find her. I know you will." Her words were comforting despite the awkwardness.

Fille and Adonis soon joined them, Adonis dragging with his head hung low. His deep-brown hair had been pulled into a small bun.

Fille broke the news before she could ask. "Donis lost one of his favorite uncles in the attack yesterday." He threw his arm around his friend.

"Ghost of Sheebah! I'm so sorry!" Kassi gasped, raising a hand to her mouth. "What was his name-eh?"

"Uncle Fozz," Adonis said softly, slowly. Kassi wanted to cry for him. If anything happened to her Uncle Sydney, Amára's dad, she wouldn't know what to do with herself. He was like a second father to her.

They quietly grabbed their food and walked to Sensei's classroom.

"I heard about your uncle," Sensei said as they took their seats. "I'm sorry, Donis!"

Adonis picked at a biscuit on his plate. "Uncle Fozz was everyone's favorite."

Sensei nodded, placing a hand on Adonis' shoulder. "What are some of your best memories with him?"

While Adonis related a few of his favorite stories, his mood lifted slightly. He finished his stories. "But now I'll never see him again," he said, slumping in his chair.

Sensei eyed the camera in the corner. "No, I believe you will, Donis. Despite what the U.N.O.E. tells you about multiple lives and rebirths as other people, I believe there's only one mortal life, one family. And that family stays with us when we die. You'll see your Uncle Fozz again."

"Yisû, my family believes the same back home on Nemal," Kassi said.

Adonis lifted his eyes, a look of surprise on his face. "You think so?"

Sensei nodded and returned to his desk. He limped, favoring his right side.

"Are you hurt, Sensei?" Kassi asked.

"Oh, I'm alright." He sat down heavily with a groan. "Nothing I haven't dealt with before."

Kassi looked to Savriah for an explanation, who said, "Any time someone contradicts the U.N.O.E., like mentioning them erasing history or sharing forbidden religious beliefs...," Savriah pointed at Sensei who dismissed it with a brush of his hand.

"The U.N.O.E. did this?" Kassi stared at Sensei, confused. "Wait, does that mean they'll do it again? Because-eh…"

"...Of what he just said to Donis?" Fille finished. "Most likely."

Kassi furrowed her brows and sat up. "But how can it be this way? How can anyone stand to live like-eh this?"

The other 400s paused mid-bite to stare blankly at Kassi until Sensei answered. "In the early years, people gave up a lot in the name of safety and protection," he said. "Now, this is the only way of life Gaians know."

Savriah finished her food and asked Kassi, "Have you ever lost someone close to you?"

Kassi shook her head. "Not twally. My great-grandma, but she was almost two hundred years old, so it was time-eh."

"Two hundred?" Fille cast her a questioning glance.

Kassi nodded, just now realizing the significance of the Fountain of Youth. She had grown up with it all her life, so she had never really thought anything of it. But Gaians didn't have anything like it. She fidgeted with the braids in her hair as she asked, "How long do Gaians usually live-eh?"

"I don't know," Fille shrugged.

"I think the average lifespan here is seventy-two years," Savriah said.

"Seventy-two?" Kassi gawked. "That's so young! Both my parents are in their 120s!"

"Does everyone live to be two hundred where you're from?" Adonis asked, speaking slowly as he lifted his head.

"More or less," Kassi said. "I don't really know what the averazhe is."

"How's that possible?" Fille scratched his head.

"The Fountain," Kassi said, thinking that would explain it. They continued staring at her curiously, apparently waiting for her to elaborate. "The Fountain of Youth?"

"Oh, Fountain of Youth," Savriah nodded. "Yisû, the U.N.O.E. talks about that all the time."

"It's one more thing Paradisers have that we don't," Fille said. "At least that's what they say."

"The Fountain helps you live to be two hundred?" Adonis asked, his word flow quickening but still slower than usual.

"Among other things," Kassi said with a nod.

"How's it work?" Fille asked.

"Could you, could you build something like that down here?" Adonis asked.

"I...think so?" Kassi's mother had shown her how it worked once. Something about adding a DNA-healing solution to the water just before she performed an Embarû Hîm, a rejuvenation song, to activate the bonding of the particles to the water molecules. Kassi couldn't recall the exact chemical makeup of the healing solution. It had been too early in the morning when her mother explained it, and Kassi only half listened. To Kassi, it was just an ordinary part of life. Now, she wished she had paid closer attention. "Or maybe at least if I had my voice-eh. But I'd still need my mother's help."

"We still need to figure out how to heal your voice," Savriah said.

"Have you chas heard of the Market Abyss healers?" Sensei asked.

"I heard that was just a myth," Fille said.

"Oh no, they're real," Sensei K said. "I used to know one."

"Used to?" Fille asked. "What happened to him?"

"*She* went back to Nemal," Sensei K explained, grazing over that detail as if it were common knowledge.

"Back, back to…?" Adonis straightened, glancing at the others.

"Nemal?" Kassi perked up. "Do I know her?"

"She went by Jarana. Don't even know if that was her real name."

"Are all the Market Abyss healers from Nemal?" Savriah asked.

"They're all from the Paradise Planets." Sensei K said.

"How'd they get here?" Fille asked.

"That's a long story, but the point is, I'm sure I can find another one."

"How?" Kassi asked.

"I've already put some feelers out," Sensei said as the bell rang. "I'll let you know. But for now, it's time for class."

They got out of their seats and took the elevators down one floor. The doors opened to the Chinpoke Squad waiting to get on. The Chinpokes shoved their way in and forced Kassi and her friends to squeeze through them to exit into the hallway.

Fille turned and shouted, "Thanks cacafuegos!" He made the hand gesture of grabbing his thumb with two fists and pulling them apart. The same one Malyra had flashed Kassi the other day in the ocean.

"Anytime, gumballs." Nikola flashed a broad smile.

Fille's face turned beet red. "What? Where'd you hear…," he started to ask when he noticed a malicious grin on Malyra's face. "YOU!"

"It's a part of who you are," Malyra said right as the elevator doors closed, giving her the last word.

"I was five!" Fille pounded on the elevator doors.

"Gumballs?" Kassi was confused.

Adonis busted out laughing. "It's because, it's because he got gum stuck on his…"

"Don't you say it!" Fille turned on him, fire in his eyes. This only made Adonis laugh harder.

"Not this again." Savriah sighed with a shake of her head. "Boys," she said as if that explained it. Kassi was still confused. Probably something lost in translation.

"He was freakin' out, he was freakin' out because he got…," he tried to say when Fille started shoving him.

"I was five! Everybody does embarrassing things when they're five!"

Adonis couldn't finish his sentence, he was laughing so hard. He laughed for the next five minutes while Fille cast him dirty looks and punched his arm. "Gumballs!" Adonis blurted out one last time with another fit of laughter. It was good to see him laugh despite his loss. Sensei's words must have really helped.

Professor Raisen taught another boring lecture in Period 5. Most of his class, *Civility and Etiquette*, was mind-numbing repetition–like some form of brainwashing–but a couple of things he said about Earth paying taxes to the Paradise Planets made Kassi wonder. Ravana, Meela, Professor Raisen–they all believed Kassi's parents and the Council collected taxes from the poor Gaians. Professor Raisen also spent a good deal of time blaming the Paradisers for a lot of Earth's problems.

No wonder they hate us!

During *Evéik*, Kassi studied her assigned readings while the rest of class practiced their grammar. It was the first time she had ever felt advanced in anything. Of course, it was also the first time she wasn't with her best friend, Amára, who was always first in their class.

After school, they strolled to the docks and met up with the

Blue Krakens. Hitting the water, they swam to Sector 13 for rehearsal. After reviewing the song playbook and running through some routes and AquaSphera drills, they faced off with a coachless team of 600s who had run their training on the other end of the field–no on-land, elite training facility for them.

Kassi started on the sidelines again as a substitute goalie, even though a few of her teammates didn't even want to play. After some of the big saves she made against the Red Squalls, she half-expected to start the match. To her surprise, they didn't sub her in until the last fifteen minutes of the game. She tried not to let it get to her. In the game, she made a few good saves, but they still ended up losing 8-0. Once the final buzzer sounded, the other team vanished. They bolted for the docks without saying a word.

"That was rude-eh." Kassi put a hand on her hip.

"You'll grow used to it," Fille said. "None of the other teams ever acknowledge us once the game's over."

"Only the Red Squalls," Savriah said.

Kassi was sure Vander was a big reason for that. He seemed like the kind of cha who genuinely respected others, regardless of their social status–one more reason why he was so bosst.

They reached the docks, changed, and said their goodbyes. "Ride the tide," Fille called.

"Tide!" they said as they parted ways.

As she walked back, she reflected on the Krakens' defeat. They needed to make real changes if they ever stood a chance at winning any matches, not to mention even qualifying for the Siren Games. They needed to claim the top rank in their league to even advance. That meant beating all the other 43 teams in the league, including the Red Squalls. It was impossible!

She made it back to the townhome without any more splashes off the slidewalks. Her balance was improving. Inside, Kyoto and Meela both waited for her at the kitchen table.

"What's for dinner?" Kassi said with some sass, tossing her school bag to the floor.

"Sheist on a shingle." Meela smiled as she plopped a dollop of gruel on Kassi's plate. She was in a slightly better mood. "How's school, hun?"

"Horrible as always." Kassi took a seat, trying not to examine her food too closely. At least they were having rice and bean chili today.

"I'm sure it'll get better," Meela said as she pulled a fresh, steaming batch of government-rationed protein biscuits out of the air fryer and placed it on the table. Kassi sighed and piled up her plate. Kyoto didn't say a word. He cleaned his plate and retired for the night.

"B'fore ya head up," Meela said. "Somethin' ya need t'know."

"What?" Kassi asked.

"Th'attack yesterday," Meela said. Kassi straightened in her seat. She tapped her foot impatiently while Meela rubbed her eyes for a good minute before continuing. "Ravana said yer folks had somethin' t'do with it. Somethin' about a rescue attempt gone wrong er 'bout 'Disers punishin' us for takin' ya'll. She didn' give details, but I thought ya should know."

"Rescue attempt?" Kassi furrowed her eyebrows. "I thought the portal was closed!"

"Ravana said someone opened th'portal on this side. One 'o the rescuers they caught b'fore we got there," Meela said.

"But wouldn't my parents have-eh been trying to rescue me?" Kassi asked.

"Might'a been 'bout one of th'other kids an' his parents. Not sure. Yer parents still might'a tried t'help 'em out. But it was them settin' off th'bombs t'create a diversion so they could grab 'em kids and take 'em home."

"I don't believe-eh that," Kassi shook her head repeatedly. "My parents wouldn't. I thought that was you."

"C'mon now, we'd never do that," Meela said.

Kassi fought down her inner trembling as she said, "You killed Macks."

"We did no such thang!" Meela stepped toward Kassi, anger rising in her voice.

"I watched it happen," Kassi said, a sudden constriction in her throat. She never liked confrontations.

"That was an accident! An' I don' appreciate yer tone!" Meela pointed in her face.

Kassi folded her arms and sulked in her seat. Meela huffed before lowering her arm and taking a step back.

"If you weren't the ones setting off the bombs, then what was your assignment about?"

"Ravana anticipated th'rescue. Sh'called us in t'help prevent it."

"But you couldn't prevent the attack that killed all those people?" Kassi asked.

"Didn' get there in time t'help those poor people." Meela's voice softened as she lowered her eyes.

Kassi eyed the discolored panel in the corner. "Does the U.N.O.E. know?"

"They always know." Meela excused herself and ascended the staircase to her room. Kassi soon followed to her own bed.

Curling on her stained, moldy mattress, she thought of home. Why would the Council support a rescue attempt that caused the deaths of innocent Gaians? It didn't make sense. Her parents couldn't have been responsible. They might have failed to help the people of Earth, but they're no murderers.

She tried to sleep, but the thought of it kept her up. Calmness escaped her. Her usual siren meditation exercises did little to help. A walk through the Royal Gardens back home would always restore her calm.

Sitting up and closing her eyes, she tried singing a song her older sister, Nasri, often performed whenever Kassi helped her manage the Royal Gardens. Nasri was a brilliant, botanical artist and the Royal Gardens were her canvas. Over the years, it had grown from a small flower patch to an awe-inspiring, biodiverse masterpiece spanning acres and even included underwater aquascapes. Despite the limitations of her voice, the melody helped Kassi picture herself walking beneath the grapevine trellis, past the hand-carved gazebo and the towering hedges of the garden labyrinth to the tulip fields. Her mind stilled, and she drifted to sleep.

Thirteen

After *Evéik* the next day, Fille and Adonis stayed behind in Sensei's class, leaving Kassi to walk alone with Savriah. "So relieved it's Friday! I could really use a couple days off after such a ludicray week!"

"What do you mean? You don't have to come in tomorrow?" Savriah asked.

"It's Saturday!"

"400s still have to come to school on Saturdays and Sundays to clean," Savriah said. "Nobody told you?"

"What? No! Nobody told me." Kassi paused in the middle of the hallway. "We have-eh to clean what?"

"The school."

"The entire school!" Kassi shouted louder than she meant to despite her hoarse voice, startling a pair of harmonizing 500s strolling by.

"What's going on?" Fille said as he and Adonis met up with them in the hallway. "Is Savvy embarrassing the 400s again?"

"I don't do that!" Savriah punched both Fille and Adonis in the arms.

"Ow, what'd I, what'd I say?" Adonis rubbed his arm where she had socked him.

"Kassi didn't know we come in on Saturdays and Sundays to clean."

"Nobody told you?" They both said in unison.

"It's not as bad as it sounds," Fille reassured her. "All the other kids and teachers are gone. We got the whole school to ourselves."

"We just, we just lollybag the whole time." Adonis said.

"Mr. Benetti is the only faculty around. He checks us in…," Savriah began.

"He checks us in, and then he checks out," Fille said, waving a hand away from his face. "You'll see." As easy as that sounded, Kassi still didn't like the idea of getting up early on the weekends. She needed to catch up on her sleep.

When 06:30 on Saturday morning rolled around, she groaned the longest groan of her life. "I zhust wanna sleep!" As she sat up and stared at the water-stained wall in front of her, she realized she had never truly appreciated everything she had back home. She missed her family, her bed, and all the freedoms she had taken for granted.

I just wanna go back to the way it was. A tear escaped her eye and rolled down her cheek.

When she arrived at school, all the 400s from her school were there, grades 9 through 12. It was the first time they had something together outside of AquaSphera.

Fille and Adonis stood in the hallway in the middle of a conversation. "…that's what I'm saying. I heard the principal talking about installing a bob wire fence! We'd be trapped here like rats in cages," Fille said.

"Yo yo, cha! Did you just call it a Bob wire fence?" Adonis laughed.

"Yisû, Bob wire fence. The fences with the spiky little sheisters on top!" Fille made a gesture with his hand to depict the spikes.

"I know I know, but Bob wire?" Adonis burst out laughing.

"You actually, you actually think it's called Bob wire. As in Robert wire. You think it's called Robert wire!"

"Cut your mouth you soft-headed sheist!" Fille shoved him. "What do you call it?"

"Cha! It's Barb wire! Like Barbara wire!" Adonis spoke slowly for once to emphasize the correction.

"It's not Barbara wire! It's Bob wire!" Fille raised his voice and stepped toward Adonis.

"I'm telling you, it's Barbara!"

"You depps, it's neither of those things!" Savriah reached forward and pushed them apart. She shot both a disapproving look and said.

"Well then, what is it?" Fille tapped his foot impatiently.

"Chas, it's barbed wire. Because the wire has barbs on it. Those spiky sheisters are called barbs. Barbed wire!"

"Oh, that…that actually makes sense," Adonis said. Both his and Fille's faces lit up with realization.

"Alright, kids, get to work," Mr. Benetti, a gray-haired man with a hunched back and green armband, called out from down the hall.

"Will do, Mr. Benetti!" Joshi said as he and a few others gave him a thumbs up.

"Kassi, you made it," Fille said. She had been standing there for a while, but they were too wrapped up in their conversation to notice.

"Let's flake off and go upstairs," Quade said.

"We outie, we outie like a belly button," Adonis said.

"Gross, would you stop saying that?" Fille shouted.

Once they were upstairs, Kassi asked, "So how long are we here-eh?"

"Til noon. Then we jet to the training pools." Catelyn said. She had thick, blue, medium-layered hair.

"Oh wait wait, I almost forgot," Adonis pulled something out of his bag. It was a blue and white AquaSphera jersey with the name Zavala on it. "I know it was yesterday, but happy birthday, Fille!"

Fille held it up and flipped it around to examine it with a pleased look on his face, "Cha, this is bosst! Thank you, Donis!" He pulled the new jersey over his head and wore it over his school uniform. The other 400s patted him on the back and wished him a happy birthday.

"I got you something, too," Savriah handed him a plain white towel.

"Oh, this looks just like our government-issued plain white towels." He held it up and flipped it around to examine it. "It is a government-issued plain white towel!"

"I thought you could use an extra one. You know, you can never have too many," Savriah said. Kassi almost thought the gift was a gag, but seeing the earnest look on Savriah's face, she wasn't so sure.

"Um, thanks?" Fille said as he tossed the towel in his bag.

"The big 16. The big 16!" Adonis bellowed, his voice echoing down the empty hall.

"Although technically I'm only 4 since I was born on February 29th!" Fille smiled. "I've only had 4 real birthdays!"

"Wait, is that real? Fille's only 4 years old?" Kassi had never considered the possibility of people born on February 29th aging slower than everyone else.

They all laughed except Kassi. Fille studied her. "We're joking. Of course, I'm not 4 years old!"

"Right, of course-eh! I was...only kidding," she lied, forcing a laugh.

They spent the rest of the time playing broom hockey in the hallway of the third floor with Coach Muzzey's broomsticks and Professor Oakey's well-polished nameplate. They were extra rough to add as many scuffs as they could.

At noon, they cruised to the training pools. After practice, they faced off against a team of 700s called the Purple Piranhas. The Blue Krakens lost. It wasn't even close. Kassi still spent most of the game watching from the sidelines. Her hopes of returning home continued to melt like a flaming, soft wax candle.

Sunday turned out to be more of the same. Eating the same government rations, lollybagging at school, watching her team from the sidelines as they lost another AquaSphera match, and crying herself to sleep at night as she dreamed of home. She wondered if Amára's situation was any better.

Amára's got a healthy voice and is probably the fastest siren on the field. She's likely helping her team win some games. The thought gave Kassi some comfort. At least one of them had a small chance, even if it took her years.

After school on Monday, they skipped to the docks as usual. In their wetsuits, Fille pulled up their schedule on his wrist's holodisplay. "What?" He exclaimed, sprinting to the officiator's kiosk where an older, female officiator sat. His voice carried across the docks. "Kicked out! How's that possible?" Fille pointed fiercely at the schedule displayed above his wrist.

"You failed to submit the proper forms on time," the woman said, her pinched voice snappish. She had a white-haired pixie cut and a condescending look on her face.

The argument ensued for another five or ten minutes before Fille finally had the woman convinced and restored the team's approval status.

Nikola's voice rang across the docks from the diving plat-form. "I've never seen someone so excited to get back in the water and lose!" He laughed before turning to dive.

Fille grabbed his thumb and pulled his fists apart in response.

After they were gone from the docks, Kassi asked him, "What does that mean?" She imitated the gesture.

"The cacasheist? It means go eat sheist and die!" Fille shouted at the lines of students where the Chinpoke Squad once stood. Many of the students returned the gesture assuming Fille's insult was directed at them.

That afternoon, they were right back in the thick of losing

another AquaSphera contest. After watching the first half from the sidelines, Kassi subbed in at the beginning of the second half. As she dove for her first shot on goal, she couldn't get Nikola's voice out of her head, *I've never seen someone so excited to get back in the water and lose!* She lost focus a number of times and allowed goals she normally would have deflected.

Maybe I don't deserve to start, Kassi shook her head. *At least, not until I get my voice back.*

The second the final buzzer sounded, the other team bolted. They were only 500s, but even to them, the Blue Krakens were too insignificant to acknowledge. Kassi and her teammates began the long swim back to the docks, humiliated by another defeat.

As they did, Kassi scanned the other sectors and spotted the Red Squalls. They were just finishing up their game. Another victory, no doubt. Kassi couldn't help but feel jealous of Vander's teammates. Not only did they get to play on the top-ranked team with the likelihood of qualifying for the Siren Games, they also got to play alongside Vander. When Kassi wasn't dreaming of home, she found herself fantasizing over the idea of playing beside him. The thought made her blush. She turned her back on the others hoping none of them noticed. Savriah studied her curiously. She opened her mouth to say something when everyone powered up their suits and took off toward the coast. Kassi powered hers up and followed loosely behind.

The next day at school, and each day that week, Kassi asked Sensei if he had received a response from the Market Abyss healer. It was always the same response, "Nothing yet." In the meantime, buzz began to circulate about the upcoming round two of the Siren Games. Round one, the AquaSphera tournament, had just barely concluded and the bottom sixteen teams had been eliminated from the Games. The forty-eight remaining teams prepared to enter the only individual event in the Games. All other rounds paired team against team, but round two, known as The Abyss, challenged each player individually. The

U.N.O.E. added this round, Kassi had learned, to make sure there were no freeloaders among the winning teams.

On Saturday, Fille came bounding down the hallway wearing his new AquaSphera jersey. Most of the 400s were already playing broom hockey in the corridor.

"This pata's wearing my present!" Adonis whooped.

"You know it! Zavala's the greatest player in all the worlds!"

"Well, I wouldn't, I wouldn't go that far. I mean, he's good, but he's no Vonahan." Adonis shook a finger in the air. He pulled a jersey out of his bag with Maroon and Black colors with the name "Vonahan" written on the back.

"Vonahan! That soggy biscuit couldn't score if his life depended on it!"

"Don't you talk about my Vonnie that way!" Adonis stepped toe to toe with Fille. "Besides, Zavala's nothing without Foster. Foster's the only reason their team even qualified!"

"Whale sheist!" Fille waved a dismissive hand.

Catelyn shouted over the noise of the rough game they were playing, "Donis, how could you root for anyone other than Team Miami? Sensei Kelipalo mentored Zavala and everyone else on that team!"

Kassi had watched round one's AquaSphera tournament back on Nemal just before she was taken. Caesar, Amára, Coltren, Evita, and their cousins and friends always watched the Games back home, cheering on their favorite teams. While their hometown pro leagues were enjoyable, nothing compared to the heated contests of the Siren Games. Champions trained their entire lives to compete against billions of Gaians to be the best. Their desperate determination drove them to excel to heights Paradisers could only dream of. Unable to watch the Siren Games live, they downloaded the broadcasts via Rosen-comm and watched them as if they were. They would curse at the refs, cheer a big play and bet on winners and losers. This season, their favorite team to win it was Barcelona, with Lula Chirico as their captain.

"Vonahan and Zavala, pshh," Kassi shouted over Savriah's shoulder. "They got nothin' on Lula Chirico!" She couldn't tell whose jaw dropped lower, Fille or Adonis.

"You chas, you chas watch the Siren Games?" Adonis asked.

"I thought you chas just made money off the Games," Savriah said, loudly enough for their other teammates to overhear.

"What are you chas talking about?" Quade paused mid-swing with his broom to ask.

"Savvy!" Fille cast her a disapproving look.

"How would Kassi make money off the Games?" Joshi asked.

"Power it down, Joshi!" Fille said with a dismissive hand. "Savvy's a loon–she always talks ludicray."

Their teammates eyed them curiously before resuming their hockey match.

"You need to be more careful, Savvy," Fille said in hushed tones.

"Sorry!" Savriah said with a huff, folding her arms.

"So you, so you chas do watch the Games?" Adonis whispered.

"Of course-eh! I knew Barcelona was gonna take palladium in round one," Kassi said. The palladium medal was first place, platinum was second, gold third, and silver fourth. They were awarded to the top four of the first three rounds. The final round, the ship races, awarded the top four winners with a Paradise passport and the rest of the teams with a silver medal. "Lula's zhust so naturally gifted," Kassi continued. "It's gotta be zheneric!"

"Generic?" Fille looked puzzled.

"I think she means genetic," Savriah said.

"Zhenetic," Kassi pursed her lips. "You know what I mean!"

"Barcelona only took palladium 'cause they didn't play against London!" Adonis wagged a finger. "London would've taken 'em."

"Either way, your favorite teams didn't get eliminated, so

what's the big difference?" Savriah clearly wasn't a fanatic like the others.

"What's the difference? Do you even watch the Siren Games?" Fille shouted at Savvy, sounding offended.

They argued for a few more minutes before pulling up different game highlights they had filmed on their hologlasses. They ended up spending the rest of their Saturday morning watching clips from the Ship Races.

Only the first four teams to cross the finish line earned a Paradise passport. Unless her parents rescued her, that's what Kassi would somehow have to do in order to return home. If she managed to accomplish the impossible in under six months and push her team from dead last into first place in the local AquaSphera league, they would only qualify to enter the Siren Games. They would still need to compete against champions from 63 other provinces in four events, ranking high enough in the first three rounds to avoid elimination before flying their ship fast enough around the world to win. If they couldn't pull it off this season, Kassi would be stuck for an additional six months before she could even try again.

All of this depended on Kassi finding a healer to get her voice back. It had been a couple of weeks since the injury, and she had barely noticed any improvements. The pain in her neck and throat had mostly subsided, but her voice had not returned.

As they watched highlights of the winning races, the cameras always zoomed in on the families of the winning champions as they jumped and danced in celebration. Immediate and extended families from the grandparents on down shared in the victory, earning a passport with their champion.

Kassi once asked her dad about this. *"What if the champions don't like their family?"*

"Well, Little Spice, they're big planets. There's a lot of space," Leo said in his melodic Evéik.

"But what if some of the family members really don't deserve it? What if they did nothing to help?"

"The majority of them help a lot. So there's really nothing we can do about the few who don't. We don't want to punish the majority for the shortcomings of the minority. All we can do is give them the opportunity."

Saturday's and Sunday's matches both ended in defeats. They had yet to win a single game, and Kassi was still starting each game as a sub on the sidelines. The hopelessness was setting in. Kassi was never going home.

On Monday, she dragged her feet to *Heroics* class, feeling down. Nikola seemed to notice, "Klutziana's such a loser, she's worse than a 'diser!"

Malyra joined in. "If there were a contest for losers, she would be second!"

Nikola laughed. DeSchuster had the blankest expression on his face like he got off on the wrong waterbus stop and couldn't figure out where he was. "Why second?" He was built like an Old World Nemalís statue but apparently had the IQ of a sock, and yet somehow he was an 800.

"Cha, because she's a loser!" Nikola said.

DeSchuster didn't seem to get it so Malyra added, "She wouldn't be first at anything, you blowse!"

Kassi tried to ignore them, slumping into her seat in the back. They didn't let up all morning, insulting her every chance they got. By the time lunch had arrived, Kassi was ready to explode. They grabbed their food and escaped to Sensei's classroom. The elevator doors opened to Sensei Kelipalo standing in the hallway, a huge smile on his face.

"I found him."

Fourteen

"You found the healer?" Kassi instantly perked up, the morning stress melting away.

"Come on. I'll fill you in." He led the way back to his classroom.

The hallways were empty during lunch, so they weren't too worried about anyone overhearing their conversation. Besides, they were 400s. No one ever paid attention to them.

Kassi could barely contain her excitement as they followed Sensei back to his room, hopping and skipping all the way there.

"How'd you, how'd you find him?" Adonis asked.

"One of my contacts got back to me."

"I wonder if I know him! What if he's from my hometown? What's his name-eh?" Kassi spoke almost as quickly as Adonis, a thousand questions flitting across her mind.

"He goes by Hira."

"Hira?"

"Probably a moniker to protect his identity," Sensei said.

"Did he agree to heal my voice-eh? What do we do next? How do I meet him?" Kassi yipped like an overactive Ducat Russell terrier.

"I sent him a message," Sensei said calmly over his shoulder.

"It took a bit to get through to my contact, and for him to reach Hira, but they say once Hira's been reached, he always gets back to you within twenty-four hours."

Twenty-four hours? Kassi forced a breath. *It's fine, I can wait that long.*

"I can't believe you found him!" Savriah said.

"Sensei K is bosst!" Fille and Adonis both pounded on the lockers, earning a glare from a professor who poked his head out of his room. They reached the classroom and ducked inside.

For the rest of lunch, Kassi envisioned herself with newly replicated vocal cords. Tomorrow, she would finally be a true siren again! The past three weeks without her family, her home, and her voice had been the longest of her life, but at least now with her voice back, she might start feeling more like herself.

Despite how boring *Civility and Etiquette* was, it went by in a blur. In *Evéik*, she had a hard time paying attention to her reading. Every few minutes, she glanced over at Sensei to see if he heard back from Hira.

The next morning, it was all Kassi could think about. *Surely, Sensei's heard from him by now!*

Malyra and Nikola both seemed to notice she wasn't paying attention. In P.E., as they ran their laps, Nikola, DeSchuster, and Malyra both took turns pelting her with spit wads. A few 700s joined in. After the tenth one got stuck in her hair, Kassi cursed at them loudly enough for Coach Muzzey to hear, the volume of her broken voice surprising her.

Within seconds, Coach was in her face. "Yash's tap-dancing sheist! It's the broomstick, Four Hundie!"

The Chinpoke Squad went from spitting wads to spewing insults. After Kassi's lengthy verbal drubbing, Malyra was handed the sonic pulse baton. Still, without a voice to perform a shield song, Kassi made a run for it as Malyra gave chase while performing her attack incantation. Within seconds, Kassi felt her bladder constrict.

She wouldn't! Kassi whipped her head back toward Malyra. The sinister look in her eyes said it all. *No, please!*

The sonic pulse caused Kassi to lose control and urinate in her gym shorts in front of the entire class. Everyone, including Coach Muzzey, erupted into laughter. Malyra, Nikola, DeSchuster, and the Chinpoke Squad looked so pleased with themselves as if they could just die of high-fiving.

Overcome with embarrassment, Kassi did her best to hold back the tears until everyone had vacated the gymnasium. Once it was empty, she sobbed, slowly skirting to the washrooms. Kassi's tears continued as she removed her soiled outfit, rinsed off, and put on her uniform. She couldn't let them see her so defeated.

Why do they enjoy watching others suffer so much? Kassi couldn't make sense of it. Running through her siren meditation exercises, she focused on the stillness of her empty surroundings. With a few deep breaths, she shuffled to the cafeteria.

"Kassi? What's wrong?" Savriah asked.

Kassi grumbled, "Those-eh cacafuegos and their yashing broomstick."

"Coach Muzzey lives for that broomstick," Fille said. "Sick, sadistic sheist!"

"I get, I get the broomstick at least once a month in his class," Adonis said. "Last time, they made me pee my pants!"

"That's what they just did to me! So embarrassing!" Kassi said. Jacen and Jaya both glanced over and snickered at this.

"Happens to the best of us," Fille said before turning. "And the worst! Laugh it up, J's! I've seen both of you pee your pants in class." Jacen scowled at this.

"Does he make you participate-eh?" Kassi asked. "You all have zhym together, right?"

"Yisû," Savriah said.

"We have to participate or else we get the broomstick the very next day." Fille gave a single nod.

"So what do you say?"

"Oh, I got plenty of things to shout at Donis." Fille poked Adonis in the shoulder. "Last time, I called him an over-spiced biscuit and a distinguishable pothole over and over again."

"Mine was better, mine was better." Adonis swatted away Fille's arm. "I called him a waterbus driver with no pants."

"That was a good one," Fille conceded. It was all nonsense to Kassi, but she liked how they used humor to turn a traumatic experience into something trivial.

Once in Sensei's room, he glanced up from something he was reading. "I heard back from Hira."

Kassi clapped, running to his desk with a bounce. "What'd he say?"

"He said he could come through this way in about three weeks," Sensei held up a small, rectangular device with text scrolled across it–Hira's message.

"Three weeks!" Kassi deflated. "He can't come any sooner?"

"Yisû, that's, that's forever!" Adonis tried peeking over Sensei's shoulder to read the message.

"I know it's a long time to wait," Sensei put the device away and shooed Adonis back to his seat. "But at least he's coming."

"I know." Kassi breathed a long sigh. "It is still good news." She pursed her lips and tried to force a smile. It was hard to suppress her disappointment.

That afternoon, while the Krakens were warming up their voices, Fille called them to the huddle. "Bad news, chas. Our match today," he paused, "it's against the Black Hydras." Groans and complaints rumbled throughout the squad.

"Who are the Black Hydras?" Kassi asked, looking at her teammates.

"Chinpoke Squad," Adonis ran a thumb across his neck.

"Oh," was all she said. She did her best to hide her inner and outer trembling.

Without a coach, typically, singing practice and AquaSphera training were half-hearted and stuffed with a fair share of lolly-bagging–not that day. Even Fille and Adonis had reined in the humor. Their upcoming match against the Chinpoke Squad loomed over them like the jaws of death.

Halfway through warmups, the Black Hydras arrived, filling the far end of the sector with foreboding. Nikola swam over to meet Fille and determine the kickoff. He looked at Kassi with the most devious grin on his face. She squirmed under the pressure of his stare, eventually breaking eye contact and turning away. He was probably picturing his team crushing the Krakens, and there was nothing Kassi could do to prevent it.

Three weeks!

"Why couldn't he come-eh sooner?" She let slip with the entire team listening in.

Her teammates gave her quizzical looks. "Who? Nikola?" Joshi asked her, eyeing the Black Hydras team captain.

"What? No!" Kassi couldn't think of a good lie. Meeting with a secret siren healer from Nemal probably wasn't the sort of thing to blurt out haphazardly.

"Power it down, Joshi! Of course, not Nikola," Fille said. "Game on in fifteen! Let's focus!"

"Fifteen!" Some of them echoed as they stepped up the intensity of their drills, did their final stretches, and went through any individual pregame good luck rituals.

Fille swam toward Kassi and said, "Kassi, you're starting as our second goalie for this one."

"Oh...I am?" As much as she had wanted to start in the past, this was one of the few games she didn't mind sitting out.

"Jacen won't play against the Hydras," Fille said with a frustrated sigh, then asked with a flick of his chin, "You with us?"

She nodded and swam over to their end gate, taking her position alongside Quade.

Quade clapped her shoulder. "You ready for this?"

"Yash, I hope-eh so!" Kassi heard her breathing pick up in her helmet. The smell of familiar green muck juice permeated her helmet. Malyra was lined up next to Nikola on the kickoff line, her hair pulled back in a tight ponytail for the game.

Hydras kicked off and launched right into an assault, clearing the center immediately and catching her team off guard. Even the black luminance of the center gate looked ominous. They barreled down the sector, kicking the disc through defenders and positioning themselves for a clear shot.

An 800 took a pass from Nikola, catching with his hands and giving Catelyn the chance to intercept. With a j-step kick, sweeping both legs out to the side, she sent the disc spiraling out of bounds. While a Hydra swam out to retrieve it, the Krakens had time to form a defensive position. Hydras maintained possession. Nikola yelled furiously at his teammate who had fumbled the disc. Kassi couldn't hear what he was saying, but it looked intense. From the sidelines, it looked like their coach was also giving them an earful.

They kicked the disc in-bounds to Nikola who set up the next drive down the field. He demonstrated incredible speed and strength, weaving through defenders and creating openings in the defense. From his left foot, he sent a bullet pass behind the defense toward goal.

Kassi saw it coming and moved to intercept. Malyra pretended to swim for the same disc and bulldozed right into Kassi before she could catch it, knocking the wind out of her. The disc pelted Kassi's arm and floundered out of bounds. Doubled over and trying to find her breath, Kassi lifted her eyes to see Malyra flash the cacasheist, her lips forming the word, "Klutziana." The referee bot apparently didn't see the foul.

This is going to be a very long game.

Only a few minutes later, Kassi got bodychecked by DeSchuster. Nikola had orchestrated the pass and sent him on a direct collision course with her. Once again, the referee bot didn't catch it. The Hydras seemed exceptionally talented at using their bodies to block the bot's view of the foul. DeSchuster held up two flexed arms and mouthed something Kassi could only guess went something like, "that's what happens when you get in the way of these." The pass wobbled incomplete, and Krakens took possession. Nikola didn't seem to mind. It was almost as if inflicting pain on Kassi was more important.

The game continued with Nikola's relentless barrage of targeted attacks on Kassi, whether it was a close-range shot to her face or a pass sending a player barreling into her. Fille switched frequencies a couple of times to curse at Nikola. Kassi's body couldn't take much more of this.

By the second half, the score was tied, scoreless. Hydras caught the disc, cleared the center, and kicked a bullet directly toward Kassi from half-court. It was a long-range shot and easy to defend. Kassi positioned herself to make the catch when Nikola blindsided her, plowing his shoulder into her shin, right where the broken shin pads exposed a vulnerable part of her leg. Something snapped. Lightning pain shot up her left leg. Her hand reached down. The bone bent at an odd angle under the wetsuit. Blood drained from her face and she went pale as a sheet. Her teammates rushed to her side to help her surface. Quade and Fille wrapped her arms over their shoulders as they swam up to a lifeboat. Kassi finally heard the referee bot sound the alarm for a foul.

"Game is canceled, chas. Head to the docks," Kassi heard Fille shout to the team. Her head was spinning.

Nikola switched to their frequency and shouted, "That means you forfeit! You know that right?"

Fille ignored him. They reached the ambulance boat, and Kassi was soon lying on a gurney inside the cabin. She watched as the medics cut the wetsuit and exposed her leg, the bone sticking out.

Someone's screaming! I think it's me.

The medic stuck a needle in her arm. In a few seconds, she was out.

"How are you feeling?" Kassi peeled her eyes open to see the same medic standing over her. He flashed a light in each eye and checked her heart rate. He had short-cropped hair, a purple armband, a broad cleft chin, and brown eyes behind a pair of black-rimmed glasses.

"Like I was hit by a mackerel shark." She pointed at her leg. "Wait, what's that? WHAT IS THAT?" The left leg of her wetsuit had been crudely cut off at the knee. In place of where her boot, shin guards, and foot thruster should have been was a hardened, white plaster cast.

"I gave you a sedative. You should be feeling groggy. These will help," the medic explained, handing her two pills the size of shalimar almonds.

"These are gargantic! How am I supposed to take-eh this?" In answer to her question, he handed her a glass of water. Kassi hated pills, especially the ones large enough to make her choke. She studied the pills in her hand before asking, "Can you cut these in fourths?"

The medic studied her curiously as if she had requested he wears a cloth diaper on his head. After a long awkward silence, he reached forward and retrieved the pills, cutting them up like she requested, and handed them back. Kassi swallowed one piece at a time.

With that done, the medic sat on a stool and said, "We set the tibia bone and put a cast on your leg. It was a clean break, so you should make a full recovery. With enough rest, you'll be back on your feet within three to six months."

"Three to six months!" Kassi nearly fell out of bed. "What? Why so long?"

"I take it this is your first time," he said, pushing his glasses back onto the bridge of his nose. "That's standard for a break like yours. Just drink plenty of health shakes, lots of rest. You'll be back up and running before you know it," he said as he wrote down a few notes and exited the room.

It wasn't her first break, or even her second or third. But it only took a couple of days to fully heal from broken bones back home. One simple graphene nanobot injection and local anesthetic, and she'd be back on her feet almost instantly, fully recovered in days.

Nikola did this on purpose! That yashing sheist, chinpoke cacafuego! Kassi fumed.

Savriah entered the cabin as soon as the medic left. "How's your leg?"

"It's broken, and apparently that means I have to wait three to six months before-eh they'll take-eh this yashing cast off!" Kassi wanted to huck something across the room but nothing was within reach.

"Yisû, that sounds about right. That's standard." Savriah lightly tapped a few spots on Kassi's cast as if searching for hollow spots.

"Ow, don't do that." Kassi flinched. "And how is that standard? Back home-eh, it would take-eh two to three days, maximum! Two or three days! Not three to six months!"

"You chas have real Siren Healers, remember? Last year when I broke my arm, they didn't even set the bone right the first time. They had to break it again and reset it. I was in so much pain, and it took even longer for my arm to heal. It was miserable!" Savriah stopped tapping her cast and stared vacantly at the gurney.

"Ghost of Sheebah! That sounds awful!" Kassi felt guilty for complaining. What seemed like a nightmare scenario to her was their everyday life. "Savvy, I'm so sorry."

"Maybe this healer cha, Hira, maybe he can do something to speed it up." Savriah smiled, patting Kassi on the shoulder— probably because she couldn't reach her neck.

"Would that be too much to ask, though? He's already healing my voice-eh."

"I don't think so. That's what he's here for, right?"

"Right. Zhust wish he would come-eh sooner than three weeks."

"Me too," Savriah said as she faced the window looking out

over the Atlantic Ocean. "I can't believe Nikola did that to you. Even for the Chinpoke Squad, that was low."

"What's his problem?" Kassi growled. "He didn't foul anyone else-eh, did he?"

"No one. It's like he has a personal vendetta against you."

"He's in most of my classes. Maybe I'm zhust the 400 he sees the most?"

"That can't be it. Gotta be something else," Savriah chewed on the inside of her cheek. "Well, we're returning to the docks. Fille and Adonis are probably already there waiting for us."

Kassi didn't respond. She stared at the bulky cast on her leg and wondered why Nikola would have a grudge against her. She grumbled, "Can I zhust get a break? Zhust one!"

"Looks like you did get a break," Savriah said, chuckling as she patted Kassi's cast.

"Not that kind of...you know what I mean!"

At the docks, Fille, Adonis and the rest of the team were there waiting for them. As soon as the boat docked, Fille hopped on to help Kassi off. A crowd of students had gathered to watch, probably curious at the sight of an ambulance boat.

"How's she, how's she doing?" Adonis asked Savriah as Fille helped Kassi to her feet.

"She's pretty upset. She was complaining a lot," Savriah said.

"I wasn't complaining!" Kassi shouted.

"You could hear that?" Savriah's eyes widened with surprise.

"Of course, I could!"

"But I was using my quiet voice," Savriah tilted her head.

"First of all, Savvy, you're standing right there." Fille pointed at her feet, only meters away from them. "Second, your voice is loud."

"Even my quiet voice?"

"You don't have a quiet voice. Your voice is always loud," Fille said.

"It cuts through, cuts right through!" Adonis sliced the air with his hand.

Kassi was handed a pair of crutches. With the slidewalks, it would be impossible to get around. It was the province's policy, she soon learned, to require schools to loan out a motorized, inflatable dinghy to injured students. Fortunately, and surprisingly, this extended even to 400s. It was the only bright side to this painful situation. She had a four-seater waiting for her at the docks. The seats formed an upside-down T—two seats side by side in back, a driver's seat in the center, and one seat in front. Black with red tips, it didn't look like much, but the motor was functional. With the state of her leg, driving would be difficult for her, so Fille volunteered to drive.

"I've always wanted to steer one of these," Fille said as he took the wheel. Kassi and Savriah took seats in the back and Adonis claimed the front. Fille roared the engine to life. They sped through the streets, rounding corners at full speed. Adonis held his hands in the air and whooped. If it weren't for her cast and the dull pain in her leg, she might have felt like a VIP parading through the streets of Miami Beach.

The sun was setting and most of the streets were empty with the exception of a few late-night waterbuses. The slidewalks were free of the daily clutter of foot traffic. Fille hit a sharp turn and Savriah nearly rolled over the edge.

"I almost fell off! Slow down!" She yelled over the loud motor. Fille didn't respond. They cruised to Kyoto and Meela's townhouse as everyone clung on for dear life. Once they arrived, Fille jumped out and tied the boat to a rusted metal railing before they helped Kassi inside.

Meela sat alone in the living room. Kyoto must have still been at work at the Desalination Plant. They rotated shifts to make sure someone was always home.

"Wha' happened?" Meela rushed over to a hobbling Kassi on crutches.

"I broke-eh my leg today during AquaSphera," Kassi said, holding up her cast as she hobbled to the kitchen for a glass of water.

"We played against a team today that likes to play dirty," Savriah said.

"Here, lemme get that for ya." Meela followed after Kassi.

"This cha, this cha named Nikola," Adonis said. "He's the worst!"

"Nikola?" Meela stiffened.

"Yisû, do you know him?" Kassi asked, studying Meela's face closely.

Meela hesitated for a split second before shaking her head. "Wha'? Nah, course not. So what'd this...Nikola boy do to ya?"

"He pretended to go in for a pass and rammed right into Kassi's shin with his shoulder blade," Fille made a stabbing motion at Kassi's cast, making her flinch.

"They say it'll take-eh three to six months to heal!" Kassi still wanted to vent about it.

"Sounds 'bout right. Well then, ya'better get on up t'bed. Ya need yer rest." Meela started pulling food rations out. "Don' worry 'bout dinner. I'll bring it on up. Nice t'meet ya'll!"

Kassi struggled to balance on crutches as she climbed the steps. Savriah remained beside her to stabilize her. Once in the room, Kassi lay on the bed while the rest of them took seats on the floor against the wall. Meela was close behind with a tray of food rations. She set them down on the nightstand and said, "G'night ya'll."

As her friends sat in silence while Kassi picked at her food, she couldn't help but feel self-conscious about her bare and battered bedroom.

"She seems nice," Fille said, and then under his breath, "for a kidnapper."

"You got your own door?" Adonis swung the door back and forth on its hinges before closing it.

"And your own bed," Savriah said, poking the mattress.

"You chas don't?" Kassi had always considered her room to be the most squalid.

"Never!" Fille said.

"And one of your parents is home. Well, not your parents," Savriah corrected herself. "I mean, adults. It feels strange to see adults at home."

"Your parents are never home-eh?"

"Both my parents work long shifts," Savriah said, "and then spend their evenings down in the Market Abyss."

"They don't come home until late," Fille explained.

"Sometimes, they come home with their wobbly boots on," Savriah said.

"What?" Kassi cocked her head to the side.

"Drunk," Fille said, tipping an imaginary bottle to his lips. "The Market Abyss is where they do all the sheist they're not allowed to do anywhere else." Fille found a small pebble on the floor and tossed it at the opposite wall.

"So you never see them?" Kassi propped herself up on her elbows.

"We do, we do," Adonis nodded. "Before school, just before bed, and their days off. Why? What's it like on Nemal?" Adonis asked.

"Hard to explain. It's zhust so different!" Kassi sat up and grabbed her knees just above her cast, picturing home. "No one works long hours 'cause we all have R.A.V.'s."

"I heard of those," Savriah nodded. "They're your little robot assistants that help with everything."

"Right!"

"Wish we had those," Fille said.

Kassi continued, "but the time-eh we do spend working, we...how do I explain?" Kassi tilted her head and stared up at the ceiling. "The chefs love-eh to cook, so their food is incredible. The clothing designers are passionate about their designs. The siren healers put their souls into every incantation to provide-eh the best service-eh to those in need. It's a society where everyone feels invested, so they give it their best effort to make it a paradise-eh. My dad always said, 'These worlds are the paradise-eh we make-eh them.'" Kassi paused. She thought back on the other night when she wondered if there was a second meaning to the phrase—one much less inspiring.

"Wouldn't that be nice," Savriah said.

Kassi sat up and continued, "You can go where you want, do what you want, be who you want, keep everything you build or create-eh.

"My family lives in a palace. Everybody on Ca'pri does. It's called the City of 1,000 Palaces. We didn't build them. They were already there when my parents and their friends first discovered the planets. Our palace is larzhe enough to fit my entire extended family. My bedroom chambers were…"

"Chambers, chambers?" Adonis gasped, shaking his head. "That sounds gargantic!"

Kassi nodded. "Mine were the size of this entire-eh town-home. Ornate-eh gold trim and paintings cover the walls, water fountains and swimming lanes in every room, and the gardens…" Kassi remembered everything with so much more fondness than she ever felt growing up. She never really appreciated what she had. "The gardens went on for days. And the kitchens…"

"Alright, we get it!" Fille grumbled, holding up a hand. His annoyed tone surprised Kassi.

"What'd I say?" Kassi asked.

"We get it. You have it all. You have a gargantic mansion on Paradise with everything you could ever want. Meanwhile, we're living in the trench as 400s, sharing beds in rooms without doors, eating meager rations, and raising ourselves while our parents work long hours for the U.N.O.E.," Fille tossed another pebble across the room. Adonis and Savriah stared at the floor in silence. They didn't seem to object. "Last week, we ran home after a yashing terrorist attack where hundreds of people died. It's a sheist life on Earth and yet we're the ones helping you."

"That's not my fault! I got kidnapped!"

"Exactly!" Fille pointed out. "You got kidnapped. You've had everything your whole life while we've had nothing, and yet we're helping you find a healer so you can get back home and leave us to this same forsaken sheist!"

"I didn't realize I was such a burden." Kassi curled up on the mattress, face toward the wall.

"You're not understanding me," Fille stood. "This is nothing personal. It's just a backward situation. We're helping you out even though we're the ones who've needed help our entire lives."

"Well, you don't need to help me if you really don't want to. I can do this on my own!" Kassi spat into the mattress, holding back tears.

"That's not what I'm saying. I have no problem helping you, I just...ugh!" Fille sat back down. "I just really wish you could help us leave this yashing planet!"

Kassi didn't respond, still hiding her face from the group. He was right. She should be the one helping them. Earth was so horrific, it needed a fundamental shift in every fabric of its society. Her friends needed to leave it and relocate to Paradise, and Kassi needed to get back so she could convince her parents to open the portal and let them.

Savriah put an arm on Kassi's shoulder. "Nobody blames you for our situation."

"Right, right. None of this is your fault," Adonis agreed, running his hands through his hair as it fell to both sides of his face.

"That's what I was trying to say," Fille sighed. "I wasn't blaming you for it. It's just a stuffed situation!"

"Maybe we should go," Savriah offered when Kassi still didn't respond.

"No, it's alright." Kassi lifted her head. "You don't have to leave-eh."

"You sure?" Savriah said.

"I know it's not fair," Kassi spoke quietly, sitting up. "It's frustrating that I can't do anything about it." She paused for a beat. "I don't know why my people never did more to help.

There should be enough space and resources for all Gaians on the Paradise-eh Planets, it zhust...doesn't make sense-eh."

"We were always told Paradisers need us working here so they can live rich from our taxes," Fille said with a half-shrug.

"That doesn't sound right," Kassi shook her head. "We don't live off anyone's taxes."

"That's just what we're told," Fille said, chucking a pebble against the wall. "Something about the need to pay Paradise back for their help during the Great Correction."

"Well, I've never seen or heard of tax money coming in." Staring at the floor, she continued, "Either way, we should have-eh been the ones helping you chas all along. It's not right for me to ask you for anything."

"No, no we don't mind helping," Savriah placed a hand on Kassi's neck.

"We wanna help. We really do!" Fille said.

Kassi lifted her head, "You do?"

"Yisû! We help you get your voice back, you...help us win the Siren Games, right? Then we all go to Paradise." Fille tried saying the words as if this weren't the most unrealistic smoke dream. Still, it helped lift Kassi's mood.

"And speaking of Siren Games, they're next week!" Adonis said, clapping his hands.

"We know! You and Fille won't shut up about it," Savriah said, throwing a pillow right at Adonis' face.

"What? We can't be excited?" Adonis threw it right back.

"I think Meela knows Nikola," Kassi said, changing the subject. She wasn't in the mood to talk about the Siren Games. "Did you catch the look on Meela's face when we said his name-eh?"

"What look?" Fille and Adonis both glanced at each other in bewilderment.

"Yisû. She flinched," Savriah said.

"I think she and Kyoto know Nikola," Kassi said, fingering the french braid in her hair.

"What are you both talking about?" Fille bounced back and forth between Kassi and Savriah.

"Maybe they hired him to keep an eye on me."

Everyone's eyes went wide as Adonis exclaimed, whipping a hand to his mouth, "Oh sheist!"

Fifteen

Bright and early Wednesday morning, Kassi listened from the kitchen table, as the rumble of the motorboat grew near. Last night, everyone had decided it was easier for everyone if Fille held onto the dinghy and picked them up in the morning. Outside, Fille's blonde hair whipped in the breeze as he tied the boat before helping Kassi on board. He gunned the engine, and they made the rounds.

Winding through a few streets, they came to Adonis' town-home. Fille shouted, "Pick up your feet or lose your seat, Donis!" His home was wedged between others of the same make and style, much more compact than the one Kassi was staying at. The paint on the lower levels had chipped and faded. The upper floors were gray and blocky like the rest of the apartments and townhomes in Miami Beach. Small and cramped, it looked like it was barely holding itself together. Adonis burst out the door barefoot before doubling back and disappearing inside. He emerged a moment later with socks and shoes in his hands.

"Almost, almost forgot my socks! Had them in the dryer to warm them up."

"Socks fresh outta the dryer are bosst!" Fille said with a thumb of approval.

They swung by Savriah's, her place nearly identical to Adonis' home. She was already outside waiting for them, school bag in hand. En route, Fille spotted Malyra walking alone. "Oh ho-ho, watch this!" Fille stood up and leaned forward, wagging like a labrador. He gunned it full throttle in her direction. She noticed only at the last second. Fille cranked the wheel hard right, dousing Malyra in street water. Shrieking like a banshee, she looked up with murder in her eyes.

The dinghy had already retreated down the street when they heard her scream, "You're gonna regret this you miserable, worthless, cacafuego sheists…" Her voice trailed off.

This could be the start of a great day.

At school, Kassi took her seat in *Heroics* class and watched Malyra storm in a few minutes late. Professor Oakey noticed and said nothing–no pinch, no lecture on punctuality in the cafeteria, not even a warning!

Malyra glowered at Kassi as she took her seat, her uniform damp and rank, her hair a wet mess. A swelling sense of justice flooded Kassi–she couldn't stop smiling.

Pulling out her hologlasses, Malyra smirked as she punched a few buttons in the air. Notifications popped up on everyone's hologlasses, including Kassi's. The students immediately clicked on the link. It was a five-second loop of Kassi urinating in her gym shorts in front of class.

The class erupted in laughter all over again. Kassi stopped smiling.

"Silence!" Professor Oakey shouted, taking her position at the front of class. All through her lecture, Malyra glanced back at Kassi with a victorious, smug expression on her face. Kassi stirred angrily in her seat.

With crutches, it was impossible to reach her classes within the allotted three minutes. Each one of her professors made a fuss about it and sent her to the cafeteria for more punctuality lectures. By lunch, Sensei Kelipalo found out and abruptly marched to the front office, returning moments later with a note that excused Kassi's tardiness. From now on, she could take her time. She could even take a washroom break in between classes if she wanted. First a boat and now this–having a broken leg apparently had its perks. Still, Kassi would have much preferred not having her leg broken.

On the way to Period 5, Kassi said, "I had the stranzhest dream last night!"

"What about?" Savriah asked.

Kassi started to relate her dream about wandering the streets of London with her niece when they all passed the front row of 800s and noticed Malyra cleaned up in a fresh, new uniform, cozying up to Nikola.

Taking their seats in the back, Adonis asked, "Are those, are those two cacafuegos a thing?" He winced in disgust.

"When did that happen?" Fille asked. "How anyone could date Malyra is beyond me!"

"How could anyone date-eh Nikola!" Kassi said with a vigorous shake of her head. "He treats everyone like sheist. That's a huzhe white-eh flag for me."

"White flag?" Fille cocked his head.

"I think she means red flag," Savriah said.

"Red flag." Kassi sighed in frustration, "You know what I mean!" Malyra and Nikola were two of the worst people on the planets. *Maybe they deserve each other,* she thought as she cast them sidelong glances throughout all the rest of class.

After *Evéik*, they took the boat to the docks for AquaSphera. Until the leg healed, Kassi was beached like a toothed whale while her friends and teammates swam to the training pools. Her siren suit hadn't been repaired since the accident, and even if it had, it wouldn't fit over her gargantic, clunky cast. If they had singing practice on land like the higher statuses, Kassi could have at least joined them for that, even with her hoarse voice.

While her friends rehearsed and competed, rather than spend the afternoon with her grips at the townhome, Kassi stayed on the docks, found a vacant bench, and read from Sensei's assigned Evéik readings. He was counting on her to complete the full list by the end of the school year, and she didn't want to disappoint. Besides, if she wanted to win the Siren Games, she would need to sharpen all of her skills. Since she couldn't improve her game in the water or exercise her vocal cords, she would have to focus on her mastery of advanced Evéik.

With her hologlasses, Kassi had already finished the first book on the list called, *Gatsby li Itor*, and was halfway through the second titled, *Li Sashir van Yeki*. They were old classics from hundreds of years ago that had been translated by Granton Macavoy, one of the original explorers who discovered the Evéik language over a hundred years ago. Kassi was fascinated by the stories of these people who lived such different lives. She found herself relating to Dorothy, a girl torn away from her home and doing everything she could to find her way back.

She was reading about a cowardly lion when Nikola burst out of the ocean alone, landed on the docks, and stormed to the lockers, fists clenched. He was staring daggers at anyone who made eye contact.

Moments later, he reappeared, still in his wetsuit and sonopack, his wavy hair pulled into a loose man bun. He whirled in her direction as if he could feel the weight of her gaze. They locked eyes. He gave her a deep scowl. She turned away, hiding her face until she thought it safe to look again. When she looked up, he was at the springboards. Nikola glanced once more in her direction before diving into the ocean.

Soon after, Malyra and the rest of the Black Hydras emerged just ahead of Kassi's friends and her own team. Kassi stood and met up with her friends at the dinghy.

"So what'd you do this whole time?" Savriah asked, taking Kassi's crutches while Fille and Adonis helped her down.

"My reading assignments from Sensei."

"Sounds more productive than losing another game." Fille untied the boat and pushed off.

"So we lost?" Kassi asked.

"What else?" Fille said.

Adonis stood up on his seat, turning to face them. "But that goal, that goal Catelyn scored was bosst!"

"Yisû, that was definitely bosst!" Fille roared the engine to life.

"Catelyn scored? From the defense-eh?" Kassi shouted over the noise.

"I mean this as a compliment, but Catelyn seems like the kinda person who collects animals in jars," Savriah said, her loud voice easily carrying over the engine. Kassi and the others stared blankly at Savriah for a few beats.

"She shot up, she shot up like a torpedo from the back," Adonis said, shooting his arm through the air. "Read the danger and caught an incredible interception just before the other team cleared the center."

"It was a ludicray catch," Fille shouted over his shoulder as he gunned the throttle and they jerked forward, nearly knocking Adonis over. He scrambled to his seat. "And then she bicycle kicked it through the goal!"

"Bosst, go Catelyn!" Kassi said. Her braided pigtails flapped in the wind as they jetted through the streets of Miami Beach. The weather was perfect. The sun was setting and the sky was radiant. For the briefest of moments, Kassi forgot about her completely stuffed situation. Then she remembered Nikola. She told her friends about it.

Fille shouted over his shoulder, "What if we followed him after AquaSphera? See where he goes."

"Solick, solick! Let's spy on that pata!" Adonis leaned on the back of his seat.

"I would, but…" Kassi pointed to her cast.

"Oh yeah, I forgot," Adonis sat back down.

"So we wait a few weeks til you're healed," Fille said.

"And then we spy," Kassi said, her raspy voice mostly swallowed by the wind and the hum of the engine.

"Only two more days 'til the Siren Games," Adonis shouted.

"Siren Games!" Fille whooped. "Friday's the day!" Fille carved through the streets as Kassi's mind raced with anticipation. As terrible as her experience on Earth had been, she had grown attached to her new companions. Kassi actually looked forward to watching the Games with her new friends.

The following day, Nikola kept to himself, brooding quietly in his seat. Whatever put him in a bad mood last night must have carried over. Whenever Malyra reached out, he shrugged her off. Kassi couldn't help but smile each time he did.

That weekend, all practices and matches were postponed for the Siren Games. At the closing bell on Friday, students rushed to change out of their uniforms. The only clothes Kassi had were the burnt orange shirt and bright green shorts she wore her first day. No matter how she begged Meela to buy clothes, she always got the same response. "Them's th'brakes. Ya'll had everythin' all yer lives. Is's time ya'll live like us fer a change."

Savriah noticed Kassi tugging and adjusting her clothes in frustration. "I've got an extra shirt you could borrow, if you want," Savriah said. Her taste in fashion left a lot to be desired, but Kassi would take anything at this point.

"I'd love-eh that, thank you!" Kassi said as she removed her shirt and pulled over the one Savriah handed her. It actually fit Kassi. The sky blue color didn't match her bright green shorts, but then again, nothing in all the worlds did. She'd have burned all her green shorts if she had a single additional option. She was half tempted to fashion her own clothes out of palm tree fronds.

Savriah also generously offered to let Kassi borrow her makeup. Some of the tones didn't match her complexion, so she only applied the eyeliner, mascara, and lip gloss, making sure to really scrub and wash the brushes before and after using them. She brushed out her hair and let it fall to both sides of her face. She had washed it the night before with some shampoo and conditioner Meela had lent her. Kassi always took great pride in her long and flowing, deep-brown hair. Back home, people always complimented her for it. She decided to show it off today.

As a special touch, she put on the diamond earrings Amara had given her. Hobbling on her crutches next to Savriah, they hurried out of the school's main entrance where Fille and Adonis were waiting in the boat.

"Where's your armband?" Savriah said as they descended the steps. She had pulled her thick, curly red hair into a french braid and wore regular clothes for the first time since Kassi had known her.

"What?" Kassi said, puzzled.

"Your armband?" Savriah tapped the yellow band she had slipped over her upper arm.

"I don't have-eh one…"

"You're not allowed to go anywhere without it. I've got an extra," Savriah said as she shuffled through her bag and pulled out a second mustard yellow band. With a shrug, she slipped it on and they finished climbing down the stairs to meet up with Fille and Adonis.

"Look at you, look at you beautiful dames!" Adonis said as he reached out a hand to help Kassi in the boat. He and Fille each wore tank tops and board shorts. Without their shoddy school uniforms or wetsuits, they looked like regular people–or, at least they would have if it weren't for their yellow armbands. Gaians couldn't allow 400s to escape their status, even for one day.

Fille roared the engine to life and floored the throttle, swerving through boat lanes and cutting corners on their way to South Pointe Plaza. The wind whipped through their hair. When he hit some of those turns and corners, water sprayed up in their faces. Kassi realized she shouldn't have done her hair and makeup before the boat ride. She had a feeling Savriah's mascara and eyeliner weren't the highest quality, and her hair was blowing into a tangled mess. With only one hand free while holding onto the boat, Kassi unsuccessfully tried to tie her hair back. Savriah noticed and used her free hand to help. Hopefully, she'd have time to duck into the washrooms and repair the damage.

Large crowds filled the plaza, balconies of apartment towers lined with people, as they cheered wildly. Projected on giant holoscreens hovering over the ocean, standing nearly a hundred meters tall, the Siren Games had already begun.

When they pulled up to the pier, Kassi whipped out a small mirror to assess the damage. Her hair was a windblown mess and her eyeliner and mascara had smeared into the crease of her eyes. She needed to find a washroom quickly before she saw anyone like….

Vander!

Vander's glistening emerald eyes looked right at her with his confident smile. As Savriah helped her out, Kassi nearly tripped on her crutches. A hand jetted out to steady her—Vander's hand. He looked so fashionable in his clean white long-sleeve shirt with the sleeves rolled up, his light blue slim pants, and white kicks. His blonde curls blew effortlessly in the breeze.

"What happened to your leg?" Vander pointed.

Kassi double-blinked nervously. "I got a cast."

"I can see that. How'd it happen?"

"Oh right, I broke it, well Nikola broke it—he was on the other team." Kassi stuttered.

"A battle wound! Happens to the best of us." Vander somehow found a way to make her injury sound impressive. "Who's Nikola?"

Fille hopped next to them on the docks, tying up the boat, and shouted, "He's a real cacafuego with the Black Hydras!"

"I don't think I know him," Vander said. "We haven't played the Black Hydras, yet."

"Well when you do, don't hold back," Fille said, holding up a fist.

"Yisû those, those cacafuegos play dirty," Adonis said.

"Case in point." Vander motioned to Kassi's leg. "Should we be worried?"

While Vander intently listened to Fille's answer, Kassi quickly faced away and whispered to Savriah. "Where are the nearest washrooms?"

Savriah didn't pick up on the social cue and responded loudly, "Do you need to pee or something?" Everyone heard, turning their heads.

"Ha ha, no." Kassi tried to play it off, then continued through clenched teeth, "I zhust got a lot of water splashed on me and want to clean up."

"Oh. The washrooms are right over there." she pointed, her voice still louder than Kassi would have liked.

"Thanks," Kassi said, positioning herself on her crutches.

"You need any help getting there?" Vander asked, stepping forward as if ready to catch her again.

"Oh no, I've got it manazhed, I can manazhe with...I'm zhust gonna go and be right back and uh..." Unable to find a natural conclusion to her sentence, she spun and hopped away.

At least the washrooms were inside the plaza, so Kassi didn't have to traverse any slidewalks to get to them. On her way, as she weaved through the crowds, Kassi ran into the Chinpoke Squad. Malyra was the first to spot her.

"Awww, did you fall in again?" Malyra feigned a nurturing tone before switching back to her normal spite. "You know, you're really not pretty enough to be this clumsy, Klutziana!" Nikola was abnormally quiet, but he still had murder in his eyes when he glared at Kassi.

DeSchuster laughed and repeated, "Klutziana," as if it never got old.

"I didn't fall in!" Kassi said, speeding up her retreat. As she did, someone gently brushed into her and bolted in the other direction. She whipped her head around to catch who it was. He had already disappeared into the crowd. Kassi instinctively checked her pockets and found something. "A holodrive?" She held up a thumb-sized, emerald-cut device the color of sapphire. "I didn't know they made these here."

Realizing she was still exposed and the Chinpoke Squad wasn't too far away, she put it back in her pocket and returned her attention to her current hair and makeup crisis.

Once in the washroom, she caught sight of her reflection and released the loudest groan. "Yash, kill me now!" The thought of Vander seeing her like this made her want to cry. Pulling the hair and makeup kit she had borrowed from Savriah, she was about to get started when Vi'ella walked in.

Vi'ella stood behind her in a solid one-shoulder crop tee and ripped, skinny jeans. There was a new blonde streak added to her deep-brown hair, which had been pulled back in her usual braided ponytail. "Girl, you look like you could use some help."

"No, I've got it handled." Kassi knew she didn't sound very convincing.

"Listen, there's nothing to be embarrassed about. Sheist like this happens to everyone. So come on, let me look at you!" She dragged a chair to the mirror and motioned for Kassi to take a seat.

Kassi sighed and sat down. "I guess you're right."

"That's why I said it." Vi'ella moved Kassi's head around to survey her hair from all angles. "Hand me that brush. You work on your makeup and I'll see what I can do about all this." She said, her hand circling Kassi's tangled hair. Kassi nodded and handed her the brush, secretly relieved to have help.

Vi'ella brushed out the first of many knots. "Such beautiful, long hair!"

"Thanks!" Kassi said. "I left all my favorite hair products back home-eh, so I haven't been able to do much with it."

"Back home? You mean where you moved from?" Vi'ella asked.

"Something like-eh that," Kassi said vaguely.

"Hmm," Vi'ella said. "So what's your story?"

"My story?" Kassi cleaned the smears around her eyes.

"Yisû, where you from?"

Kassi wasn't sure she wanted to go into it, especially with

strangers cycling through. The washroom had roughly a dozen stalls, a row of sinks and mirrors, and an adjacent shower room. They weren't crowded, but they weren't empty either. Not much for privacy. "You probably wouldn't believe-eh me."

"Try me!" Vi'ella paused her brushing as if waiting for an answer.

If anyone could help her win the Siren Games, it was the Red Squalls. They were the top team in the province, and Vi'ella and Vander were their best players. However, Vi'ella might hate Paradisers. Telling her might turn her against Kassi, making things worse.

On the other hand, The very fact that Vi'ella offered to help Kassi, a 400, proved she didn't fall into the same groupthink as the majority of Gaians. She might be more open-minded. Telling her the truth was a big risk. She took a deep, heavy breath and said quietly enough for only Vi'ella's ears, "I'm from Nemal–Ca'pri to be precise."

Vi'ella eyed Kassi curiously. An uncomfortable silence stretched for a few beats before she smiled. "You're pushing my waves!"

"I'm not," Kassi said. The door swung open, startling Kassi, as a few more people burst into the washroom and disappeared behind stalls. "That's where I'm from."

"Mm-hmm." Vi'ella resumed brushing Kassi's hair. "Let's just say I believe you. Why in Yash and Sheebah's names would you come here?"

"You want the whole story?"

"That's what I asked for," Vi'ella said, raising both eyebrows.

Kassi started from the beginning, avoiding any buzzwords that might attract the attention of those circulating through. She related her story while they worked on her hair and makeup. Every now and then, someone would cast curious, disapproving looks in their direction. At first, Kassi thought it was something she said until she saw them eyeing their armbands. They were a low number and a high number associating with each other.

Vi'ella wasn't shy with any of them. She glared right back, daring them to say or do something. Kassi finished recounting everything.

"Your story's something else!" Vi'ella said. "Either you're making up some elaborate tale to get attention, or you're actually fallen from paradise. I don't know yet."

"I know it sounds ludicray," Kassi said. "Not sure I would believe it either."

"And your little friends out there," she pointed with the hairbrush, "they believe you?"

Kassi nodded. "One of our professors helped with that. Sensei K."

"Sensei, huh?" Vi'ella chuckled. "And what did he say about it?"

"He said my Evéik sounded zhust like the Evéik spoken by other Nemalís."

"How does he know what they sound like?" Vi'ella asked as she braided Kassi's hair.

"He mentors champions at the Siren Games. Says he talks with the officiators all the time." Kassi intentionally left out the part about Sensei once living on the Paradise Planets.

"What's his name?" She asked.

"Professor Kelipalo."

"Oh I know Kelipalo," Vi'ella said, finishing up with Kassi's hair. She was good. The French braid looked better than anything Kassi could do. It reminded her of Amára when she used to style Kassi's hair. Kassi had also finished cleaning her face and reapplying makeup.

"Hmm," Vi'ella washed her hands in the adjacent sink. "If Kelipalo says it's true..." Kassi stood up and put everything back in her bag before hobbling out the door on her crutches. Vi'ella followed her out of the washroom. "If you're really from where you say you're from, then that'd probably make you the fastest siren in the province. I heard stories about Nemalís swimmers."

"Not like this," she said holding up a crutch.

"I'mma have to think about this. Let's head back." Vi'ella said.

They rejoined the group and took their seats on folding chairs that had been set up for the crowds. The seat next to Vander was vacant. As much as Kassi wanted to take it, she hesitated.

"Kassi, welcome back," Vander said. "Bosst earrings! Where'd you get those?"

Kassi felt her cheeks flush. "They were a gift, a birthday present from my best friend—well she's also my cousin—back home-eh, from...where I'm from."

"She must be a good friend," Vander smiled, turning his attention back to the screens as commentators were reviewing the morning's events. After their exchange, before she could talk herself out of it, Kassi set aside her crutches and sat next to Vander, his leg mere centimeters from hers. Even with all she'd been through, it felt like the bravest thing Kassi had ever done in her life.

The kiosks at the center of the plaza were alive and bustling with business. Hovering holoscreens stretched along the coastline giving every seat a great view of the action. The rich taste of roasted peanuts ribboned through the air. The voices of animated commentators reverberated across the plaza.

"Got you a bag of peanuts," Savriah said as she handed Kassi a small paper sack and took a seat on the other side of Kassi.

"Where'd these come-eh from?" Kassi opened the bag as a salty, nutty aroma filled her nose.

"The U.N.O.E. stands. They always have free food kiosks at the Siren Games," she said.

"Huh." Kassi grabbed a handful and tossed them in her mouth. Compared to what she had been eating for the past few weeks, the roasted peanuts were mouth-watering.

"It also came with a juice box." Savriah reached down to grab a small grape-flavored energy water with a tiny plastic straw. Kassi poked the straw through a small hole in the box and took a sip. While it wasn't freshly squeezed melongo juice or cream 'n sodas like she drank every day back home, compared to their "health shakes," it was sweeter than rajabee honey. "Isn't it so good?" Savriah asked as she slurped it down.

"It's bosst!" Even though it wasn't cold, the juice was refreshing on such a hot day. Kassi wiped sweat off her brow as she emptied it after only a few sips.

Squeezing the last few drops out of her juice box, Kassi watched her friends do the same with theirs. This was as good as it got for them. A small bag of dry-roasted peanuts and a kid-sized grape energy water. If only she could take them to Paradise and introduce them to a Nemalís feast. Imagining the look on their faces as they piled their plates with food prepared by the greatest chefs in all the worlds—made Kassi smile.

Her thoughts were abruptly interrupted when Vander jumped to his feet and shouted to no one in particular, "That's some razzle dazzle right there!" Caesar used to jump out of his seat like that. Vander stood posed like a chiseled Nemalís statue as he stared at the screen.

Two girls walking by asked him, "Excuse me, do you have a watch?"

"Sure do," he replied without taking his eyes off the screen. "Tells the time and everything."

The girls giggled. "Well, could you tell us the time?"

He broke from the screen to look at his watch. "Oh alright. It's 15:45."

"Thank you!" They laughed some more and walked off, glancing back a few times to check him out.

"Keep walking," Kassi said under her breath as she glowered at the girls.

The holoscreen feed cut to a commercial break. Once again, Kassi saw advertisements from the U.N.O.E. as they streamed more slow-motion faux happiness mixed with inane slogans, closing with "the U.N.O.E. where your safety is our greatest concern!" Somehow, just hearing it in this context of the dangerous Siren Games made it seem like the opposite was true.

A few other Red Squalls joined them, as well. It was an unusual, but welcome sight. All of them mingled with Fille, Adonis, and Savriah, treating them like equals rather than inferior "Four Hundies."

Adonis planted on the other side of Vander and said, "You know, you know why the sun's yellow, right?"

"I do, but I'm curious to hear what you're gonna say," Vander said with a smirk.

"Don't encourage him," Fille shouted.

"Because it's made of gold!" Adonis said, pointing.

"Oh right, ha ha." Vander's laugh seemed about as real as the U.N.O.E. commercials they just watched. "So what's the punchline?"

"What? I'm telling you, it's gold!" Adonis said, his voice rising in pitch.

Vander studied him as if waiting for Adonis to burst out laughing. When he didn't, Vander said, "You can't honestly believe that."

Savriah interjected, "He's serious. He really thinks it's made of gold. We already tried convincing him otherwise."

Adonis shrugged. "Why else would it be yellow?"

Kassi and others listening in just laughed before returning their attention to the Games.

"... *world-class teams and players come together from all corners of the world for the 156th semi-annual Siren Games!*" Shouted Kassi's longtime favorite commentator, Leron Roust. His gray hair parted down the middle, and he wore a simple, red button-down shirt, nearly hiding his red armband.

"*I expect to see sparks fly from Team Barcelona, this year,*" a female commentator by the name of Lisi Houstine responded. She had mahogany-brown skin and wore a sleeveless, form-fitting dress, exposing very toned shoulders, a purple armband over her bare, right arm. Blonde streaked her deep-brown hair in perfectly even box braids, and she had eyebrows and a jawline made for the camera. Her beauty was stunning and almost intimidating.

"Barcelona always has a few tricks up their sleeve, Lisi, but my money's on Miami. They're out for blood, hoping to earn a place in the Vampire Hall of Fame," Leron said.

Savriah leaned forward and eyed Vander on the other side of Kassi. She chewed on the inside of her cheeks for a moment before stating, "You know, you'd look really great in an off-shoulder dress."

Vander whipped his head in all directions as if to make sure the compliment was directed at him. "That right there's probably the strangest compliment I've ever gotten."

Fille and Adonis stood and yelled, "Next wave's starting!"

Each of the holoscreen displays split into quadrants, displaying four camera angles simultaneously. Four athletes wore full siren wetsuits, helmets, sonopacks, and a sonic cannon mounted on one of their shoulders.

The champions took their positions, standing on diving boards over one of four gargantic, above-ground water tanks. Their names were displayed at the bottom of each quadrant with a clock zeroed out next to their names. Lula Chirico, the athlete Kassi favored to win, was standing on a platform in the top right quadrant of the giant holoscreen. Her brown hair was pulled back in a Dutch braid, framing her flawless skin and a sharpened jawline. Stadiums full of fans and the families of champions surrounded each pool and cheered loudly. Sirens brought in from the Paradise Planets to officiate were in the process of lightly narcotizing the four athletes with a Humav Hîm, a siren narcotic song, to temporarily disorient them.

"Oo, I love-eh Lula Chirico's wettie! Bosst design," Kassi said. It was one of the best Gaian designs she had seen, despite the mandatory, purple 700s collar. It was still no Marcano—Kassi's favorite Nemalís wetsuit designer–but no one could really compete with him, Gaian or Paradiser. The purple collar stood out to her. All her life, she had seen these colored collars on sirens, and never knew what they were for. Lula was a 700. The other athletes in this wave were all 800s. She got a closer look at all the Nemalís sirens on screen. "Wait, that's my old *Astrophysics* professor, Professor Rockwall!" Kassi shouted without thinking.

"*Astrophysics*? The U.N.O.E. banned that study over a decade ago." Vander said, eyeing Kassi suspiciously. "What kind of school did you go to?"

"Oh...uh, I didn't mean *Astrophysics*, it was..." In a panic, her mind went blank. She couldn't think of a single course study.

"It's too bad we can't learn *Astrophysics*. That would be a fascinating subject! Much better than the useless *Civility and Etiquette* classes they made us take at Appel Senior High." Vander said.

"They make us take the same at Miami Beach High," Savriah said.

"Careful what you say, Vander," one of his Red Squall team-mates warned, flicking his chin at a nearby discolored camera panel. Vander gave a subtle nod of acknowledgment and turned his attention back to the Games.

On-screen, each of the four Siren athletes were now heavily in a daze and on the brink of sleep just as the platforms gave way and dropped them into the water below. Their initial reaction was always comical. Cameras zoomed in on their faces as athletes responded with a spectrum of shock, panic, and confusion. They each tried to quickly take in their surroundings.

In the second quadrant, Kassi watched as the LifeBot, a convincingly lifelike, robotic version of Lula Chirico's younger sister, plummeted deep into the water with chains tied to her ankles. Because of the Humav Hîm performed by the Nemalís officiators, Lula was convinced the LifeBot was her sister. The anthropomorphic bot of the sister wasn't equipped with a breathing apparatus, so Lula believed she would drown within seconds. Singing a powerful Mendari Hîm, a siren domination song, Lula powered up her sonopack and lit the first two bulbs before speeding downward to catch her sister. Just before she could reach her, a second LifeBot in the shape of a gargantic sea dragon intercepted, blocking her rescue attempt. The monster was the size of a small mountain. It charged Lula, wrapping its tail around one of her arms and flinging her through the water. She quickly repositioned herself to face the beast.

On the other screens, similar situations played out with different creatures preventing siren athletes from rescuing their loved ones. Lula Chirico's clash with the dragon was more exhilarating.

Lula danced in the water gracefully as she pivoted and twisted to dodge the onslaught of teeth and claws. She caught the creature off balance just as she increased the intensity of her Mendari Hîm and lit the third and fourth bulbs on her sonopack. Firing off a flurry of blasts from her shoulder-mounted sonic cannon, she produced enough force to break the skin causing the dragon to recoil long enough for Lula to dart downward and collect her sister. Scooping her up, she tried propelling toward the surface, but the weight of the chains on her sister's ankles held her down. The sea dragon returned for vengeance.

The third and fourth bulbs had dimmed and the energy from Lula's sonopack was mostly depleted. Bellowing a powerful chorus, she relit the third and fourth bulbs as she simultaneously eluded attacks from the monster. With a quick slicing motion of the hand, Lula shattered the chains with an energy blade from her palm thruster before expending the last of her energy to torpedo to the surface. With a burst out of the water, Lula crashed onto the diving platform and cradled the lifeless bot.

Removing her helmet, she studied the bot in her hands, the effects of the Humav Hîm wearing off. Her head lifted, her eyes sweeping over the crowds in the stands, the cameras pointed at her, and her face on the giant holoscreen behind her. Standing up, she dropped the bot and held a victorious fist in the air as the crowds roared. Lula Chirico had just completed the second round of the Siren Games.

Rankings flashed on the holoscreen with the twenty-eight athletes that had already competed that morning. The top time so far was 02:13. The worlds record in The Abyss was currently 01:54, held by Fierro Divinci.

Crowds held their breath, anxiously waiting to see Lula's time posted. After a long pause, the giant numbers 01:52 flickered to life, floating and rotating on the screen. The stands erupted in applause.

"Fantaseismic!" Leron's voice cracked with excitement as the commentator's voice roared over the noise. *"Sinking a flaming dagger into the heart of the competition!"* His passion was contagious.

"She sets an incredibly high bar for the rest of the competition," Lisi said.

"Lula just broke-eh the worlds record!" Kassi exclaimed.

"That's your girl, Kassi," Fille clapped.

With forty-eight teams remaining after round one's eliminations, and nineteen to a team, there were a lot of athletes competing. Over three days, they would broadcast 228 waves of the second round, four athletes competing at a time. The aggregate scores of players from each team determined where teams ranked, including which four won medals, and which twelve got eliminated.

One by one, the other athletes surfaced to complete their rounds, ranking them well below Lula on the scoreboards. Another wave of athletes took their positions on the springboards and waited for Nemalís officiators to perform incantations on them. Kassi reflected back on some of her favorite moments from The Abyss in previous Games. Each season, they tried to change things up a little, but it always revolved around the rescue of someone the champions cared about. Although one year, one of the athletes apparently didn't care for anybody, so they just dropped a treasure chest full of U-

Coins for him to hoist up to the surface. He didn't get very far in the Games.

The most terrifying challenge was the underwater labyrinth. It reminded her of the one her sister Nasri designed in their family's Royal Gardens back on Nemal. In one of the labyrinth years, Fierro Divinci lit the fourth bulb during Round Two and set a Worlds Record–the record Lula Chirico just broke. Kassi still couldn't figure out how he managed to find his way through the maze so quickly. Amára theorized that he sent out low-frequency pulses through the maze and followed the quietest. "Echoes would bounce off the dead ends," Amára explained, "so those paths would be the noisiest." In the past, they had seen a few Sirens attempt this and have some success at the very end of the maze. But Fierro was the only one in history to pull it off from the very start. Somehow, he figured out how to detect the slightest of all differences in sound wave intensity.

Kassi and her friends watched heat after heat with hundreds of champions trying to surpass Lula's time, as the sun lowered in the sky. So far, the closest was an athlete by the name of Harlin Scarlotti, who scored a 2:01. Lula maintained a solid hold on first place. Day 2 would bring hundreds more knocking on that door.

With the final heat for the day concluded, the holoscreens showed broadcasters standing in front of the giant waterfields as they interviewed a few of the previous winners who currently resided on the Paradise Planets, but came to Earth to officiate the Siren Games.

"Sela Romane, your team won the Games back in '26. Tell us about life on Paradise." The journalist said.

Vi'ella shouted at the screen. "Girl, looks like you got a bun in the oven,"

"I didn't say it," Vander was quick to say, holding out both hands.

"Only one bun?" Kassi asked Vi'ella. It struck Kassi as odd that someone would only bake a single bun.

"You know, a bun in the oven," Vi'ella arched her hands

around her own stomach to indicate a pregnant belly. "You never heard that expression?"

"Oh, pregnant? No, I've never heard that before-eh." Referring to pregnancy as baking a bun in the oven made Kassi giggle.

"Guess they don't have that saying on Nemal, huh?" Vi'ella probed, almost as if she were trying to catch Kassi off guard and see if she was really telling the truth. Kassi whipped her head in all directions to see if anyone overheard. Fortunately, no one noticed or seemed to care except for Vander.

"Nemal? What you chas talking about?" Vander shot Vi'ella a questioning glance.

"I'm just teasing her," Vi'ella said, brushing it off.

Kassi gave her a subtle shake of the head, her eyes trying to say, *Please don't tell Vander!*

The crowd slowly dispersed. Kassi and her friends made their way back to the docks, and Fille drove them home. They rode in silence, everyone tired from a long day under the hot sun. One by one, they said their goodbyes, shouting, "ride the tide," as they parted.

Kassi opened the door to find dinner left out on the kitchen table. She carted it upstairs to her room. As she changed her clothes, she realized she hadn't returned Savriah's shirt.

As she changed out of her shorts, she stumbled across the holodrive in her pocket from earlier that day. With all the day's excitement, she'd completely forgotten about it. Putting on her hologlasses, she held the smooth, sapphire drive up for her glasses to scan. They immediately detected and imported a file titled, "For Little Spice."

Sixteen

Clicking open the file, a video opened, and she was suddenly joined by a life-size projection of her family in the cramped bedroom—Vidara and Leontari, Nasri, Kairos, and Caesar. Kassi's heart leaped! She had missed all of them so much.

"*Hi, Little Spice,*" Leontari, Kassi's dad, said in Evéik as he brushed long curls out of his face and tucked them behind his ear. Kassi had never seen her father like this–unkempt beard, grimy hair, dark bags under his eyes. "*This past month has been just agonizing, for all of us. Even though Ravana promised you'd be safe, day and night, we're working on a way to get you back. I can't believe she still went ahead with her plan. We told her it would be too dangerous,*" Leo tensed, balling his fists, "*the U.N.O.E. closed the portal until recently with the Siren Games. Getting anyone through even for the Games was extremely difficult. But we are working on a plan. We will get you back, Little Spice,*" Leo said, his eyes watering. He took a deep breath and continued, "*I'm sorry you're the one who has to go through this. If I could take your place, I would in a second.*"

"*We all would,*" Caesar said quietly.

"We miss you, Kassiana," Leo's voice wavered. *"Nothing's the same without you."*

"Kassiana." Vidara, Kassi's mother, was already a little choked up. Her hair fell to both sides of her face in swoopy layers, still immaculate considering the circumstances. *"I'm deeply regretful! I should have known Ravana would try this. I had a feeling she might, but I dismissed it. I got distracted. I'm so sorry,"* she said, burying her head into Leo's shoulder.

Her oldest brother, Kairos, spoke next. He had chopped off his long, wavy hair since Kassi had last seen him. *"You can get through this, Kassi. We love you. We believe in you. If anyone can survive this, it's you!"*

"We miss you, Kassiana." Nasri held both hands close to her chest. She was nearly ten years older than Kassi, and she also had long, wavy hair. All their lives, people remarked on their striking resemblance. Today, Nasri looked tired, her hair in a quick high bun. *"We've got everybody on this. We're coming to get you. None of us will rest until you're home safe."*

Caesar was the last to speak. Other than his puffy eyes, he looked exactly the same. His eyes traced the floor for a beat before starting, *"Ah, Kass, I let you down. I was the one in charge of keeping an eye on you, and I...I wasn't there for you when you needed me the most. I'm sorry, Kass!"* She had never seen Caesar cry before, but when he sniffed and a tear rolled down his cheeks, Kassi felt the warmth of her own tears. A few errant tears turned into sobs as she hugged her knees so tight, she almost couldn't breathe. Caesar took a breath and continued, his voice trembling, *"I know you think you're the weakest siren among us. I teased you about it all the time, but I only let myself do it because I figured you'd eventually realize how strong you are. I never said it, but I always thought one day you would be the best of us."* He forced a brave smile, blinking away the tears.

"He's exactly right." Kairos nodded.

"We love you, Little Spice," Leo said with sadness behind his blue eyes. *"It won't be much longer!"* They all started singing the

song Leo began writing for Kassi when she was born, adding verses through the years. As was tradition in Nemal, he and their extended family, friends, and neighbors sang for Kassi on her first day of school, her elementary graduation, her recent coming-of-age celebration, and other major events. It was Kassi's song.

ASHKANA TUV (REMEMBER WHEN)

Remember when you'd dance to my vinyl records from my past
You would spin with both arms wide open, bouncing as you
*   laughed*
If I sat down, you'd grab my hand and make me dance with you
That was you, and ashkana tuv

Remember when you'd run through the palace playing hide
*   and seek*
You would hide behind the same old curtains thinking you'd
*   fool me*
You would squeal
When you were revealed
Giggling like you do
That was you, and ashkana tuv

All the days I spent far away were hard to be without you
The memories I didn't get to see - missing out on things
*   you'd do*
When I'd come back
You'd run to dad
And be the girl I knew
'Cause you loved me, too - you

Remember when you grew up so fast right before my eyes
If only we could go back in time to moments of our lives
I wouldn't change

A single thing
Even the hard times, too
That was all still you, and ashkana tuv

IN EVÉIK

Rikordûtu máti olis pareludu shi nayalí biníl luþitóbé dari
    nayalí sahul tuvat
Olis kwídu kin amos rukûtó brít kík tuvat, kertsésách áz
    ritudu tuvat
Lô bekala fichi nayat, olis viposudu nayalí shoho tuvat, i
    hulitu parelutu kin tuvé mwat.
Budu tuvé sîmat, i ashkana tu

Rikordûna máti olis koorudu méso li sarébé neltudu
    bisabé i kimé tuvat
Olis bisadu gésh li mara taman atanóbé tuvat, pensách
    olis jilizu mwabé tuvat
Olis sikadu tuvat
Máti budu keshefudu tuvat
Basamách áz daidu tuvat
Budu tuvé sîmat, i ashkana tuv

Dur poþ kehevala amni li tagóbé/ôeróbé nayat, budala
    sabun shi kehevala kimun tuvat
Daila néz prapala shi tazala li dakiratóbé nayat – téa néz
    fizanala kwam shi nayat
Da olis vaksala nayat
I tum olis péudala nayat
Van amni li miharitóbé olis daizu tuvat
Budu méshû tuvé sîmat, tuvat

Rikordûna máti wasînudu nak hûn kásh vikolak dávor
    nayalí potóbé tuvat

Lô hanya téa píbi lersûbi lev agité shi shukanó van bizí
   vitó bizat
Olis néz sorjana nayat
În tani shéané
Pun li sabu agitó, gam
Budu amni orla tuvé sîmat, i ashkana tuv

As the song concluded, they all said, "Ashkana tuv!" and the video ended. Kassi stared into space, wiping the last remaining tears from her eyes. Curled up on her mattress, she replayed the video, paying closer attention to Leo's mention of Ravana's plan.

What did he mean that he was sorry she was "the one to go through this"? And that Ravana still went ahead with her plan? Did they know about this? Kassi was confused and a little frustrated. Her parents still treated her like a little kid, never telling her anything. Kassi wished she could use the Rosen-comm and ask them the million questions that swarmed her mind. Instead, she watched a few more times until she fell asleep.

Conflicting emotions from the previous night carried over into the next morning. There were so many questions she needed to ask her family. *Why are the Games set up this way? Why do Gaians have to win a passport to Paradise?* While her head spun with concerns, she heard heavy tactical boots marching up the stairs–Kyoto.

He stood silent, silhouetted in the doorway. Even the way he planted himself was intimidating. Kassi threw her ratty blanket off and grabbed her things. Kyoto retreated down the stairs without a word.

At school for their Saturday cleaning, Adonis slapped Fille in the chest. "You ever wonder, you ever wonder why Saturday has the word "turd" in the middle of it?"

"It's-a-turd-ay?" Fille said, over-emphasizing each syllable.

"Maybe, maybe the pata who named it also had weekend cleaning duty," Adonis said.

Savriah examined Kassi's face. "You look way more tired than usual."

"Uh-huh." Kassi wasn't in the mood for her blunt observations.

Fille seemed to notice Kassi's mood. "Making 400s get up early on Saturday mornings is a yashing joke! As if we don't have enough of their sheist to deal with!"

"I hate-eh Saturday mornings," Kassi grumbled in agreement.

They lollybagged the rest of the morning away, waiting for the final bell which rolled in at a banana slug's pace. At 12:00 on the dot, they bolted for the motorboat, anxious to join the others at the plaza and continue watching the Siren Games. Fille sped as quickly as he could. When they docked, they noticed long lines leading to some food kiosks.

"It's free taco day!" In his excitement, Fille almost forgot to tie the boat down.

"Tacos! Tacos!" Adonis chanted.

"Tacos, huh?" That was a big step up from roasted peanuts. Her stomach rumbled. The last taco she had, August—one of Ca'pri's finest chefs—made crispy, homemade tortillas, plucked fresh tomatoes and peppers from their gardens for the salsa and cooked savory, beef basil with a zip of spice. It had been royalty!

As they waited in line, the holoscreens looped a U.N.O.E. video between every possible break in the Siren Games. Actors held hands as they sang a sentimental song about the U.N.O.E. standing by its citizens. The advertisement irritated Kassi more and more with each viewing. It concluded with, "Courtesy of the bountiful generosity of our great United Nations of Earth, welcome to the Siren Games. Have a taco on us. Enjoy the rest of your day and remember, your safety is our greatest concern!" As unnerving as they were, Kassi wasn't about to let it ruin her appetite for tacos. She missed real food, and she was always hungry.

They waited for nearly an hour, watching the holoscreens

from their spot in line as the hot sun beat down. More than half of the siren athletes had finished round two, and Lula still remained on top. A few Barcelona teammates ranked highly, as well, helping the overall team score.

Reaching the taco stand, a boy and girl only slightly older than Kassi handed her a package with two small tacos and a boxed energy water–this time passion fruit flavor. With a soggy tortilla and faux beef–beethe–it was a far cry from August's work of art, but Kassi didn't care. Before taking another step on her crutches, she crammed the first taco into her mouth. It tasted as average and disappointing as it looked, but after a month of food rations, it was a delectable delicacy.

"You're holding up the line!" someone shouted, interrupting her short-lived moment of bliss. She closed the box with the second taco in it and hopped over to rejoin her friends. They were already a few paces ahead and hadn't noticed her stop.

Before she could reach them, someone violently rammed into her, sending her sprawling and her food spilling onto the platforms. Nikola, Malyra, DeSchuster, and another 800 named Calandra appeared. Nikola stepped over her and stomped on her fruit punch, spraying some innocent bystanders.

"What the sheist?" they yelled at him.

"Whatcha gonna do?" He opened his arms, inviting the confrontation. They sized him up and backed down.

Malyra snatched the taco box. "Here let me help you with this!" She stuffed the taco into her mouth, chewed it up, and spat it out into the box. "Much improved," she tossed it to Kassi who was still struggling to get back to her feet. Calandra laughed a maniacal, obnoxious laugh.

Fille was first to notice Kassi missing. He spotted her amidst the Chinpoke Squad, sprawled on the floor. Nikola caught his gaze and taunted him. "Hey Gumballs, still yashing ugly huh?"

Breaking into a full sprint, Fille tackled Nikola to the ground, Savriah and Adonis close behind. Adonis took wild swings at DeSchuster who seemed amused at the attempt. Savriah elbow-shoved Calandra away, grabbed Malyra, and put her in a head-lock, shoving her face into the splintered wooden platform.

Malyra managed to look up just enough to glare at DeSchuster. "Well? What are you here for?"

DeSchuster threw a right hook that knocked Adonis to the ground before running to assist Malyra. He easily pulled Savriah off and tossed her to the ground. Nikola had Fille pinned, his fist raised as the armed mediation officers arrived. They paused to eye everyone's armbands before giving Nikola a subtle nod. He landed the punch, hitting Fille in the nose. Blood spurted out, and Fille grunted in pain.

"Alright, that's enough! What's the meaning of this?" one of the officers asked.

"These Four Hundies picked a fight with us, unprovoked," Nikola said with a cold sniff.

"Unprovoked?" Fille spat blood. "These cacafuegos jumped our friend on crutches!"

The mediation officers helped Nikola up to his feet, leaving Fille to fend for himself. "Four Hundies pickin' a fight with elites? You little sheists need to learn your place!" The officer in charge flexed. His nameplate read *Officer Locard*. He had a mullet and a sizable amount of black neck hair exploding out of his collar—no armband. In fact, none of the mediation officers wore armbands! "You're comin' with us!"

"What about them?" Fille pointed at the Chinpoke Squad.

They ignored Fille and let the Chinpoke Squad go without so much as a warning. One of them even gave Nikola a pat on the shoulder. Malyra dusted herself off, huffing in frustration. Savriah had apparently rattled her. Nikola stared at them like he was just itching to finish the fight. DeSchuster kissed his biceps and flashed his usual idiotic grin.

Kassi's blood boiled. Her fingers squeezed her crutches tightly, wanting nothing more than to crash one into Nikola's head. Instead, she limped alongside Savriah, Adonis, and Fille as they were ushered to a nearby squat building. It was an old hotel that had been repurposed as an administrative office for local authorities. Plain on the inside as it was on the outside, it featured monochromatic walls and floors with hard metal chairs lining the empty wall. Behind a tall counter, they could barely see over a dark-haired woman shuffling files on her hologlasses. The four of them took a seat. Adonis nursed a swollen lip. Savriah fidgeted with a new tear in her pants. Fille pinched the bridge of his nose and was still riled up. Kassi had never seen Fille so angry.

"Those chinpokes started it. Why don't you punish the real criminals?" Fille shouted to no one in particular. Everyone behind the counter pretended to be preoccupied.

After a few minutes, Officer Locard returned. "We've notified your school of the disturbance. They'll determine a fair punishment. You'll be escorted off the premises and banned for the remainder of the day," he explained.

"And what about the ones actually responsible? You gonna ban them?" Fille yelled, pointing in the general direction of the crowds outside.

The officer clenched his jaw before he continued, "You chas should be grateful you're only banned for the day. If it were up to me, you'd be banned for life for that kind of shameful behavior." He puffed out his chest and smoked a fumer as he stared down at them. He opened his mouth as if to say more, but a head shake from another mediation officer, probably a superior, convinced him otherwise. Instead, Locard blew fumer steam and grumbled, "You're free to go."

The four of them stood to leave. Fille glared at Officer Locard who inched forward and smirked as if begging Fille to do something stupid. Adonis hooked an arm around Fille, guiding him to the exit. "Cha, cha let's flake off before they ban us for life." Fille resisted briefly before leaving with the rest of them.

$$\mathcal{S}\text{eventeen}$$

They stomped out of the building in muted fury. Savriah helped Kassi onto the boat, and Fille stood at the wheel and revved the engine. Vander and a few Red Squalls spotted them from their seats and strolled over.

"Leaving already?" Vander asked.

"The cacafuegos banned us, they banned us for the day," Adonis said, kneeling on his seat and pointing an accusatory finger at the mediation officers.

"Banned? Didn't take you for common criminals. What'd you do?" Vander asked, shoving his hands in his pockets before quickly retracting them, eyes darting up at a nearby camera panel. Even Vander, a favored 800, was careful to follow U.N.O.E. policy.

"After I got my tacos, the Chinpoke Squad knocked me over and stole my food!" Kassi shouted from her rear seat on the boat, surprised she didn't stammer this time in front of Vander.

"Chinpoke Squad?" Vander asked.

"800s from our school," Savriah said.

"Bullies," Adonis added.

"They rammed right into me. Nikola stomped on my enerzhy water and Malyra chewed up and spat out my tacos," Kassi said.

"These-eh chas were zhust helping me out. Now, we're banned for the day and our school's supposed to punish us next week." Kassi kicked at the back of the driver's seat with her good leg.

Vi'ella heard the commotion and came over to join them. "What'd ya'll do? Steal some tacos? I keep saying they don't give us enough."

Vander ignored Vi'ella's interruption and asked, "And how'd they punish the 800s?"

"Not even a warning," Savriah answered.

"One of them even applauded them for it," Kassi said, growling.

"See, that's the kind of miscarriage of justice I keep saying is the cause of division in our society," Vander scowled, shaking his head. "The way these choads treat 400s is just a blatant disregard for human decency." He turned to Vi'ella and filled her in.

"Feverin' Sheebah!" Vi'ella shook her head.

"We're gonna miss the rest of the day." Kassi slumped.

As they idled there on the docks, two officers marched toward them, likely to make sure they vacated the premises.

"You're awfully quiet, Fille. What do you say about all of this?" Vi'ella asked.

"I don't wanna talk about it." Fille stood in the boat and glowered at the oncoming officers, his upper lip and nose still spattered with dried blood.

"You chas should probably flake off," Vander said as the officers had almost reached them. "Before you do, tell us who these choads are."

"Malyra, Nikola, Calandra and DeSchuster," Savriah said.

"Nikola's the one who broke-eh my leg," Kassi said. "He's got some-eh vendetta against me."

"And what'd you do to him?" Vi'ella asked, hands on her hips.

"We've been trying to figure that out," Kassi shrugged. "I never even met him before I started school here a month ago!"

Fille unhooked the boat and pushed off. Vander and Vi'ella

walked down the street, Vi'ella's arms folded as she spoke inaudibly to Vander.

"Can't we just wait til they're gone and sneak back in the crowds?" Kassi asked.

"Cameras will spot us," Savriah said, pointing to the small black panels on the building corners. "We've been marked. They'll detect us if we get anywhere close to the plaza."

"Or any other public watch parties," Fille added.

Fille stared ahead and drove aggressively, but this time it wasn't for the thrill of the ride. Cutting a corner, he splashed a couple of pedestrians on the slidewalks. They shouted curses and shook their fists. Fille ignored them and sped off without a word.

He dropped off the others and steered toward Kassi's townhome. He hadn't said a word the whole trip. Kassi wondered if he blamed her. As he docked and hopped out to give Kassi a hand, she said, "Thanks for helping me today. I got you chas in trouble."

"You didn't do anything. We got punished because the U.N.O.E.'s full of insecure pieces of ripe sheist who need someone to beat down so they don't feel so small!"

"I thought you weren't...," Kassi glanced at the nearest camera.

"I'm too tired to give a sheist," Fille grumbled.

"Oh." Kassi worried the U.N.O.E. might hurt Fille like they had Sensei. Opening the front door to the house, she gave a somber wave, "Ride the tide." Fille gave a single nod and sped off.

Meela looked up from her holopad at the kitchen table when she heard the door swing open. "Ain't ya goin' t'Siren Games today?"

"We got banned," Kassi grumbled.

"What for?"

"For being 400s!" Kassi shouted as she stomped up the stairs. "Some 800s attacked us and we got banned for it!"

"Tha's normal 'round here. Ya see, Ravana's right!" Meela called up the stairs. Kassi groaned and stomped down the hall to her room, slamming the door.

Sunday morning, Fille swung by to pick her up, a fresh shiner over his right eye. He limped onto the porch and clutched his right side, just like Sensei.

"What happened?" Kassi asked, concerned.

"I got whipped—same as always," Fille said, turning to hide his face.

After picking the others up on their way to school, Kassi asked, "So what happens if we don't go?"

"For school, for school cleanup?" Adonis asked. Kassi nodded.

"Detention," Fille said over the roar of the engine.

"Aren't we already punished for yesterday?" Kassi asked.

Fille locked eyes with Kassi, a pensive look on his face. After a beat, he pulled the dinghy to the side of the street. "She's right."

"Right about, right about what?" Adonis said.

"What difference does it make if we go or not?" Fille said with a half-shrug. "We're already punished."

"They could make the punishment worse," Savriah said.

"What's worse, what's worse than this?" Adonis said. "Let's go catch the last day of the Games!"

Fille nodded and turned the dinghy around, cruising to the South Pointe Pier. When they pulled up, Officer Locard spotted them, spinning on his heels and marching directly toward them.

"What now?" Fille said.

Once Officer Locard was within range, he growled, "You chas really wanna test me? Pick up your sheist and beat fins or I'll getcha banned for life!"

"But we were only banned yesterday! Why can't we watch today?" Savriah asked.

"You've got school cleaning! Don't think I don't know you're skippin'," he said, veins popping out of his forehead.

Fille groaned, revved the engine, and pushed off the docks. "Maybe Sensei left his holopad so we can still catch some of the Games."

At school, they were a full hour late for cleaning. Mr. Benetti scowled and said, "You better have a good excuse for making me wait." After a few empty threats, he only made them stay an extra hour. He probably didn't care enough to do more.

In Sensei's classroom, they searched for his holopad–no luck. Kassi deflated. No one had the energy to lollybag. Instead, they found a clean floor space, stretched out, and tried to nap on the hard rubber floor.

Monday morning, Fille rounded up the gang, and they drove to school to face the music. Principal Purves waited for them on a balcony in a dark pants suit, her hair pulled back even tighter than usual as if her face wrinkles were growing heavier. She glowered at them as they ascended two flights of stairs to reach her, Fille leading the way with a stubborn slowness.

Before the principal could open her mouth, Fille shouted, "What'll it be, Ol' Purvy?"

"What'd you call me? You little sheist!" Yanking Fille by the arm, she dragged him to her office, Savriah, Adonis, and Kassi following close behind.

"I thought you weren't supposed to say that," Fille sassed.

Once in her office, she sank into her chair and studied the four of them from across her desk. "If it were up to me, you'd all be expelled. Unfortunately, I'm not lucky enough to be rid of you. But I still can make your lives miserable."

"You mean more miserable than it already is?" Fille apparently wasn't done.

"You're really asking for it," she said, stabbing a long, poorly-manicured fingernail in the air.

"Fille, maybe we should..." Savriah started to say.

"What? We already clean on Saturdays and Sundays." Fille threw his arms up. "We don't get enough to eat, and we have teachers giving us the broomstick at every turn. We sit in the back with the wonky, broken desks. Should I go on?"

"Oh, it could still be worse!" Purves said. "I could tell your professors to give you the broomstick for every class period!"

"Solick idea! Then nobody will ever learn anything in your school. Your school will be the dumbest in the whole province! I'm sure Supervisor Kenett would love that." Principle Purves shifted in her seat, anxiously tugging on her blazer. Fille was getting under her skin.

Principal Purves considered the four of them for a moment before patting the top of her desk, a smile creasing her mouth. "I have something better. Irene?" After a beat, Irene popped her head in. "Send these four to the first floor for the remainder of the day." She smiled, looking pleased with herself.

"But the first floor is flooded," Irene said. "Those rooms are completely empty."

"Don't you think I know that!" Purves shouted. She patted her hair as if checking to make sure no strays escaped from her rigid bun.

"That's the best you got?" Fille didn't back down.

"Just wait. You'll beg for mercy by the end of the week!"

Outside, a security guard by the name of Officer Jerold waited to escort them. He stood at least a head taller than all of them, his wiry frame a reminder that no one on Earth ate enough. He led them down the stairs, Kassi falling behind as she hobbled with her crutches.

They reached the bottom as Kassi carefully slipped into the cold ocean water. It rose halfway up her shin. Bending at the knee to keep the cast dry, her toe kissed the water as she sloshed through the doorway and into the flooded corridor.

It was dark, drafty. Dim light forced its way through clouded windows that hadn't been wiped in years. The smell of mildew and rotted fish permeated the air. Kassi took caution with each step, making sure her crutches gripped the floor below. The others waded ahead.

"What Yash-forsaken filth!" Irene's complaint echoed off the walls.

"C'mon you!" Officer Jerold shouted at Kassi when he noticed her lagging behind. "Get up here!"

"I'm trying to keep my cast from getting wet!" Kassi stumbled and almost crashed.

"Don't make me drag you!" He blinded her with his high-beam flashlight.

She picked up the pace, nearly submerging her cast more than once. Jerold shoved each of them into their separate rooms.

Just before locking them in, Irene gave them final instructions. "You're still expected to virtually attend class while you're down here. Your professors will send a feed directly to your hologlasses."

Kassi surveyed her room. It was barren of all furniture and the windows were sealed shut. "What about a chair for my leg? Or a washroom?" Kassi asked.

"You get neither," Irene said.

Kassi held her leg up and tried balancing in the water. Her armpits were sore, her leg was already feeling heavy, and they hadn't even started the day yet. She would have to stand in this for the next six hours, all because Nikola had attacked her and Fille had come to her defense.

Nothing makes a speck of sense on this yashing planet!

With her hologlasses on, she saw the feed from *Heroics* class. It was impossible to focus. After holding her position for thirty minutes, her leg gave out and her cast splunked into the water. The cold ocean seeped in and soaked her cast.

Mirific!

Three more hours had passed and Kassi was more miserable than ever and feeling dizzy. Leaning against walls, shifting positions every couple of minutes, both feet were numb from the cold. Her body shivered violently. She had already tried pounding on the windows with the rubber end of her crutches.

Sifting through the water in search of something harder, she came up empty.

The sound of a key inserting into the lock cut through the silence. The door pushed open against the water, sending a ripple across the room. Kassi saw a broad, hulking figure fill the door frame. He scanned the room with a flashlight.

"There you are!" he said. Kassi would recognize his friendly voice anywhere. Sensei Kelipalo had found them! "Let's get you outta here before you catch pneumonia!"

She sloshed across the floor and hugged Sensei, one of her crutches falling into the water in the process. "How'd you find us?"

"You chas never showed up for lunch, so I poked around to find out what happened," he said as he bent down to retrieve the crutch. Fille, Adonis, and Savriah already stood in the hallway, their teeth chattering.

Together, they followed Sensei outside, squinting as they entered the bright sunlight. As soon as Kassi's eyes adjusted, she glanced over at her friends. Their lips had all turned purple.

"Sorry you chas had to be down here this long. If I had known." He shook his head. "I'll have a talk with Principal Purves. Convince her to swap your sentence to something that isn't life-threatening."

They found a place on one of the balconies to stand in the sunlight and thaw their stiff limbs. If they were on Nemal right now, they could jump in a warm bath and drink hot cacao to warm up. They didn't have those here. Taking a seat on the warm cement, Kassi removed her dripping wet sock and shoe and examined the damage to her cast. The bottom half was completely water-logged, ruined.

The blood started to return to her feet. At least Miami Beach had a warm, tropical climate. Even in March, temperatures ran high. The others bounced on their feet to increase the blood flow. Kassi decided to join them. Standing up, she stretched what she could with her clunky, sopping cast.

"Think we'll have to go back down there?" Kassi asked.

"I don't, I don't think I could survive another hour like that," Adonis said, jumping from side to side.

"Sensei will get us out of it," Fille said with a brush of his hand.

"Maybe you shouldn't mouth off so much," Savriah said. "Principal probably would've given us an easier sentence."

"We don't deserve any sentence!" Fille shouted.

"I'm just saying. Let Sensei do all the talking."

"Savvy's right, Savvy's right on this one," Adonis said, pointing.

A few moments later, Sensei emerged from the front office. "Well, I had to pull a few strings from the higher-ups. Good thing for you chas I'm still helping train champions and Supervisor Kenett still listens to me." He eyed Fille before continuing, "She really has it in for you chas today. I've never seen her so stubborn. I convinced her to give you detention for the rest of the month. That's the best I could do."

"Anything, anything beats going back down there," Adonis said.

"What do we have to do for detention?" Kassi asked.

"Cleaning," Savriah said. "After school, we have to stick around and clean for a couple of hours. Scrub toilets and wash floors."

"So more lollybagging," Kassi said.

"No, detention isn't with Mr. Benetti. It's with Officer Jerold. And sometimes Principal Purves sticks around to inspect everything after we're done," Savriah explained.

"Oh," Kassi said sniffing, her nose runny.

"So that means Blue Krakens will miss AquaSphera for a whole month?" Fille asked. "The rest of our team won't have enough players without us, so they'll have to forfeit our matches. And for what? We shouldn't even be punished in the first place!"

Sensei placed a hand on his shoulder. "Now before you do

something stupid, maybe you should take a moment. If you go poking the bear again, it's back to the first floor."

"Why do we always have to take everybody's yashing sheist? It's not fair!" Fille shouted, kicking the air.

"I know. That's just how things are," Sensei said. "You just have to ride the waves that come."

"Until when?" Fille threw his arms out. Sensei didn't answer, a pang of sadness in his eyes. He obviously wished he could do more. Kassi wished she could, too. These were her friends. They were only in this predicament because they rushed to help her. She needed to get them off this barbarous planet.

"Well, there's still a few more minutes left of lunch. You might as well come upstairs and eat." Sensei waved them back inside.

They ate what they could before rushing off to Period 5. Just before she left, she asked Sensei about her cast.

"Go to the Healer's office and tell them you need it recast."

While the others dashed to class, Kassi followed Sensei's advice and visited the Healer's office. However, the boy at the front desk reported her for skipping class and had her escorted out.

Despite her crutches excusing her tardiness, when she arrived late to Professor Raisen's class, he paused his quiet lecture, stepped forward, and pinched her arm hard.

"Ghost of Sheebah! Can you not do that?" Kassi shouted.

"How dare you blaspheme, you filthy 400! BROOMSTICK!" He shouted.

For the first time, Kassi heard him clearly. She never took Professor Raisen for a devout Universalist. Most Gaians cursed using the names of Yash and Sheebah. It was the one show of U.N.O.E. disrespect that everyone got away with, simply because nearly all Gaians did it. Yash and Sheebah were the male and female deities of the only religion allowed on Earth–Universalism. The U.N.O.E. leaders were its highest-ranking members, and they tried to mandate Gaians to observe their practices.

They built shrines of either Yash–the male deity–or Sheebah–the female–in all of the major cities and province capitals, requiring all Gaians to attend. However, only the elite class and those with political aspirations–like apparently Professor Raisen–ever showed up.

The kids lined up and spent the rest of class shouting a barrage of insults. All except her friends, who just made up nonsense when it was their turn to participate. Even Fille participated, making his best attempt to lighten the situation for Kassi. They shouted things like, "cast-lovin' biscuit", "silent howler monkey," and "collapsible side table." Kassi bit into her tongue to keep from laughing. Fortunately, no one used a sonic pulse baton on her this time–probably because of the broken leg.

After class, Fille playfully cuffed Adonis on the shoulder. "Collapsible side table. Ha! That was a good one, Donis." His mood seemed to be lightening.

"I got, I got more." Adonis smiled.

In Evéik, Sensei walked to the front of class and jumped right into his lecture. "We left off last week with present tense conjugations of the verb, *fizan*, which means "to discover" and talked about how to put it into a question. Now, who can translate this into Evéik?" Sentences popped up on everyone's hologlasses, except for Kassi's. She was about to dive into her next book when she glanced over at the display floating above Sensei's holopad.

QUESTION: How did we discover the Evéik language?

Answer: Leontari and Vidara Rivernova discovered the Evéik Language while digging in Antarctica.

"MISS LINEA, would you like to give it a try?" Sensei pointed to a 600 on the far right.

Linea stood up, and with the help of her hologlasses,

fumbled over the translation. After a few corrections from Sensei, he applauded her effort and she sat back down. A 700 raised his hand.

"Yisû, Mr. Atley."

"But Professor, Evéik was discovered by Dr. Kilbourne of the Paradise Foundation. And then it was stolen…," he said.

"Stolen by Leontari and Vidara. Yisû, I've read the lies the U.N.O.E. put in the curriculum. Not a word of it's true," Sensei said with a dismissive wave of his hand. The students gasped, shooting quick glances at the camera panels, apparently shocked someone would dare contradict the U.N.O.E. Sensei flashed an emboldened glance at the camera in the corner. "I wonder, do any of you know the truth of what really happened?"

The classroom remained silent. Sensei flipped through some notes for what was probably today's lecture. Stacking them and tossing them aside, he said, "Well, we can't have that. It's time you learned." Kassi decided to put her reading aside for the day to listen in on the lecture.

Sensei projected a new display to their hologlasses and repositioned himself in the center of the room. "Back in the late 2020s, two Penn State students by the names of Leontari and Vidara Rivernova, a husband and wife duo, dreamed of exploring new worlds in the cosmos, but at the time, that was only science fiction. Other than trips to the Moon and Mars, no one had ever ventured beyond to the outer reaches of space. As students, Vidara was working on her Ph.D. in archeology and Leo his Ph.D. in acoustic engineering, but they both had a fascination with space exploration. They never would have guessed their fields of study would provide the catalyst for intergalactic expansion.

"It all started with Vidara. She and her professor, Dr. Catarine Fresia were particularly excited to explore the glaciers of Antarctica. They were granted a permit to excavate near Lake Vostok. For three years, they reached new depths in the ice until they finally struck gold! Well, sedimentary rock, to be exact."

Everyone in the classroom leaned in, hanging on to every word. It was quite the contrast from all their other professors who lulled them to sleep.

"On October 28th, 2029, after more than three years of hard digging through blocks of compounded, thick ice, under some of the harshest weather conditions imaginable, and surviving multiple attempts on their lives - a story for another time - they made the discovery of a lifetime!

"Carved into the side of ancient iron tools, dating back thousands of years, possibly tens of thousands of years, they found curious writings of an unknown language. This find ignited a new passion from the team to expand the dig site. Leo and a few others joined them, at this point. They swore everyone to absolute secrecy among their small team until they gathered more evidence to present to the world. After six more weeks, they had uncovered the remains of half a dozen tools and two large boulders containing inscriptions of this same ancient and immortal tongue. These two slabs are what we now call the Stone Scrolls of Evéik.

"They secretly recruited a very talented young linguist by the name of Granton Macavoy and took him to the excavation site to show him the scrolls. Mr. Macavoy tried piecing it together based on his knowledge of other ancient languages. He found some commonalities to known dialects and, after many months of research, successfully deciphered the first few sentences of Evéik. But this isn't where all the real magic begins," Sensei Kelipalo said, speaking in hushed, dramatic tones.

"During a night of let-loose revelry and celebration over their discovery, Vidara started singing the sentences they had translated and something magical happened. Leo had been sipping on a glass of glacier water while she sang. He suddenly detected a sweetness that revitalized his tired body. It awakened him. Dr. Fresia, who had reluctantly agreed to join them after experiencing a terrible headache, felt a soothing sensation flow to the four corners of her brain. It relieved her pain. They couldn't believe what they were witnessing firsthand. Vidara had just unlocked the healing properties of Evéik and become the world's first siren!" Sensei paused to let that sink in. The silence was thick until a 500 let out a restrained cough.

"They discovered an ancient language that had the power to heal. But that's not all. Leo had been researching possible ways to harness the energy produced by sonoluminescence. Introducing Evéik into the acoustic frequencies, he enhanced and stabilized the energy output, allowing his team to convert the light and heat into consumable energy. It's this breakthrough in nuclear fusion that provided clean, renewable power for the entire planet. It's what powers our sonopacks, our power grids, and the G.D.C. in Antarctica where the Rosenbridge connects our world with the Paradise Planets."

"So why's it called Evéik?" A 700 asked.

"Good question, Mr. Atenza," Sensei said, "Apollo Ducat and Dr. Fresia were the ones responsible for the name. Apollo was a historian who hypothesized Evéik to be the language spoken by the first intelligent human beings on Earth. Dr. Fresia belonged to a religion that's now outlawed on our planet, and it was her belief that the first intelligent human beings were a man and woman by the name of Adam and Eve. She started calling the language Evéik, after Eve, and the name stuck."

Kassi had heard all of this before. She grew up on this knowledge. It was fascinating to see the astonished expressions on the faces of the other students. They were so entranced, none of them noticed the time. When the bell rang, the whole class let out a groan. "That's alright! We'll pick it back up tomorrow morning. Quiz Friday on Chapters 3 and 4 of your textbooks." Kelipalo shouted as the kids flooded into the hallway.

As Kassi left, she turned to see a row of armed mediation officers filing into Sensei's classroom from the emergency exit. One of them rushed to the front door and shut it before Kassi could see more.

Eighteen

"What are they going to do to him?" Kassi asked, shaken by the scene, her inner trembling bubbling to the surface.

"Same as always." Fille placed a reassuring hand on her shoulder. "It's better you just put it out of your mi..." Fille stopped abruptly. Savriah stood beside them, toothbrush in hand, brushing her teeth. Fille pointed, "What are you doing?" He whipped his head in all directions as if to make sure nobody was watching. No one was. They never paid attention to 400s.

"What?" she said, her voice muffled by the bulky, pink toothbrush.

"WHAT ARE YOU DOING?" Fille repeated, louder and even more embarrassed.

"I had something stuck in my teeth." She shrugged as if confused by Fille's uproar.

"Then go to the washrooms, you loon! Normal people don't brush their teeth in public!"

"I already got it. I'm done." Savriah stashed the toothbrush away in her backpack.

"This, you see, this is why they bully us!" Fille tossed his arms up.

"They bully us because we're 400s," Savriah said.

"Other 400s don't get bullied as much as we do!" Fills shouted as he stormed down the hall toward the front office.

Detention was much different from their weekend routines. Kassi was suddenly even more grateful for Mr. Benetti's negligence. Officer Jerold brought with him two 500s, as well as Jacen and Jaya who had volunteered for extra credit. He tossed Kassi an old toothbrush, not unlike the one Savriah used moments ago. "You're on floor polishing duty starting with this lobby," he said gruffly before leaving her and taking the other three to their assignments.

A 500 boy named Wulff stayed behind to supervise, closely watching Kassi. He had a crooked nose and a light brown Edgar hairstyle. The first time she rolled onto her back to stretch, he jumped in her face and screamed, "No breaks or we add a day!" Kassi reluctantly resumed scrubbing. Wulff added, "And just remember what you did to deserve this, Four Hundie!"

"What I did?" Kassi looked up and glowered at Wulff. "I didn't do a yashing thing. We're punished because some-eh coward blindsided me. He attacked me and I got punished! How is that fair?"

"Don't," Wulff said, pausing to shake his finger as if to buy himself time to put words together, "don't talk back or we add a day." Kassi wanted to jam the toothbrush in his mouth and make him eat dirt, but instead, she kept her head down and cleaned.

By the end of the day's penance, Kassi's fingers were rubbed raw and her back ached with an unfamiliar stiffness. Sore muscles were far from foreign to her, and she had always pitched in with the cleaning back home in the palace—everyone did. But R.A.V.'s did most of the physical labor. They were even entertaining to watch, rinsing and wiping everything so thoroughly—it was relaxing. They only required simple instructions, light supervision, and occasional upkeep—nothing like manual scrubbing with a smart-less toothbrush.

Before Kassi could leave, Principal Purves had to inspect her work. "Unacceptable," Purves said with a crooked scowl. "It's no different from before. Make her do it again tomorrow," she told Jerold. Kassi groaned–the very thought made her knotted muscles throb.

She hobbled back to the front entrance where her friends were waiting. Jacen and Jaya leaned against the wall, both smirking at the four of them.

"Traitors!" Fille spat as the four of them hopped in the dinghy and took off. Kassi and her friends rubbed their shoulders and backs from the pain—something that was completely unfair for them to endure. She couldn't help but feel guilty.

Slowing to dock in front of Savriah's house as the engine idled at a low hum, Kassi said, "I'm sorry, chas. This is all because of me. If I hadn't stopped to eat my taco…"

"It's not, it's not your fault," Adonis was quick to dismiss.

"It's like I said before, it's nothing you did," Fille said as he tied the boat to a post.

"The Chinpoke Squad's to blame," Savriah agreed.

Kassi nodded soberly, but she wasn't just referring to the specific incident. It was her fault, along with every paradiser, for not insisting they open the portal to the Gaians. Ravana was right to bring them here to see it for themselves. Life on Earth was almost unbearable. Gaians needed to experience the peaceful, orderly existence on Paradise.

The next day in *Heroics* as she walked in late as usual with her crutches, Nikola shouted, "Who let you out?" Kassi heard the others snickering behind her as she hobbled to her seat.

When she walked into *History of the Worlds*, he threw another jab. "You really smell like ripe sheist today!" More giggles. Kassi tried miserably to ignore them.

On her way to her desk in *Mechanical Engineering*, Nikola said, "It's impossible to underestimate 400s. The bar could be all the way to the floor and these depps would bring shovels."

In *P.E.*, he got the whole Chinpoke Squad to spit at her every time Coach Muzzey turned his back. When Nikola got in her face, Kassi mustered a sliver of bravery and stood her ground. She shoved Nikola, or at least she tried with her crutches. Nikola hardly moved–barely affected by the shove–and yet it was enough to earn Kassi the broomstick.

After more ear-blistering shouted insults, Nikola used the sonic pulse baton to knock Kassi to the floor with a sonic punch to the stomach, her crutches crashing to the ground. His strike was strong–much more powerful than Malyra's.

They reached Sensei's classroom for lunch. Kassi complained for most of it, needing to vent. She said, "I zhust need a sonic rifle."

"Get in line, get in line," Adonis said.

"Once you're healed, you'll have your chance to stand up to them," Sensei said as he stood and limped across the classroom, holding his side. Kassi had almost forgotten about the mediation officers. She suddenly felt bad for complaining.

In Period 6, Sensei K began his lecture with his usual enthusiasm, as if unphased by the most recent beating.

"*Gaté bébulak máþetító. Mish Biki, gîlara li lista van Evéiké i wéka loro li luþibé bizat. Hûn anish buvi prap bébulak shi doshosách li linggwûbé bizat.*" Ms. Kassiana, would you care to translate for the class?" While the other professors treated 400s like lepers, Sensei seemed to enjoy showing her off to the class. Kassi translated it out loud.

"Very good. Before we continue, did anyone have any questions about the history lesson we covered yesterday?"

A 600 raised his hand. "So where does Dr. Kilbourne come in?" the boy asked.

Another hand shot up. It was Malyra. "Dr. Kilbourne was there with Granton Macavoy. He deciphered the first runes and called the language, Evéik. He was also the first one to try singing the language. It wasn't Vidara and it wasn't an accident at some party."

Sensei gave a half-shrug and said, "Ms. Malyra, you can believe what you want."

"My father is an assembly member for the Provincial Department of Interplanetary Diplomacy and is good friends with Dr. Kilbourne's grandson, and he says Leontari and Vidara are nothing more than common criminals." Malyra huffed, crossing her arms.

Fille leaned back in his seat and shouted, "We all know who your yashing father is, you buttshark. You won't shut up about it!"

Malyra faked a laugh as she whirled on Fille. "I see your lips are moving, Fille. You might wanna look into that."

"And you might wanna keep it to a dull roar! Why you shouting?"

"You're the one shouting!" Malyra pointed a wicked finger at Fille. "I'm articulating a point with sophistication! Like a dame." She said, straightening her posture as if to emphasize her classiness. "Something a Four Hundie blowse wouldn't know anything about."

"Oh yisû, you're a real ball of the bell." Fille reached up his hand as if ringing a bell above his head.

Malyra snorted. "Don't you mean belle of the ball?"

"Nope!" Fille said.

"Alright, that's enough," Sensei K said. "In answer to your question, Ms. Malyra, everything I detailed to you yesterday was the truth."

"That's not the truth. That's a lie! My father will hear of this!" Malyra stomped. "He'll get you fired."

"Well, he can certainly try." Professor Kelipalo flashed his usual, confident grin before jumping right back into his lecture as if Malyra's threats were about as concerning as a dead housefly on the outside windows. "Now, let's go over the nominative, accusative, genitive, and dative cases for a noun…" Sensei said, switching gears. He spent the rest of class going over Evéik grammar until the bell rang.

Once in the hallway, Malyra ranted to Calandra, an 800 and

new recruit to the Chinpoke Squad. "Just wait til my father hears about this traitor!"

"I can't believe they let a 'diser-lover teach here!" Calandra said, her face twisted in disgust. She had a blonde, tousled lob hairstyle with pink highlights and mimicked all of Malyra's mannerisms like a crazed sycophant.

"Who gives a fiery sheist!" Nikola said, looking bored. "The cameras already saw everything. The U.N.O.E. already did what they're gonna do regardless of what you tell your father."

"They're not doing enough!" Malyra fumed. She noticed Kassi glancing back at them and announced loudly, "My father will make sure Professor Kelipalo is out on the street before you can say Evéik three times!"

"Evéik. Evéik. Evéik." DeSchuster couldn't help smiling as he chanted with a couple 700s gathered around.

"Yash and Sheebah, you're juvenile!" Malyra stormed off.

"What's got her covered in spiders?" Kassi overheard Nikola say just before she turned the corner to catch up with Fille and Adonis.

They dragged their feet to the office for another day of detention. "Could Malyra really get Sensei fired?" Kassi asked.

"Not a chance!" Fille said without hesitation. "This school needs him way more than he needs this job."

"And he won the Siren Games. He can go back to Astera any time he wants!" Savriah said.

"He's doing, he's doing the whole school district a gargantic favor by sticking around," Adonis widened his hands for emphasis.

"That's funny coming from you, Team London!" Fille jabbed a finger at Adonis who just shrugged.

"How's he doing them a favor?" Kassi asked.

"He mentors and brings new champions to the Siren Games every season. And he had more champions win the games than any other Evéik teacher on the entire yashing planet. It brings a lot of pride…"

"...and money, and money," Adonis added.

"...and money to the district he represents," Fille finished.

"I see," Kassi said, still feeling uneasy.

"Malyra tries so hard to be a wet blanket. In the end, she's just a half-digested biscuit."

They walked into the office to receive their detention assignments and were ushered into the principal's office. When they opened the door, Principal Purves and Professor Raisen pushed away from each other, guilt written on their faces. Kassi and her friends instantly spun on their heels and ducked out of the office.

"Let's zhust pretend we didn't see that," Kassi said as they took their seats to wait for their detention assignments.

Officer Jerold put them to work. With her back and fingers still sore from the previous day, Kassi struggled to make it through the entire two hours. By the end, she was so stiff, she could barely get back to her foot and hobble to the front entrance on her crutches. They rode home in silence, completely spent.

The next day, Nikola continued his barrage of insults, starting with the horrid smell seeping from her cast. He was right about that–it smelled of rotting fish. She had tried on multiple occasions to convince the school Healer to recast it. Each time, they told her she would need to come back right after school, which was during her assigned detention, so it was impossible. If she didn't get it recast soon, she would likely contract some kind of infection.

That afternoon during Evéik, Professor Kelipalo paused his lesson and read a message to the class. "Sorry to be the bearer of bad news. I have to read this message aloud:

It is our deepest regret to inform you that another coordinated terrorist attack has disrupted our peace yet again. Multiple cities across the globe have fallen victim to these atrocious acts of senseless violence, and all students are to return home and be counted with their families immediately. Parents have been notified and will be coming to pick you up. May the U.N.O.E. find a resolution to these matters and restore the peace."

ANOTHER COORDINATED TERRORIST ATTACK—DIFFERENT cities, same pattern.

It was pandemonium. Students erupted in confusion and burst from their seats, flooding the halls. As they did, Kassi overheard them shouting things like, "How could someone be so violent?" and, "Why hasn't the U.N.O.E. stopped them yet?" Kassi and her friends remained at their desks until the classroom emptied.

"Who could be doing this?" Fille asked Sensei once the room had cleared.

"I don't know, Fille," Sensei said, a hint of tension in his broad shoulders. He looked up from the news reports and seemed to notice the worry lines etched on their faces. "I know it's a horrific situation, but you're safe for now. You should all go home and check on your loved ones."

Kassi kept quiet, reflecting on her conversation with Meela after the previous attack. She wondered if this meant there was another rescue attempt.

"Wait, wait, don't we still have detention?" Adonis asked.

"Not today. Your parents should be waiting for you at the front," Sensei said.

Not mine, Kassi sagged in her seat.

They unfolded from their seats and headed for the door. Adonis and Savriah left with their parents. When Fille saw his father, he said, "Hi Pops, I need to take her home first." He pointed at Kassi. "Is everyone safe?"

"Yisû they're safe, no thanks to Yash!" Fille's father said. "Meet me at home?"

Fille nodded before helping Kassi down the front entrance stairs. On their way out, they passed a mother who was crying as she embraced her son, a 700. In her eyes, she saw a fear that most Gaians were likely experiencing today.

While riding on the water, the wind of motion wasn't enough to lift the heaviness Kassi felt. She wondered if Ravana's plan might actually work. It would help the Gaians. Maybe after Kassi was fully healed, she could write new songs for her team, lead them to greatly improve and come together, maybe even recruit some better players to join. It would probably take longer than six months which meant they would push for next season. Kassi wondered if she could last that long on Earth, or if it would ever be enough to actually win the Games. Then again, it was clear her family was trying to get her back. If they coordinated a successful rescue, Kassi could convince them to open the portal and let the Gaians through. At the very least, she could get her friends through. Unless the rescue failed. It all seemed so impossible. The hopelessness of her situation stressed her out. *"You can't change the past, but you can ruin the present by stressing about the future,"* her brother, Caesar, would always say. Out of instinct, Kassi turned to a siren meditation exercise. She focused on her surroundings, tilting her head backwards as her eyes traced the blue, cloudless sky. Amára was under the same sky. The tension dissipated. Kassi had been so focused on her Gaian friends, she hadn't thought of Amára in several days. She felt guilty for not remembering and hoped her best friend was safe. Maybe Amára would find a way to win the Games and help the rest of the captives and Gaians.

Fille helped her to the front door. As they drew closer, they heard a heated exchange inside.

"Should I stick around?" Fille put his ear to the door.

"You don't need to."

"I should," Fille said, opening the door.

They walked in as Kyoto shouted, "It's not your place to…" He abruptly stopped at the sight of Kassi and Fille in the doorway. Meela mumbled something under her breath and retreated upstairs. Kyoto lingered for a moment to glare at Kassi before following. Their bedroom door shut and locked, and a muffled argument ensued.

"Thanks for checking," Kassi turned to Fille. "I'll be safe."

Fille nodded, closing the door behind him. The roar of the engine shrank into the distance. Kassi took a plate of food to her room and spent the evening forcing herself to focus on home-work. If the ever-present threat of more detention didn't hang over her head, she would have skipped homework, but every missed or failed assignment earned a day of detention.

She wanted to know what they were arguing about. It clearly had to do with the terrorist attack. Questions and concerns soaked her mind. It took Kassi three times as long to finish her assignments before she collapsed onto her mattress.

The next morning at breakfast, Kassi asked Meela, "So...what were-eh you two arguing about yesterday?"

"That's none of your concern!" Kyoto said, pressing a firm hand on the table.

Kassi would have to wait until Meela was alone to get answers.

On their way to school, a news update looped on all of the screens throughout Miami Beach. Kassi and her friends listened as they weaved through traffic.

THIS JUST IN: a video has been circulated by the terrorist organization known as the Hel Mafia claiming responsibility for both attacks," a woman in a smart suit and a slicked back ponytail announced. *"While little is known, recent intelligence has revealed the terrorists are 'disers from Nemal and Aruna."*

FILLE, Adonis, and Savriah whipped their heads toward Kassi. She shook her head vehemently, confused by the accusation. Despite what Meela had said from the previous attack, Kassi still couldn't believe anyone from home would have anything to do with this. The news continued:

YOU CAN REST ASSURED *that the U.N.O.E. is doing everything within their power to capture these 'disers. Grand Deputy Jone Wynbell proposed they assign a new leader to its elite, anti-terrorist task force to root out the Hel Mafia and bring them to justice. By majority vote from the senate and grand assembly, they have elected Griffonage Li, a highly decorated Siren and top of his class. He has accepted the post and will begin immediately. Top officials are optimistic that under new leadership..."*

KASSI HAD BEEN STARING at the black, synthetic rubber floor of the dinghy when she heard his name. She jerked her head up to see a face she almost didn't recognize. It was the same Griffonage who aided in their kidnapping, but much thinner and with short-cropped hair.

Savriah studied Kassi and asked, "What is it?"

"That man," she pointed. "The one they just appointed," she said as Fille and Adonis turned their heads to listen in. "He's one of the chas who brought me here-eh!"

"You sure that's him?" Fille asked.

"Yisû, that's him. He was there that night," Kassi said. Seeing his face triggered the memory of Macks lying on the ground. The thought of it caused Kassi to breathe heavier. She had to force herself to inhale and exhale slowly to prevent another panic attack.

"Wow, he didn't waste any time!" Fille said, idling the engine to stare blankly into space for a beat. "Huh," he said, revving the engine and continuing down the street.

"How did he climb the ranks so fast?" Savriah asked, staring at the holoscreens.

Kassi wondered the same thing. She also thought the name of

the terrorist organization–Hel Mafia–was curious. It was a reference to Norse Mythology. Leo, Kassi's father, had spent countless hours studying Norse and other mythologies. The Hel Mafia, coincidentally, sounded like a name he would come up with. But there was no way he was involved. Kassi was sure of it.

Thursday night, Kyoto worked the late shift. Kassi found Meela alone in the kitchen. "So was there another rescue attempt?"

"There was." Meela nodded. "We stopp'd 'em again."

"Huh," Kassi sank into the seat next to Meela.

"What?" Meela asked, eyeing Kassi.

"If it didn't work the first time-eh, why would they try again?" Kassi asked. "My dad's always reading books on history and military strategy. I know he'd never use the same tactic twice if it failed the first time."

"I don't know. Just did what we's told and kept another child from escapin'. Tha's all I know." Meela said, handing Kassi a plate.

"Well at least I know it wasn't my parents," Kassi said with a sigh as she filled her plate with a biscuit and some rice. Meela studied her for a beat, silent. Kassi took a bite and asked around a mouthful of rice, "But you didn't stop any bombs from going off?"

"Didn' get there in time."

"So you didn't actually see who set off the bombs?" Kassi asked, raising an eyebrow. Meela didn't answer. "Is that what you and Kyoto were arguing about?"

Meela cast a sidelong glance at Kassi, "Nah, that was b'cause I let one of 'em go."

"Who?"

"Ol' friend o' mine. A grip like me to another kid who needs watchin'."

"She tried helping one of us escape-eh?" Kassi couldn't picture Kyoto or Meela lifting a finger to help her.

"We caught her trying t'use th'Rosen-comm for her hossty.

She was jus' confused, so I spoke some sense, an' she agreed t'change 'er ways if I let'er go." Meela said. "I prolly shouldn't be sayin' any of this."

"Wait, did she set off the bombs?" Kassi stood and leaned over the kitchen table.

"Wasn' her," Meela shook her head. "Prolly why Griff didn't make a fuss when I let 'er go."

"I saw Griff on the news today," Kassi said. "He's in charge of the anti-terrorist thingy now. How'd he get that position so fast?"

"Not really sure, t'be honest," Meela shrugged as she climbed the creaking staircase to her room. "Anyhow, you best be gettin' on t'bed."

Kassi climbed the stairs behind her. "Does the U.N.O.E. know about all of this?"

"They always know," Meela said. "They might be arguin' with each other now it's gone s'far, but they always know."

Once Kassi reached her room, she plopped onto the mattress. Staring at the dangling ceiling fan above, she tried to process everything–the terrorist attack, Meela's claim it was another rescue attempt, Griff's high appointment. She tossed and turned for hours until she finally dozed off.

Once they reached Sensei's classroom for lunch the next day, she filled them in.

"So these chas are setting off bombs and killing hundreds all so they can save one of their own?" Fille asked.

"And Ravana, Ravana is stopping them?" Adonis looked just as confused as Kassi felt.

"That's what she's saying, but I can't believe-eh that!" Kassi said, shaking her head.

"So what do you think it is?" Savriah asked.

"I don't know. But my parents would never allow anyone from the Council to do something like-eh this." Kassi rubbed her temples. "And I can't picture any of them killing innocent people."

"How well do you know them?" Fille asked.

Kassi shrugged. She had met all of them only briefly. Other than her Uncle Sydney, the Council of Creators was spread out across planet Nemal.

After lunch, she finally convinced the school healer to recast her leg, even though it was during class. Maybe they couldn't bear the smell.

Thankfully, there was no detention on weekends. They were back to their usual mornings with Mr. Benetti, giving their bodies a couple of days to recover.

Monday morning, Nikola and the Chinpoke Squad were at it again, doing everything they could to badger Kassi. She wasn't sure how much more harassment she could take.

In line at the cafeteria, Fille and Adonis joked around trying to rope in Kassi, but she wasn't in the mood. They grabbed their food and took the elevator up. The doors opened to Sensei waiting for them, a huge grin on his face. "Good news! Follow me," Sensei said, leading them through his classroom and small office to the emergency exit. A red warning sign said something about an alarm should the door be opened. Sensei pushed it open and ushered them outside. A rusted metal ladder ascended to the rooftop on one side and on the other, concrete stairs descended, hugging the side of the building until it fed into the slidewalks down below. The platform was barely big enough for two of them, let alone four teens and Sensei K, so they each took a step and sat, leaning against the wall.

"I heard back from Hira! We've got a rendezvous point for Kassi," Sensei said.

Kassi exclaimed, "Thank the elyon sky!"

"Hira?" Adonis asked.

"The healer! Did you already forget?" Kassi cuffed him playfully on the shoulder.

"Oh, right right."

"He's here early!" Kassi had been counting down the days, and it had been almost two weeks since his message.

"Good news, right?" Sensei smiled.

"It's bosst news! But why out here?" Kassi looked down over the flooded streets below.

"No cameras," Sensei said, pointing.

"Yash, I can't even believe I've lasted this long!" Kassi let out a loud sigh of relief. It had been a month and a half since she lost her voice, and while some raspiness had diminished, her high range had never recovered. During vocal exercises, the high notes were wispy squeaks. At least the hideous burn on her neck had mostly disappeared.

Sensei continued, "Saturday at 1400, Hira will meet you at the South Pointe Pier. He said he'll be wearing a red hat."

"Saturday at the Pier, at 1400. Got it," Kassi said with a nod.

Opening the door, Sensei led them back into the classroom. They took their seats at the front of class, and Fille began the process of dividing up the food.

Kassi bounced in her seat as she brushed the hair out of her face and twisted it up into a loose bun. She wanted to cry. *I can't believe I'll finally have my voice back!* Kassi lifted her cast. *And my leg.*

"Guess what?" Sensei sat on the edge of his desk. "Friday is your last day of detention."

"What? How?" Fille jumped to his feet, his mouth full of biscuit.

"I made a convincing argument to the school board about letting all of our teams have a fair chance at becoming champions and representing the region. With my track record, they know to listen to me. I told them two weeks was more than enough, and the Blue Krakens deserved to compete."

"No more detention! No more detention" Adonis and Fille chanted as they pumped their fists in the air and danced around the room.

"Good, 'cause I don't think I can scrub any more shower stalls," Savriah said, examining her fingertips.

"Or floors." Kassi rubbed the cracked skin on her palms.

That afternoon and for the rest of the week, detention was much easier. They were on the final stretch. By Friday, the two hours of detention flew by as Kassi scrubbed her last hard rubber floor. Principal Purves had never been satisfied with the work, so Kassi had spent all two weeks washing the same lobby. It made as much sense as everything else on this yashing planet. Wulff had remained her volunteer supervisor for the duration of the two weeks. When she left, she flashed him the cacasheist. He scowled, knowing he no longer had any authority to add extra days. Maybe he never had.

Kassi regrouped with the others. No more sore backs and fingers–detention was over.

"I'm in the mood to do something, today," Fille shouted over the roar of the boat engine as he drove them through the streets of Miami Beach.

"The balconies at my grips' townhome are always empty," Kassi said. "We could go there."

"Why are they called grips?" Savriah asked, tilting her head to the side. Kassi just shrugged.

"Chas?" Fille asked Adonis and Savriah. They both nodded in agreement. Fille gunned it for Kassi's townhome.

Kyoto barely looked up from an article he was reading at the kitchen table when they burst in the front door and ascended two flights of stairs. Old and rusty lawn chairs littered the balcony. Sturdy enough to sit on, they each snagged one.

Once they were settled, Adonis said, "Ok ok, so not to be Johnny Raincloud or anything, but what if this pata, Hira, is a fake? You know? What if he's not the real deal?"

"You're skeptical?" Fille stared at Adonis, wide-eyed. "Why, because he's not one of your cousins' contacts?"

"I'm just, I'm just saying. You know. What if?"

"I have a good feeling about it," Kassi reclined in her lawn chair. "I have a fifth sense about this sort of thing. I don't think there's anything to worry about."

"Fifth sense?" Adonis cocked his head to the side.

"She means sixth sense," Savriah said.

"Sixth sense-eh! You know what I mean!" Kassi threw her hands up and barked under her breath. "Ruff!" After a beat, Kassi changed the subject. "Why are there so many mediation officers here? They're everywhere down here!"

"So many 500s sign up because of the no-armband thing," Fille said. "They get a power trip out of punishing the rest of us."

"There are, there are actually more mediation officers than there are people on all the Paradise Planets combined," Adonis rattled off.

"Is that another one of your cousin's fun facts?" Kassi eyed him suspiciously.

Savriah pulled out a small bag and started fidgeting with it. "Donis is actually right about this one. Mediation officers outnumber all 'dis…paradisers almost two to one."

"Hold the sails! What in the flying Sheebah is that?" Fille said, pointing to Savriah's bag.

"What's what?" Savriah asked, whipping her head in all directions.

"THAT!" Fille stood up and leaned forward, pointing centimeters from the bag.

"My fingernail clippings." Savriah held up the bag with pride. Kassi, Adonis, and Fille recoiled in disgust.

Fille coughed. "Why?"

"Helps me think. Why does it matter?" Savriah asked.

"It's nasty as sheist! That's why!" Fille staggered back to his seat.

Adonis scooted farther away. "It's gross, disgusting!"

Kassi shuddered and skidded her chair back.

"I don't see what the big deal is," Savriah said as she tucked the bag back into her pocket.

Adonis changed the subject. "So Kassi, Kassi, you've been here almost a month now. Do you like anybody?"

"What do you mean?"

"You know, you know, do you *like* anybody?" Adonis repeated the question.

"Of course! She likes Vander," Savriah said. "You didn't know?"

"I do not." Kassi flushed red.

"Of course, I didn't know. How would I know?" Adonis held his hands out.

"Why do you think I like-eh Vander?"

"We've all seen the way you look at him," Fille said.

"Well, what about you? Who do you like-eh?" Kassi tried to shift the attention off of her.

"Ganna's the one for me!" Fille leaned back, hands behind his head. "She's royalty if I've ever seen one."

"Whatever, pata, I already, I already called dibs," Adonis slapped Fille's chest.

"You can't call dibs on a girl!" Fille shouted.

"Who's Ganna?" Kassi asked.

"She's an 800 on the Red Squalls," Savriah said.

Adonis and Fille continued swatting at each other. Kassi asked Savriah, "What about you?"

"Oh, I don't like anyone right now," Savriah said.

Fille shouted, "You've had a thing for Joshi ever since Grade 6!"

"Yisû, but I don't any more!"

"I don't believe that." Fille tossed two dismissive hands.

"Have any of you...ever dreamed of winning the Siren Games?" Kassi asked. Even though they always scoffed at their chances, she wondered.

"Of course," Fille said with a half-shrug. "Who doesn't?"

"All the time, all the time," Adonis said. "I'd love to be a champion."

"I've dreamed of winning palladium medals ever since I was little," Savriah said. "I always wanted to walk to the podium wearing a cape and have someone there to take it off for me."

"A cape? Why a cape?" Kassi asked, raising one eyebrow. Savriah just laughed to herself and shrugged.

"I used to dream about crossing the finish line first. But any time I mentioned it around my parents, they always said the same thing," Fille stared at the ground. "Don't quit the day job!"

"What day job?" Kassi asked, confused.

"It's something they always say," Fille said, picking at a piece of paper and flicking bits into the air. "Not that any of them could quit their day job since it's mandated by the yashing U.N.O.E."

Kassi shook her head at all the U.N.O.E. enforced and did to their citizens. "Maybe one day, we'll leave Earth and all this behind."

The others stared into space, clearly not so confident.

Saturday morning, with detention over and Hira on his way, they were happier than usual. Mr. Benetti eyed them curiously while taking roll. He retired to his room and they skipped to the far end of the school to resume their lollybagging. Adonis and Fille chased each other around while Savriah tried to join in. Still, in her cast for a few more hours, Kassi took a seat and spent the morning fantasizing about enacting some retribution with a sonic rifle. With her new voice, she could put all the bullies in a trance and escort them outside right into the street water. Or she could frame students for pranks against teachers that would earn them the broomstick. Kassi also thought about chewing up all the 800s' food, so when they woke from their stupor, they would find piles of pre-chewed food on their plates. Her mind ran wild with ideas, and even though she would never enact them, she still felt guilty for thinking them. The noon bell rang.

"So Sensei told you to go alone?" Savriah asked.

"Yisû, but I still need a ride-eh to the pier," Kassi said.

"I can do that," Fille said with a single nod.

After dropping everyone off, Fille and Kassi made their way to South Pointe Pier. She could hardly contain her excitement. Maybe she'd recognize Hira from home. They sped through the streets and Kassi couldn't stop repeating over the hum of the engine, "I can't believe it's finally happening!"

When they arrived, there were only a handful of people out on the pier. "Good luck, Kassi! I'll be waiting around the corner just in case." Fille pointed to one of the four apartment towers.

Kassi hopped to the end of the pier on her crutches. They pinched under her arms, like always. She couldn't wait to chuck them into the garbage receptacle.

Kassi paced the four corners of the large, wooden pier. It was gargantic, built to house thousands of people, so it took Kassi a good amount of time to circle the full perimeter. Scanning faces in all directions, she anxiously searched for a man in a red hat.

A bag was slung over her shoulder with her newly-repaired rental wetsuit tucked inside. Kassi planned on catching the tail end of their AquaSphera match after the healing, anxious to return to the waterfield after spending three weeks out of the water. Once healed, she'd be able to power all four thrusters once again. The drag created by the rips and tears in the old suit would keep her from reaching her previous best, but it would still be a major improvement.

An hour went by—Kassi grew worried. She wondered if there was a chance she missed Hira, or worse, if he had reconsidered. Squinting in all directions, she rubbed her eyes and blinked hard, scanning all the faces again and again—no red hats.

Doubt crept in. *Maybe he's not coming. What if the U.N.O.E. did something to him?* Kassi fretted, unable to find her calm as more doubts flooded her mind.

Just then, a voice startled her from behind, almost causing Kassi to trip and spill onto the pier. *"So you must be Lesley's student,"* he said in fluent, Nemalís Evéik. A short man with tawny-brown skin in a red hat appeared out of nowhere.

Nineteen

The man stood behind Kassi calmly, as if he had been there all day. He wore a simple, black wetsuit with a black collar, held his helmet in his hand, and smiled with kindness in his hazel, deep-set eyes. His bushy, brown eyebrows matched the short curls on his head.

Kassi sighed with relief and said, switching to Evéik, *"Yisû, I'm Kassi. And you're...?"*

"Hira. Call me Hira." he bowed. *"Are you ready to swim?"*

"I would be, but my leg..." Kassi pointed at the cast.

"I noticed that. I've got something for it, but first, we need to get you out of camera range," he said, hugging the corner of the pier. He hadn't moved since she spotted him, likely standing in a blind spot.

With tight form, he leaped over the railing and vanished under the water. When he surfaced, he beckoned her in.

"With my school uniform on?"

"That's up to you." He smiled. *"Leave the crutches and jump in."*

Kassi whipped her head around to see if anyone was watching. The pier was empty. Stripping down to her under-bikini, she stuffed her uniform into her bag, took a deep breath, rolled over the railing, and splashed into the Atlantic.

With a cast on her leg and one hand holding a bag, she sank. Hira dove after her and brought her up to the surface, just under the pier. When at high tide, the water would kiss the underside of the pier and even spill over at times. However, it was low tide, so they had about a meter of space between the surface of the water and the underside of the pier–the perfect hiding spot. Large cement beams formed X's to make up the pier's foundation. Hira clamped a camouflage climber treestand onto a slanted post to provide Kassi a seat, then did the same on another post and took a seat across from her.

Whipping various items out of his bag with smooth efficiency, he said, *"Let me see that leg."* Kassi lifted her water-logged cast out of the water. With a pair of laser-edged scissors, he sliced the cast open and tossed it into a canvas bag at his side. In the same fluid motion, he wrapped her leg with a robotic brace that automatically tightened to perfectly fit her calf. *"This'll hurt. Since this isn't a new injury, I have to re-break the leg in order for the nanobots to find the break and form the graphite bone graft."*

"Wait, you have to wha…," Kassi didn't finish before the rods in the brace abruptly folded, snapping her leg, before straightening again. The sharp pain caused her to scream, tears welling up in her eyes.

"Sorry," Hira apologized. *"I've found that it's better to surprise people with the pain so they don't have any time to fret over it,"* he said casually as he swiftly poked her with two injections before replacing the leg brace with a sleeve. One of the injections was a painkiller that quickly numbed the leg. Within seconds, the pain dissolved.

"Why didn't you do that first?" Kassi wiped her eyes.

"The numbing agent sometimes confuses the nanobots," he said. The sleeve he slipped over her calf was thinner than the hydrophobic material of the wetsuits and would easily fit under her wettie. It tightened her leg and provided strong support. *"It'll be sore for a couple of days, but with the sleevecast, you can immediately walk on it, run on it, and swim."*

"So much better than the cast they gave me," Kassi said, stretching and rotating her newly freed foot.

"We'll test it out on the beach where we're headed. Slip into your wetsuit, then meet me in the water." Hira said as he packed his bag, sealed his helmet, and dropped into the water.

Seated on the climber treestand, Kassi wriggled into her wetsuit. With the helmet on, she plopped into the ocean and powered up her suit. Hira treaded just below the surface and held out his wrist. Kassi hovered her arm over his and their audio frequencies linked.

"Now, let's take care of that voice. Follow me." Hira took the lead at a leisurely pace, but with Kassi's broken voice, she still struggled to keep up. Still, with her new leg and the anticipation of a healed voice, she was jittery with excitement. After roughly twenty minutes of swimming, they reached an empty beach on a remote island and surfaced.

"We should be safe here." Hira removed his helmet and scanned the horizon.

Once Kassi stepped onto the sandy beach, she tested out her leg. Other than some stiffness and a dull ache, it was back to normal–just like last time after she had jumped off of Sofiû Falls. She had just turned thirteen and wanted to try dancing in the air. At eighteen meters high, it had been a reckless jump. Her leg was outstretched when she had hit the water, snapping her femur and knocking her unconscious. If Amára hadn't been there to rescue her, she might have died that day.

Kassi wobbled forward, taking one step, then another. Picking up the pace, she jogged and then started to dance and twirl along the beach. After three weeks, she was finally back on her feet! She wanted to sing for joy, but she didn't have her voice back yet. Kassi bounced to Hira.

"How's the leg?" He asked.

"Wonderful!" Kassi said with a pirouette. *"Thank you so much!"*

"We're just getting started," he said, his Evéik naturally rhyming.

Kassi paused for a beat to look out over the deserted island. *"Where are we?"*

"It's an abandoned Marine Reserve from before the Great Correction—completely off the grid. Since the U.N.O.E. thinks I'm dead, I can't be caught on camera or by any of the functioning deep water sensors," he said as he climbed to a level clearing and unpacked his bag.

"They think you're dead?" Kassi asked.

"We faked my death when I came here as a Siren Games officiator. It's the only way to stay on Earth as a siren healer," Hira said as he laid down a tarp over the sand. *"So Lesley tells me your vocal cords were ruptured by a sonic cannon."*

"Yisû, one of Ravana's soldiers."

"Ravana. I heard what she did to Macks Sinclar. He and his family were good friends of mine." Hira paused to stare out at the wide open ocean, deep sadness in his eyes. After a beat, he returned to his setup, pressing a button to inflate a clear-plastic tent.

"Have you come across any others like me?" Kassi hoped he might have some news of Amára.

He shook his head, *"I haven't."* Kassi slumped. She stretched her eyes out across the water as if she could see her best friend in the distance. Hira finished setting up his workspace. *"I'm sorry I couldn't get here sooner. There are a lot of people who need my help."*

"I believe it," Kassi said. *"I'm just grateful you're here."*

"I'm sure your parents are working on a way to get you back home," Hira said. Kassi thought about the video message they had sent. *It won't be much longer,* Leo had said.

Once inside the tent, Hira closed and sealed them in to keep out the sand. The transparent walls and ceiling gave her a clear view of their surroundings—white clouds in a deep blue sky and relaxing ocean waves crashing onto the beach. Unfolding a small polypropylene table, he had her lie down on the hard surface. He extracted a long glass tube with devices on both ends known as Stem Cell Cloning Devices or S.C.C.D.s. He proceeded to do an ultrasound scan of her throat to acoustically map all angles of her vocal cords. The SCCD buzzed to life, creating an exact holographic replica. Hira pushed a button to insert the stem cells as the process of creating a brand new pair of vocal folds began. The printing operation was always fascinating to watch. Hira applied a powerful numbing reagent to her throat and commenced the surgery. As he did, Kassi stared at the sky, making shapes of the clouds, reminding her of life on Nemal.

Oftentimes at the Rivernova Academy, Dame Helena Zenra taught class outside under the laminated sunshade glass. The cool breeze carried the aromas of nearby flowers and the gentle sounds of ocean waves crashing on the distant shore. Beach cats and jungle wulves playfully snuggled up next to Kassi and her classmates. Kassi and Amára had a great view of the sky, and while they listened to passionate lessons on ecosystem ecology, they made shapes in the clouds. Leontari peeked in on their studies to see how Kassi was doing. He always reviewed her assignments or school projects and praised her progress. It was the same with all of Kassi's underwater dance recitals in the waterfield arenas. Leo was always in the front row.

Last year, in the middle of performing their big annual recital, one of the other dancers had lost control of his sonopack's energy output and shot forward in a sudden burst of speed. Kassi had been directly in his path, and they collided. Leo was the first to dive into the pool and pull her out of the water, Vidara close behind. The impact had broken Kassi's arm just above the elbow. Kassi had been screaming from the pain as Leo did his best to calm her. Vidara had performed a healing incantation while Leo injected the nanobots. Within minutes, Kassi had a healed humerus bone and only minor stiffness where the graft had formed. Only hours later, she was back in the water playing AquaSphera with her friends.

Kassi had no idea how long she had been daydreaming when she felt Hira shake her shoulders. *"Kassiana, I'm finished."*

"That was fast," Kassi said, the tone escaping her lips feeling as smooth as mulberry silk. *"My voice!"* A wave of relief

cascaded through her as she instinctively reached for her throat as if her fingers could graze the brand-new vocal cords beneath her skin. Instead, she found a small row of stitches.

"Maybe for you," he smiled as he put away his tools.

"Yisû, I drifted off," Kassi said.

"Most people do. It's actually easier for me." He pulled out a bottle from his pack and handed it to her. *"Drink this. You'll notice some soreness at first, but that should go away by the time you finish this and the water I put in your hydro-cask."*

She uncapped the bottle and pressed it to her lips. Liquid poured down her throat as cool as ice and sweet as rajabee honey–like nectar straight from the Fountain of Youth. Each sip transported her back home to warm sunny beaches where she and Amára would bask in the sun with their two-liter jugs of Jarna Water from the Fountain.

"Is this from…" Kassi held up the black, metal water bottle.

"The Fountain? No, I enhance my own water. I admit I'm not as good as your mother, but my rejuvenation solutions and incantations are still effective."

"It's so sweet!" Kassi tipped the bottle to get the last few drops.

"Thank you," he nodded. *"Try out your new voice. Let's see how we did."*

Kassi began singing a few basic warm-ups, starting with what she called "bubble lips." She rolled her lips as she sang arpeggios stretching to the top of her range and back down to the very bottom. Every note resonated effortlessly–it was literally music to her ears. Her voice was back! Her cheeks were wet with tears before she realized she had been crying.

"I wasn't sure I'd ever be able to sing again," she said as she blubbered. *"It just feels magical to have it back."* Her fingers continued tracing the stitches as she sobbed. A few beats passed as she regained her composure. She threw her arms around Hira, hugging him as she sniffed and said, *"How can I ever thank you enough!"*

"The pleasure is all mine. I'm just sorry you had to lose it in the first place," Hira said. *"But I'm sure you'll appreciate it that much more now."* Kassi nodded. She would never take her voice–or her leg–for granted again.

Hira threw on his helmet. *"Well, I must be off to my next patient. You know how to get back?"*

Kassi stretched her eyes across the ocean. *"I need to get to Alice Town. You know which direction that is?"*

"Alice Town? That way," he pointed. *"But your suit's GPS should be able to locate it."*

"This old suit doesn't have a functioning GPS," Kassi said, patting her helmet.

"Oh," Hira eyed the suit as if noticing its sad and battered condition for the first time. *"Need me to guide you?"*

"Could you?"

"Certainly." He marched down the beach and into the water.

Following close behind, Kassi said, *"You've given me my life back. I just wish there was some way to pay you back!"*

"No need," Hira said. *"But you can help me by helping the Gaians."*

"Of course!" Kassi promised.

"Let's dive!"

Kassi fastened her helmet, joined Hira in the water, and torpedoed toward Alice Town. Her new voice was so rich and full, she had no trouble lighting up the third and fourth bulbs on her sonopack. She could sing with sháloor once again. Exploring her new voice, Kassi sang siren incantations she hadn't performed in ages. The first one that came to mind, probably because of Hira's enhanced water, was the melody her mother sang every morning in front of the Fountain of Youth.

The Fountain of Youth towered from the center of the Royal Gardens of Palace Rivernova. It was the source of all DNA healing and reverse aging. On the rare occasion when Kassiana woke up early enough to witness it, she would come outside to watch her mother Vidara perform an Embarû Hîm, a siren rejuvenation song, into the Fountain. Her melodies were always so beautiful. Whenever Kassi listened in, she felt a calm come over her, along with a renewed sense of life spread through her entire body. It was like natural hot springs soothing every muscle while drinking the most refreshing, ice-cold melongo cream 'n soda, all while someone was softly rubbing the soles of her feet.

Looking back, Kassi wondered why she didn't visit the Fountain of Youth every morning. Oh right, because it was early in the morning, and back then, mornings were for sleeping. Now, Kassi would give anything to get up early just to hear her mother sing. En route to Alice Town, she performed her mother's incantation. As she did, she pictured her mother's powerful voice rippling through her mind, inspiring Kassi to sing it with sháloor.

FOUNTAIN OF YOUTH

Life might pass me by again
Time can happen so fast, when
Hours seem long but the years are soon gone
And you're left wondering where all the time went

With a Fountain of Youth we can be young forever
When the old becomes new we can make our own heaven
Sound out the truth to rejuvenate body and soul
For everyone
And we'll always be young

Maybe the good things don't have to end
Saving up all our tomorrows
Let's spend the day like it won't fade away

Like there's time in a safe we can borrow

With a Fountain of Youth we can be young forever

When the old becomes new we can make our own heaven
Sound out the truth to rejuvenate body and soul
For everyone
And we'll always be young

I never thought we would find the solution
What if we outlive the stars and the sun
Don't spend the time without loving someone
So we're not the only ones

IN EVÉIK

Lagi neblarosh év mwabé viat
Hûn kásh yonash agitat, máti
Vud nubri ôeróé, da mak píba bud li odunóat
I nohosách miharách tuv ubi píba amni li agitat

Ma'ferna budosh nios kin în jarna van înshûbé bizat
Máti gorûd li tamanáf nuvo hulish bizí édînek nemalé
    bizat
Mun fuigáb shi enbarûd tané i suléé li vîrûfat
Ma tajojang
I kudad méshû budách nios bizat

Fortas dai néz mit shi ikiré li agaþ shéanóat
Nak zînarách amni bizí zatrasotóat
Feníd kehevíd li tagé biz síl kuda néz poþ pítharíd famat
Síl ebi bud lev în zînáfé agit amprantish bizat

Ma'ferna budosh nios kin în jarna van înshûbé bizat
Máti gorûd li tamanáf nuvo hulish bizí édînek nemalé
    bizat
Mun fuigáb shi enbarûd tané i suléé li vîrûfat
Ma tajojang
I kudad méshû budách nios bizat

Nukwam pensala olis pata li ojutubé bizat
Té lô muvibíd li ástarûtóé i li solyaé bizat
Fortas bud agité shi dimar ashkách nezobé famat
Hûn bud néz li hanya zobé nayat

When the training pools zoomed into view, Hira waved a goodbye salute before steering northward. She bowed low before spinning and blasting toward the twenty-four illuminated AquaSphera waterfields. After a quick scan for an end gate in robin-egg blue, she spotted them in Sector 20.

They were in the middle of a heated contest with the Yellow Sharks. She cut the jets and glided next to Royce, the other sub on the sidelines. Casting her a sidelong glance, his eyes bulged briefly before shaking his head, clearly trying hard to suppress his shock. When Kassi extended her wrist to link audio with him, he pulled away, making her chase. But she was faster and held her wrist in place long enough to link with the team. Her helmet was instantly flooded with her teams' voices singing a Mendari Hîm, a siren domination song.

"Notice anything different about me?" Kassi asked Royce. He stared forward and sniffed. Kassi tossed up a dismissive hand and said, "Still the wettest blanket on the team!" She wasn't going to allow "his highness" to ruin her moment.

The holographic clock floating at the top of the arena indicated there were only a few minutes left in the first half. Everyone was fully engaged in the song, but they noticed Kassi on the sidelines and were pointing her way, waving and cheering. At halftime, they swarmed her with a flurry of questions.

"I thought you broke your leg?" Joshi said, examining her left calf as if trying to find the hidden cast beneath the wetsuit.

"I did. It's healed," Kassi kicked and twirled in the water.

"Healed? Already?" His eyes went as wide as U-Coins.

"That's right," Kassi said.

"And your voice!" Savriah exclaimed.

Kassi nodded. "I'm back, chas!" She said as she performed a fluid backflip.

"Woo-hoo!" Fille and Adonis both shouted. Savriah clapped enthusiastically, which was pointless since no one heard clapping underwater.

"Show us how it's done, Kassi!" Fille shouted. "You'll be center forward. Johnes, move back to center mid. Jacen, you're on the bench."

"You want the goalie to play striker?" Johnes looked confused.

"Just trust me," Fille said. Johnes nodded and took his new position.

Jacen scowled. "Why am I sitting out?"

"Because you're the softest, ripest piece of sheist, that's why!" Fille shouted, pointing right in his face.

The second half commenced and Kassi was ready. They started with the disc. She swam circles around the midfielders. Fille kicked a perfect arc through the center gate, and Kassi quickly beat everyone else to it. The sphere beamed a bright blue as Kassi sent a bullet pass forward to Simmone, their right forward. Once again, Kassi outpaced her opponents, lighting the third and fourth bulbs. Simmone kicked it back. It wasn't the cleanest pass, but Kassi still easily snatched it, catching the disc with her left foot. A defender sped to intercept. Kassi spun, pulling the disc away just in time, sending the defender sprawling. Popping up the disc and using her right hand thruster, she pushed off and performed a beautiful Macaco kick and rocketed the disc through the end gate between two very surprised Yellow Shark goalies.

It was only the first drive of the half, and Kassi had already scored the first two points of the game for her team, providing a much-needed equalizer. It was now 2-2.

"She lit, she lit the fourth bulb!" Adonis pointed at her sonopack. "Did you chas see it?"

The other Krakens stared in disbelief as Kassi's fourth bulb shined. The opposing team also paused for a moment of admiration.

Kassi soaked up the positive attention–something she'd had precious little of. *Is this how Amára feels every day?*

Feeling a swelling hope from her teammates at the prospect of winning their first game, Kassi maintained her momentum for the next few minutes until she missed a pass. It should have been an easy catch, but the disc slipped her grasp and landed in the hands of a Yellow Shark.

Kassi cursed as she burst toward the player to try and recover the disc. He passed it off quickly and they made their counter. Kassi weaved and blasted through players, trying to force a turnover. They managed to slip it through other Blue Krakens, clear the center, and take it downfield for a shot on goal. Still frustrated from the missed catch, Kassi lost control of her speed, plowed into Catelyn on defense, and caused an error that gave them an open goal. They shot and scored.

"Sorry," Kassi said as she kicked herself. She couldn't picture Amára missing passes or colliding into teammates.

On the next opportunity to score, Kassi took a shot that veered wide and went out of bounds. "Ugh, I can't hit the broad side of sheist!" Kassi wanted to tug at her hair, but couldn't with her helmet on.

"You're swimming faster than any 400 we've seen! Just focus and you'll get the next one," Fille said, trying to sound encouraging.

Kassi battled with herself for the rest of the game. She made a few interceptions and scored an additional goal, but it was far from enough for her team to win the game. They ended up losing 5-4 to the Yellow Sharks, one of the lower-ranking teams in their league.

"Sorry chas, that was my fault. We should've won," Kassi said, hanging her head. Even with her voice back, she still couldn't lead her team to victory against one of the easier teams in the league. Speed wouldn't be enough to lead her team to win the Games. It would take years of training to have any kind of real shot. Despair set in as she realized her chances of even qualifying for the Games were none.

"Kassi, you scored four points! That was more points than we've ever scored before!" Savriah said.

"And that's the longest I've ever seen anyone maintain the fourth bulb," Catelyn said with admiration.

"Yisû, I thought Vander and Vi'ella were the only ones around here who could do that," Joshi said. Many others on her team complimented her, trying their best to make her feel better. It was a nice sentiment, but Kassi knew she had let them all down.

As they headed back to the docks, Kassi replayed the game in her mind. Back on Nemal, she had always played better than that. Of course, that's also because she had Amára on her team, and her opponents were just playing for fun. AquaSphera matches on Nemal weren't nearly as competitive as they were on Earth. All the same, Kassi needed Amára. Amára always knew how to help Kassi shine on the waterfield.

Twenty

En route to the docks, flooded with frustration, Kassi pushed her tattered wetsuit to the limits. The rush of cool ocean water helped take Kassi's mind off the game. With an explosion of speed, she shot past Vander, Vi'ella, and their team just before jetting out of the water onto the docks.

The Red Squalls landed right behind her. Kassi heard Vander's voice shout, "Where'd those jets come from?"

"Huh?" Turning around, she saw a swarm of siren athletes approaching her, Vander and Vi'ella leading the charge. At first, she wondered if she had done something wrong.

"Since when could you light the fourth bulb?" Vander asked, his beautiful, emerald eyes locking with hers. Vi'ella stood beside him, a knowing smile on her face.

Kassi's heart fluttered off the beat before she answered. "Um...since I was ten?" Her teammates still hadn't arrived.

"You're pushing our waves!" Another 800 said—a boy Kassi didn't recognize. Kassi shrugged nervously, half expecting the usual ridicule she had grown accustomed to on Earth.

Vander studied her for a moment. "How fast do you swim the 5k?"

"Minute-eh two," Kassi said, shying away from his gaze. "Well, probably not in this wet...."

"Minute two?" Vander's eyes widened.

"I believe it," Vi'ella said.

"But that means she's faster than the province record," Vander said.

"Yisû, it does." Vi'ella gave a confident nod.

"You know something," Vander eyed Vi'ella suspiciously.

"I know something," Vi'ella said, her smile broadening.

The Blue Krakens finally emerged. Many of them rushed to Kassi, probably noticing the attention she was getting.

"Did you, did you see it?" Adonis asked. "She lit the fourth bulb. Had it lit for the entire second half of the game!"

"Huh," Vander stroked his chin, eyeing Kassi. Her cheeks flushed redder than an overripe toma-cherry. "Lighting the fourth is hard enough, but keeping it lit?" Vander raised his eyebrows. "That's a feat only champions attain. Impressive!"

"Thanks." Kassi kicked her feet. Speed was her one Nemalís advantage, but she still wasn't coordinated enough to win a low-level game. Of course, she didn't want to bring that up when she was getting showered with Vander's praise.

That's when Nikola, Malyra, DeSchuster, and the Black Hydras muscled over. "What's all this about?" When Malyra spotted Kassi at the center of it, she smirked. "What'd Klutziana do this time? Break another bone? I told her she isn't pretty enough to be this clumsy."

Kassi clenched her fists and took a step forward, itching to slap the smile off Malyra's face. Malyra flinched. Her eyes widened at seeing Kassi without crutches.

Vander placed a hand on Kassi's shoulder. "I've got an idea." He turned to Malyra. "I hear you currently hold the speed record in the Miami Province." The Miami Province covered over an 800 km radius and was one of the sixty-four provinces of Earth.

"You heard right," Malyra said, flashing the most despicable grin. Her hair had been pulled back into a small ponytail. She reached back and set it free, shaking her textured blonde hair down. Even with the ponytail kink, it still looked stylish, which was infuriating. "Why, you wanna race me?"

"But do you really deserve that record, that's what I'd like to know?" Vander ignored her question and continued, his eyes lighting up with the possibility of a race. "I mean, the fastest swimmers weren't even in that race."

"What do you mean fastest swimmers? They were there," Malyra crossed her arms, narrowing her eyes. "I defeated all those blowses!"

"And if someone were to challenge you...," Vi'ella said, folding her arms.

"If anyone dares challenge me, I'll race them any place, any time!"

"Well good, then I call a Race for Blues!" Vander shouted across the docks for all to hear. Sirens from all directions heard it and came running, cheering loudly in approval.

Malyra shifted slightly as if trying to hide her nerves. "It's your funeral." She raised her voice to address the gathering crowds, "Just don't go crying to me when you get pulsed out and lose your wetsuit to me."

"Oh you're not racing me," Vander said. "You're racing her," he pointed to Kassi.

The sudden shift of eyes on Kassi pushed her back a step. "What? Me?" She shook her head vigorously. "Oh no, no, that's a very bad idea. A very bad idea." Kassi had never been good under pressure.

"You can't be serious!" Malyra scoffed. "Klutziana? A four hundie with rags for a suit and croaks for a voice? She's not even worth the time!"

"Sounds like you're afraid," Vi'ella said, poking Malyra in the shoulder.

Malyra swatted her hand away. "Afraid of her? Don't make me laugh!" She looked down her nose at Kassi. "And besides, why would I ever race her for that ratty piece? It doesn't even have gills." Malyra's wetsuit was one of the best models U-Coins could buy. Sleek, well-designed, equipped with all the advanced features. Meanwhile, Kassi's was from pre-Evéik times.

"She's right, why would anyone want this suit?" Kassi fingered one of the more obvious stitched tears in her sleeves, drawing attention to it. She searched for anything to get her out of racing Malyra, even if that meant agreeing with a chinpoke.

"What about mine?" Vi'ella asked. Vi'ella's suit was even better than Malyra's, featuring numerous upgrades you could only earn from winning tournaments.

"No, Vi'ella. Please-eh, listen to me! This is a bad idea," Kassi said, doing her best to fight down her outer trembling. "Maybe you should be the one to race Malyra."

"It's gotta be you, Kassi. I can tell you two have some history," Vi'ella said. "Besides, you can't just sit back and let her push you around like that."

"You'd really put your pride and joy on the line for Klutziana?" Malyra sneered. Kassi wondered the same thing. Why would Vi'ella risk her suit for Kassi?

"You're gonna stop calling her that." Vi'ella poked her shoulder again.

Malyra flinched at the threat, taking a step back. Her eyes swept over the sea of faces surrounding them as she ran a hand through her blonde hair, tucking it behind her left ear.

Vander seized the moment to rally the crowd. "What do you say, chas? Race for Blues?" The crowd erupted into raucous applause and began chanting, "Race for Blues! Race for Blues!"

Malyra shrugged with a subtle nod to Vi'ella, "It's your loss!" The cheers grew louder. "Maybe you should let her race in your suit–give her a fighting chance."

"No, we adhere to the rules," Vander interjected.

"And besides, she doesn't need it," Vi'ella said.

"I'll be expecting that suit when I return," Malyra said to Vi'ella.

"You gotta earn it first," Vi'ella said.

As much as she wanted to finally yank Malyra off her high cloud, Kassi wasn't ready—not for this. If she lost, Vi'ella would give up her prized wetsuit. Vander and the Squalls would never regard her the same, and she would never live down the embarrassment of losing to the queen of the Chinpoke Squad.

"Alright, chas, link frequencies and go shave the bed!" Vander cupped his hands and shouted. The way he said it reminded her of Caesar. It was something he always said.

Everyone latched their helmets and dove back into the water to swim to the finish line. Nikola and Vander volunteered to remain behind to officiate a clean start to the race.

"Finish line is the first boundary of Sector 1," Vander explained as he and Nikola took their positions on the edge of the docks. "First place wins the other's wetsuit. No fighting or attacking your opponent. We'll give 'em five to reach the finish in time." Vander checked his watch before noticing Kassi's oxygen tank. "Do you need to refill that?"

"What?" She followed his gaze to her sonopack. "Oh yisû, I almost forgot. It's empty." Malyra rolled her eyes and sighed as if she couldn't believe she let herself get talked into this. Kassi ran to the oxygen kiosk and refilled her tank. If only she could keep running, far away from here, but there was no way out of this now. With a full O2 tank, she returned to the diving platform.

Kassi's hands were clenched together, wringing each other tightly. Her mind raced to find the right incantation—nothing. Vander turned to her, possibly detecting her uneasiness. "Before every match, I say to myself, 'singing small doesn't serve the worlds'. I feel it always helps me channel my focus on the challenge directly in front of me."

Kassi thought about this. *Singing small doesn't serve the worlds.* As she did, a Haraki Hîm, a siren acceleration song, popped into her head.

"Good luck, Kassi!" Vander faced the others and shouted, "On your marks!"

"I'll call it," Nikola said, eyeing Vander suspiciously. He had pulled his dark brown, wavy hair back into a man bun. "On three!" Kassi inhaled a deep breath as they lined up to dive. "One, two...THREE!"

Kassi dove and launched into an incantation in fluent Evéik, immediately causing cavitation in four of the five bulbs on her sonopack. She and Malyra blasted off.

Malyra took the early lead with Kassi close behind. Kassi was hoping to catch Malyra's tailwind and decrease the drag caused by her suit's patches and tears. She couldn't help admiring Malyra's wetsuit. It was streamlined and hydrodynamic, with flawless hydrophobic material for zero resistance against the water–superior in every way to Kassi's clunky rental. But Malyra only used her foot thrusters, so Kassi hoped her hand thrusters would be enough to give her the edge. It was a lot to overcome, and the race would take over ten minutes. She tried to focus, but the image of Vi'ella relinquishing her suit over to Malyra plagued her mind.

Calm, she reminded herself, pushing those images to the back of her mind.

Kassi needed a strategy. If she could remain in Malyra's blindspot for the first leg of the race, she could catch her by surprise, enter her tailwind, and propel herself to the finish line ahead of her. She focused all her energy on staying close, directly behind Malyra.

Malyra gained speed and an air pocket formed behind her– the tailwind. Just behind it was an air pocket collapse. If Kassi timed her entry incorrectly, or if Malyra saw her coming and shifted at the last second, Kassi could get caught in the collapse and get pulsed out. If that happened, the race would be over. Kassi would spin out and Malyra would forever rub it in her face. Precision timing was crucial for this strategy to work.

Malyra's suit effortlessly carved through the water. Kassi felt the drag pull against hers, forcing her to exert more energy. It wasn't enough. Malyra gradually pulled away. Increasing her output, she tried her best to sing with sháloor and keep the fourth bulb lit. It kept her in the race for the moment, but she knew she would need to do more.

Even though she could normally sing this incantation in her sleep, she found herself forgetting some of the words. Her confidence waned. The disappointed faces of her friends popped into her mind again and again–the look of regret on Vi'ella's face at losing her prized suit, or Vander's face when he realized he was wrong about her. Finally, she was in a position to impress him, and here she was, about to fail miserably in front of everyone. The fourth bulb sputtered. Kassi felt her palm thrusters giving out. Without her hand propulsion, she didn't stand a chance.

Find your calm!

If anyone deserved to lose a crushing defeat, it was Malyra. Kassi had to readjust. Rather than finish her Haraki Hîm, she switched to a different incantation. The break between songs slowed Kassi, giving Malyra a wider lead. Kassi had a lot of ocean to make up. The new incantation breathed life into her sonopack, illuminating the third and fourth bulbs.

Kassi closed the distance, gaining on Malyra and feeling the momentum turn in her favor for the first time in the race. Maybe this once, Kassi could win on her own–without Amára. They were more than halfway through as Kassi torpedoed forward, gliding up next to Malyra. Malyra's face soured at the sight of Kassi. She probably assumed the race had already been won.

Kassi pulled ahead and took the lead. *Maybe I don't need to ride her tailwind,* she thought. Malyra pulled behind Kassi out of eyesight. Kassi bellowed her incantation, her body straight as an arrow, and propelled forward with all thrusters on full blast.

Almost there!

They reached the final stretch. In her peripheral, Kassi spotted Malyra gaining on her. The finish line closed in. Kassi sang with sháloor and pushed all four thrusters to the max. With only seconds to go, Malyra sliced through the water, blasted her foot thrusters, and passed Kassi.

As she passed, Kassi caught sight of the air pocket behind Malyra. She still had a chance to catch her tailwind and slingshot past her. It was now or never.

With a final burst of energy, Kassi gunned it and made her move. Malyra noticed and swerved away from Kassi, forcing Kassi to miss.

Sheist!

Kassi brutally collided with Malyra's air pocket collapse and was pummeled sideways as if struck by a gargantic watery fist.

With a loud grunt, Kassi took the blow and spun out. She glanced up just in time to see Malyra cross the finish line, winning the race. Suspended in the water, Kassi floated motionless and watched the crowds cheer while her friends and teammates hung their heads.

Her life was over.

Twenty-One

Kassi had given her all.

It wasn't enough.

She couldn't face any of them now.

As she floated a short distance from the finish line, Kassi turned away, wishing she could disappear. She needed Amára. Amára would've swam circles around Malyra. That would've shifted the focus off Kassi and onto Malyra's miserable, embarrassing failure.

"Kassi, you with us?" Fille was the first to reach out. Adonis and Savriah drifted next to him.

Her eyes felt puffy, her cheeks wet. She must have been crying. Quickly blinking back the tears, she said, "Yisû," still hiding her face.

"That was actually a much closer race than anyone was expecting," Savriah said.

Mirific, everyone expected me to fail even worse than I did.

"Sheist happens," Fille said. "Especially to us."

"That's why I zhust wanted this one time-eh…," Kassi turned and searched the crowd for Vi'ella.

"Let's flake off back to the docks," Fille said with a flick of his chin.

They powered up their suits and swam back, singing their incantations. It was a long fifteen minutes of shame before they reached the landing platforms. They removed their helmets and took a seat to wait for everyone else. Kassi wanted to leave, but she needed to apologize to Vi'ella for losing her suit.

Soon enough, the others surfaced and gathered on the docks. Malyra was more obnoxious than ever. "Easiest win ever!" she said. "I didn't even have to try."

"She almost got you at the end," Vi'ella said, folding her arms.

"What are you blind? She wasn't even close!" Malyra whipped her hand out. "Now, hand it over!"

Vi'ella looked like she wanted to say something, but held back. She walked to a nearby locker, removed her wetsuit, and threw on a casual outfit before returning, her wetsuit in hand. "Take it. Even if you did get lucky."

"Don't be a sore loser," Malyra scoffed, snatching the suit.

Vi'ella shook her head, clearly done for the night.

Vander exited the water alongside Nikola, both huffing for air. Nikola seemed pleased with himself. Vander was ruffled. Kassi had never seen him lose his composure. He was always so calm and collected. Was he that upset about Kassi losing? The expression on Nikola's face hinted at something else going on. Vander stormed into the washrooms, avoiding everyone in the process. Kassi looked at her friends who all witnessed it with raised eyebrows.

Vi'ella was about to leave when Kassi caught up to her. "I'm sorry, Vi'ella. I really stuffed it." Vi'ella paused, silent for a beat. Kassi continued, "For a moment, I thought I had her, but I zhust timed it wrong, and…"

"Listen, it's not your fault," Vi'ella said. "We put this on you. You said it was a bad idea. I was the one that didn't listen. I just hate bullies," she shook her head and scowled in Malyra's direction.

Kassi lowered her eyes. "What about your suit?"

"Don't worry about it. I'll check out a rental until you win mine back for me." Vi'ella said, the corners of her mouth hinting at a smile.

"Win it back?" Kassi popped her head up and eyed Vi'ella curiously.

"You'll get her next time." Vi'ella patted Kassi's shoulder and walked away.

Kassi wasn't so sure. The crowds gathered where Malyra was still incessantly gloating. It was nauseating. Kassi knew she would never hear the end of it.

After changing their clothes, Kassi and her friends loaded into the boat. They had the dinghy until Principal Purves saw her without crutches, which wouldn't be until Monday, so they decided to make the most of it. Fille took them on a detour, speeding through the streets until they reached the open ocean.

A sticky wind flapped Kassi's braided hair, the boat jumped the waves, and they watched the sunset paint the sky the color of newly-forged bronze. By the time Fille stalled the engine and set them adrift, they could barely see the coastline. A passing U.N.O.E. patrol yacht slowed as Kassi and her friends all felt strange eyes scrutinizing them for a few awkward beats. To everyone's relief, the U.N.O.E. watercraft sped up and left them alone for the moment.

"We need a coach," Fille said once they were alone, leaning on the driver's seat from the side so he could see everyone.

"We've always, we've always needed one," Adonis said, kneeling backward on the front seat to face the others.

"Kassi needs one. She's got real potential," Fille said.

"Chas, I appreciate the idea, but it really won't make a differ-ence-eh," Kassi said.

"Fille's right," Savriah agreed. "We need to talk to Sensei on Monday about getting a coach."

"Isn't it too late? We've lost so many games already," Kassi said.

"We haven't lost too many," Fille said. "We can still make the

Final 16 tournament." At the end of the season in May, the top 16 teams in the league enter a championship tournament to determine the Miami League title winner.

"If we, if we could get one, that would be bosst!" Adonis said. "We'd actually have a chance of becoming champions! Or at least start winning games."

"We'll ask Sensei on Monday," Fille insisted with a nod. Kassi shook her head and was about to voice her objections. Fille cut her off, "You need to trust us, Kassi. I've never seen anyone light up four bulbs as long as you. Your speed is ludicray!" He reignited the engine and shouted, "You just need a little direction from a good coach."

With a coach, they would get their hopes up, and she would just let them down all over again. She wished they would reconsider, but Fille seemed determined. They reached the townhouse. No longer needing help, Kassi hopped off the dingy and said, "Ride the tide."

"Tide!" they said as Fille gunned it.

Inside, Kyoto and Meela waited for her at the dinner table, as usual. Kassi took a seat and started eating as if nothing were different. Kyoto's voice startled her when he lifted his head and said, "We know you saw a healer from Nemal today." His expressions were inscrutable as always.

"How?" Kassi asked, her mouth full of sticky rice.

"We always know where you are." He lit a fumer and puffed before continuing.

"Tracker in your siren suit," Meela said.

Kyoto cast Meela a disapproving look.

Kassi leaned forward. "Did I do anything illegal?"

"We thought you should know in case you're planning on escaping," Kyoto said, pointing a flexed finger. "And we're not the only ones who know."

"I wasn't trying to escape-eh!" Kassi pressed both hands on the table.

In response, Kyoto popped a fumer in his mouth as he

collected his holopad, stood, and retired upstairs to his bedroom. Meela got up to follow him.

Monday morning came too soon. Principal Purves waited for them on the steps, hand outstretched until Fille handed over the keys to the dinghy. Kassi expected videos of her defeat to be circulating before she found a seat in Period 1. She was right. Malyra hadn't wasted any time. Students giggled incessantly, mocking Kassi and reenacting the pulse out as they pointed and laughed in her direction. It didn't end with Period 1. It was as if the entire grade had nothing else swimming around in their brains.

"Don't these chas have anything else-eh to smack their lips at?" Kassi grumbled when she saw her friends in line in the cafeteria.

"They never do," Savriah said, shaking her head.

"Sick, sadistic sheists!" Fille shouted, kicking the air in their direction.

"Let's zhust flake off to Sensei's class." Kassi sighed.

Adonis said, "We outie, we outie like a…"

"No. Just no," Fille said, cutting him off.

Passing a singing trio of 600s and dodging five 700s rehearsing a new dance move, they walked toward the counter to grab their food when DeSchuster blindsided Kassi, hammering her to the ground and shouting, "Pulsed!" Her head hit the floor hard. DeSchuster flexed both arms to the raucous applause of the students in the cafeteria.

"DeSchuster, just because your parents met at a family reunion doesn't mean you gotta take it out on everyone else," Fille shouted at him.

"What'd you say to me, Four Hundie?" DeSchuster got in Fille's face.

"You're probably too dumb to understand the insult." Fille didn't back down. He flicked DeSchuster's forehead and said, "Your elevator doesn't reach the top floor." Even though they were close to the same height, DeSchuster had at least ten kilos on Fille in pure muscle mass.

Kassi slowly got back up to her feet, shaken. DeSchuster had his back to her, his focus on Fille. His ridiculous burst fade hair looked like a bleached-blonde ferret on his head. Something came over Kassi. Without thinking, she kicked DeSchuster as hard as she could from behind, right between the legs. DeSchuster grunted in pain, doubled over, and went down.

"Oh sheist!" Adonis whipped a hand up to his mouth. He tugged them toward the exit and said, "Let's flake off, let's flake off before we get in trouble."

They bolted.

Kassi and the others slid inside the elevator. It slowly swallowed them up and ascended. The stairs might have been a better option for a quick getaway.

Once they caught their breath, Savriah said, "I can't believe you did that."

"Me neither." Kassi shook with adrenaline.

Reaching Sensei's room, Fille checked the hallways to see if anyone was in pursuit. It was empty.

"What'd you do this time?" Sensei eyed Fille from his desk.

"Nothing," Fille said, leaning against the door frame with forced casual ease, casting glances down the corridor.

"Uh-huh." Sensei held Fille's gaze as if patiently waiting for the real answer.

Fille squirmed. "He started it! He smashed into Kassi. Knocked her down in the middle of the cafeteria."

"Out of nowhere," Savriah said.

"Who?"

"DeSchuster!" Fille said.

"800s, 800s never get punished for anything," Adonis said.

"So what'd you do about it?" Sensei asked.

"I kicked him," Kassi said.

"Right between the legs," Savriah added.

"He went, he went down like falling timber," Adonis said, bringing one arm crashing down for effect.

"It was bosst!" Fille said.

The drumming of fast footsteps from down the hallway grew near. DeSchuster shoved Fille out of the way and pointed at Kassi, murder in his eyes. Sensei was quick to his feet, jumping up to intervene.

"Watch yourself, DeSchuster! Remember how quickly I could get you expelled from this school," Sensei said.

"But she kicked me right in my...my jingle bells!" DeSchuster said, huffing.

"From the sound of it, you only got what you deserved," Sensei fired back. "You know what you did."

DeSchuster was probably the biggest student in school, a body full of bulging muscles, but as he cowered in the hulking shadow of Professor Kelipalo, he looked tiny. Like someone could just pluck him up with a pair of chopsticks and stuff him in their pocket.

"But...she kicked me!" He repeated, clearly unable to think of anything else to say.

"Lay a hand on her again, and I'll see to it you're relocated," Sensei stepped forward, his fists clenched. DeSchuster took the hint and scurried away like a frightened puffrabbit.

Once he left, Kassi leaned back in her seat. "Thanks, Sensei!" Sensei nodded and took a seat at his desk.

Once they were gone, Savriah asked, "Could you really get an 800 expelled?"

"I think I could, but it wouldn't be easy," Sensei said. "It would take some convincing and trading of favors, which I wouldn't be too excited about."

"Like what? What kind of favors?" Adonis asked.

"Everyone wants their kid on the next winning team," Sensei said.

"Even if their kid is the worst?" Fille asked.

"Especially if their kid is the worst," Sensei said.

After a beat, Fille asked, "Sensei?"

"Hm-mm?"

"We need a coach!" Fille broached the subject.

"That's really not necessary," Kassi said, shaking her head.

"Fille, we've been through this," Sensei said. "The coaches I work with aren't allowed to manage any teams with a losing record. On top of that, the PAC really pushes back any time they apply to manage a team with no 800s."

"PAC?" Kassi asked.

"Provincial AquaSphera Committee," Savriah said.

"But Kassi got her voice back and can really turn on the jets," Adonis said. "She lit, she lit the fourth bulb and kept it for the entire second half of our game."

"She's got some real potential," Fille added. "I think one of those coaches could really help us get there."

"I'm glad to see Hira helped," Sensei said to Kassi.

"He did," Kassi said. "Thank you so much for arranging it!" Kassi couldn't believe she had forgotten to thank him sooner.

"All the coaches I know are already with other teams this season," Sensei said.

"Isn't there something you can do?" Fille asked, a hint of desperation in his voice.

Sensei studied each of them, Kassi in particular. "I might know one. I'll see if I can call in a favor."

Fille clapped his hands in excitement. He and Adonis both shouted, "Sensei K is bosst!"

At AquaSphera that afternoon, Kassi took the striker position once again, hoping to improve her control and accuracy. She agreed to trade off with Joshi on goal at halftime. They played against the Maroon Minnows, a team of 500s who were tied with the Blue Krakens for last in the league and the only other team without a single win.

"Alright bubbleheads, let's sing it today. We gotta win this one!" Fille shouted.

Kassi went through a series of mental exercises to find her

inner calm. *Singing small doesn't serve the worlds.* Vander's words resonated in her mind.

At the start of the game, Kassi sped past the defense for an incredible catch and easy shot on goal, scoring their first two points. 2-0. She felt like she was getting her rhythm until she missed a crucial pass that turned the disc over. The Maroon Minnows counter-attacked with a shot on goal, but fortunately, Quade made the stop.

Kassi found herself getting more and more frustrated as the first half progressed. She continually misfired her shots and dropped her passes. By halftime, they were still 2-0. Kassi switched to goalie for the second half.

The rest of the contest was scoreless. Kassi blocked a lot of shots, but the Kraken offense failed to put any additional points on the board. By the end of the game, they barely won, 2-0, with Kassi's early goal the only score of the game. The team was elated with their first victory, congratulating Kassi for her game-winning goal, but Kassi had a hard time seeing their win as a real victory.

We barely won against the yashing Minnows!

Kassi kicked herself all the way back to the docks. With a healthy voice, she played much better, but not nearly good enough. She replayed all her missed shots, dropped passes, and turnovers again and again. By the time they surfaced, she was ready to shred her wettie and call it quits.

Savriah sensed Kassi's darkened mood. "You played good, Kassi. And just imagine how much better you'll get with a coach!" Kassi didn't share in her optimism.

The next day, people were still chatting about Kassi's humiliating Race for Blues fiasco. Savriah said she heard a few 600s in the halls talking about how close the race was, but everyone else seemed to focus on Kassi getting pulsed. She tried her best to ignore them and focus on her class assignments. At least those were easy enough. As long as she painted the U.N.O.E. in a positive light, she scored well on her tests and worksheets. Everything else was basic–it didn't require too much time or effort to keep up.

In the halls, she kept a watchful eye for anyone else looking to blindside her. DeSchuster left her alone, likely heeding Sensei's warning.

During lunch, they arrived at Sensei's classroom, but he wasn't there. The room was empty. A plate of extra food sat on his desk.

Fille snatched the rations. "I'm sure he'll be back."

Kassi needed to recharge, so she put on her hologlasses and watched her family's video message again. She jumped when she heard Adonis' voice directly behind her.

"Whatcha watching, whatcha watching?" He snagged her glasses and put them on. "Why you watching a video of the savrîn and bôri of Paradise?"

"What? Oh, this?" Kassi retrieved her hologlasses from his hands and put them away. "It's zhust a video messazhe from my family. Some cha at the Siren Games slipped it into my pocket when I wasn't looking."

"Your family?" Savriah asked.

"Yisû." Kassi wondered why they gawked at her with such wide eyes.

"You're a, you're a Rivernova?" Adonis shouted as his jaw dropped. Savriah stared right through Kassi as if completely dumbfounded. Fille put down his own hologlasses and joined them.

"Didn't I already tell you chas that?" Kassi asked.

"No! You never, you never told us!" Adonis stood, turning to Fille. "Did you know?"

"I thought you said your parents were in the Nemalís Guard!" Fille rose to his feet next to Adonis.

"What? I never said that." Everyone was up on their feet, stepping back from Kassi. Her eyes bounced between each of their faces. "Chas, I'm still zhust Kassi."

"Your family rules the Paradise Planets," Savriah said.

"Savvy, whisper!" Fille said, tilting his head in the direction of the camera.

"I am whispering," she almost shouted.

"The U.N.O.E. already knows," Kassi said with a shrug.

Sensei returned to the classroom. "Good news, chas!"

"Sensei, did you know Kassi's a Rivernova?" Fille pointed. "As in daughter of Vidara and Leontari, savrîn and bôri?"

"Is that right?" Sensei studied her. "Huh, you do look just like your mother. I don't know why I didn't connect that before."

"Yisû, I get that a lot," Kassi said, twirling her long hair into a high bun to get the heat off her neck.

"I met your oldest brother, Kairos, when he was just a baby," Sensei related. "He was their only child at the time when I left, so I never met their other kids."

"That was a long time ago. He's almost thirty-five-eh, now!" Kassi said.

"How many are in your family, now?" Sensei asked.

"There are six of us," Kassi said before changing the subject. "By the way chas, I've been thinking about our songs. I have some ideas that'll showcase the strength of our voices better. Would anyone mind if I work on new arrangements?"

Fille and Adonis studied Kassi. She wasn't sure if they were still stuck on her being a Rivernova, or if they were mulling over her question.

"That's a great idea, Kassi," Sensei interjected. "Especially considering my good news."

"So what's, so what's the good news?" Adonis asked. Kassi joined them on their feet, tired of craning her neck to see everyone.

"I figured out a way to help train you," Sensei smiled his usual broad smile. "I spoke with a good friend of mine–Coach Rockson."

"Coach Rockson! THE Coach Rockson?" Adonis asked, wildly running hands through his hair.

"I've helped many of his teams, including this season's Team

Miami," Sensei said. "After the team's training yesterday afternoon, we chatted about your situation."

Kassi knew of Coach Rockson. He held the record for coaching the most Siren Games winners. Back on Nemal, they often cheered for his champions. The thought of working with him engulfed her with both anxiety and excitement. As much as she appreciated the opportunity to work with a worlds famous coach like Rockson, she wondered how everyone would react when they realized Kassi still wasn't good enough.

"He agreed to coach us?" Fille shouted.

"To train you, yisû. He agreed as long as I'm there with him to help out," Sensei said. "Just the four of you, for an hour or two after your matches."

"That's so bosst!" Adonis, Fille, and Savriah danced around the room. They roped in Kassi and she reluctantly joined in. The bell rang, cutting their celebration short.

As her friends dashed for the hallway, Adonis turned and asked, "So when do we, so when do we start?"

"This evening, right after the rest of your team leaves for the docks," Sensei said.

During the next two class periods, Kassi caught her three friends shooting her curious glances. She didn't see the big deal about being a Rivernova. Even though her parents ruled Paradise, everyone on Nemal shared everything, so it didn't really make that big of a difference. They all had palaces and everything they could want. If anything, being a Rivernova only meant having more duties and responsibilities to serve the people of Paradise.

When the final bell rang, they rushed to the docks and blasted to their sector. All of Kassi's friends were bursting with excitement at the prospect of their upcoming training, they played a much better game than usual. It was still a close game, but they pulled off the victory against a team of 500s, 3-2. Kassi scored the goal, but it was Fille's ricochet point that put them over the top. Despite her disappointment in herself, once again, she was happy for Fille. He was elated to score the winning point.

"What got into you chas today? Ya'll seem amped!" Joshi said with raised eyebrows as the rest of the team and most sectors cleared out.

"Power it down, Joshi! We're just feelin' the momentum from our last win," Fille lied. "Go head back—we gotta school assignment to work on."

With the rest of the Krakens gone, they swam to the U.N.O.E. cutters floating on the surface to refill their oxygen tanks and change frequencies.

Once back in the water, they scanned the area and noticed three people floating on the far end of their sector. They swam in their direction. As they drew near, Kassi recognized him. Next to Sensei was the same Coach Rockson she had seen on the holo-screens. He was really there and he was even bigger in person. His bulging muscles stretched the threads of his sleek, yellow, and black wetsuit with a red collar. His flawless caramel-brown skin accented his bright white smile, and there was a light behind his eyes just like Sensei Kelipalo. Sensei and Coach were close in size. A younger version of Coach Rockson floated next to him, with a gray collar. Kassi assumed it was his son. While his dad was bald, his son sported a tight, burst-fade mohawk.

They waved their arms over Fille's wrist and linked audio. Sensei spoke first, "Chas, allow me to introduce you to my good friend, Coach Rockson, and his son Kiowa."

Coach Rockson bowed and said, "We came a little early to catch some of your match."

"You saw my ricochet?" Fille said, excited.

"We missed it. It was already 3-0 when we got here," Coach said.

"I can't believe-eh you're really here to train us," Kassi said. "My family and I always cheered for your champions."

"Thank you. You must be Kassiana Rivernova. I've heard a lot about you." Coach Rockson extended a bow underwater. "I can't begin to imagine what you're going through. Being ripped from your family, your life, like that."

"Thank you," Kassi said softly.

"Is there anything we can do to help?" Coach asked.

"Not really," Kassi said with a shake of her head. "The U.N.O.E.'s involved."

"There is something we can do," Sensei said with a nod. "Help you chas win the Siren Games. If not this season, then the next. Now that your voice is healed, I can finally do something."

"We can do something–that's why we're here," Coach Rockson nodded. "I'm already managing Team Miami this season–with Sensei's help–so our time is limited. But we can train you for an hour or two in the evenings until our time commitment with them frees up. My son, Kiowa, will assist." He threw a hand on his son's shoulder. "He's only 14 now, so next year's his year to win it."

"That's the truth," Kiowa clapped silently. "You chas ready for a transformation?"

"We're ready to sing it," Fille said. Kassi and the others nodded.

"Good! I expect great things. In this training, I expect you to become the best version of you. But that's something you can't do until you know who YOU are. That usually requires stumbling down a road of mistakes and acceptance until you discover the most natural, original person inside." Coach smiled a big, bright smile as he spoke with infectious enthusiasm. "Once you find that, you've got your foundation."

"And that's when we build you up!" Kiowa added, matching his dad's passion.

"That's the truth!" Coach patted his son's shoulder. "Each practice, Kiowa here will help you with your dancing while Sensei and I focus on your vocals and team play. We're gonna hit it hard on all fronts and turn you into champions. So go out there and give me everything in the tank!"

They started with vocals. Sensei and Coach took turns

teaching them new exercises. Sensei said, "Set up your high notes with an early consonant. This means knowing the language well enough to write in these changes. Go into it early and don't be afraid to build up some energy before hitting it."

Coach followed it with, "And don't sing the high note like it's the destination. You're passing through it. The less fuss you make of it, the better." Kassi had always stressed over her high notes. Their approach made sense.

Kassi and her friends were all a little self-conscious at first. They didn't want to embarrass themselves in front of their new coaches. Coach and Sensei were quick to praise their efforts, offer encouragement, and make them feel more comfortable. They gave them constructive feedback and helped them over-come their fear.

After vocal exercises, they jumped into dancing. Kiowa took lead on this. "I'mma teach you underwater ballet."

"Ballet?" Fille cocked his head to the side. "What does that have to do with AquaSphera?"

"Ballet provides athletes with fundamentals you can't get anywhere else. Flexibility, body awareness, controlled move-ment. You'd be surprised!"

They rehearsed positions and routines over and over, building up muscle memory. Kassi had done many before, but she was far from mastering them. He spent extra time with her on moves that involved hand thrusters. "Always use your hand thrusters, Kassi. Those are key for controlling your flow of motion," Kiowa said.

Lastly, they worked on their team play. "You gotta read the danger on the field just as much as spot the opportunities," Coach said. They ran some drills and worked on their waterfield awareness. When Kassi missed some passes, she cursed under her breath and kicked herself. Her frustration grew, causing her to commit more mistakes–just like in her previous matches.

At the end of practice, they rounded everyone up and gave them their final notes. To Kassi, Coach said, "Mistakes happen to the best of us. We all do it. But champions bounce back quickly. After the game's over, review your mistakes and learn from them. But in the moment, kick that sheist off the waterfield and get back in the game. And never, ever beat yourself up because of it."

"But what if I can't bounce back quickly?" Kassi asked.

"If you have to, close your eyes and take a moment," he said.

At the docks, they thanked their new coaches and said their goodbyes. Without their dinghy, they were back to walking. Adonis bounced on his feet and said, "You patas feeling it? You feeling it? It's like the air is electric! We're finally doin' it!"

"We're becoming champions," Savriah said.

"It's no longer just a far-fetched dream," Fille said in agreement. Kassi remained quiet. As nice as it was to see her friends have hope for once, Kassi had her doubts.

They said goodbye, "Ride the tide!"

"Tide!"

Once alone, Kassi tuned out the quiet bustle of evening foot traffic. Even with the best coaches, could they really improve enough to make it to the Final 16 this season? If not, would they have the stamina to continue pushing for another six months and try for next season? They had players on their team who didn't even want to play. Although, Sensei did say something about recruiting players to the team. Kassi really wanted to recruit a specific player to their team. The thought made her blush as she entered the townhome.

Kyoto and Meela sat quietly at the kitchen table. "Yer home late," Meela said.

"We added new practices to help our team," Kassi explained. "They're after the games, so I won't be home until around 1900 from now on."

"Arrighty, then," Meela said. Kyoto didn't look up, but at least he didn't object.

Each day that week, her friends couldn't wait to hit the water. Kassi enjoyed her training with Coach Rockson, even though she still didn't believe it would make the difference they were hoping for. After each training session, Coach and Sensei asked Kassi more about her past, her relationships with her family, with Amára. They grilled her as if trying to unlock secrets. Kassi answered all their questions but didn't really see the benefit of it.

They spent every free moment during their classes going through the mental exercises their new coaches assigned them. Some from Sensei, some from Coach Rockson, and even a few from Kiowa. "If you can't envision yourself doing it the right way beforehand, you won't when it matters," Coach had told them.

During their individual notes, Coach told Kassi, "You've got great speed and good instincts, but you're hesitating–second-guessing yourself. You gotta learn to let go and trust those instincts." Kassi tried implementing their advice. She spent all day and night practicing what Coach had given her. During their afternoon matches, she actually started to see results. When she dropped a pass or kicked a wild shot, she got frustrated. However, instead of reacting, she paused to find her calm. It allowed her to bounce back and lead her team to score more points.

On Friday afternoon, they played a mid-ranked team of 600s and actually won! It was a close contest against the Silver Hammerheads. It was only their third win of the season, but it was at least enough to shift momentum.

"That's it, chas. You're doing it!" Sensei, Coach, and Kiowa applauded their victory.

After their next practice, Coach pulled Kassi aside, "Kassi, you're starting to silence that fear that's been holding you back. Your next step is to realize your potential as a supernova siren."

"What? There's no way I..." Kassi began to object.

"Listen, you told me how back home, you were only better because of Amára or Caesar. You've been living in their shadow," Coach Rockson said. "You borrowed their light because you thought you needed it. But trust me when I say this. Kassi, you don't! You've got more than enough right here," he said as he pointed to her voice. "If you believe it, you'll find a reason to shine bright enough to light that fifth bulb!"

Kassi forced a nod, still doubtful. She thought about it all the next day during their Saturday morning cleaning. Instead of lollybagging the day away, the four of them reviewed Coach's notes, AquaSphera strategies, and techniques. It was during this when Kassi finally decided to show them her new incantations and arrangements. She had written a few new songs and revamped all their old ones–some with new choruses, others with added intros or outros, and all of them with newly restructured lyrics. With their hologlasses on, she forwarded them the files.

"I think this'll help you sing with sháloor," she said, anxious to see if they liked her changes.

They took some time to listen through them. After the third song, Fille asked, "When did you have time to do all this?"

"I've been working on these ever since I got here-eh," Kassi said.

"Since you, since you got here?" Adonis asked.

"I was worried no one would like-eh them," Kassi shrugged.

"Kassi, these are bosst!" Fille said. Savriah and Adonis nodded in agreement.

"So how, so how do we sing with sháloor?" Adonis asked.

"You gotta get lost in the words and melodies. Clear your mind, dig deep, and believe every word you sing," Kassi said.

During the match that Saturday afternoon, Kassi saw the field more clearly, felt the rhythm, and fell right into the pocket. They played against the Teal Fins, a team of 600s, and opened with one of Kassi's new songs after they had rehearsed it with the team earlier that day in training.

"Singing small doesn't serve-eh the worlds," Kassi said to her friends, using Vander's words. "To become-eh champions, we need to sing it with sháloor." Fille, Adonis, and Savriah nodded. Their other teammates seemed confused.

"Just follow our lead," Fille told them before pointing at Adonis. "Kick us off, Donis!"

Adonis sounded off a four count.

CHAMPION OF MY DREAMS

How many times must I fall down before I get this
Only the voice inside will take me to the finish
How much abuse must I ignore before I break free
Why does it take so long to win the smallest victory

I will rise from the lowest lows
I'll take what you've never given me
Yeah I feel it within my bones
I'll be the champion of my dreams

How many strings must I unwind to be untangled
Been in their web of lies for far too long to handle
How much arrest can I allow before I realize
Even the least of us deserve a chance at Paradise

I will rise from the lowest lows
I'll take what you've never given me
yeah I feel it within my bones
I'll be the champion of my dreams

Life in the deep, the trench - it's all I've ever known
I'm gonna leave it all - go as far as I can go

I will rise from the lowest lows
I'll take what you've never given me
yeah I feel it within my bones
I'll be the champion of my dreams

Champion of my dreams

Champion
Champion of my dreams
Champion

IN EVÉIK

Kwam dua agitó fichi káthosh naya dávor prapíd ramé
    nayat
Lénûfa shi li þoji hanyaþi li zish levoat
Kwam nui lamosh kuzuné naya dávor harijíd vuraj nayat

Dag dai lénû famé hûn nubrif shi ris li petilu nasaraat

Arugafa dari li yostiklu yostikáfó
Lénûfa té mita nukwam yiva mwaé tuvat
Nam, rasa famé kilev nayalí sumukó nayat
Budafa li juarabé van nayalí sînyotóat

Kwam dua varzó shi budíd bervarîm kiramoshîm nayat
Budala ma dur gam nubrin lev jukí zuwané van zánitó-
    jang shi yantir
Kwam nui lofûsh gréfaré naya dávor sedaríd nayat
Varim în mokaé par Shargojang li mînim van bizat

Arugafa dari li yostiklu yostikáfó
Lénûfa té mita nukwam yiva mwaé tuvat
Nam, rasa famé kilev nayalí sumukó nayat
Budafa li juarabé van nayalí sînyotóat

Vi lev li handof, li shant – mita ferna sápéréba bud amni
    famé nayat
Þarpafa amni famé – píd áz dur áz písh nayat

Arugafa dari li yostiklu yostikáfó
Lénûfa té mita nukwam yiva mwaé tuvat

Nam, rasa famé kilev nayalí sumukó nayat
Budafa li juarabé van nayalí sînyotóat

Juarabé van nayalí sînyotóat
Juarabé
Juarabé van nayalí sînyotóat
Juarabé

The Blue Krakens dominated possession for the majority of the game. Savriah, Adonis, Fille, and Kassi were in sync from the kickoff, with Adonis on defense making incredible stops, Savriah clearing the center again and again, and Fille and Kassi swimming circles around the Teal Fins taking shots on goal. They won a sound victory over them, 6-3.

That evening, Coach clapped them on the backs. "You chas are doing the work! You're seeing results. A few more months and you chas could be real contenders! But don't let a few victories go to your head."

Kassi had never been the type to motivate herself on her own–she always needed that support around her. With all the encouragement from her coaches and friends, Kassi was starting to believe in herself. Her friends were focused and determined, and her new coaches were inspiring. It made all the difference.

They won another game on Sunday against a team of very surprised 500s, 11-4–their highest score of the season. Their opponents still vanished after the game without acknowledging the Blue Krakens, but that didn't bother them as much. They were winning and climbing the ranks.

"What's happened to you chas?" Joshi asked after Sunday's victory. "It's like something clicked inside the four of you and now you're clowning everybody!"

"It's Kassi's new songs. We found our rhythm!" Fille said, bouncing to an imaginary groove.

"The new songs are a huge improvement, Kassi," Joshi said. A few other teammates nodded in agreement. Royce, Jacen, and

Jaya gave Kassi the stink eye and swam silently back to the docks. Even winning games wasn't enough to un-prick the prickly chas.

That Sunday, Coach swam up to Kassi. "I think you're ready for the Race for Blues rematch," he said.

"How do you know about that?" Kassi asked.

"Sensei filled me in," Coach said. "I wasn't there, but I'm betting you lost because you doubted yourself. You're past that now. Remember, if you believe it, you'll have a reason to shine bright enough to go supernova! Winning something like that could earn you a recruitment letter from a better team—something that hasn't happened to a 400 since Kimaya Angelle."

"But I could never leave my team, my friends," Kassi said, shaking her head.

"That's something you're gonna have to figure out," Coach said. "It might be your only chance. But don't worry about that. Focus on the race!"

A rematch against Malyra—just thinking about it made her palms sweat. Ever since her defeat, she had fantasized about redeeming herself. Doubts flooded her mind, telling her she wasn't ready.

Silence those fears, Coach always said. Kassi forced herself to trust her coach. The next morning, she would issue the challenge.

In Period 1, Malyra sneered at Kassi as she walked in. Kassi paused in front of the classroom, her stomach in knots. Nikola glowered at her and she shrunk under his stare. She couldn't do it. Scurrying to her seat, she cursed under her breath and spent the rest of class motivating herself to do it before Period 2.

The bell rang, they ran to class. Once again, Kassi paused in front of class, eyeing Malyra. Dr. Jibu stepped into view and stared curiously at Kassi before pointing her to her seat at the back. Another missed opportunity. For the rest of class, Kassi anxiously stared at Malyra, bouncing her leg or tapping her foot as she waited for her next opening.

The three-minute break before Periods 3 and 4 had their moments, but Kassi got cold feet. Malyra seemed curious as to what Kassi was up to. During *P.E.*, she shoved and jostled Kassi at every opportunity. Rather than rattling Kassi, it lit a fire. It was time to confront the bullies. At lunch, she would issue the challenge.

Before entering the cafeteria, Kassi stopped in the washrooms. Staring at her reflection in the scratched-up mirror, she took a deep breath.

Silence those fears, Coach's words echoed, giving her courage. Kassi marched into the cafeteria, straight to the front of the line, and shouted before she had time to reconsider, "MALYRA!"

Twenty-Two

All the 800s in line, along with crowds of students nearby, turned to face Kassi. Their jaws dropped when they saw it was a 400 who demanded her attention.

"MALYRA, I CHALLENZHE YOU TO A RACE-EH FOR BLUES!" With her healthy voice, she could really crank up the volume.

Malyra squirmed for a moment before scoffing. "And why would I do that?"

Some of the students were already chanting "Race for Blues," eager to see a rematch. Most of them probably wanted to see Kassi embarrass herself again.

"You afraid you'll lose-eh?" Kassi said with a boldness that surprised even her.

"I'm afraid you have nothing to offer," Malyra said, rolling her eyes.

Kassi removed the earrings from her ears. Jewelry was rare on Earth. The elite class hoarded all of it, leaving nothing for the rest of the Gaians. "I have-eh these diamond earrings." Kassi held them up. They were the only thing she had from home, the one possession she prized. She had pulled them from the inside of her mattress that morning.

"Where did you get those? Stolen, no doubt?" Malyra said, stepping forward to get a closer look. There was a hint of jealousy in her eyes.

Kassi kept her distance, holding up the earrings for Malyra to see. "Inherited from my family back home-eh."

The chant, "Race for Blues" grew louder. Malyra started to feel the pressure of those around her. Kassi caught the slightest glimpse of fear behind Malyra's eyes before she masked it with her usual smugness.

"You said you'd race anyone, any time-eh. So race-eh me!"

Nikola and the Chinpoke Squad were all uncommonly quiet throughout the exchange. They must have been waiting for Malyra to make up her mind before they chimed in. Nikola stared intently at Kassi as if trying to read her mind.

"Fine," Malyra said, rolling her eyes. "If you really want to lose again, Klutziana, then who am I to get in your way?" The cafeteria erupted with excitement.

"At the docks after school," Kassi said.

Cheers continued to ring throughout as Kassi and her friends left for Sensei's classroom.

"That was solick, Kassi," Fille said.

"Ghost of Sheebah, that was scary!" Kassi shook with nervous excitement.

"Did you see, did you see Malyra squirm? I think she's afraid," Adonis said.

"It was bold, but I think you can beat her this time," Savriah said.

"I have to," Kassi said.

"You will," Fille said.

When they told Sensei what she did, he applauded her. "I knew you had it in you," he smiled. "I'll have to jump in the water and see this for myself!"

"You'd come watch?" Kassi asked.

"Of course!"

The next two classes went by in a blur. Kassi had her song

picked out the night before and rehearsed it in her mind, envisioning her strategy to defeat Malyra. She pictured Sensei and Coach giving their usual pep talks as she let their words boost her confidence. Vander's words also rang in her ear, *Singing small doesn't serve the worlds.* By the time the final bell sounded, she was ready to face Malyra.

At the docks, a crowd had already formed, lining up to dive down and swim out to the finish line. Many of them chatted in anticipation of the race. They were arguing over who would get the better camera angle of Kassi's second debacle on their helmet cams. Kassi pushed their doubts out of her mind and focused.

Calm.

Malyra showed up with the Chinpoke Squad, parading across the docks like reigning champions prematurely celebrating another victory. Rather than watch the obnoxious spectacle, Kassi retrieved her wetsuit from her locker. Savriah followed her in.

"You look nervous," Savriah said. She could always read Kassi.

"Of course I'm nervous," Kassi said.

"You're faster than she is, Kassi," Savriah said, patting Kassi on the neck. "You can win this." As awkward as Savriah was, her faith in Kassi was inspiring.

Kassi wished Amára or Caesar were here, but Coach was right. All her life, she had lived in their shadow. Neither of them was here to lend their light. Kassi had to shine her own.

Back on the docks, only Vander, Malyra, and Nikola remained behind. Vander seemed unusually quiet as Nikola smirked in his direction. *What happened last time between them?* Kassi put it out of her mind and focused on the race.

"How'd you find out about this?" Kassi was surprised to see him.

"Word spreads fast when it comes to a Race for Blues. And I wasn't about to miss Malyra's much-deserved moment of humiliation!" Vander smiled at her. Kassi still glazed over a little every time he smiled in her direction. She knew his smiles were the same for everyone else, but she still wanted to believe he reserved the best ones for her.

"Thanks." Kassi suppressed a smile. Nikola glared at her, seemingly unhappy about the whole idea of a rematch.

"Is your oxygen tank full?" Vander asked.

"Yisû, I just refilled it."

"Then let's launch these rockets!"

Without her entourage, Malyra looked less confident. Glancing down at Malyra's suit, Kassi recognized Vi'ella's old wettie. Kassi scowled. Malyra grinned when she saw how much it bothered her. "It's only fitting you should lose against your friend's threads." She tried staring Kassi down, but Kassi braved her stare. Malyra wouldn't intimidate her this time.

Nikola gave the count off. "On three!" Lining up on the springboards, Kassi and Malyra prepared to dive. "One, two...THREE!"

Kassi cut through the water like a knife, powering up her sonopack with the Haraki Hîm she had prepared. Singing with sháloor, she lit four bulbs and blasted into the Atlantic right alongside Malyra.

SUPERNOVA

Ay - The distance had dimmed all my shine
I felt like I'd fallen behind
The sparks I had left couldn't start my fire

Oh - I held to the last of my hope
I found a new light in me grow
Speaking a language I've always known

Bright as the sun all my starlight's begun to erupt
I finally believe it

They're just within reach all my treasures and dreams that I lost
And now I can see it
My supernova
It's all that I needed
My supernova
I now have a reason to shine

When so many have gone where I've been
To help me find power from within
Where would I be without all of them?

Hey - now it's my turn to be brave
To trust in the choices I made
Remember what I learned along the way

Bright as the sun all my starlight's begun to erupt
I finally believe it
They're just within reach all my treasures and dreams that I lost
And now I can see it
My supernova
It's more than a feeling
My supernova
It's given me reason to shine

I wondered if I'd never know
Who I'm supposed to become
I've waited so long on my own - alone
Hoping I'd find my way home - back home

Bright as the sun all my starlight's begun to erupt
I finally believe it
They're just within reach all the faces and things that I loved
Why couldn't I see it
My supernova
From the beginning

My supernova
Was all I was needing
My supernova
It's more than a feeling
My supernova
It's given me reason to shine

IN EVÉIK

Ay - loma amni nayalí berké li riketat
Rasaba síl gésh mita kátha nayat
Mita nohosách li kítóbé téabam dimar nayalí vierat

Hí – gréma shi li mish van nayalí eswabé nayat
Pataba în nuvo daveré / orûbé lev mwajang wasîn nayat
Semách în linggwûbé méshû mita sápéréba nayat

Roni áz li solya, pesara shi revîn amni nayalí ástarû'orûat
Dîmin truvîn famé nayat
Tikû kilev tordo amni nayalí helorianóbé i sînyotóbé sîm
    perdoba nayajang jukat
I anish buvi taz famé nayat
Nayalí mipoakaat
Bud amni sîm naya jôba famat
Nayalí mipoakaat
Anish mit în loshiné shi berk nayat

Máti mita píba hûn duabé ubi mita buda nayat
Shi witíd patad dari kilev kuasibé mwaat
Ubi olis bud kimun amni van jukabé nayat

Hé – anish bud nayalí valé shi bud ándrijang famat
Shi fidat lev li weringóbé huliba nayat
Rikordû té péudaba samé li modobé nayat

Roni áz li solya, pesara shi revîn amni nayalí ástarû'orûat
Dîmin truvîn famé nayat
Tikû kilev tordo amni nayalí helorianóbé i sînyotóbé sîm
    perdoba nayajang jukat
I anish buvi taz famé nayat
Nayalí mipoakaat
Bud mas sé în rasapé famat
Nayalí mipoakaat
Yiva în loshiné shi berk mwaat

Mihara lô olisíd budíd én nayat
Perdor i kin ne'ubi shi píd
Hûn nubri rukoba hanya shi sápéré nayat
Lô ferna olisíd patad nayalí modo hémé nayat – bébulak
    hémat

Roni áz li solya, pesara shi revîn amni nayalí ástarû'orûat
Dîmin truvîn famé nayat
Tikû kilev tordo amni li lootzûtóbé i shéanóbé sîm ashka
    nayajang jukat
Dag téam taz famé nayat
Nayalí mipoakaat
Dari li pesarup
Nayalí mipoakaat
Buda amni buda jôsách nayat
Nayalí mipoakaat
Bud mas sé în rasapé famat
Nayalí mipoakaat
Yiva în loshiné shi berk mwaat

KASSI TRIED A NEW STRATEGY. Rather than swimming in her blind
spot, she kept pace right alongside Malyra for the first leg of the
race. Malyra tried to speed up and swerve in front to catch Kassi

in her air pocket collapse, but Kassi dodged and remained steady. Each time Malyra made a move to gain the advantage, she used a similar pattern of maneuvers. Kassi realized she could mimic them to ride her tailwind.

They reached the halfway mark of the race and Malyra started to pull ahead. The drag on Kassi's suit slowed her down once again, despite the extra thrusters. Trailing behind, she would need to make a move for the air pocket. It wasn't her initial strategy, but she had taken Coach's advice and imagined alternate scenarios so she could adapt.

Malyra could see Kassi in her peripheral and continued the same moves and motions in an attempt to pulse out Kassi. Performing from her diaphragm with all her strength, Kassi blasted her thrusters and boosted forward. She closed the distance between them and aimed directly for the air pocket.

Malyra moved at the last second, swerving in front of Kassi and nearly pulsing her out. Kassi managed to veer off slightly and avoid it, but the swerve knocked her out of the lane. Rather than festering with frustration, she bounced back quickly. With another boost of vocal power, she closed the distance and found another opening. Malyra didn't see her in time, probably assuming Kassi had already been pulsed out.

Kassi timed her entry and belted a long note for continuous energy. Speeding up, she acted quickly before Malyra could take evasive action. This time it worked! Kassi slipped directly behind Malyra and successfully entered the air pocket. Resistance against her suit lessened significantly, requiring much less exertion and allowing her to prepare for a final burst of speed. With the finish line fast approaching, she had a tight window. Gathering momentum from the tailwind, she put everything into her final chorus and blasted ahead to Malyra's left side. As she did, something unexpected happened.

Kassi lit the fifth bulb!

It was the first time in her life she had managed to light the fifth bulb, and everyone was there to witness it. It ignited the central thruster on the pack. With an immense boost she had never before experienced, she torpedoed right in front of Malyra and through the finish line!

The faces in the crowd were wide-eyed with surprise, their mouths gaping open. Kassi's friends and coaches threw their hands up in the water, cheering wildly in celebration. Sensei and Coach Rockson beamed with pride. Adonis, Fille, and Savriah squeezed their teammates and even shed a few tears of joy.

Malyra was somewhere behind her, but Kassi couldn't see her until she swung her legs forward to hit the brakes and spun to look behind her. The crowds weren't just shocked because she had lit the fifth bulb.

Malyra had been pulsed out.

Twenty~Three

Kassi had dreamt of this moment so many times, she wasn't sure if it was real. Frozen with shock, she remained suspended in the water as her friends were quick to surround her.

"MALYRA GOT PULSED!" Many shouted in disbelief as they swarmed Kassi and congratulated her.

The cavitation blast where the air pocket collapsed would have hit Malyra like a bullet train. It might have even knocked her unconscious. Kassi couldn't believe it. In front of everyone, Kassi faced her bully. She pulsed out Malyra, lit the fifth bulb, and won the race, all in a broken rental suit.

Someone shouted, "Please tell me someone got that on video!"

"Everybody got that on video. Listen, that's gonna be the most watched video for years," Vi'ella said. "I've never seen someone get clowned like that!"

"That was so bosst!" Fille said.

"I can't even, I can't even handle how bosst that was!" Adonis shouted. They were dancing and spinning in the water, completely awestruck.

"That was the single. Greatest. Moment of my life!" Fille emphasized each word with his hands.

"You really smashed her," Savriah said. "I've never seen someone get hit that hard!"

Kassi was still processing everything when Vander and Nikola joined them a few moments later. They could still see Malyra floating off in the distance. It was clear who had won. Nikola reached Malyra and checked on her. He grabbed her hand and examined her face closely. Kassi could only see Malyra angrily whip her hand back from him.

"Malyra got pulsed?" Vander whooped. "This I gotta see. Who filmed it on their helmet cam?"

Kassi wanted to see it, too. She and Vander gathered around Joshi who was the first to pull it up. He captured the shot from a great angle. His helmet projected the holovid directly in front of them, depicting the moment Kassi went supernova past Malyra on the final stretch. As Malyra tried to catch Kassi's tailwind, she collided with the air pocket collapse as the cavitation blast slammed into her like an invisible wrecking ball. The open-mouthed expression of horror and shock on Malyra's face was so priceless.

"Pulsed the dead sheist right out of her!" A boy watching over their shoulder shouted. Kassi laughed to the point of tears.

"Wow, that's absolutely embarrassing for the Miami Province title holder." Vander laughed. "Not only suffering a crushing defeat but also getting pulsed by a 400 with a broken wetsuit. Sirs and dames, this is one for the books!" Kassi blushed at all the attention she was getting from Vander.

"I knew you could do it!" Vi'ella patted Kassi on the shoulder. "She won't be calling you Klutziana anymore."

Joshi played the video a few more times for those who wanted a replay.

"Joshi, can you send me a copy?" Kassi asked. She planned on watching it on repeat all night long.

"Alright, chas, let's shave the bed and get back to the docks!" Vander said.

"I'mma hang back and make sure Malyra doesn't make a run for it," Vi'ella said.

"Good idea. There's a high probability she would do just that," Vander said.

"Thanks, Vi'ella!" Kassi said as they swam back to the docks to continue their celebration. The return trip was a fifteen-minute-long victory lap. Once on the landing pad, they awaited Malyra and Vi'ella. After a few long moments, both arrived. Vi'ella dragged Malyra who stood as if poised to flee. When she couldn't, she threw a tantrum like a toddler.

"Get your yashing hands off me!" Malyra shouted, practically trembling with rage.

"Not until you give that suit to my girl," Vi'ella folded her arms and blocked her exit.

"I'm not giving that Four Hundie sheist!" Malyra screamed.

"You're not going anywhere until you do," Vi'ella said, planting her feet directly in front of Malyra, nose to nose.

Malyra grunted so loudly under her breath, Kassi could feel the grinding itch in her own throat. "Fine. Is this what you want? Is this what you want?" Malyra began tugging and pulling her suit off right in front of everyone.

"Oh, you're gonna do it right here?" Vi'ella stepped back to give her some space.

Within moments, Malyra was standing in her high-neck bikini. Kassi forgot how perfectly toned her abs were. Malyra fiercely threw her wetsuit directly at Vi'ella who caught it with ease. Storming to her locker, she screamed at the top of her lungs, "All you sheist muppets were in on this!" A few of the kids filmed Malyra's ridiculous outburst.

"It looks like her days of looking down on people are coming to a middle," Fille said, chopping a hand through the air.

Vi'ella handed Kassi the wetsuit. "Here you go!"

"It's yours. I can't take it," Kassi said, trying to hand it back.

"You earned this," Vi'ella held her hands up, refusing to take it back. "I'm fine with my new rental. This one's yours!"

Kassi held it up. It was magnificent in so many ways–nearly to the quality of Nemalís suits! No more oxygen tanks, no more rips and patches that caused drag, no more boring designs.

"Try it on," Vi'ella said. "Give it a test drive."

The day was still young. With the Race for Blues, most had skipped the day's rehearsal, but they still had their AquaSphera matches. Kassi hurried to her locker, stripped off her old suit, and put on the new one. It fit so perfectly as if tailored just for Kassi. She and Vi'ella were the same height, and although Vi'ella was more muscle-toned than Kassi, they wore the same size. The suit was so beautiful, it practically sparkled. Kassi couldn't stop admiring it.

"My baby has a new home," Vi'ella said when Kassi returned to the docks.

Kassi stretched and flexed, fingering the threads on her arms as she soaked in the moment. After all she had been through these past months, Kassi had finally earned a victory.

Twenty~Four

In her new wettie, Kassi could cross the worlds, even after expending so much energy on the Race for Blues. Adrenaline pumped through her veins. With a clean dive into the Atlantic, she torpedoed toward the training pools. Her friends and teammates were also energized. After a few short drills, they faced off against a team of 700s called the Tinsel Tiamats–ranked fourth in the local league.

"Singing small doesn't serve-eh the worlds," Kassi said to Fille who turned to face the team.

"That's right bubbleheads, so let's sing it with sháloor!" Fille shouted. Kassi had been educating them on how to sing with sháloor ever since they started performing her songs. They broke from their huddle and took their positions.

During the game, Kassi connected pass after pass and shot with incredible accuracy. Fille, Savriah, and Adonis were on the level. All game long, they stymied their opponents' promising drives, turning many of them into scoring drives for the Krakens. The Tiamats still proved their rank by putting many hard-earned points on the board, but by the end of the contest, the Krakens pulled off the win, 12-10. Even more surprising than the defeat of the fourth-ranked team in the league was the response they got after. The Tiamats acknowledged the Krakens after the game.

"Where'd that come from?" Hensey, their team captain, asked as a few of her teammates swam up alongside her.

"We've been trying out some new incantations and strategies," Fille said, keeping it vague.

"I'm sure it doesn't hurt that you got the fastest siren on your team, although you might find it hard to keep her," she said, pointing at Kassi. Word got out fast! Kassi looked down, unsure how to respond.

"That we do," Fille said, a hint of concern behind his smile. "Good game, chas!" He bowed, and to Kassi's surprise, Hensey and her teammates bowed in return, the bow one gave an equal.

After such a big victory, many of the Krakens were hesitant to swim back to the docks. They were becoming more and more suspicious about why Fille, Adonis, Savriah, and Kassi always remained behind after the games.

"So what is it you chas do here after the games?" Joshi asked. "It's time you tell us!"

"Power it down, Joshi! I'll tell you later," Fille said, doing his best to convince them to return. They eventually did, reluctantly.

On the U.N.O.E. cutters, her friends refilled their oxygen—something Kassi no longer had to do. Fille said in the open air, "Not sure we'll be able to hold them off much longer."

"Let's ask, let's ask Coach if we can invite them to these," Adonis said.

They dove below the surface. Sensei Kelipalo, Coach Rockson, and Kiowa swam into view, big smiles on their faces. Sensei spoke up first, "You did it, Kassi! You lit the fifth bulb!"

"And you won a big victory, today!" Coach added.

"All thanks to you three," Kassi said with a deferential bow.

"Don't discredit your efforts, Kassi," Coach Rockson said. "We showed you how, but you chas did the work!"

Kassi still couldn't believe she lit the fifth bulb. If only Amára could have seen her.

"We've been thinking," Sensei said. "It might be time to bring in the team."

"I was, I was just about to ask," Adonis said.

"Before we do that," Kiowa said, "You'll wanna make sure every player is willing to go all in. If you need to replace any of them, now's the time."

"Oh, we need to replace some," Fille said. "There are three, in particular, I can't wait to dropkick to the beach!"

"Now that you have a few impressive wins under your belt, you could probably recruit a few players from some of the better teams," Coach said.

"Like-eh the Red Squalls?" Kassi squeaked, unable to hide the excitement in her voice at the prospect of having a very certain player on their team.

"It's very rare for higher numbers to join a lower-numbered team, but it doesn't hurt to ask," Coach said with a half-shrug. "Then again, you might get recruit attempts from higher ranked teams you should probably consider."

The thought had crossed her mind since Coach had first brought it up. She couldn't leave her friends. "I wanna stay here," Kassi said. Although, if an invitation from the Red Squalls came, she might have a really hard time saying no.

"That's up to you, Kassi," Coach said. "Now, let's get to work. We've got a full schedule for you chas, today."

After everything that day, Kassi was exhausted. But their coaches didn't ease up—they pushed everyone to their limits. It was a long and grueling session of vocal exercises, ballet training, and waterfield drills. By the time they swam back to the docks, Kassi was dragging, wanting only sleep. Judging by the hanging heads and sluggish steps of her friends, they felt the same. With one more congratulations to Kassi, they said their goodbyes.

On Wednesday as she walked into *Heroics* class, Kassi overheard many of the students gossiping about Malyra's embarrassing defeat and childish breakdown on the docks. Throwing on her hologlasses, she found a holovid Fille had sent to the entire school showcasing Kassi's moment of triumph. Malyra, once the queen of this school, now cowered in the corner, shielding her face from class. After dishing insults for so long, she was now on the receiving end. Nikola quietly sulked in the seat next to her.

Kassi floated on clouds all morning as if rays of sunlight cascaded down through the ceiling to bless her every step. With each passing period, she continued to watch as 700s, 600s, and even lowly 500s replayed their race and openly teased Malyra. She felt a little guilty for enjoying it so much, even if Malyra did deserve it.

Kassi arrived early to *P.E.* that day and overheard Malyra shouting at Coach Muzzey in his private office. "Send one more nude pic to my glasses and you'll be hearing from my father!"

Kassi froze in place, shocked. *Why would Coach Muzzey, a grown man, be sending…pictures to Malyra?*

Kassi took longer to change into her frumpy workout clothes. The washrooms emptied. She thought she was alone until she heard sniffling in the corner. Peeking over a bench, she found Malyra curled on the floor, crying.

She almost turned to leave but paused. Glancing at a vulnerable Malyra, Kassi recognized the pain she felt. The hate in Kassi's heart started to dissolve. Taking a seat on the adjacent bench, Kassi broke the silence. "It doesn't feel good, does it?"

Malyra whipped her head up, startled. She probably thought she was alone. Her puffy eyes focused on Kassi for a few beats before she responded. "Everyone's so awful!"

"So were-eh you," Kassi said quietly.

Malyra faced forward and stared into the open as if pondering on this. She glanced back at Kassi and said, "But you're a Four Hundie. They shouldn't treat an 800 like this!"

"No one should treat anyone like this," Kassi said. "Why should 400s be any different?"

"Because you're 400s," Malyra said, raising an eyebrow.

"400s disregard the rules. They…you break laws and defy U.N.O.E. policies. It's why you're 400s!"

Kassi was confused by this. She had never quite learned how star scores were tabulated. "But, I didn't break any rules."

"Maybe not you, but your parents or your ancestors did," Malyra said, furrowing her brows as if judging Kassi.

"My ancestors? So all this time-eh you've been punishing us because of something people did before-eh we were even born? How is that fair?" Kassi fired back.

"That's just how it is," Malyra folded her arms and faced the wall. "Now beat fins. I'm done with you!"

To think I almost felt sorry for her! Kassi huffed and rushed out and into the gymnasium.

For the first half of class, Malyra remained in the washrooms. In her absence, Calandra took a more active role in harassing Kassi, kicking her whenever Muzzey had his back turned. One kick struck the back of Kassi's knee, sending her to the floor. Rather than roll over and ignore her, Kassi jumped up and charged Calandra with a hard shove.

Coach Muzzey was quick to intercept, getting right in Kassi's face. "Yash's tap-dancing sheist! What do you think you're doing, 400? It's the broomstick!"

Malyra entered the gymnasium, joining them just in time to participate. Of course, Coach Muzzey didn't do anything to punish her for being so late.

For the last thirty minutes of class, Kassi took the barrage of bellowed insults. No matter how many times they did this, she never got accustomed to it. Her ears buzzed. Her nails bit into her palms. Spit covered her face.

At the end, Calandra aimed the sonic pulse baton at Kassi and fired away. This time, however, something changed in Kassi. She became defiant–the same defiance Malyra had just accused all 400s of earlier. Rather than run for it, she planted her feet and performed a powerful dodge riff, deflecting the majority of the pulse, turning it into nothing more than a breezy gush of wind.

Calandra stood with the class as everyone waited for Kassi to double over. When nothing happened, Coach Muzzey yanked the sonic baton out of her hands to inspect it. Calandra pouted and stomped, clearly upset. The class broke into chatter, many blaming Calandra for not using it correctly. While they were preoccupied, Muzzey adjusted some settings and test-fired the baton, accidentally aiming a widespread high-frequency pulse at all the other students. A collective grunt sounded as everyone received a simultaneous sonic uppercut that sent them thumping to the ground. Tall students like DeSchuster received the blow below the belt and fell harder than the rest. Malyra whimpered, Calandra cried in pain, Nikola whipped his head up from the ground and glowered at Kassi.

Coincidentally, Kassi was the only one out of range and unaffected by the pulse. The bell rang and she bolted out into the corridors just as she overheard Coach Muzzey exclaim, "Yash's tap-dancing sheist!" Kassi almost fell over with an uncontrollable fit of laughter, howling all the way to the cafeteria where she joined her friends in line.

"What happened, what happened?" Adonis asked, wide-eyed. Kassi recounted Coach Muzzey's mishap between giggle fits.

"Wha-hat!" Fille shouted louder than ever. "Did anyone film it?"

Kassi said, "I don't know. I hope-eh so!"

After school that day, they raced off to AquaSphera. "I feel another win in the wind," Fille said.

"A win in the wind, a win in the wind," Adonis echoed.

At the docks, Kassi was surprised to find Vander and Vi'ella waiting for them. Vander called out, "Chas! We've caught news of your winning streak and your most recent surprise victory against the Tiamats. They were completely dumbfounded by the upset."

"We discovered a little secret as to why the turnaround," Vi'ella said.

"What secret is that?" Kassi asked, feigning ignorance.

"A certain coach who will not be named," Vander said as he eyed the passing crowds of students, all of whom were conspicuously paying attention to their conversation.

"Should we discuss this…," Fille nodded his head toward the ocean.

"Good idea," Vander said. They changed into their wetsuits and dove into the water, telling their teammates to swim ahead. Once out of camera range and tuned in to their own private frequency, he continued, "So how'd you convince a high-profile coach like Rockson to train you when he's already coaching Team Miami?"

Kassi and her friends cast each other sidelong glances. Fille asked, "How'd you know?"

"I stayed late after one of our games to practice some speed drills. Spotted you chas in the far sector," Vander said.

"Sensei Kelipalo is friends with him and called in a favor," Kassi said.

"He's one of our professors," Savriah explained. "He assists in training a lot of champions for the Siren Games."

"I know of Kelipalo," Vander said. "But I feel there's a crucial detail you're withholding."

Kassi cast a look at Vi'ella who responded, "I didn't say anything." Vander's eyes bounced from Vi'ella to Kassi, curious. Kassi and her friends exchanged glances.

"Tell him, tell him," Adonis said. "He should know."

Kassi started from the beginning, telling her story one more time. She rushed through the details of her near drowning, hoping to keep the trauma at bay. Just the thought of it still made her hyperventilate–especially while underwater.

After she finished relating everything to Vander, he stared off into space for a few silent beats passed before he said, "That's almost so outlandishly unbelievable, you'd have to be the most imaginative storyteller, or…," He eyed Kassi for a moment who shied away from his deep gaze, before he continued, "or you're speaking the truth. The sheer fact that you've got Kelipalo and Rockson in your corner speaks to your credibility. It makes sense why Coach would train you chas."

"What about you, Vi'ella?" Kassi asked.

"It was Sensei's involvement and Kassi's speed that tipped the scales," Vi'ella said. "After hearing her story, then seeing her blast past us, I knew she was telling the truth, which is why I knew she could win the Race for Blues."

"So that's why you wagered your wettie," Vander said with a nod. He then looked at Kassi, sizing her up. "So you're Nemalís. And a Rivernova at that. You're certain we shouldn't notify the authorities?"

"They already know," Kassi said. "They say we have to win the Siren Games if we want to go back home."

"I can't imagine the kind of trauma you've experienced being abducted like that. Ripped from your home to be treated as pawns in a convoluted game of politics," Vander said with a shake of his head.

"It's wrong what they've done," Vi'ella said. "You don't abduct people just to prove a point."

"So let's get to why we pulled you aside," Vander said. "We heard Rockson was helping you out. Now I understand why, and I want in."

"We want in," Vi'ella emphasized.

"You what?" Kassi pinched herself in case this was a dream, causing a jolt of pain by accidentally pinching a scab where one of her professors had drawn blood earlier that week.

"We wanna join your team and help you qualify for the Games. And I know a few of our fellow Squalls who will insist on accompanying us should we make the move. That is," he paused to look each of them in the eye, "if you'll have us."

"Red Squalls are first in the league," Fille said, scratching his head. "You'd really be willing to leave and join us? One of the lowest-ranked teams?"

"We're only halfway through the season," Vander said. "As

long as Krakens win most of their games between now and the end of May, you can still enter the Final 16 tournament for the Miami League title."

"Yisû but as a Red Squall, you're practically guaranteed that spot. Why risk it for us?" Kassi asked.

"Because what they've done to you is wrong," Vi'ella said as she folded her arms. "We gotta set that right. And we know Coach Rockson can get you there."

"Your situation needs to be redressed," Vander said. "We wanna help you get back to your family."

"Even though the U.N.O.E. says my parents might be the reason so few Gaians even make it to Paradise?"

"First of all, you're not your parents," Vander said. "And second, we don't know the full story. Who really knows for certain why things are the way they are."

Kassi was stunned. Two of the most powerful sirens were willing to sacrifice their own chances at leaving Earth to help her get back to her family–first, Sensei Kelipalo, Coach Rockson, Fille, Savriah, and Adonis, and now Vander and Vi'ella. Her eyes grew misty. She was the one who should have been helping them all along. Well, now she could at least try her best to help them win the Siren Games. That's what Amára would do. Softly, she said, "Thank you!"

"We're with you, girl," Vi'ella said, throwing her arm around her in a side hug.

"So what do you chas say?" Vander asked.

Fille said, "Without a doubt, we want you on the team!"

"And our teammates?" Vander asked.

"How many?" Fille asked.

"There are at least three Squalls who will be interested."

"Who you thinking? Ganna for sure. Who else?" Vi'ella asked Vander.

The name Ganna sounded familiar. Fille and Adonis exchanged glances of suppressed excitement. That's when Kassi remembered their conversation on the townhome balcony. Ganna was the girl they squabbled over.

"Ganna, Murrey, and Tallie," Vander said. "If there's room on the team."

"We can make room!" Fille said a little too eagerly.

Savriah added, "We've been needing to make cuts for a while."

"Yisû we have," Fille said, a devious grin spreading across his face.

"So cutting players is allowed?" Kassi asked, confused. "I thought playing AquaSphera was mandatory for all students."

"It is, but there are always some players who can't find a team," Savriah explained. "When that's the case, those players are forced to practice drills by themselves until they have enough to form their own new team."

"Oh," Kassi said. "Sad!"

"It's not sad," Fille said, jittery with excitement. "I've been waiting all year to do this!"

"Good, then it's settled," Vander nodded. "Let's break it to the teams!"

Vander and Vi'ella surfaced–their team currently rehearsing in one of the elite studios–while Kassi and her friends stroked to the training pools where the Krakens had gathered in their sector.

Fille pulled Catelyn, the Krakens' other team captain, aside and explained everything that was going on. After he filled her in, they called for a huddle.

"Due to some new additions to our team, we can finally make some much-needed cuts!" Fille said, pumping his arms as he floated in front of the team. Pointing at each of them in turn, Fille shouted, "Jacen, Jaya, Royce–after you've grown enough phytoplankton to replace all the oxygen you've wasted, you can all take a long walk off a short pier, sink to the depths of the ocean and POUND SAND! You're off the team!"

"Like we care," Jacen grunted. "Just because you won a few games doesn't mean anything!"

Royce said nothing as usual and only flashed them the cacasheist.

"Like we ever wanted to be here, anyway," Jaya sneered as the three of them swam toward one of the empty sectors

After practice, they played against the Neon Nessies, a team of 700s from their school. They were lower-tiered bullies with obvious aspirations of joining the Chinpoke Squad. Kassi was eager to pummel them. Rules allowed for teams to play with fourteen, so Blue Krakens readjusted their positions to accommodate for being down one player on the field with no subs.

Kassi, Fille, Adonis, and Savriah were world-class throughout the contest. 700s who had laughed at her and called her "Klutziana" on the regular found themselves getting dispossessed again and again by Kassi and her friends. Kassi and Fille made fools of their defense, racking up the points. By halftime, they were cruising for a clean sheet. The Nessies had spent most of the game screaming at each other. Two of their own players almost came to blows after one of Kassi's goals.

Despite the disadvantage, Blue Krakens won 7-0. Without saying a word of acknowledgment, and with their tails permanently tucked between their legs, the Neon Nessies retreated to the docks.

"Good game, bubbleheads! Now line it up," Fille shouted. As the team formed a floating line, Fille continued, "We have some bosst news! Kassi, you wanna tell 'em?" Fille waved her to the front.

"We have some-eh new additions to our team," Kassi announced with excitement. "Vander, Vi'ella, Ganna, Tallie, and Murrey from the Red Squalls are joining us!"

"Wha-hat," Joshi chuckled. "You chas are pushing our waves!"

"Power it down, Joshi," Fille said. "Just listen!"

"And, I'm not done-eh," Kassi continued, ignoring their skepticism. "Coach Rockson will be our coach!"

The team floated in silence, straight-faced. Kassi wasn't sure if they were shocked or still waiting for the "real news." At that moment, Coach Rockson, Sensei K, and Kiowa swam into view, as did Vander, Vi'ella, Ganna, Murrey, and Tallie. It was the first time Kassi saw Ganna. She had medium-length auburn hair with highlighted waves, beautiful jaw definition, and gorgeous eyes. It was clear why Fille and Adonis fought over her.

Jaws dropped among their teammates at the sight of these celebrities. Star athletes from the top team and the most famous coach on the planet were all here to join them, the team that had spent the entire season in last place.

"What? But how?" Joshi asked, both gloved hands brushing over the top of his helmet.

"Some of us, even some 800s, believe everyone deserves a real chance at winning the Games despite their star score. Coach Rockson and I have been watching you, and we see real potential. Even if we don't make it this season, I think we can turn the Krakens into a league champion!" Sensei said, swimming forward. "We wanna transform you into a powerhouse team that has a real shot at winning a Paradise passport!"

"So what do you say, chas? You ready to win this?" Kiowa shouted. To that, they cheered loudly, whooping and hollering with excitement, many with tears in their eyes. A team of 400s who never had much hope of amounting to anything in their lives now had a chance. They'd still have to win most of the rest of their games just to qualify, and then from there, they would have to compete against the greatest champions in all the worlds to win. The odds were heavily stacked against them, but for the first time in their lives, it was no longer impossible.

"Go get some rest. You're gonna need it!" Coach said.

They bolted for the docks where they continued their celebration. Vander led the new team in a chant:

Awaken, awaken, awaken the kraken
Awaken, awaken, awaken the kraken
If I'm not mistaken, we no longer lackin'
I said awaken, awaken, awaken the kraken

As THEY DID, Fille pulled Kassi aside. "This all happened because of you, Kassi! Because of you!" He locked eyes with Kassi, a look of sincere gratitude on his face.

"He's right, Kassi," Vander shouted, his deep emerald eyes making her heart flutter. "You brought us together and made this happen!"

Kassi bounced with pure elation, grateful to have found a way to finally help them.

Twenty-Five

"Chas, you're all invited to my house to celebrate!" Vander shouted over the Kraken chant.

Kassi had never been invited to any of their houses before. Getting invited to Vander's house of all places– her pulse raced with the possibilities. *Maybe we'll get the chance to talk alone.* The stars twinkled in the night sky as Kassi followed her teammates along the slidewalks to Vander's.

On the way, Savriah asked Vander, "So what happened between you and Nikola after Kassi's first race? You looked upset." Kassi always wondered the same thing but didn't have the audacity to ask. This was one moment she was grateful for Savriah's bluntness.

Vander paused briefly on the slidewalks to glance back at Savriah before answering, "You chas saw that, huh?" He resumed leading the way to his house, speaking over his shoulder. "Nikola–that choad! We were the last two to swim back to the docks, and he cranked up the speed," Vander said. "I thought he was just looking for a little friendly competition, so I followed suit and turned on the jets."

Everyone listened intently as they trailed quietly behind. Vander's voice carried over the water and echoed off of nearby townhouse walls as he continued, "Without warning or provocation, he sideswipes me—deliberate cheap shot! It knocks me out of my lane, and before I can reposition myself, he jets in front for another low blow, pulsing me out for no reason."

"That cacafuego!" Fille shouts. "He's the worst of the chinpokes!"

"He's the one who broke my leg," Kassi said.

"Ah, so he's the one. I remember you mentioning that, now," Vander said as they pulled up to his townhouse.

His home was similar to Kassi's, only bigger, and the decor more extravagant and inviting—the house of an 800. Only his younger sister was home, and she seemed preoccupied on the living room couch watching a dramatic series on her holopad. Kassi couldn't help wondering if the series was contraband or U.N.O.E. approved.

They climbed two flights of stairs to the sun parlor, sandwiched between two balconies at the top of the townhome, a similar but expanded layout to Kassi's top floor. The walls of the parlor were smothered in a patchwork of multicolor vinyl record jackets. After spinning a record, Vander opened a small fridge and pulled out a case of energy waters and a basket of apples—real apples!

"How'd you score these?" Joshi asked as he held up a juicy, red apple.

"Shh," Vander held a finger to his lips.

He handed Kassi a couple of apples and waters, his fingers grazing hers. Her heart leaped with excitement as she bounded toward the first balcony and ran right into the screen door. With a grunt, she almost fell backward but caught herself at the last second. Whipping her head in all directions, she hoped nobody noticed. Everybody noticed—including Vander. They were staring awkwardly at her as she tried her best to shrug it off, open the door and slip out onto the balcony.

Unlike her mismatched, rusty balcony chairs, Vander had current, coordinated patio furniture. A full moon splashed light across the balconies. Music from the record player was piped through a couple of small speakers, playing big-band swing music from hundreds of years ago. Even though Kassi had never heard it before, it helped restore her calm after her embarrassing debacle minutes earlier. She missed listening to music. They only had access to the song playbook they performed and the pre-approved playlist of generic songs that came with her holo-glasses.

Kassi hoped to strategically position herself close to Vander when he entered the balcony. As she waited for him to finish divvying out apples and waters, she listened in on Adonis' and Quade's conversation.

"Yash and Sheebah, that moon's huge!" Quade observed.

"Yisû, it's even bigger than the sun!" Adonis said.

"No, no it's not," Quade said, shaking his head

"I'm telling you! The moon is bigger than the sun!" Adonis said, his finger flexed at the moon. "Did you see the solar eclipse last year?"

"I did," Quade said, casting Adonis a sidelong glance.

"See? You see? The moon covered up the sun. So it's bigger!"

"No, it covered up the sun, because it's closer," Quade said.

"I'm telling you, it's because it's bigger." Adonis didn't back down.

"Help me out, Kassi," Quade noticed Kassi listening in on their conversation. Savriah was there, as well, but remained quiet.

Kassi turned to face them. "I've never really been good at astrology, but even I know the sun is bigger than the moon," Kassi said.

"Astrology?" Quade cocked his head to the side.

"She means astronomy," Savriah said.

"Astronomy, you know what I mean!" Kassi said with a frustrated sigh, barking under her breath. "Ruff!"

Whipping her head back toward the sun parlor, Kassi noticed Vander was gone. She quickly scanned the balconies and found him on the other side in a conversation with Ganna, her hand resting on his arm! *Is she flirting with him?* He leaned in awfully close for someone who wasn't interested. They both laughed at something he said. As they did, Vander swung his arm around Ganna and pulled her in even closer. Kassi's heart sank to the floor. She suddenly didn't want to be there.

Opening the parlor doors, she ducked down the stairs and slipped out the front entrance, passing Vander's sister who was laughing hysterically at something on her holopad. Everyone else was having a great time tonight!

Brooding as she clomped back to the townhouse, she stubbed her toe on a plank and almost knocked an elderly 600 man into the water. After a quick apology, she hobbled the rest of the way in pain.

Inside the townhome, she padded quietly up the stairs, hoping to avoid conversations. Once the door closed behind her, she curled up on her lumpy mattress. Fortunately, no one came upstairs to check on her. Kassi wanted to be alone.

Maybe they were just really friendly with each other, she tried to convince herself.

Her mind dwelled on it for too long, her emotions a kaleido-scope of changing colors. Besides, she really didn't have time for a relationship. Getting home was all that mattered, and Vander was just a distraction. She needed to write it out–put it to melody. Pulling up a blank page on her hologlasses, she poured her feelings into a song. Ideas flowed as she typed quickly to keep up with them. It was therapeutic. When it was finally over, she collapsed on her bed and dreamed of her former life back on Nemal until she fell asleep.

The next morning, the bliss of peaceful dreams faded as her thoughts were soon drenched with last night's disappointment.

I always get my hopes up, no matter how many times they've crashed and burned to smoldering ash. Back home, the boys she always liked ended up only pretending to be interested in her to get to Amára. Although Amára would turn them down after realizing Kassi was interested. Boys never came between them. If only Amára were here now.

Of course, if Amára were here now, Vander would probably be interested in her!

Kassi grumbled her way through breakfast, her cold shower, and her walk to school. When she passed Nikola in *Heroics* and he flashed his usual scowl, she recollected the conversation with her friends about spying on him.

That could help get my mind off…things.

At lunch, she brought it up. "I should tail Nikola today after AquaSphera."

"I completely forgot about that," Fille said, running a hand through his hair.

"Why do we, why do we wanna follow him again?" Adonis had also apparently forgotten.

"To see where-eh he goes after AquaSphera," Kassi said with a yawn.

"And because Meela might know him," Savriah said.

"Right, right," Adonis said.

"You seem a little down today," Savriah said. She always knew–just like Amára did. Today, Kassi really wished she would stay out of her head.

"I'm fine," she lied. Savriah eyed her as if she were peering directly into her brain.

"Shouldn't we all go?" Fille asked.

"Your suits all have trackers," Sensei said. "If Ravana's monitoring Kassi's suit, she's likely monitoring yours, as well."

"She's monitoring my old suit," Kassi said. "My grips don't know I won the Race-eh for Blues. They have no idea I even have a new suit, which is why I need to go now!"

"Is it because Vander was with that Red Squall dame?" Savriah wouldn't let it go. Kassi wanted to scream at her but instead suppressed a pout.

"Vander was what? Vander was what?" Adonis asked.

"One of the new recruits - I don't remember her name,"

Savriah didn't seem to notice Kassi staring daggers at her. "They were cuddling on the balcony the whole night."

Mirific! I didn't need to know that detail.

"Speaking of which, where'd you run off to last night, Kassi?" Adonis asked.

"I...wasn't feeling well," Kassi said, her hand on her stomach.

"Remember? She likes Vander," Savriah whispered loudly enough for everyone to hear.

"Not anymore!" Kassi tried to sound convincing.

"The two new girls from the Squalls are Ganna and Tallie. Which one was it?" Fille demanded, tapping his foot impatiently.

"Probably, probably Ganna knowing our luck," Adonis said, slumping in his seat. Everyone apparently liked Ganna.

"Yisû, it was Ganna!" Kassi shouted with a dismissive swipe of the hand just as the bell rang. She bolted ahead of the others for class. During the next two periods, she turned away from them, and they left her alone. She just wanted the day to end so she could follow Nikola and distract herself with something perilous. It was exactly the kind of mission she would have dragged Amára into.

In the open locker room at the docks, Kassi bumped into Ganna. It didn't help that she was gorgeous–her perfectly-styled hair, her naturally long lashes, her full lips. And when they changed into their suits, Kassi couldn't help but notice how toned her abs and legs were–the body Kassi wished she had. Of course Vander was interested in her! Kassi searched for a reason to dislike her. Maybe she was cruel and insufferable like Malyra.

"Hi Kassi, I'm Ganna." She bowed respectfully and smiled. "We never officially met, but I saw your Race for Blues–so impressive! You're so brave doing what you did. I could never do something like that in front of a huge crowd." Her smile seemed genuine.

Sheist, Ganna's nothing like Malyra!

"Oh, you saw that? Thanks," Kassi said, forcing a polite smile.

Kassi changed into her new, heavily upgraded siren suit. It was magnificent. But even her brand new wettie wasn't enough to cheer her up.

Vander and Fille were now the two team captains, and Vander led today's dive. Kassi avoided eye contact with him. "We always dive together," Vander shouted as they reached the springboards. "Last one to Sector 11 is on suit cleaning duty. Now, let's shave the bed!" The light turned green and they dove.

On Nemal, whenever Caesar told them to "shave the bed," they would descend low enough to graze the ocean floor and touch the bottom with their fingertips. She and Amára would always grab a handful of sand. As Kassi dove into the cool Atlantic with her new team, she plunged to the bottom and combed a hand over the seabed in memory of better days.

Powering up her suit, Kassi lit four bulbs and blasted off into the Atlantic. With Vander and Vi'ella close behind, the three of them reached The Turq well before the rest, so Kassi decided to revive another old tradition from home. She swam laps around the waterfield just like she did before every game back on Nemal. She didn't notice it until now, but none of the Gaians ever circled the pitch before a contest. It gave her the lay of the land, a chance to assess the crowd, and it helped her acclimate to the pool and find her calm before the game. Seeing the crowds would always energize her. Her dad was always cheering her on from the stands. He never missed a game. Staring out into the deep ocean, Kassi felt so far away from home.

"Whatcha doing, Kassi?" Vi'ella asked.

Kassi returned her focus to the game. "Taking in the pitch before the game. Back home, we did this to find our calm."

"Mind if we join you?" Vander asked.

No, please don't, she wanted to say. "Uh, I don't mind." Kassi didn't want to sound rude.

They joined her for her second lap. As the other players

started showing up to the Sector, they saw the three of them swimming laps.

Vander filled them in before they could ask. "Kassi says they do this back where she's from before every game."

"Ok bubbleheads, huddle up!" Fille shouted. His voice was always loud like blaring trumpets in her helmet. He really didn't need to shout. They gathered in for position assignments. "Since this is our first game together, we'll probably have a few of you playing positions you don't normally play, and now we have four subs instead of two." He then issued them out one by one. Sandt, Nida, Starwell, and Simmone were on the bench to start out.

"You want me as Gater?" Johnes asked.

"Don't worry about it, Johnes. You'll get yours," Vi'ella said, patting him on the back.

Coach Rockson, Kiowa, and Sensei joined up with the team. "Alright chas, good news! With your recent wins and recruits, we've been given permission to officially coach the Krakens!"

Many whooped and cheered at this. "Now, we still coach Team Miami, and they take priority since they're in the Games, so any days we can't train during the regular time, we'll continue holding practice after our matches."

"Wish I could've seen Ms. Kofsky's face when you registered!" Fille said. Ms. Kofsky was the female officiator at the registration kiosk who had once refused to allow the Krakens to compete earlier in the season.

"Her head, her head probably exploded," Adonis said with wild hand gestures.

"Let's get to work!" Coach Rockson shouted, jumping right into their training.

Their match that day was against the Gray Orcas, the second-ranked team in the league. Orcas won the kickoff. Kassi took her position on the midway line.

"A little something I say before every game: singing small

doesn't serve the worlds," Vander said as he took his position next to Kassi.

"So let's sing it with sháloor!" The Krakens shouted in response. They had gotten used to Fille shouting this before every match.

Vander nodded with an approving look on his face, "You chas know about singing with sháloor? Bosst!"

With her sonopack powered up and four bulbs lit, Kassi was a nocked arrow, ready to fire. She hoped a brutal game of AquaSphera would help her forget about Vander and Ganna. However, with them both on her team, that would likely be impossible.

Vander took lead on the song playbook, picking one of Kassi's new songs. It was a different kind of Mendari Hîm, one of her recent additions, and Vander was eager to sing it. Kassi couldn't help but read into it, wondering if he meant something by selecting her new song.

She glanced over at him, hoping he would give her some kind of sign. Instead, she saw him look at Ganna and mouth something along the lines of "this one's for you."

I always get my hopes up!

Now she just wanted to tune him out. He was a very talented siren, and the song suited his voice, but Kassi didn't want to hear it and sing along. If only she could sing her own incantation, but they were a team and needed to be in sync. She was stuck providing support vocals in Vander's singing of her song as a love serenade to Ganna.

"Listen chas, when you get to that hook, you gotta really shmooze it!" Vander said. With a four-count, he jumped into it. Music and a choir of voices rang through Kassi's helmet, with Kassi's personal suit settings pushing her voice just above the mix.

HOP, SKIP, AND A JUMP

Baby, I've been missin' you for weeks I said

Baby, I've been missin' you
I've been callin' holophone
And wonderin' if you're home
So I'm gonna get there fast

A hop, skip, and a jump
And I'm with you
A hop, skip and a Jump and I'm there
A hop, skip, and a jump

Baby, we've been far apart for too long
Baby, we've been far apart
I'm worried that you'll find
Someone else is on your mind
So I'm gonna get there fast

Please believe me when I say
That I'm right on my way
And to show you that I care

A hop, skip, and a jump
And I'm with you
A hop, skip and a Jump and I'm there
A hop, skip, and a jump

IN EVÉIK

Pinokat, mitách budách lukosách tuvé ma osétó nayat
Diréla, pinokat, mitách budách lukosách tuvé nayat
Mitách budách hísînách dar li dînwabé nayat
I miharana lô bud hémé tuvat
Hûn píd shi prapíd ebi káshin nayat

În kers, chado, i în sultarû bud kin tuvé nayat
În kers, chado, i în sultarû i ebi bud nayat

În kers, chado, i în sultarû

Pinokat dur rutiv gam nubrin mitách budách bizé
Pinokat dur rutiv mitách budách bizé
Teryana sîm kudad patad tuvat
Bud dar tuví kilibé nezo neviþi
Hûn píd shi prapíd ebi káshin nayat

Bîtû truvîn mwabé máti diré nayat
Sîm anish bud dar nayalí modobé nayat
I shi most tuvé sîm flegîn nayat

În kers, chado, i în sultarû bud kin tuvé nayat
În kers, chado, i în sultarû i ebi bud nayat
În kers, chado, i în sultarû

As he sang it, Kassi imagined he was secretly singing for her. She couldn't help herself. Maybe he would be so impressed by her songwriting skills, he would realize his mistake and ditch the other dame.

Ugh, just focus on the game!

Gray Orcas spread out to form their first attack formation, marching toward the center gate. Kassi positioned herself to make a run on goal in case the Krakens managed to intercept and clear the center. Orcas connected a few passes and circled the gate as blue gaters rushed them to force a turnover. Ganna caused an interception, quickly bouncing a pass off her boot through the center gate. Vander waited for it on the other end. The second the center gate lit up bright blue, Kassi bolted for goal. Vander seized the opportunity, kicking a precision pass that threaded the defense. Onside when the pass was struck, Kassi swam behind the defensive line and retrieved it, tapping the glowing disc forward with her right foot for a clear shot on goal.

Swinging her right leg forward, she faked a shot that sent both goalies sprawling before propelling to the left. With a left-footed side bicycle, she sent it right down the middle for two points. Defenders swarmed to block any ricochet attempt.

After that, she got lost in the game. Zoned in, she scored a brace and helped her team win, 9-7. Once again, the other team stuck around to offer their congratulations. The tides were changing.

On the far end of the training pools, the Black Hydras concluded their own match. Kassi kept an eye on Nikola and waited for her moment to follow. He remained behind with Malyra as the rest of their team swam back to the mainland. They looked to be in a heated argument. She crossed her arms and wagged a finger at him. He turned and swam away. Malyra stomped and kicked like a spoiled child who was given the wrong flavor of iced cream. With him gone, she eventually swam back toward the docks.

That's my cue. Kassi blasted off after Nikola to catch up.

"Where you going, Kassi?" Joshi shouted into her comms.

"Power it down, Joshi, she's just going for a swim," Fille said before Kassi could think of an acceptable response.

Thanks, Fille. Kassi aligned herself directly in Nikola's swimming lane, careful to stay in his blind spot at a safe distance. He had intentionally broken her leg before, the last thing Kassi wanted was another physical altercation knowing how brutal Nikola could be.

He lit four bulbs, using his hand thrusters for maximum speed. Kassi matched it. *So you can light four bulbs!* Nikola only lit two during their game against the Black Hydras.

After almost forty-five minutes of supersonic speed, Nikola finally slowed and approached a nearby beach. Without gills, Kassi never would've made it this far. Her new suit was also equipped with a satellite-based radionavigation system, and it indicated that they were approaching a city named Charleston of the Atlanta Province.

Nikola surfaced, climbed a rusted metal ladder onto a small dock, and removed his helmet. Kassi kept low to the water and waited. The sun was only beginning to set–still plenty of light for Nikola to spot her. Since most of the streets here were also flooded, Kassi took advantage, powered down her suit, and silently swam alongside Nikola undetected as he made his way through Charleston.

He entered an old, abandoned building, its first floor completely submerged. Kassi found an entrance through an underwater doorway that reached a staircase to the upper floors. Careful to avoid any cameras, she silently ascended the rotting wooden steps underwater until she surfaced. As soon as she removed her helmet, she heard voices just up ahead and around the corner. Kassi froze like a woolly-possum playing dead.

Nikola and another male voice from the adjacent room echoed off the flat walls. "Have you heard anything from mom or dad?" The other voice asked, clearly Nikola's brother.

"Dad and Step Mom, Janine," Nikola corrected him. "They never spoke to me before, why would that change now?"

"I just thought it might be different this time," Nikola's brother said.

"You know they never cared about me. None of the family did. Wanna know the last thing they said to me?"

"What?" his brother said.

"Janine said she and dad were tired of pretending to love me. That my existence has always been the reason for dad's misery and depression," Nikola said.

Kassi silently gasped, quick to cover her mouth. *What kind of parents say something like that!*

"Sheist!" His brother said. "They were always so cruel to you. I'll never understand it."

"You were the only one who ever stood up for me," Nikola said. "And look where that got you–banished to Earth."

"Well, you're also the reason I made it to Paradise in the first place, winning the Games and all," his brother said.

"Funny how I thought that would be enough for the family to finally accept me as one of them," Nikola said. He paused for a beat before asking, "So how you holding up?"

"It could be worse. Charleston's no Paradise, but I'm managing," his brother said. "I'm helping my hossty make her way into the Siren Games. She's got real talent!"

"You're helping yours? Why in the worlds would you do that?" Nikola asked.

"Amára didn't do anything. Neither did your hossty," he said. "It's not their fault!"

Hearing Amára's name almost made her squeal out loud, but she smothered her mouth with her hands.

Ama's here!

"Isn't it?" Nikola raised his voice. "Their parents don't lift a finger to help the Gaians, they're too busy living on Paradise. Amára and Kassiana are just like them. Maybe not now, but they will be."

"How do you know that?"

"Because that's how they were raised, Enzo," Nikola said. "Brainwashed and lied to all their lives. Ravana brought them here to change all of that. Show them firsthand just how everyone else lives so maybe they'll convince their parents to open the portal."

"And they've seen it, haven't they? Why keep them here?" Enzo asked.

"Seeing it isn't enough. They need to experience it. They need to know the desperation we all feel every day!" Nikola shouted.

"For how long? Do they really need to stay here for years until they win? I don't know about your hossty, but Amára gets it. She's determined to help Gaians. Give her a chance to go back and talk to her parents about it," Enzo said.

"If she's really determined, have her prove it by winning the Games. Until then, we can't let her go back," Nikola said.

"But why are we imprisoning them?" Enzo asked. "Forcing them to do this isn't gonna win any of them over."

"Because they have to understand the full scope of it. If we just let them go, they'll hop back home and forget all about us behind their high walls and royal gardens."

"You should have more faith in them, Nikola."

"And you should have less, little brother," Nikola said. "People never do what they say. I'm not about to entrust my life and future into the hands of some 'disers just because they say they'll help us."

"Well I trust Amára," Enzo said. "And I want to help her get home so she can start the process. I don't wanna live down here forever."

"And I trust Ravana's methods. She'll get a quicker response from the Council of Creators," Nikola said.

"Her methods?" Enzo shouted. "She killed one of them the day they arrived."

"You know that was an accident…" A wooden step creaked loudly under Kassi's elbow, causing Nikola to stop short.

"What was that?" Enzo shouted.

Footsteps drummed in her direction. Kassi threw her helmet on and dove, swimming as fast as she could. With her heart leaping out of her chest, Kassi sang the first words that came to her mind, powered up her suit, and blasted off into the Atlantic.

Panic overcame her. She struggled to sing her incantation, heaving and gulping air in between phrases. Her suit sputtered, her palm thrusters fluttered and choked, but with the first and second bulbs lit, she managed to keep her foot thrusters on.

After ten minutes of broken subsonic speed, without thinking, Kassi twisted to glance back. At her pace, the rushing water spun her out. Tumbling and flipping with her arms flailing, it took her longer than it should have to revert to her training and use her hand thrusters to regain control. Disoriented, she squinted in all directions as fast as she could, trying to spot anyone rushing toward her. No one was in pursuit, but Kassi still couldn't relax. Her last underwater chase ended with her almost drowning. Her leg ached at the thought of Nikola breaking it again.

Her navigation system put her forty minutes away from the docks. Her breathing steadied enough to make the swim back. Every few minutes, on the way back, she paused to sweep her eyes in all directions and make sure no one was in pursuit.

The docks were empty by the time she landed. Dark and vacated, the lockers looked haunting. Her jagged pulse still raced. *Silence your fears!* Kassi rehearsed her siren meditations until she found her calm. She snatched her clothes and hustled home, still feeling a little vulnerable.

Once inside, with her back to the door, Kassi heaved a sigh of relief.

"C'mere a minute." Meela's voice startled Kassi.

"Ah! Don't sneak up on me like that!" Kassi placed a hand over her chest.

"Sneak? I'm jus' sittin' here!" Meela said. After a few deep breaths, Kassi took a seat next to Meela at the kitchen table. "Kyoto an' I've been thinkin' bout what you said 'bout th'last attack. 'Bout it bein' th'same exact diversion tactic an' all."

"Oh?" Kassi perked up.

"Th'story we been hearin' from Ravana don't add up," Meela shook her head. "Somethin' else's gon' on. Cain't be yer parents."

"That's what I've been saying!" Kassi threw her arms up. She never believed that accusation, but it still bothered her.

"We don't think Ravana's th'one behind it, neither. Don't make sense why she would. But somethin' else's goin' on. We gon' do some diggin' t'find out. Jus' thought ya should know."

"Glad to hear it," Kassi said as she rose to her feet.

"Hey, where'd you get that?" Meela pointed at Kassi's heavily upgraded wetsuit.

"Won it in a Race-eh for Blues," Kassi said, spinning to show off her new threads.

"Hmm," Meela nodded. "Well done, missy!"

"Thanks," Kassi said as she retreated up the stairs. Once in her room, she immediately passed out on her mattress, exhausted.

The next day before Period 1, she tracked down her friends in the halls and pulled them aside, eager to tell them everything.

"What happened, what happened?" Adonis asked.

"I followed Nikola up to Charleston."

"Up the coastline?" Fille asked.

"Yisû. He met with his brother, Enzo. They almost caught me, but I zhust barely got away!" Kassi exclaimed.

"So is he, is he a spy?" Adonis asked.

"He is!" Kassi said.

Everyone gasped. "So it's true!" Fille said.

"What a, what a dirty cacafuego!" Adonis said.

"But guess what?" Kassi bounced on her feet with excitement as a trio of singing 600s strolled past, eyeing her curiously. "I found her! I found Amára!"

"You actually, you actually saw her?" Adonis said.

"Well, no. Enzo zhust mentioned her. He's the one keeping an eye on her. But now I know where Amára is."

"Do you know where in Charleston? That's a big province," Savriah said.

"Well, no. But I'm sure-eh we can find her, right?"

"Hmm, they probably use the northern training pools for their AquaSphera games. Maybe we could swim up there after school."

"Yisû! Northern training pools!" Kassi clapped. "This afternoon!"

"When? We can't miss a game," Fille said. "We're on a streak. We just climbed two spots on the rankings with our win yesterday."

"We have four subs now–if we play a really easy team, you chas could probably win without me," Kassi said.

"Too risky," Fille said. "We can't take that chance right now."

"He's right, he's right," Adonis said. "We need you, Kassi!"

Kassi slumped. She knew they were right–Kassi needed to stick with her team. If only she didn't have to choose between her team and her cousin.

"We better get to class!" Fille said, checking the clock on the wall.

Kassi nodded and shuffled to Period 1, sinking into her seat in the back. Pulling out her hologlasses to prepare for the day's lecture, Kassi noticed something taped to the bottom of her desk. It was a small handwritten note that said:

I know it was you!

Twenty-Six

The words hit her like a thousand simultaneous rajabee stings. Whipping her head up, she saw Nikola glowering at her from his seat in the front row.

Kassi shrunk, beads of sweat trickling down her neck. During class, she nervously scratched her nails against the battered wooden desktop, wondering what Nikola might do about it. Her leg ached where he had broken it. When the bell rang, she hung back and waited for Nikola to leave first–he didn't. He let the Chinpoke Squad go on without him. Kassi didn't want another tardy with more assignments. Reluctantly, she got up from her seat and beelined for the halls.

Nikola stood to intercept, reaching her just outside the classroom. "I know it was you," he said again, his jaw muscles tightening. Kassi tried to pick up the pace, but he was tall and had long strides. "What did you hear?"

"What?" Kassi shot him a quick, nervous glance.

"My conversation with Enzo. What did you hear?"

"Nothing," Kassi lied.

"Tell me or I'll report you to the mediation officers!" Nikola growled. "They always listen when an 800 reports a 400. Or I could just tell Ravana you were trying to escape."

"I heard Enzo talking about my friend Amára," Kassi said.

"What else?"

"I heard what you said about your parents." Kassi made an attempt to sympathize.

"Sheist!" Nikola whirled on her, stopping them in the crowded hallway as students continued rushing past. Many cast them curious glances. "That was none of your business! What were you doing there?"

"You've been spying on me this whole time, and now you're upset I spied on you once?" Kassi huffed, her hands on her hips.

Nikola shook his head. "You had no business being there. I should report you."

"Enzo wouldn't report me," Kassi said softly.

"Why do you think I haven't already?" Nikola scowled and stormed off.

At lunch, Kassi shuffled to the 400s line and waited for her friends. She cast a glance at Nikola in line with the 800s. He locked eyes with her for a brief moment. Instead of his usual wicked glower, he studied her curiously. Kassi shifted, smoothing the wrinkles in her uniform. She was at least relieved that he wouldn't report her. Enzo's words must have affected him.

During AquaSphera practice, Kassi went through the motions. She couldn't stop thinking about Amára. Now that she knew where she was, she was desperate to find a way back up to Charleston.

Their game that day was against a weaker team of 500s. The first half dragged, which was unusual for Kassi. As the first half concluded, Blue Krakens led 7-0. It wasn't even close. Coach Rockson swam up to them. "Alright chas, meet me topside."

Kassi joined them on the U.N.O.E. cutters that floated just above the surface, climbing the metal steps to the aft deck of the boat where the rest of her team were grabbing green protein biscuits and refilling their O2 tanks and hydro-casks. With an untouched biscuit in hand, Kassi stared out across the water as if searching for her friend.

"You with us, Kassi?" Vander asked from behind her. Kassi turned to see the genuine concern in his beautiful emerald eyes. The day had been an emotional rollercoaster, and all she wanted to do was curl up in his arms and tell him everything. But then she saw Ganna clamp onto his arm and join the conversation. She smiled kindly at Kassi, too nice to dislike.

"Yisû, I zhust...miss my best friend from home-eh," Kassi sighed.

"I can only imagine," Vander said. Kassi nodded and pretended to smile, trying to hide her jealousy as she eyed Ganna at his side.

"Vander told me your story," Ganna said, her fingers sliding into Vander's. "I'm so sorry, Kassi! If you need to take a break and clear your head, you should."

"Ganna's right. This game's as good as won," Vander said. "Do what you need to do."

Kassi thought about that as she stared more intently at the open ocean around her. Maybe she didn't have to choose between her team and best friend. They could finish this game without her. She could still make it in time if she left now for the northern training pools.

This could be my only chance to see her!

Glancing back at Vander and Ganna, she saw understanding in their eyes. "Go," Ganna said with a smile. "We'll tell the others."

Kassi nodded and said, "Thank you!"

With a hiss, her helmet sealed and she dove back into The Turq. Powering up her sonopack, Kassi torpedoed northward, entering the coordinates as she sliced through the water.

The water of the northern training pools was darker than the ones near Alice Town. Teams were concluding their games in all sectors–Kassi barely made it.

Her eyes swept over the waterfields as she swam above each

of them. Sirens noticed Kassi hovering above the sectors and eyed her curiously. However, they paid her their respects as she passed, bowing low. For a 400, that was a very strange response. Maybe they treated 400s differently up here. As she took a breath and extracted oxygen through her suit's gills, the realization hit her. They thought she was an 800! And with all the upgrades Vi'ella earned over the years, they must have regarded her as a very elite 800.

By creating a spectacle above the training pools, athletes paused to look directly at her before resuming their matches, giving Kassi a clear view of their faces.

"C'mon, Amára! Where are you?" She had scanned over half of the training field with no sign of her.

Reaching one of the last sectors, Kassi strained her eyes. *Amára!*

"Ama! Ama!" Kassi shouted, frantically waving her hands, her arms, her legs, and anything else she could shake.

Amára's hair was longer now, pulled back in a tight, low ponytail. She was floating near her opponent's end gate as gaters fought over control of the center. From the looks of it, Amára's team was well in the lead and the game was nearly over. One of the gaters was a boy that looked just like Nikola with short curls. *Enzo!* Amára lifted her gaze and spotted Kassi. Her eyes grew wide as saucers as her lips mouthed, "Kassi? KASSI!"

Amára bulleted toward the sideline and pointed to one of their subs. He immediately took her spot, a bewildered look on his face. She then swam to Kassi, her eyes welling with tears. Kassi heard a mixture of giggling and crying escape her own lips. They embraced, nearly squeezing the air out of each other. When they parted, Kassi saw Amára's mouth moving, muted. Kassi held her wrist to Amára's to link audio. As soon as she did, Kassi heard her best friend's voice for the first time in months.

"I can't believe it's you," Amára said in Evéik, holding both of Kassi's arms as they floated in the water. Her voice was rich and melodic like a dazzling viola solo.

Kassi smiled, unable to wipe her tears. *"I found you!"* Games all around them ended and sirens were swimming back. Enzo was quick to join them and link to their frequency.

"Yisû, but how?" She asked.

"I just followed his brother." She looked over at Enzo, who soon realized who she was.

"That was you!" He said in broken Evéik, raising both eyebrows.

"You must be Enzo," Kassi said, switching back to English.

"Yisû," He said, studying Kassi closely.

"Enzo's brother, Nikola," Kassi told Amára, "he's the one who watches and reports everything I do."

"He let you follow him?" Amára asked.

"No! He didn't let me," Kassi said. "In fact, he threatened to report me."

"Yash, he would do that," Enzo said.

"But as soon as I found out where you were-eh, I had to come-eh see you," Kassi said, staring at her old friend. This reunion felt like a dream.

Amára did the same and chuckled as she said, switching back to Evéik, *"So how do you like the early mornings?"*

"They're the absolute worst! I can't even sleep in on the weekends! And the food?"

"It tastes like a party in my mouth…" Amára began.

"…and everyone's throwing up," they said in unison. Something they said whenever they drank Caesar's vegetable juices. He would juice tomatoes and red peppers with celery and drink it straight. At the time, she thought they were disgusting, but compared to the Gaians' muck juice–bleh! They were still gross.

"It's nothing like our spreads at the palace," Amára said.

"I miss those so much!" Kassi said, her stomach rumbling.

"So who's there to make sure you get up? You don't have me there to pull off the covers."

"I don't even have covers," Kassi said. *"I barely have a blanket."*

"Same."

"At first when I got here, my grips installed the most obnoxious alarm clock. It would beep and fly around the room until I could swat it down," Kassi said, swatting at the ocean water as if imagining her old alarm clock. *"Fortunately, I talked them into giving me a normal alarm clock. And you? What do you do with yourself now that you don't need to take care of me in the mornings?"*

"My grips have a cat, so I take care of her."

"You got a kittee? No fair!" Kassi pretended to pout.

"Yisû, I guess." Amára's smile faded. *"I miss home!"*

Kassi nodded, her voice soft, *"I know, me too."*

"Amára always talks about you," Enzo said, bringing the conversation back to English. "Good to finally put a face to the name!"

Amára examined Kassi's suit and raised her eyebrows. "Ghost of Sheebah! You're an 800?"

Kassi shook her head, "No! I'm a 400. I zhust won this suit in a Race-eh for Blues."

"Bosst, me too!" Amára said. Kassi noticed the crimson-red stripe on her collar. "Wish I could've seen it! Who'd you race-eh?"

"This bully in my school–Malyra," Kassi said with a smile. "You'll never believe it, Ama! I lit the fifth bulb and pulsed her out!"

"Great Sheebah's ghost!" Amára exclaimed.

"I still can't believe I did it!"

"I can't believe I missed it!" Amára said.

"What about you? Who'd you race-eh?" Kassi asked.

"This boy named Marcasa. He wasn't a bully, but he was pompous," Amára said. "He needed a good dose of humility, and I needed a better suit. So I challenzhed him the first week I got here-eh."

"The first week?" Kassi was right. Amára was instant royalty down here.

"Your voice-eh sounds healed." Amára inspected Kassi's neck.

"I had to wait a month and a half, but I found a healer from home-eh," Kassi said, rubbing the neckline of her suit. "He printed me new vocal cords."

"It's ludicray you had to go through all that!" Amára said, furrowing her brows.

"And it sounds like my brother hasn't been making it easy on you," Enzo said.

"You chas are nothing alike!" Kassi said.

"Don't judge Nikola. He's had it rough his whole life," Enzo said. "He's hellbent on taking revenge on somebody. It should be my parents, but for now, it's you."

"At least I finally know why," Kassi said.

"What does he do?" Amára sounded concerned.

Kassi filled her in on some of the highlights of Nikola's relentless bullying. Amára clenched her fists as she listened. Nikola was lucky he wasn't here right now. Amára would have likely unleashed fury on him.

"I've been so worried about you!" Kassi said.

Amára relaxed her muscles and shrugged. There was a sadness in her eyes Kassi had never seen before. Amára had always been so upbeat and optimistic. It broke her heart to see her like this. "I've been worried about you, too, Kassi." They floated in silence for a brief moment before Amára added, "You think we'll ever get back home-eh?"

"I hope-eh so," Kassi said quietly. She wished she could be more encouraging. But Amára had always been the hopeful one. With her down, Kassi was lost.

Amára asked, "Did you get a messazhe from your family?"

"Yisû," Kassi said. "During the Siren Games, someone slipped me a holodrive."

"Me too."

"I think our parents knew about Ravana's plan before she kidnapped us," Kassi said.

"They did?" Amára cocked her head to the side.

"My dad said something curious," Kassi said.

Enzo interrupted, "Chas, I hate to rush the reunion, but we gotta flake off if we're gonna get back before anyone notices we're gone. Especially now that Nikola is onto you. You don't want him to report you."

"I love that you came-eh! I would have come sooner if I knew where you were-eh," Amára said, her eyes growing misty.

Tears welled in her eyes–Kassi didn't want to say goodbye. They powered up their suits and swam toward the coast. En route, Kassi swerved in front of Amára. "Whoosh."

Amára smiled and sped up to weave in front of Kassi with a "Whoosh." Back on Nemal, they would do this back and forth as they spiraled and danced through the water. It brought her back home, even if just for a brief moment.

"Ashkana tuv!" Kassi said.

"Ashkana tuv, ashté!" Amára said back as Kassi banked left and torpedoed southward back to Miami.

Kassi sang a variety of Evéik incantations for the journey back to Miami Beach, arriving at the docks. They were empty once again. She grabbed her uniform and ran home.

As she did, her attention shifted to Ravana and her methods. Ravana wanted them to convince their parents just how difficult it was for Gaians to make it to Paradise. That part made sense, even if she didn't like it. But why did she have to separate them? Why did Kassi have to sneak off to Charleston to see her best friend and then worry about serious repercussions if she got caught? After seeing the sadness in Amára's eyes, Kassi wanted to be there for her. But she couldn't. It made her angry at Ravana for keeping them apart.

Frustrated, her steps quickened as the soles of her shoes gripped the wooden planks of the slidewalks and propelled her forward. Reaching the townhome, she burst through the door and stormed inside. She glanced up and nearly tripped over herself.

Two strangers waited for her at the kitchen table.

Twenty-Seven

A moon-pale man with dark eyebrows, high and tight black hair, and deep-set eyes stared at Kassi as he smoked an unusually fat fumer–probably Market Abyss contraband. Indecipherable tattoos crept up both sides of his neck. The woman seated next to him had a brunette pixie bob and a weasel face. Kassi recognized her immediately–the face that haunted her dreams.

Ghost of Sheebah!

Images flooded Kassi's brain of this same woman blasting her with a sonic cannon just before she nearly drowned. The trauma resurfaced. Kassi felt her throat constrict and her breathing quicken. It took every effort to focus.

Inhale. Exhale. Inhale, exhale–breathe, Kassi! She told herself. The woman flashed the same thin-lipped smile, probably noticing Kassi's discomfort.

When Kassi finally regained her calm, she asked, "What's going on?"

No response.

"Where are Kyoto and Meela?"

"They're gone," the man said, scratching the side of his nose. "You got us, now." The woman eyed Kassi as if she were some live squirrel she couldn't wait to dissect. Even though Kassi was fully clothed, she felt the need to cover up. "I'm Moza, and this is my girlfriend, Farra. We're your new grips." He spoke with his eyes half open.

"What happened to Kyoto and Meela?" Kassi asked again.

"You snuck off to Charleston." Moza puffed his fumer and leaned forward. "Are you planning an escape? Think you'll get away with your little friend?"

Farra sauntered over to Kassi and circled her like a hawk looking for the perfect angle to descend on her prey. She fingered Kassi's braided hair, stroked the skin on the side of her neck, and patted her waist. Kassi recoiled, trying to distance herself.

"Answer the question, princess," Farra said. Her voice was scratchy, as if from screaming all day. She lit her own fumer without breaking eye contact with Kassi.

"Escape-eh?" Kassi's eyes darted back and forth between them. "I didn't...I was zhust visiting my friend. Making sure she was..."

"LIAR!" Farra lunged forward, finger pointed centimeters from Kassi's face. "We know what you're up to!"

"I'm telling the truth!" Kassi pleaded.

Like a woman possessed, Farra lurched forward and yanked Kassi's arm toward her, stabbing it with her burning fumer. Kassi howled. Pain like electricity shot up her arm as she retreated until her back was against the far corner of the room, a fresh red burn on her arm.

"Quit lying you little penchode! Tell us your plan!" Kassi barely heard it over the pain. She didn't move, cradling her arm.

Moza stood, a full head taller than both of them. Studying Kassi closely, he said, "Kyoto and Meela were too lenient. We won't be. We've got eyes and ears on you at all times, and we'll be watching."

Kassi huddled in the corner.

Farra finally broke her gaze and meandered into the kitchen

as she said to Moza, "She'd fetch a good price." Kassi noticed the scarlet red armband on Farra's arm. Moza had the same.

They're 800s?

"You know Ravana won't approve of that," Moza said, taking another casual puff of his fumer as he leaned against a countertop.

"I'm just saying." Farra perched on one of the seats and flashed a predatory grin at Kassi. "Things are gonna be different from now on, princess!"

As hungry as she should be, Kassi lost her appetite and escaped upstairs. Her bedroom was deplorable, but it was her only sanctuary. Once the door was shut, Kassi stared at her arm. The angry red of her skin was still painfully hot and starting to itch with ferocity. As bad as she had been treated as a 400, she couldn't believe someone would be so barbaric as to stab her with a burning fumer.

Farra was the last person in the worlds Kassi wanted as her grip. A moonstruck sadist, she was supposed to have been "dealt with" by Ravana. Apparently, instead, Ravana put this raving lunatic in charge. Kassi might not have any love for Kyoto and Meela, but they were familiar, predictable. They had even started doubting the information Ravana fed them.

Could that be why they were replaced? Kassi wondered.

Kassi tossed and turned all night. She had barely fallen asleep when she was awakened with the ominous sense that someone was staring at her. Peeling her eyes open one at a time, she turned her head just as Farra pounced on top of Kassi and rolled her onto her stomach. A strong hand gripped her braided hair and yanked her head back.

Snip snip.

Released, Kassi scrambled to her feet and against the wall, feeling where her hair should have been.

It's gone!

Her fingers trembled as they reached higher and higher until they finally found hair. She pulled the rest out of her braid–uneven lengths that didn't even reach her shoulders!

For as long as she could remember, she'd had long, thick hair down to her waist. It was one of the few things she took pride in. It took years to grow and, within seconds, it was hacked off. Kassi stood for several beats, fingering the new ends of her hair in disbelief.

The shock was soon replaced with anger. Kassi clenched her fists and glared at Farra.

"You wanna take a crack at me? Go ahead!" Farra's gravelly voice cut through the darkness like a bone saw, the stench of her morning breath invading the air. She took a fighting stance and held up the pair of scissors like a cobra ready to strike. Kassi took a step back and unclenched her fists. "You've got five minutes to be downstairs, princess!" Farra whisper-shouted and disappeared down the hall.

Kassi's entire body was shaking. Starlight seeped through the lone window. The clock glowed in the darkness, reading 05:15–more than an hour before she needed to get up. Her quivering hands reached for her phantom hair. She flipped the light on in the washroom and assessed the damage. Jagged hair fell to her collarbone. Angry tears escaped her eyes as she pulled up what was left of it into a ponytail and tried to process what happened.

Downstairs, she found Farra lounging on a sofa seat in the living room, a fresh fumer in her hand. Moza wasn't there. The silence was thick at this unworldly hour. Kassi lingered on the bottom stair as if descending the final step meant entering Farra's lair.

"See that box over there?" Farra asked as she pointed at a large cardboard box at the base of the stairs. "Bring it here!"

Kassi reluctantly did as she was told, wishing instead she could hurl the box right at Farra's head. The box was heavy–probably too heavy to throw. She hefted it to the living room coffee table, trying to stay as far from Farra as possible.

"Open it," Farra demanded. Inside, Kassi found a small grinder, dried flower buds, filters, and rolling paper. "You're gonna roll fumers for me to sell," Farra said. "I'm asking top U-Coin for these on the Market Abyss, so they better be rolled to perfection!"

"Why would I do that?" The words slipped out before Kassi could stop herself. Farra leaped forward and snared Kassi's arm, pressing another burning fumer down onto her bare skin. Kassi screamed and collapsed to the ground in pain.

"Now get rolling!" Farra shouted, raising her fumer up as if to burn her again. Kassi scrambled to her feet.

Withdrawing the contents from the box, she fumbled with the papers, the buds, and the filters. "I don't know how," Kassi said as she examined it.

"Figure it out!"

Kassi made a pile of rolling paper and a second pile of the buds she apparently needed to grind as filling for the fumers. The grinding was easy enough, but when she tried rolling the first one, leaves scattered everywhere and the wrapper didn't stick. It was a mess.

"You have to lick it you dumb penchode! Haven't you ever smoked a fumer before?" Farra scoffed.

"Uh, no. Never had any interest," Kassi said. "Why would anyone buy these-eh? They already get free ones from the U.N.O.E."

"Sheebah's shrine, you're dense!" Farra shouted. "The U.N.O.E. fumers are weaker than dirt. These are top grade. Don't you know anything?"

After a few more tries, she rolled the first acceptable fumer. As the initial shock of the new burn subsided, all Kassi could think about was enacting revenge on her psychopathic new grip.

As if Farra could read her mind, she said, "And don't you get any ideas about asking anyone for help. If someone comes for me, I'll make sure you never swim again!" Farra shouted from her armchair. "Or maybe I'll make sure you end up just like those friends of yours who tried to escape."

"My friends?" Kassi paused.

"You heard about the bombings?" Farra asked. Kassi gave a subtle nod. "Both were escape attempts. What do you think we did to your friends and those helping them?"

"What?" Kassi found herself asking the question, not wanting to know the answer. Farra just smiled a devilish grin.

For the next hour, Kassi rolled as many as she could while Farra hovered, inspecting each new fumer closely. As soon as her own fumer burned out, she replaced it with a new one from Kassi's pile. If Kassi ever thought to take a breather, Farra held her lit burner up as an ever-present threat.

"You should be grateful to Ravana, you know." Farra blew steam in Kassi's face. Fortunately, fumers were odorless, but they did little to mask Farra's foul breath. "If it weren't for her, you'd be entertaining my guests. And you're lucky Moza won't let me break the rules."

The skin around the burns continued to itch. The scars looked hideous. Her school uniform sleeves weren't long enough to cover them. It was almost 06:30 when she was supposed to get ready for school. Moza finally awoke and descended the stairs to find them in the living room.

"What's this?" he asked, one eyebrow raised.

"Don't give me that look," Farra sneered. "We're just having a little fun!"

"She needs to go to school," he said, shooing Kassi away like an annoying fly. "You, go get ready. Breakfast will be ready in a minute."

Kassi didn't wait for a second invitation. She shoved past the cardboard box on the coffee table and climbed the stairs to her room, overhearing Farra as she did.

"You're such a buttshark, Moza!"

"Ravana entrusted us with a prime hossty! Don't you dare stuff this opportunity for me!" Moza said, raising his voice.

Whether from exhaustion or fear, Kassi's hands shook as she pulled out her ponytail and roughly braided two short pigtails.

They barely reached the base of her neck. She wanted to cry, but there was no time.

At the kitchen table, she inhaled her food rations and bolted out the door for school. There were no more rude surprises from Farra before she left, most likely due to Moza's presence.

On her walk to school, Kassi couldn't stop trembling–she almost fell into the street water more than once. Her hands continued grasping for hair that was no longer there.

The holoscreens flashed a news update:

"BREAKING NEWS: *the Counter-terrorist elite forces have captured the first Hel Mafia terrorists. In a worldwide effort to restore safety to our planet, the U.N.O.E. has worked tirelessly to bring those responsible for these heinous crimes to justice. The date of their public executions will be announced shortly. We expect these two to be the first of many...*"

KASSI GLANCED up at the photos of two familiar faces plastered on the giant holoscreens. It was Kyoto and Meela!

Twenty~Eight

"**F**our Hundie, keep it movin'!" Came grunts of protest from behind her. Kassi had apparently stopped to stare at the screens, creating a foot traffic jam.

She resumed her walk to school, trying to make sense of the news. Kyoto and Meeta had questioned Ravana's explanation behind the bombings and were now its prime suspects. None of it made sense—it only filled Kassi's mind with questions. The scorch marks on Kassi's arm continued to itch, but at least the pain had mostly subsided.

In *Heroics*, Nikola was surrounded by the Chinpoke Squad, laughing and lollybagging before class. But when he glanced over at Kassi, his usual smugness was gone.

"What happened to all your hair, Klutziana?" Calandra shouted for all the class to hear.

Malyra joined in, "Didn't anyone ever tell you it's dangerous to run with scissors?" The class erupted in laughter.

Racing to her desk, Kassi buried her head, instinctively reaching again for her phantom hair. Since the Race for Blues, Malyra had mostly left Kassi alone. Kassi thought her bullying days were done—apparently not.

"Alright, settle down," Professor Oakey said, sounding tired. "We have a lot to go over today."

Near the end of class, Kassi raised her hand. In her bustle to get ready and leave the townhome, Kassi forgot to use the washroom. She desperately needed to, and lunch wasn't for a few more hours.

"What is it?" Professor Oakey asked, her hands on her hips.

"May I be excused to use the washrooms? It's an emergency!"

"We all know what that means!" Malyra shouted as the class rippled with snickers and stifled laughs.

"Come here," Oakey said. Kassi thought she might actually give her permission. Instead, once Kassi was within range, Oakey reached out and pinched her extra hard right on her newly burned skin. A yelp escaped Kassi's mouth. "I'm giving you a warning this time, Miss Katiana," Professor Oakey said. "Next time you ask, it'll be detention!"

"It's Kassiana," Kassi said under her breath as she blinked back tears of pain and returned to her seat.

When the bell rang, Kassi bolted for the door. Calandra stuck her foot and sent Kassi spilling onto the floor. As much as she wanted to rip Calandra's pink and blonde hair out, every second counted, so she popped back up and beelined for the washrooms. They were completely empty. The only good thing about the limited time between classes, the washrooms were always unoccupied.

By the time she reached *History of the Worlds*, Dr. Jibu was already into his lecture. "You're tardy! Go to the cafeteria." Kassi groaned. Now she would have extra assignments due by tomorrow–they were easy enough, but still took up valuable time. If she failed to turn those in on time, it was detention, and she didn't want to miss any AquaSphera games.

As she watched the mind-numbing presentation on punctuality, she tried to process everything that had happened that morning. She was still in denial, expecting to find her long hair intact.

Things had finally been looking up–new voice, new team, new wetsuit, and she had found Amára. But now, a maniacal Farra pulled her under a new riptide. Kassi dreaded returning back to that townhouse.

After getting the broomstick in *P.E.*, again, Kassi joined her friends in the cafeteria.

Savriah said, "I saw Meela's face on the news update."

"Yisû. I got new grips last night." Kassi nodded. "Moza and this perverted cacafuego named Farra. Look what she did!" She flashed her arms' scars, then turned her head, flicking her short braid.

"Your hair!" Savriah gasped, covering her mouth.

"Are those fumer burns?" Fille pointed.

"Does it, does it still hurt?" Adonis asked, grabbing Kassi's arm for a closer look.

"It mostly itches," she said as she scratched the fringes around the scar. Kassi was more upset about her hair. It would take her years to grow it back.

In his classroom, Sensei K examined her burns closely as Kassi detailed her traumatic morning. "Why is she like this?" Kassi asked, tugging on her sleeve to try and cover the burns. It didn't help. "First my voice-eh, and now this! What did I ever do to her?"

Professor Kelipalo furrowed his brows, stood up, and walked to the classroom windows, staring out over the flooded streets. He spoke without turning, "You know when I was a boy about your age, I went to school in a small town called Kahului," Sensei began. "Lars, a dear friend of mine, always came to school in long sleeves, no matter how hot it was outside–always long sleeves." Sensei looked back at them and continued, "I often asked him about it. He gave me the same deflective answer each time, 'Gotta hide these guns so I don't make the rest of you chas jealous,' he'd say as he patted his biceps.

"But one day, we were out on the beach and some girls were daring us to swim with them in the ocean. My friend, Lars, really liked the girls but was giving them some bogus excuse about needing to walk his dog or something. The girls knew he was making it up. They tried to corner him and take his shirt off. He dodged and ducked playfully, trying not to ruin the mood, but got tripped up over a branch in the sand and the girls got him—tugged that shirt right off. And that's when I saw it." Sensei grew quiet, and when he turned to them, his eyes were misty. "Lars had fumer burns all over his body, just like those. All this time I knew him, I had no idea he was being abused by the very people who were supposed to protect him."

Kassi and her friends patiently waited while Sensei paused for a few beats to stare over the ocean, heaving uneven breaths and wiping a tear from his eye, before he continued, "The next day, I sat him down and told him what I'll tell you." Sensei sat Kassi down and looked her in the eye. "You did absolutely nothing to deserve this. Every day you're gonna find yourself at a crossroads. You can choose to let their perverse actions darken your bright future, or you can leave them behind, get on the other side of this, and become an inspiration to others."

Kassi stared at the floor, holding her knees to her chest.

Sensei studied her for a few beats before he stood, shoulders tense. "I always wish I could go back and help Lars get away from his abusers. I'll find a way to help you with yours."

That afternoon at the training pools, Vander noticed Kassi yawning. "Looks like somebody's burning the candle at both ends," he said.

"Her new grips are the ones burning things," Fille said. "Like Kassi's arms with their fumers."

"Wait, who's doing what?" Vander asked, his deep emerald eyes locking with hers. He eyed Kassi's arms, which were now fortunately covered by her wetsuit. She didn't want him to see her hideous scars.

"What happened to all your hair?" Vi'ella asked.

Kassi looked at Vander, opening her mouth to try and explain. But she couldn't say it out loud, not again, not to him.

When Kassi couldn't answer, Fille recounted everything and filled them in.

"I would've killed her where she sat," Vi'ella said. "In broad daylight, I don't care."

"Forcing a minor to participate in illegal activities," Vander said, "and physical abuse. Both are against the law. She should be reported."

"We're 400s, we're 400, remember?" Adonis said. "Authorities won't do sheist!"

"Wouldn't authorities already know?" Kassi asked. "There are cameras." All this time, the U.N.O.E.'s lack of intervention had been a relief, but now, Kassi actually wanted them to step in and do something.

"That's true," Vander said. "They always know."

"Well we gotta do something," Vi'ella said. "We can't just float here and let some lunatic burn holes in our friend."

"If you try to help, Farra will just make it worse," Kassi said softly.

"Is there anything we can do?" Vander asked.

When Kassi remained quiet, Fille said, "We can help Kassi win the Siren Games!"

Vander nodded. "You heard them chas, let's go out there and win another one for the Krakens!" The team grunted and took their positions.

With Kassi still rattled and tired, it wasn't her best match, but Kassi still made two assists to help her team win another victory.

After the game, Coach pulled her aside. "I'm impressed by you, Kassi. With all you got going on in your life, you still show up to play."

"Thanks, Coach," Kassi said.

Once at the docks, Kassi watched her friends leave as she stood paralyzed, dreading the monster that awaited her at the townhouse. Slowly, she made her way back, trying to think of an excuse, any excuse to be somewhere else. Eventually, she found herself at the front door. With a deep breath, she went inside.

For the next hour, Kassi rolled fumers from the couch. Her fingers started to cramp, and the quality of her rolling worsened. Without warning, Farra's hand shot out, pressing a lit fumer into Kassi's right forearm. Kassi shrieked.

"You're getting sloppy!" Farra said.

"They're going to notice all these burns!" Kassi said.

"Just remember what I'll do to you if anyone interferes!" Farra said. "Now, pick up the pace or the next one's on your neck!"

Moza walked downstairs and surveyed the scene, scowling at Farra.

"Don't look at me like that," Farra said, rolling her eyes.

To Kassi, Moza said, "Grab your dinner and go."

After grabbing a plate of rations, Kassi rushed to her room, as if hiding behind her bedroom door would be enough to keep Farra away. She sunk heavily onto her mattress and set the plate on the nightstand.

After another early morning of rolling fumers, Kassi headed to Saturday cleaning at the school. By the time she arrived, Fille and Adonis were already dancing around with excitement. "Next weekend is round three of the Games–Sonic Battles!"

"Yash, that's next week. I almost forgot," Kassi said. With all she was going through, Kassi had lost track of time. Back on Nemal, she and Amára always counted down the days for each round of the Siren Games.

"You almost forgot?" Fille shouted, whirling on Kassi. He seemed to notice the fresh burns on her arms. "Oh, right. Sorry, Kassi!"

During AquaSphera, Kassi was too physically and emotionally drained to contribute. After another Blue Kraken win, Kassi didn't dare go anywhere but straight back to the townhouse, its gaping jaws open to consume Kassi. She could almost sense Farra's eyes boring into her from the other side of the front door. Her hand trembled as she opened it. In the doorway, Farra counted stacks of U-Coins she had likely earned from Kassi's hard work.

"Do I get any of that?" Kassi asked without thinking. She immediately regretted it.

Farra snatched Kassi's arm and pressed her smoldering fumer into the skin just above her elbow. Kassi howled. She instinctively scanned the room for a weapon to retaliate.

Farra must have noticed the anger in Kassi's eyes. "Remember, you touch me and you'll never swim again! So start rolling, princess!"

Her fingers were almost numb by the time Moza returned home from work. Sleep was nothing more than a short break as she was at it again early Sunday morning.

On her way to school for Sunday cleaning, a news update flashed on all of the holoscreens.

"...HIS mysterious death comes as a shock to us all. Grand Deputy Arthur Doss died of an unknown disease never before seen. Before and after photos from the past few months indicate some form of accelerated aging, but experts are baffled as to the cause..."

FROM HER STUDIES ON NEMAL, Kassi had learned that Grand Deputies made up the top inner circle of the governing body just below the three presidents of the U.N.O.E. They were some of the most powerful chas on Planet Earth, and one of them had just mysteriously died. Judging from the responses of those walking on the slidewalks around her, nobody cared. Kassi's nose itched. She let out a loud, disruptive sneeze. Practically the entire street whipped their heads in her direction and scowled.

Apparently, me sneezing is bigger news.

At the front entrance of the school, Kassi sneezed again. Reaching her friends in the corridor, she sneezed a third time. "Ugh, I'm so sneezy today!"

"It's allergy season," Savriah said. "I get it, too." Kassi had never had allergies before. Life on Earth was chock-full of foreign, wretched experiences.

After Mr. Benetti checked all the 400s in, Jacen, Jaya, and Royce disappeared as usual while the rest of them spent the morning playing hallway hockey on the top floor with Professor Oakey's nameplate. For as long as she had known them, Jacen, Jaya, and Royce had never participated in their lollybagging. But ever since they were cut from the team, it seemed they made a much greater effort to avoid everyone completely.

Following their training with the coaches, they won another match in AquaSphera and climbed another notch up the ranks. Returning to the townhome, Farra wasn't there—only Moza! Kassi let out the biggest sigh of relief. Moza snored loudly on the couch, his holopad resting on the coffee table. As long and thin as a pencil, his holopad was a pearly white with gold trim on both ends.

Maybe I could message Ravana—the one person who could stop Farra. She clearly wouldn't approve of how I'm being treated.

Kassi tiptoed toward him, breathing silently while aware of every tick and creak in the floorboards. She had never tread so quietly in her life. Skirting the long coffee table, crumpled fumer papers and flecks of dried bud leaves still dusting its surface, she squatted down and delicately retrieved the holopad.

Powering it up, she held it in front of Moza's face to unlock the home screen—nothing. She wasn't close enough. She inched closer and stretched to hold it directly in front of his face, A bead of sweat tickled her nose. She felt a sneeze coming.

Sheist, not again!

The holopad lit up, recognizing Moza's face. The welcome screen projected into the air above the thin device.

The tickling sensation in her nose overwhelmed Kassi. She couldn't stifle it. Taking two muted, bounding leaps toward the kitchen, holopad in hand, she let out a loud sneeze.

Moza woke for a brief second, turning toward Kassi and

studying her face. "Gesûn!" He said before rolling over and resuming his nap. Kassi exhaled, realizing she had been holding her breath.

From her kitchen seat, Kassi pulled up his messaging application. She found Ravana listed in his contacts. Starting a new message, Kassi typed quickly, describing in as much detail all that Farra had done over the past few days. Moza continued snoring.

Kassi concluded her message and reviewed everything. She reviewed it again, and a third time. The send button hovered within reach.

"What are you doing?" Moza's voice punched through the silence. Lightning quick, Kassi's hand swiped closed the messaging application. Moza's clothes rustled against the old leather fabric as he rolled over to face her. He eyed the holopad and jumped to his feet, closing the distance with two quick strides to snatch it from the table. "Why do you have this?" He asked, shaking the device in the air.

Kassi blinked, her tongue in knots. She could feel the sweat soaking through her school jumper.

Moza clutched the holopad and eyed Kassi suspiciously. Without another word, he retired up the stairs to his bedroom. The door locked behind him.

Slumped in her chair, Kassi stared vacantly at the floor. She had almost gotten the message off. If only she hadn't reviewed it so many times. Frustrated, Kassi stomped upstairs and collapsed onto her lumpy mattress.

The next morning, at 05:15, Kassi jolted awake with a bucket of ice-cold water in the face. She gasped for breath.

"Aww, did you think I was gonna let you sleep in?" Farra chuckled and walked out of the room just as she growled, "Five minutes!" After another morning of rolling fumers, Kassi dragged her feet to school.

As she fell heavily into her seat at lunch, Kassi exclaimed, "I can't do this much longer!"

"I'm so sorry, Kassi! We'll find a way to get rid of her," Sensei said, furrowed brows. He offered Kassi a salve from his drawer for the burns.

"I almost got a messazhe off to Ravana yesterday," Kassi said, her words slurred a little. Her brain was in a fog from sleep deprivation.

"You think that'll help?" Sensei asked.

"Ravana said our grips are supposed to treat us with honor and respect," Kassi explained. "And she mentioned punishing Farra when she attacked me with her sonic cannon. Maybe she zhust needs to know what's going on."

"Worth a try," Sensei said, rubbing his chin.

That afternoon in the locker room, loud and obnoxious as usual, Malyra and the Chinpoke Squad stripped off their school uniforms and lingered, as if on display with their curves and well-toned muscles. Kassi grunted with pain as she slid her wetsuit on over all the scars.

"Girl, I'm hurting just listening to you," Vi'ella said, sitting on the adjacent bench as she twisted into her own wettie.

"Farra never lets up. Early mornings and late-eh nights," Kassi said.

"You're working harder than a one-legged dancer in a kick-line," Vi'ella said, shaking her head. "You need to sit this game out. Let your body rest."

"But the team needs me," Kassi said.

"We got an easy team today–the Crystal Caimans. They're third to last," Vi'ella said. "Simmone needs more experience, anyway."

"You think I should?" Kassi didn't want to let her team down, but Vi'ella was right.

"Listen, you're no good to us if you're dead," Vi'ella said. "You gotta take care of yourself."

The team dove without Kassi. Lying on one of the steel benches, she accessed her reading material from Sensei's Evéik assignments. Under the warm, sunny weather, with waves crashing in the distance, she didn't get through more than a few paragraphs before she was out.

Kassi woke with a start to someone gently shaking her. She was ready for Farra, but it was just Savriah. "We're done. Didn't want you to be late getting home."

"Wow, I slept the whole time-eh?" Kassi peeled herself off the hot, metal bench and stretched. A sleep indentation had formed down the side of her face.

"Yisû, you slept for almost four hours," Savriah said with a chuckle.

"I needed it," Kassi said, feeling groggy. Once she could walk a straight line, she made her way back to the townhouse.

As soon as she stepped inside, Farra yanked her by the collar and slammed her against the wall. "I thought I told you not to tell anyone!"

"What? I didn't…"

"Don't lie to me!" Farra shouted. "I went by the docks and overheard your coaches talking about 'Kassi's abusive new grip'," she said with air quotes. "Just wait til Moza gets home and hears about this!"

"But Moza told you not to…"

"Moza disapproves, but he's still my boyfriend," Farra said. "He'll defend me against your little penchode coaches!"

I'd give anything to see him try! Kassi chuckled at the thought of Moza trying to take on Sensei Kelipalo and Coach Rockson.

"What's so funny?" Farra spat, lighting a fumer. When Kassi didn't answer, Farra said, "Get over there and start rolling!" She shoved her toward the coffee table.

By 22:30 that night, after hours of fumer rolling, Kassi went to bed. She curled up and rewatched the holovid from her family until she fell asleep.

Twenty~Nine

It was Friday, and round three of the Siren Games had begun. There was no AquaSphera or training that weekend. Their teammates joined them on the South Pointe Pier, including Vander…and Ganna. Ganna was too kind for Kassi to hate, but she couldn't shake the jealousy every time she saw them together.

When they arrived at the plaza, people didn't hide their objections to a mixed group of 800s and 400s. The 500s and 600s watched with downturned lips and furrowed brows, while 700s and 800s vocalized their strong disapproval. Vander and the others tuned them out like live-background musicians.

Kassi had learned from a conversation with Savriah earlier that week that even after school graduation, everyone continued associating exclusively with those of the same status. "Why is it so taboo for 400s to be friends with 800s?" she had asked Savriah.

"If anyone from a higher status befriends someone from a lower status, their star score gets 'corrected' to a lower score by the U.N.O.E.," Savriah emphasized in air quotes. Since then, Kassi had looked at the 800s on their team with newfound admiration. Vander, Vi'ella, Ganna, Tallie, and Murrey were risking more than she had realized.

Ushers handed out free popcorn and energy waters as they arrived. Hopefully, Kassi would get a chance to eat hers this time. She spotted the same security guard from their previous scuffle–Officer Locard. He made eye contact with her and immediately clenched his fists as if readying himself for another scuffle. Then, his expression drastically changed as he looked at her present company of 800s. Straightening himself up, he held an air of deference towards the 800s and eyed Kassi curiously as if she were some mangy alley cat in the midst of magnificent, purebred savannahs.

Officer Locard addressed Vander and the 800s, his voice carefully subservient, "Pardon me. It's routine to ask, but we're on the lookout for any suspicious activity. Have you seen anything unusual?" He glared straight at Fille when he said it.

Murrey spoke up. His brown, disconnected pompadour hair, held firm despite the strong breeze. "I saw a dolphin with a hat once."

"I mean around here." The officer said.

"Nah, that dolphin was somewhere in the Pacific," Murrey said, pointing westward. They walked past Locard who glowered at Kassi and her 400 friends as they took their seats. For now, he left them alone.

The Games had already begun, and the first wave of round three–the Sonic Battles–had already concluded with four teams advancing. Now only thirty-six teams remained to compete in round three.

They were airing the next wave, and in the lower left quadrant of the screen was Team Shanghai versus Barcelona–Lula Chirico's team! In the previous two rounds of the Siren Games, Team Barcelona had claimed a palladium medal and a silver medal.

"We always wondered back home-eh," Kassi said to Savriah, "why does it matter if a team wins a medal?"

"Medals boost the status of the entire family," Savriah explained. "That's how 800s become 800s. Someone in their family line won medals but didn't win the Siren Games, so they're still here on Earth but as a higher status."

"I see. Is that the only way to increase your score-eh?" Kassi asked.

"No, it mostly comes from the yearly stimulus dividend," Savriah said. Kassi cast her a quizzical look, so Savriah continued, "Each member earns one status point for the family as a stimulus dividend," Savriah explained. "That is, unless someone in your family disobeys a U.N.O.E. policy. Then the family earns demerits, instead. Status points get deducted."

"The whole-eh family?" Kassi raised her eyebrows.

"Families rise or fall together," Savriah said.

The Sonic Battles featured a different map each year. This year, they had formed boundaries around four separate locations within the underwater ruins of the ancient megacity once known as Jakarta. Lining walls with sound-deadening material, these old skyscrapers littered the underwater landscape and provided strategic shielding.

Teams were given sixty seconds to familiarize themselves with the territory and claim their position. Shoulder-mounted sonic cannons were all adjusted to non-fatal decibel levels. With only the highest of frequencies in use for these weapons, each blast required pin-point precision aim. Players wore star-shaped targets no bigger than their hand on the center of their chest, lit up with their team's colors.

The gong rang and the battle commenced. Shanghai immediately went on the offensive. They split into multiple formations to surround Barcelona, but Barcelona evaded their advances. Firing back and forth, two Barcelona members were pulsed– knocked out of their positions as if punched by an invisible fist in the chest. Their star-shaped targets were exposed, and Team Shanghai lit them up. Once hit, their targets changed colors from

Barcelona's golden yellow to white. It was now nineteen players to seventeen.

While Shanghai swarmed the two Barcelona players, Lula Chirico capitalized on the distraction. Dividing into two groups of eight, they flanked Shanghai. The first squad opened fire. Shanghai scrambled to take cover, but the second squad was ready for them. With many Shanghai players exposed, Barcelona managed to eliminate nine of their opponents, making it 10-17.

"Fantaseismic maneuver by Barcelona!" Leron shouted wildly from the holoscreens. *"Eliminating half their team with a decoy and flanking maneuver. Lula Chirico starts all the dominoes falling."*

With four battles on at once, there were eight teams. That meant eight different Bátel Hîms–siren battle incantations–going on simultaneously. The feed rotated between them, and whenever they played one of Lula's hîms, Kassi took mental notes. They were powerful and showcased the teams' strengths. Caesar's voice rang in her mind, *"Teams that know how to craft lyrics and melodic phrasings to their own vocalists' strengths–they're always the ones to beat."* It was Kassi's goal to do exactly that for her own team, and the advanced reading assignments from Sensei were helping.

Shanghai was disjointed, interspersed, and isolated throughout the underwater ruins, and Barcelona didn't waste any time tracking them down and eliminating them one by one. Only Shanghai's team captain had proven challenging as she tagged three Barcelona players before they pulsed her and blasted her from all sides. The target on her chest changed to bright white, and Barcelona was crowned the victor, advancing to the next bracket in the tournament.

After their defeat, those on Team Shanghai hung their heads, many even sobbing. Lula and her teammates swam to them and tried consoling their former opponents. Teams always took defeat very hard in the Games, but it wasn't until now that Kassi realized why. This was their only path to earn a spot on the Paradise Planets and a better life.

Even though they lost, they did still have one final chance. All teams that lost their first battle would face off in the sudden death round. It was a chaotic, royal brawl. Eighteen teams battled on the same field simultaneously until only six teams remained.

It must have been demoralizing for all the champions who got so close, only to fail. Out of the sixty-four teams that entered each Games, sixty had to stay on Earth. Since only those ages fifteen to eighteen could compete, many champions aged out, their hopes and dreams of a better life shattered. As much as she had always enjoyed watching them, Ravana's words rang in her mind, "There shouldn't even be a Siren Games!" Kassi was starting to realize Ravana was right.

She turned away from the holoscreen, observing the crowds around her as they stared up at the screen. While there were a few purple and red armbands speckled throughout the crowd, the vast majority wore either blue or green. Their eyes twinkled with hope as they watched their fellow Gaians inch closer to Paradise. This was all they had to cling to. Kassi wanted to cry for them.

"Whatcha looking at?" Vi'ella followed Kassi's gaze to the surrounding masses.

"Huh? Oh, nothing." Kassi whipped her head toward the screen, pretending to follow the commentators' recap.

By the end of the day, eighteen teams advanced in the tournament, including Team Miami–the team Coach Rockson and Sensei Kelipalo were training. The remaining eighteen would face off in sudden death the following Sunday. Even though winning teams already qualified for the final round of the Games, they would still continue to battle for one of four medals in round three.

After all the excitement, Kassi reluctantly returned to her psychotic grip. She almost didn't. At one point, she thought it might be worth it to just sleep under a bridge and avoid her grips altogether. A jet-black, ominous U.N.O.E. patrol yacht slowed next to her as she was considering this. They drifted closer to her side of the street. It scared her enough to scurry back to the townhome.

Entering through the front door, the lights were off. For a brief moment, Kassi thought everyone might be asleep until Farra jumped out of the shadows and stabbed Kassi's arm with a burning fumer. Kassi howled.

"You're late!" Farra shouted, her harsh voice tearing through the silence, her breath ripe with the smell of muck juice burps.

"We were-eh watching the Siren Games," Kassi said, nursing her arm.

"Who said you could do that?" Farra jabbed at her again. This time Kassi recoiled and almost avoided a second burn– almost. It was enough to infuriate Kassi to the point of lashing back. She kicked Farra in the shin as hard as she could. Farra grunted but responded quickly with a hard slap in the face, knocking Kassi to the floor. She then grabbed Kassi's wrist and yanked her to the living room sofa. "You've got a lot of catching up to do, princess, so you better get started!"

The sting fresh on Kassi's face, she held a hand to her throbbing cheek as she stared in disbelief at a room full of boxes. It was way more than she ever had done before. "All of these-eh?"

"That's right," Farra kicked back on the sofa. "And if you don't finish them tonight, you'll be sleeping on the ground floor."

"But that's flooded!"

"I set up a table for you above the water." Farra flashed a wicked smile as if she were already imagining Kassi rolling off into the water mid-sleep.

For the next three hours, Kassi rolled furiously. Farra had fallen asleep on the couch, and Kassi took advantage of that time to roll quick, sloppy joints and stash them at the bottom of the pile. It allowed her to knock out a few more boxes in less time.

The front door swung open and Moza stumbled through it,

startling Kassi and causing her to spill freshly ground buds. She thought Moza was already upstairs in bed.

"Alright, go to bed," he said, slurring his words.

Farra woke at the sound of his voice. With a lazy stretch, she said, "Always popping the fun balloons." She then inspected Kassi's work, her face souring at the poorly rolled fumers.

"She said she was going to make-eh me sleep downstairs if I didn't finish," Kassi pointed at all the boxes in the room.

"You're not sleeping downstairs," Moza said as he stumbled into the kitchen, pulled government rations out of the cupboard, and stuck them in the air fryer. Farra huffed at this and stormed over to the kitchen. Kassi still couldn't get a read on Moza since his expression never changed, but she was always glad to see him. He was the only reason Farra hadn't worked Kassi to death.

"You will not undermine me!" Farra shoved a finger in his face. For a couple, they really fought a lot. Kassi wondered if they even liked each other. It was nothing at all like the married couples Kassi had grown up around on Nemal–always supportive pairs and the best of friends.

"Look, I'm just trying to stick to Ravana's plan. She entrusted us with…"

"Entrusted us with a prime hossty, yisû! You've said it a million times!" Farra shouted, waving her hand dismissively before storming up the stairs to the bedroom.

Thirty

There were no days off with Farra. After another early morning of manual labor and fumer burns, Kassi dragged herself to school for Saturday cleaning. They meandered to Sensei's classroom to watch the Siren Games on his holopad. Kassi watched for only a few minutes before sleep deprivation claimed her. She spent the rest of the morning lying on the classroom's hard, vinyl flooring.

At the stroke of noon, she muscled herself up and they rushed back to the South Pointe Plaza. It was free taco day, and this time, Kassi collected her tacos and juice without any hassle. They took their usual seats at the rear of the plaza, their backs to the apartment towers.

Kassi instinctively scanned the crowds in case Amára stroked to Miami Beach for the Siren Games. It was likely an impossibility, but she looked for her all the same. Even though it had only been a couple of weeks, it felt like forever since she had seen her best friend. Farra had threatened to send mediation officers to Amára if Kassi ever tried to sneak off to Charleston again.

She turned her attention back to the holoscreen to watch more battles from round three. They already missed a few today, including Barcelona's match with Lima. Lula Chirico had led

Barcelona to a swift victory. Kassi caught select highlights throughout the day whenever the commentators pulled it up between ads.

The current battle playing out was between Miami and Sydney. Sensei K and Coach Rockson would likely be at the underwater Jakarta arenas in person. Miami had just made a big advance against Sydney, pulsing out and tagging five of their players in the process. Ganna sat next to Vander who was transfixed to the holoscreen, her hand on his leg. Kassi tried to ignore them, unsuccessfully.

"That's soon gonna be us, chas," Vander whooped.

Kassi tried picturing herself on holoscreens competing in the Siren Games. After watching them every year since she was born, it would be surreal to actually be in them. The thought of it made her knees bounce with nervous excitement. At the same time, Ravana was right–there shouldn't be a Siren Games.

Miami won their battle, advancing to the next bracket, and would be matching off with Team Auckland later that day. Barcelona was scheduled to battle Tripoli in a few hours. As lively as the crowds were around her, Kassi teetered in her seat, ready to pass out. She had reached the seventh level of exhaustion, courtesy of her relentless tormentor.

Miami and Barcelona both won their matches that evening and advanced into the top four–the medals round–wrapping up the day's events. The Games would resume on Sunday.

At the townhome, after receiving two fresh scorch marks on the back of her hand, Kassi resumed rolling. Knowing Moza would eventually intervene, she only pretended to hustle this time to avoid more burns. Scars covered her hands and arms– hideous reminders of the abuse she had endured over the past nine days. It had been little more than a week and yet she could barely remember life before Farra.

After another morning of sleeping on the hard school floor, Kassi and her friends zoomed to the plaza for more Siren Games. She was upset to hear they had already missed the sudden death sonic battle. The sheer chaos of hundreds of sirens swarming the ruins while scrambling to piece together any kind of strategy was always exhilarating. Six teams advanced and twelve teams were eliminated. Meanwhile, Barcelona was set to face off against Miami for palladium. The excitement from the crowd was enough to give Kassi her second wind.

It was a grueling battle between the top two teams, and Barcelona barely pushed ahead with only Lula and a few of her teammates left standing. They claimed palladium while Miami took platinum.

"I'm sure Coach and Sensei won't be happy about that," Fille said.

"That blunder in the third act by Hauser cost them the contest," Vander added. "I'm sure he'll never hear the end of it."

Round three came to an end, and they said their goodbyes. Kassi watched them leave, staring at the flooded streets and contemplating her options.

I need to find a way to get a message to Ravana, she thought. She contemplated stealing Moza's holopad again the next chance she got.

"What are you still doing here?" a familiar voice asked from behind her.

Kassi turned around to find Ganna alone, Vander and the rest of her friends already gone. "I...uh, was zhust thinking of how to get rid of my grips."

"They seem awful! Do you need a place to stay?" Ganna asked. "You could stay with me for the night."

She thought about Ganna's offer. "Farra never said I couldn't stay somewhere else-eh," Kassi thought out loud. "I zhust can't go to Charleston."

"Then it's settled," Ganna said with a bounce. "It's a sleepover!"

"It's a sleepover," Kassi echoed with a smile. Of all people, she couldn't believe her first sleepover on Earth would be with Vander's girlfriend. But Ganna was so nice to offer, and Kassi didn't know if she could survive another night with Farra. She wasn't breaking any rules.

They reached Ganna's townhouse–like Vander's but pastel blue and with different porch furniture. Ganna reached for the front door.

"400!" Came a shout from the shadows, the voice gruff and deep. Kassi jumped, nearly tripping into Ganna. Armed mediation officers emerged and surrounded Kassi. "You have been reported missing by your legal guardian and must be returned to your domicile immediately," a man said. He had high and tight red hair and freckles, was a full head taller than Kassi and Ganna, with broad shoulders and a sonic cannon aimed at Kassi. With furrowed brows and a thin-lipped scowl, he looked coiled like a cobra ready to strike should Kassi make a run for it.

"She did nothing wrong!" Ganna shouted from the doorstep.

"This is none of your concern, 800," the man said. "Stand clear or it's twenty demerits against your family!"

Two officers reached forward and clamped firm hands on each of Kassi's arms to cart her away. Twisting to glance over her shoulder, Kassi saw Ganna, dread etched onto her face.

Around the corner, a U.N.O.E. patrol ship floated. The officers nudged her on board, stuffed a gag in her mouth, bound her wrists behind her back, and shoved her through a door into the extended cabin.

On the other side of the tinted windows, she finally saw what was inside. Thick pyramid acoustic foam layered the walls, ceiling, and most of the flooring, with only a small, circular clearing in the center. The door shut behind her. An officer covered in all black, thick padding wearing heavy ear protection advanced on Kassi, aiming a sonic rifle in her direction.

Kassi instinctively tried performing a shield song, but her voice was muffled by the gag. The officer sent a sonic pulse that struck her like a heavy-fisted punch to the thigh, knocking Kassi to the ground. He then performed a series of sonic strikes while Kassi lay pressed to the floor, grunting with each blow.

Aiming the rifle at Kassi's arms, legs, and torso, the officer unleashed a sonic beating that bruised and battered Kassi's entire body.

With her wrists bound and her mouth covered, Kassi was helpless. The onslaught continued, relentlessly. When Kassi was just about to pass out from the pain, the assault finally ceased. The officer exited, leaving Kassi strewn across the floor.

The boat slowed to a stop as the door was thrown open and strong hands gripped Kassi. They ripped off her bindings, yanked out the gag, and tossed her over the edge onto the hardwood porch of her townhome. Before she could rise to her feet, the boat gunned the engines and drove into the distance.

The front door was already open, and Farra stood in the doorway with arms crossed, a thin-lipped smirk on her face. "You thought you could avoid me, eh princess? You just bought yourself double duty!" While Kassi still struggled to her feet, Farra reached out and pressed a fresh fumer into Kassi's left wrist. It was the last straw and Kassi passed out from the pain.

At 05:15 Monday morning, as if from a recurring nightmare, Kassi woke to find Farra silently staring at her from the corner. For a brief moment, Kassi thought she was imagining it as if Farra were some demon spirit sent to haunt her.

In a flash of movement, Farra sprang forward, covered her mouth, and jabbed a fumer into the softest skin on Kassi's neck. Searing pain sent her heart racing as she let out a muffled scream.

"Shhh," Farra whispered, pinning Kassi down as she held the burning fumer centimeters from Kassi's left eye. Her bruised ribs screamed under Farra's weight.

She wouldn't.

Kassi froze. After a few slow beats, Farra finally retracted her hand and stood. "Be down in five minutes, princess!" She wasn't just burning arm skin anymore.

Kassi's legs trembled as she hobbled down the stairs. Everything hurt. It was more pain than Kassi had ever experienced.

Once at the coffee table, her fingers shook as she struggled to roll fumers for the next hour until Moza retrieved her for school.

Breakfast rations weren't enough to wake her. Between extreme exhaustion, shock, and pain, Kassi limped to school like a zombie. In a daze at school, she went through the motions, class after class, until she dragged herself to the cafeteria.

"You look like a phantasm from one of my warzone dreams," Savriah was the first to say. "Are you sick?"

Kassi shook her head, too tired to respond.

"What'd she do this time?" Fille started examining her arms for new burns.

Pulling her short hair back, Kassi showed the latest burn. "She also threatened to burn my eye. But it wasn't just her this time. The mediation officers…"

"You got whipped? You got whipped?" Adonis' eyes went wide.

Kassi nodded, clutching her side.

Once in Sensei's classroom, Savriah filled him in. As she did, anger flared in Sensei's eyes, his fists balled up and ready to plow right through the classroom walls.

Out of one of his drawers, Sensei withdrew a small device and dialed a few numbers. "Tolin," he said into the device, "meet me at Kassi's. Right now."

Thirty-One

Sensei marched with a speed and determination Kassi had never seen before. She and her friends struggled to keep up.

"Fille and Donis," Sensei shouted over his shoulder.

"Sensei?" they both said.

"Keep an eye out for patrols while we're in there."

Reaching the townhome, Sensei Kelipalo crashed through the front door without breaking stride. He barreled toward Farra who skittered to the back of the kitchen like a startled munchkin cat.

Moza, who had been sitting in the living room, jumped to his feet and moved to intercept. Tall and lean, built like a soldier, Moza was strong but no match for Sensei K. Moza swung a few punches and even landed one or two, but Sensei brushed them off and swatted at him like an enraged bear, flattening Moza to the ground with a single blow.

Farra bolted for the backdoor. Sensei moved in to grab her, but Moza cut him off with a desperate lunge, allowing Farra to slither out the back.

Kassi tried to give chase, but she was in no condition to catch Farra. Her bruised, tired legs wouldn't carry her fast enough. By the time she and Savriah pushed out the back door, Farra was out of sight.

Savriah locked her hands behind her head and heaved. "Should we go after her?"

"She's found a U.N.O.E. patrol by now," Kassi grumbled.

They returned inside to find Sensei K and Coach Rockson both towering over a defeated Moza.

"What have you done?" Moza glared at Kassi. "Ravana will hear of this!"

"That's actually the point," Sensei said. "Let's find that holopad of yours and let her know how her assigned grips have been treating Kassiana."

"No, wait." Moza tried jumping to his feet. Coach Rockson placed a strong hand on his shoulder and anchored him down to the floor. Despite Moza's protests, Sensei rummaged through Moza's things until he found the holopad.

Sensei carried the holopad to Moza. "Lift him up, Tolin, so I can scan his face."

"No, no, that's not necessary!" Moza said. Coach lifted Moza to his feet. "Listen, it was all Farra! I tried stopping her."

"Not nearly enough," Sensei said, casting Moza a hard stare.

"He's right," Kassi said. "Moza did stop Farra whenever he was around."

Holding it to Moza's face, Sensei unlocked the holopad and pulled up the messaging application. Moza turned to Kassi and said, "Look kid, I'm sorry I didn't do more to stop her."

"Why didn't you?" Kassi asked. "You knew what she was doing."

Moza didn't respond, his gaze downward to the floor.

"U.N.O.E. patrol! U.N.O.E. patrol!" Fille and Adonis both shouted as they burst in through the front door.

"Alright, I'll make a deal," Sensei said. "You tell the mediation officers there's nothing to see here, and I won't mention you in this message. You ok with that, Kassi?"

Kassi fingered the braids in her hair before answering with a nod.

A few silent beats passed as Moza looked to be weighing his options. He lifted his head and said, "Deal."

Sensei nodded, turning his attention to the holopad. He spoke clearly, allowing the holopad to transcribe his words, "Ravana, this is Professor Lesley Kelipalo. One of your grips, Farra…Farra?" He glanced at Moza.

"Monark," Moza said.

"Farra Monark has been physically abusing Kassiana for weeks and forcing her to participate in illegal activities. We understand you've promised these kids grips who would treat them with honor and respect. If you meant what you said, please deal with Farra. Sincerely, Lesley Kelipalo." They all watched as Sensei pressed the floating send button on the holographic display.

Coach released Moza who stood to his feet and rubbed his shoulder. "Thank you for not including me," he said.

Mediation officers marched through the front door. Moza held up both hands and approached them, "It's alright. This was all just a big misunderstanding."

The captain—a black-haired man with a five o'clock shadow and a jagged scar on his cheek eyed Moza suspiciously. "Is that right? Where's the woman?"

"Farra? She's stepped out," Moza said with a shrug. "Not sure when she'll be back."

"Check with dispatch," the captain barked to one of his subordinates. "What about that?" He pointed directly at Moza's red, inflamed eye.

"Like I said. A misunderstanding."

The subordinate returned and said, "They've found her. A little out of breath, but otherwise unharmed."

The captain nodded and surveyed the room, studying each of their faces and armbands one by one. He stopped on Kassi, his jaw clenched. For a moment, Kassi thought they would take her away. After a few uncomfortable beats, the captain spun on his heels and marched back to the patrol boat, his officers in tow.

When the door closed, everyone breathed a huge sigh of relief. Kassi hobbled to the couch and took a seat. Her friends joined her on the couch.

"Now let's see if Ravana's a woman of her word," Sensei said. "If Farra comes back tonight, it might be a good idea for your friends to stay the night and keep you company. After AquaSphera, think you chas can all sleep here for the night?"

"That's not necessary," Moza said.

"I think it is," Sensei said with intensity. Moza nodded.

"My parents, my parents should be good with that," Adonis said. Fille and Savriah also nodded.

With a score of 8-6, their game that day was closer than it should have been. Kassi only lasted the first ten minutes before asking Simmone to sub and take her spot. Fortunately, they pulled ahead in the end after Savriah dispossessed the disc and sent a through pass to Vander for a beautiful game-winning goal.

True to their word, Kassi's friends joined her in the empty townhome for a sleepover. Farra hadn't returned. Staring at the boxes of fumer materials, dried leaves, and crumpled rolling paper strewn across the coffee table, Kassi tried processing all she had suffered over the past weeks.

Her friends wanted to sit on the balcony and chat for a while, so Kassi joined them. "Thanks chas," Kassi said. "It's been nice-eh to have you here. I really needed someone to consult me through all of this."

"Consult you?" Fille asked. "Consult you about what?"

"I think she means console," Savriah explained as she pulled out a bowl filled with what looked like orange cat fur.

"Console-eh! You know what I mean!" Kassi sighed, frustrated she could never find the right word.

The three of them eyed Savriah curiously as she sorted through the giant bowl of fur. Fille spoke up, "Do I even wanna ask?"

Savriah looked up, realizing the question was directed at her. "Ask about what?"

"The bowl of cat fur?" He leaned in and pointed, his finger centimeters from the bowl.

"I've been saving it up for months," Savriah said, beaming. "I finally have enough!"

"Enough for what?" Kassi let slip the question before she could stop herself.

"My dolls," Savriah said. "I'm gonna make dolls with it." No one had a response to that.

Eventually, they grew tired and spread out across the townhome, sleeping on couches and the floor. Curled on her lumpy mattress, Kassi rewatched the holovid from home. She kept wondering how much her parents knew about this plan.

Moza was already in the kitchen by the time Kassi came down, her friends seated around the table for breakfast.

"You chas have bean chili?" Fille exclaimed over a mouthful of beans. "And melon energy chews?"

"Lucky!" Adonis shouted.

Seeing her friends there, with no sign of Farra, Kassi was relieved almost to the point of tears. She sank heavily into her kitchen seat, too tired to be bothered by all the chomping and slurping sounds everyone made. Once she was done, she asked Moza, "Is Farra coming back?"

"I heard back from Ravana," he said. "She's not happy with Farra. They're looking for her now." Moza puffed on a fumer and stared at the table, the left side of his face completely swollen.

Kassi nodded to her friends and they left for school.

By the end of the day, she was ready to get back into the water. On the docks, Vander stood with the rest of the team, his hair pulled back in a small bun. It highlighted his perfectly sculpted face.

"Alright bubbleheads," Fille shouted "Let's dive!"

They lined up and dove into the Atlantic, swimming out to

the training pools. Blue Krakens were on a winning streak, climbing the rankings. Starting out dead last in the league, they currently ranked twenty-eighth out of forty-four. They only needed to make top 16 to enter the tournament for the Miami League title. Kassi couldn't believe it, but as long as they kept winning, they had a chance.

In their match, they took an early lead against a team of 600s when Kassi threaded the defense, caught a well-positioned pass from Vander, and scored with a helicopter kick. Her goal swayed the momentum in their favor, and they maintained it for the entire first half.

At halftime, Coach surfaced with them onto the boats. "You chas are looking more and more like champions!" He tossed them bags of roasted peanuts and boxed grape energy waters.

"Whoa, where'd you, where'd you score these?" Adonis asked as he ripped open the bag.

"Stole it from the Siren Games food cache," Kiowa laughed. "Someone left it wide open. Couldn't pass up the golden opportunity!"

"Bosst!" Fille shouted.

Kassi and her teammates gathered around and tore into their food. Two players were noticeably absent–Vander and Ganna. Kassi's eyes swept over the other two U.N.O.E. cutters floating above the training pools and spotted them.

They were alone on the farthest boat from the team. Kassi didn't like the looks of it. She squinted in the sunlight and watched as Ganna reached up and Vander leaned in. Kassi stopped breathing. They kissed. Kassi's shoulders sagged as she released an audible groan.

"What's wrong?" Fille asked her. Kassi had forgotten about the rest of her team around her.

"Wrong?" Kassi couldn't think of a lie. Her mind went blank.

Savriah followed Kassi's gaze. "Is that Vander and Ganna?"

Other teammates paused their own conversations and whipped their heads in the direction of the farthest boat.

"Atta boy, Vander," Murrey cupped his hands around his mouth and bellowed. "Woohoo!"

"So it's official?" Tallie asked no one in particular. Her blonde, shoulder-grazing hair flapped in the wind. By that point, the entire team had lined up against the railing to watch the canoodling session.

"Thanks, Savvy!" Kassi grumbled under her breath. Now that Kassi was finally free of Farra, she should be happy, but seeing Vander and Ganna together like this was like a fumer burn to the heart.

When they returned to the water for the second half, Kassi just wanted to bolt for the docks. Coach seemed to notice. He pulled her aside and had her switch to a private frequency.

"What's got you down, Kassi?" Coach asked. Kassi didn't know where to start. "I thought you'd be happy now that Farra's gone."

"I'm definitely relieved about that," Kassi said.

"So what's wrong?"

Her eyes instinctively went straight to Vander and Ganna, who continued flirting with each other as they drifted to their positions on the waterfield. Coach must have read her expression.

"I think I know what this is about," he said. "Young love. You wanna give your heart to someone, but they're already spoken for."

"I zhust thought he would...I don't know," Kassi said quietly.

"It's hard. Feels like you'll never get a chance to have what they have," Coach said. "I remember when I asked a girl out for the first time. Mikkel Tates. She was a year older than me and she was royalty! Couldn't ever stop thinking about her. Each time she passed me in the halls, took my breath away. After a few weeks of it, I finally mustered up the courage to go talk to her," he laughed as he pictured it. "She was outta my league–by leaps and bounds. But that didn't stop me from trying."

Kassi looked at him as they floated on the sidelines, curious to hear how the story ended.

"One day in the cafeteria, I walked up to her while she was standing in line with her friends. It was so intimidating to approach her while surrounded by her friends–they always group together like that–but I did it anyway." He paused.

"What happened?" Kassi asked. His anecdote was proving a nice distraction.

"Turned me down faster than a cheetah can run. Had to cross the cafeteria in the long walk of shame as kids on all sides laughed at me. It was the single most embarrassing moment of my life," Coach said, shaking his head.

"Did you ever try again?" Kassi asked.

"With Mikkel? Nah. In the end, she wasn't the girl for me. Found me someone better." He smiled.

That wasn't what Kassi wanted to hear. She didn't want someone else.

Coach continued, "I know you're disappointed, but you can't let it keep you from reaching the Siren Games and returning home to your family. You need to channel the frustration. Use it, then leave it all on the field."

Kassi wanted to return home to Nemal. But she had secretly hoped to return with Vander at her side, as a couple. Without that possibility, it was hard to put her heart into the game. But, Coach was right. She needed to find a way to focus. "Can I pick the next song?"

"Of course, you can!"

"Supernova," the song that turned everything around for Kassi, played in her helmet. It reminded her of the strength she found within herself that day when she won the Race for Blues. Getting lost in the music, Kassi returned to the field and ended up playing one of her best games, scoring two goals and a rico-chet, and getting one assist.

After AquaSphera, Kassi returned home to find Moza alone in the kitchen. He barely paid attention to her. Still no word on

Farra–apparently, they were still looking for her. Kassi just hoped she never returned.

Grateful to have her evenings back, Kassi took the time to push through her reading assignments from Sensei as well as review Coach Rockson's latest critiques.

Three weeks passed–their winning streak continued. With their latest victory over the Charcoal Nessies, they climbed into the nineteenth spot on the rankings. Doing the math, if they won the next week of games, and a few teams directly above them lost at least one of theirs, the Blue Krakens would claim one of the sixteen qualifying spots for the championship tournament.

The following week, Blue Krakens had some close calls, but they pulled off a series of wins and reached the top 16! It was the first time in provincial history that a team of mostly 400s had come from last place midseason to claim a spot in the Final 16 tournament for the Miami League title.

On Thursday afternoon, the last game of the regular season, they held onto sixteenth place, barely qualifying for the championship tournament. "You chas pulled it off! Congratulations to every single one of you. You earned this!" They cheered in celebration.

At the docks, Sensei, Coach Rockson, and Kiowa offered to walk her home once again. She didn't mind the company, especially after their victory.

"You've been through a lot these past few months," Sensei said from behind Coach Rockson. Kiowa trailed quietly behind.

"More than anyone," Coach added. "I can't believe what you had to deal with!"

Kassi nodded.

"How are you handling things, right now?" Sensei asked.

Kassi thought for a moment before answering, "I don't know. Better now that we're in the tournament."

"And about Farra?"

Kassi shrugged.

"Has she come by?" Coach asked.

"No," Kassi said.

"That's good," Coach said.

"What she did to you," Sensei said, pausing as if to find the right words. "It's hard to let go of things like that. She left without ever making things right. No apologies, no remorse for all the pain she caused you."

"No punishment," Kassi mumbled under her breath.

"People who survive traumatic experiences like that can get scarred for life," Coach said.

"I've had my share of people who wronged me," Sensei said. "Some did unforgivable things, and they never made amends." They continued walking as Kassi's townhome came into view. Sensei continued, "Even after they were gone, for years it continued to weigh me down. My wife would always try to convince me to let it go, but I couldn't."

"So what happened?" Kassi asked as she hopped across the planks of the slidewalks.

"An old friend of mine passed along some wisdom. And I later passed it along to Coach Rockson here," Sensei said. "My friend told me to accept the apology they never gave me."

"Huh?" Kassi paused midstep.

"I created a scenario in my mind where each of these people genuinely felt remorse and apologized to me, and I accepted it. Even though I never saw these people again, and they never said those apologies, I realized I didn't have to let their lack of remorse prevent me from finding peace. Forgiveness liberated me from the heavy weight of hate, and I was finally able to move on with my life."

Kassi resumed crossing the planks as she listened.

"It worked for me, too," Coach said. "When I was a kid, I was the victim of violent discrimination. Mediation officers pulled me aside to question me for crimes I didn't have the slightest thing to do with just because I looked suspicious. It wasn't the first time. In fact, it happened quite often. A couple of times, they even gave me severe beatings with their sonic pulse batons. On one occasion, they broke a few of my teeth, and I spent a few years with chipped teeth until I was finally selected for dental cosmetic surgery. Bullies at school made fun of me for it.

"I hated all of them, and held on to that grudge for many years," Coach Rockson recounted. "When Lesley told me about his method, I realized how much it had negatively affected me over the years. It was a big reason why I never won the Siren Games. I couldn't reach my full potential when I still clung to that need for vengeance. It's like an ancient proverb I once heard: if you wish to fly, you must give up everything that weighs you down."

"That's Buddha. Another figure the U.N.O.E. erased from written history," Sensei said.

"I zhust can't picture Farra ever offering a sincere apology," Kassi said.

"It's hard, and it'll take time to imagine that unlikely scenario, but you need to try," Coach said.

Kassi thought about this. Farra's actions were unforgivable–rupturing her vocal cords, burning her with fumers, hacking her hair off. Kassi continued sleeping with the fear of another brutal awakening. By the time they reached the townhome, Kassi finally answered, "I don't know if I can, Sensei."

"I don't expect you to do it right now," Sensei said. "I just want you to consider it."

Thirty-Two

The tournament for the Miami League title–the Final 16–wouldn't start until next Monday. In the meantime, it was the weekend of round four of the Siren Games. It had been the talk of the school all week long. Coach Rockson and Sensei had already left a few days earlier to be with Team Miami for the final round. After twelve more teams had been eliminated in round three–the Sonic Battles–the twenty-four remaining teams in the Siren Games would face off in a deadly race that traversed land, air, and sea.

Kassi had played AquaSphera all her life, but the other three rounds were very unfamiliar to Kassi. She only hoped the skills she had learned from AquaSphera would carry over. Of all four events in the Games, the Ship Races were the most daunting. Teams had to build their own ships and race around the entire planet–it relied heavily on one's ability to construct and customize the optimal ship–a skill that Kassi had only begun to develop in her studies on Nemal.

During lunch, Kassi and her friends chattered about the current standings. They all had their favorites picked out and argued over who would take first.

"Barcelona for the win!" Kassi shouted, pounding her desk.

They were currently in first place. "And Team Miami." She wanted to see Sensei Kelipalo and Coach Rockson's team earn a Paradise passport, as well.

"My cha, my cha Vonnie's gonna bring it home for London," Adonis said.

"Not a chance!" Fille argued. "I could see Lula's team pulling it off. But Vonnie? Nah! Miami's the real frontrunner. Ship racing is Zavala's strength."

"Why are you even rooting for a team other than your own home province?" Savriah asked Adonis.

"What? It's not like, it's not like I'm rooting against Miami," Adonis pointed both hands to the ground. "Can't I be a fan of other teams, too? There are four winners!"

After school, they raced to the South Pointe Plaza, catching the waterbus down to the pier. Once they arrived, they stood in line for fruit cups and energy waters before meeting up with the rest of their teammates. A few Krakens had gotten there early to save seats, and they took their usual spot against the back railing of the pier on basic folding chairs provided by the city.

A U.N.O.E. news update played on the giant holoscreens:

"Today marks a glorious day! Sirs and dames, we have a wonderful announcement. Our very own Grand Deputy, Xandria Doss, has agreed to marry Captain Griffonage Li, leader of U.N.O.E.'s elite, anti-terrorist task force. These two will tie the knot in the near future with wedding dates soon to come!"

"Wow, he's really moving up," Kassi thought out loud.

"So he's the one who brought you here?" Savriah asked, studying the faces on the screen.

"One of them, yisû," Kassi said.

"That cha's making waves at the top," Fille said.

"Is this how you're hoping to change things?" Kassi asked

the screen. The feed switched to the commentators, and Kassi turned her attention to her fruit cup. This was the second time since coming to Earth that she had fruit of any kind, the first being the apple Vander handed her at his townhome. The only way to buy fruit here was on the Market Abyss, and Kassi never had any money.

It was a very small portion, but as Kassi took the first bite of a strawberry, she thought it was the sweetest fruit she could ever remember tasting. But then again, it had been almost three months since she ate Nemalís food.

"*Sirs and dames across the universe, we have arrived at the fourth and final round of the 156th Siren Games!*" Lisi announced. She was in a sleeveless red dress with her hair up as if dressed for a fancy ball.

"*This is the round we've all been waiting for,*" Leron added. He wore a blue and white tuxedo. Compared to the rest of Earth's simple and plain fashion, theirs looked like the most extravagant outfits, even with their armbands on.

"*The efforts of our top contenders have been absolutely worlds class!*" Leron continued, "*with Zavala leading the charge for Miami, they've razzled and dazzled audiences in the previous rounds. The question is, will it be enough to pass Lula Chirico's Barcelona to claim palladium.*" The crowds all around Kassi cheered wildly at the mention of Team Miami.

"*I think Barcelona will prove hard to beat,*" Lisi voiced. "*They've shown incredible stamina throughout the previous rounds. We might see fireworks from them this weekend!*"

"*A bold statement, Lisi! Only time will tell…,*" Leron continued. Round four was officially called the *Karaba Ágonas*, but more commonly known as the Ship Races. Teams had spent the past month customizing their ships and running drills with their crews to prepare for the race. These ships were built to harness the collective energy from all nineteen team members' sonopacks. It was the most dangerous round of the games, costing many athletes' lives in previous years. Siren healers invited from the Paradise Planets stood at the ready to hopefully prevent any more tragedies.

The ships were all stretched across the starting line–twenty-four teams ready to launch. Only the top four to cross the finish line earned a place on Paradise. The race would start at 1700 hours on Friday and end around the same time on Saturday evening. Kassi hated the fact that she would have to miss so much of it while sitting around at school on the following Saturday morning. Some of the best moments in the races happened during that time.

While they waited for the race to commence, commentators reviewed previous rounds, showing many inspiring highlights Kassi and her friends had missed. She caught Lula's initial round two tussle with the giant sea dragon LifeBot as she rescued her sister. She also rewatched Barcelona's sonic battles against Shanghai, Lima, and four other teams. The highlights reminded Kassi of all the times she had gathered with Caesar, Amára, and many of their family and friends to cheer on their favorite teams. It felt like a distant memory of a different life.

"Throughout the Games, it's been Lula in the sky with diamonds," Leron shouted. *"But I still think we've yet to see the best from Miami's Zavala. In the Races, he just might leave the competition with their knees on backward."*

When it was finally time, Kassi and her friends rose to their feet, eyes sparkling with anticipation. The balconies and plaza were filled to the max with crowds cheering for Team Miami. The screens displayed a countdown to the ship reveal when all the teams would roll out their newly designed ships to the public. Kassi wondered what Lula's team had created.

The countdown reached zero, and the crowds went wild as all twenty-four teams uncovered their ships for the race. Screens split into quadrants and displayed four ships at a time with the team banner below. Most ships were some form of rocket on wheels with retractable airfoils. Some large, some sleek, some lightweight. But when they arrived at Lula Chirico's ship, crowds gasped. Team Barcelona's ship was a single giant wheel with the cabin directly in the center.

"Interesting choice from Barcelona," Lisi commented.

Drums thundered with a battle rhythm as all the ships powered up and prepared to launch. The first stretch of the race was on land. Locations changed with each season, and this time they would be racing across the rolling desert sands of the African Sahara. The rules stated they had to have at least one wheel touching the ground at all times. The drums crescendoed as they slowed for the final hit, signaling the beginning of the race. With a loud boom, ships blasted forward.

Barcelona and Miami took the early lead, dodging initial attacks as they pushed the limits of their speed. After a long stretch, Barcelona settled in behind Miami and remained close behind. Cameras cut to a large cluster of ships fighting to break out from the horde and steer clear of the fray. Many were firing on each other, trying to cripple the others.

Non-lethal sonic cannons were allowed to be mounted on these ships, but firing them required rerouting energy away from the ship's speed. Since teams typically equipped their ships with layers of sound absorption materials, it required a very powerful sonic pulse to make an impact.

Team Shanghai, Lima, and Sydney were caught in a crossfire that ended with Sydney blasting Shanghai right into a giant sand dune. Shanghai's ship overturned and crashed upside down, requiring team members to exit and make quick repairs in order to reenter the race. Team Rome blasted Manaus and sent them spinning out as they collided with Toronto's ship. With each crash, the crowd reacted with shouts, gasps, groans, and cheers. Siren healers rushed to each crash site to check on the players and tend to the wounded.

Team London had been clawing their way into third position when a concentrated sonic blast from Team Rio de Janeiro smashed a dent in their side and sent them spinning out and upside down. They buckled hard against the sand dunes.

"Yeeeaaaaoooow!" Leron's voice cracked as he shouted with pure enthusiasm, *"Rio de Janeiro sinks their flaming dagger into the heart of Vonahan's London to take third!"*

"There's no coming back from a crash like that," Lisi agreed.

"Sheist, sheist, sheisty sheist!" Adonis cursed. "Get up, get up, get up!"

The crowd remained on their feet as they watched more ships battling it out for top positions. Meanwhile, Miami and Barcelona continued increasing their lead as the distance between second and third place grew farther and farther apart. By avoiding the fray altogether, they were able to devote all nineteen of their sirens to power the ship's thrusters for top speed. Kassi hoped they could keep it.

The sun grew low and their long shadows spilled across the plaza. In previous rounds, crowds would dissipate by this time. Not for round four—nearly everyone stayed.

"We always pull an all-nighter for the Ship Races," Fille said.

"We already, we already gotta miss so much of it with school cleaning," Adonis said.

"Solick!" The prospect of staying up all night was exciting.

In her seat next to Savriah, she got as comfortable as she could in the folding chair and settled in for the night. As extra chairs became available, people grabbed more so they could kick up their feet and lounge. Kassi snagged one.

Vander and Ganna were cuddled up together under a blanket, talking in indistinct, hushed tones. Vander said something. Ganna giggled. Kassi forced herself to turn away. As she rolled over in her seat, she noticed Savriah studying her.

"What?" Kassi asked.

"It's alright, Kassi," Savriah said. "You'll find your someone." How did she always know what Kassi was thinking–just like Amára had?

Many others from her team had surprisingly also paired off with someone. Kassi had been so focused on Vander, she never realized Adonis and Tallie hitting it off. They were sharing a blanket, flirting with each other.

"When did that happen?" Kassi asked Savriah, flicking her chin toward Adonis.

"Today, I think," Savriah said with a suppressed giggle.

As she scanned her circle of teammates, she found Fille sitting next to Simmone, in what looked like an exciting conversation. His voice carried, as did Vi'ella's as she chatted with Murrey while sitting across from him, rubbing his feet. Some of the Krakens were with people Kassi didn't recognize, but it seemed as though everyone else had paired off except Kassi and Savriah.

"What about you?" Kassi asked Savriah. "You like anyone yet?"

"No," Savriah said.

"I find that hard to believe," Kassi said.

"It's true," Savriah said.

An awkward silence followed as a white pelican landed by her feet. "You know, I haven't really seen a lot of animals since I got here-eh."

"They hide, mostly," Savriah said. "Sometimes, I'll spot dolphins or even a manatee on the way to the training pools, but they mostly steer clear of the main swimming routes."

"Huh," Kassi said. "Back home-eh, there was always some bird or animal that wanted to play. If we ever attempted AquaSphera in the ocean, the golden dolphines would always get in the way."

"I wish we had animals like that here," Savriah said. "I've always wanted an underwater pet."

"You'll have your pick on Paradise once we've won," Kassi said, staring at the clear, starry night as if she could see her home nestled among the constellations.

"I can't believe we actually have a shot at qualifying this season!" Savriah pulled out a small bag from her pocket and fidgeted with its contents. It looked like the same bag of fingernail clippings. Kassi decided not to look too closely. Savriah asked, "Did you have a boyfriend back home?"

"No," Kassi reflected back on the boys back on Nemal. "I had a crush on this boy at school–Dario. Amára really liked his older brother, Tullio. We talked about them all the time-eh."

"Why didn't you do anything about it?" Savriah asked.

"Amára did," Kassi said. "They probably would've gotten together if we hadn't come here first. Me? I just didn't have-eh her confidence."

"And now? When you go back?" Savriah asked.

"Hopefully, I'll never let that get in the way again," Kassi said. "Although, I'm not really into Dario anymore-eh." As Kassi thought of him, none of her old feelings returned. She'd moved on. Her eyes naturally drifted to Vander and Ganna again.

"Well, I'm gonna try and get some sleep," Savriah said. "You should, too. Here's an extra blanket I brought from home if you want it."

"Thanks, Savvy," Kassi said, taking the blanket and throwing it over her legs. She was still jealous of all her friends and team-mates coupled together.

"Goodnight," Savriah called out. Kassi said it back and they both rolled over and tried to get comfortable.

It took Kassi a while to power down. A new pair of commen-tators took the night shift and continued reporting updates on the race. Kassi did her best to curl under the blanket, but it was an awkward position, and she couldn't stop peeking over at Ganna and Vander as they fell asleep in each other's arms. Finally, after tossing and turning for hours, Kassi dozed off.

The sun woke them on Saturday morning as Leron and Lisi welcomed everyone to day two of the Ship Races. It was just after 07:00.

Kassi felt her hip pop as she stood to stretch. "Whoa, did you hear that?" Kassi asked Savriah.

"Yisû, that was loud. Sounded painful."

"Felt good!" Kassi said.

All the 400s said goodbye to their teammates as they plodded to school for cleaning. Ganna continued sleeping next to Vander as he poked out of the blanket to watch the holoscreen.

Kassi eyed him for a moment before rushing off with her friends back to the school. They snatched some government biscuits from the cafeteria before they checked in with Mr. Benetti. For the rest of the morning, they talked about the Siren Games and waited anxiously for the noon bells to chime.

As soon as it did, they made a break for it to the plaza to see what they missed. Kassi hoped Barcelona and Miami were still in the lead. They reclaimed their seats among the crowds to watch the final hours of the race.

"What'd we miss?" Kassi asked.

"Barcelona's been firing on all cylinders," Vander said. "They pulled ahead of Miami once they hit the water."

"Your girl Lula's been keeping them on the run," Vi'ella said. "They've been throwing everything they got at her. She just keeps on blowing it back at them!"

"Bosst! GO LULA!!" Kassi cheered.

Barcelona had the lead, but she could see Miami and Sydney were giving her chase. Vonahan's Team London had reentered the race and somehow closed the distance to pull in behind Rio de Janeiro in fifth place.

"These chas have been sailing all night long without a solitary break," Vander said. "It's a tight race to the finish and no one's easing off the throttle!" Kassi could almost picture him as a commentator saying those exact words from the big screen.

Savriah stared at Vander for an awkward amount of time before blurting out, "You know, Vander, you have a perfectly shaped head."

Vander blinked at her for a moment before saying, "Thanks, Savvy, I'll add that to my resume!"

Kassi heard Leron shout with pure exhilaration, *"It's been a nonstop theater of stupefying magnificence as the top teams battle for a medal!"*

"C'mon, Lula, you've got this!" Kassi said to herself, on the edge of her seat.

Fille shouted, "Chas, isn't that...?" He jumped up with excitement, "It is! It's Sensei and Coach! They're on the holo!"

"Coach and Sensei are so bosst!" Adonis couldn't hide his admiration.

They whipped their heads up to see the camera focusing on their coaches' box. Sensei Kelipalo stood right next to Coach Rockson. Both were barrel-chested with broad shoulders and nearly a head taller than the other coaches around them–like two Great Danes amidst a pack of dachshunds. Neither of them noticed the camera on them and seemed to be in an intense conversation with a short man in a bowler hat to their left. It didn't look friendly. The short man was angrily pointing at Coach Rockson. The cameras switched back to the race. Commentators focused on the middle of the pack where the largest clump of ships was in a tangle.

"Wonder what that was about," Fille said, scratching his head.

"That cha looked angry," Kassi said.

Leron continued from the commentator's box, *"unless one of these teams flies from the pack free as a bird in a park, I don't think anyone else comes knocking on Barcelona's door!"*

Next to Leron, Lisi was about to respond when blood-curdling screams erupted from one of the stadiums. The cameras quickly panned toward the commotion. It was the same coaches' box as before, but now that box was littered with fallen bodies, the scene of an atrocious crime–another Hel Mafia sonic bombing!

Thirty~Three

Kassi breathed sharply, suddenly as if stabbed with pain. Covering her mouth, she stared at the gruesome picture on the holoscreen.

Bodies lay in almost an exact circle, forming a blast radius that faced away from the hypocenter. Just beyond the initial radius lay an outer circle of injured victims slowly getting to their feet, blood trickling out of their ears, as their moans and cries filled the air. The camera operators lingered on the scene as if stunned, then abruptly cut away to the race before Kassi had the chance to scan their faces.

Shock turned to fear, and fear turned to panic as the crowds began to scream and wail, their eyes glued to the screens for updates.

"You don't think…?" Fille tried to ask, his voice wavering.

"Sensei, Sensei, and Coach…?" Adonis trailed off.

"Maybe they left before it happened," Kassi said, her heart thumping in her chest.

"They were just there," Savriah said.

"I"m sure they weren't when the bomb went off," Vander said, his voice strained.

The feed on the screen cut to a news anchor with cropped

blonde hair and glasses in a more formal suit. "*Stadium 2 of the Siren Games has just been hit in what is presumed to be another horrific Hel Mafia attack. Reports are coming in with a casualty count and...,*" he stopped abruptly to read an update. "*It appears additional blasts detonated near the training facilities in the Dubai and Abidjan provinces. We encourage all global citizens to remain calm.*"

Sitting next to him was a woman in a burgundy, high-collared dress, and suit jacket who added, "*So far, the confirmed dead now total at 41, with an additional 162 injured, many of whom are in critical condition and have been taken to St. Delfina's hospital. As soon as bodies are identified, loved ones will be immediately notified...*"

"So we have-eh to wait?" Kassi said. "What if they really..." As she considered the very real possibility, the world began to spin beneath her feet. She could hear Adonis shouting something about it all being a mistake, but his words were muffled by the fog that filled her mind. Collapsing to the ground, she hugged her knees and buried her face. Her breathing quickened and she heaved louder and louder as the world around her grew to an immense size, swallowing her up. She felt smaller and farther away with each labored breath, until...

A gentle hand touched Kassi's shoulder. A familiar voice said, "Kassi. Kassi, just focus on your breathing. Slow it down," Tallie said as she continued rubbing her shoulder. "You are in control. You are safe." She repeated over and over.

Inhale. Exhale. Inhale, exhale–breathe!

Lifting her head, she found herself surrounded by Vander, Vi'ella, Ganna, Murrey, and Tallie. A few paces to her left, Fille, Adonis, and Savriah hugged each other, tears streaming down their faces.

"What was that?" Murrey asked, studying Kassi.

"She was having a panic attack," Tallie said. "My mom gets those."

"What do we do?" he asked.

"Kassi, are you with us?" Vander stooped down to get a

closer look, genuine concern in his eyes. Embarrassed, she desperately wanted to disappear from his sight almost as much as wanted him to comfort her.

Ganna stooped next to him and said, "You're safe, Kassi. Nothing is going to happen to you."

She couldn't find words, so she nodded to acknowledge them. As jealous as she had been of Ganna, she was grateful to her and the rest of them for being there, with Kassi. Wiping her eyes, she realized her cheeks were smeared with eyeliner. Her whole body was shaking. "Thank you," she managed to say, her voice quivering.

Fille, Adonis, and Savriah embraced as they buried their heads and wept. Seeing that Kassi was above water, Tallie, Ganna, and the others drifted over to them and consoled them. Kassi soon joined in.

Everyone had forgotten all about the Siren Games. Crowds had gradually dispersed. Barcelona, Miami, Sydney, and London still crossed the finish line in time to claim one of four Paradise passports that earned them and all their families a place on Paradise. While the world mourned another horrendous tragedy, these siren athletes won the Games and would be taking their families through the portal–away from it all. On all the holo-screens, their victory was a footnote to the breaking news alert.

Sunday morning at school, Kassi and her friends took the elevator to Sensei's classroom and sat in silence until noon. Kassi had to believe he wasn't gone.

"Have-eh we heard anything yet?" She asked.

"I haven't seen Kiowa," Fille said. "He'd know."

On Monday morning, Kassi rushed to school with hopes of finding Sensei there in his classroom. When she burst through the door to his room, his seat was empty. Other students had also paid his classroom a visit, likely hoping for the same confir-mation. Many sank into vacant seats, regardless of their status, and waited. She took a seat as well and was soon joined by Fille, Adonis, Savriah, and many of their other teammates.

They sat in silence all throughout the first period, skipping class. Other students stayed while many more peeked their heads in intermittently to see if there were any updates. Kassi was surprised to see students of all statuses deeply concerned. Apparently, he was more than just another professor to them, as well.

One student who couldn't care less–Malyra–went out of her way to find Kassi and bump shoulders with her in *P.E.* class. She scoffed, "Awww, do you miss your Sensei? He got what he deserved for defending you Four Hundie sheist muppets!"

Kassi turned on a U-coin and pounced on Malyra, throwing her to the floor. She placed a palm against her chin, twisted her head, and slapped her furiously. Students stood frozen in shock for a brief moment before one of them yanked Kassi off. Coach Muzzey was slower to respond than usual–likely shocked–but eventually jumped right in Kassi's face.

"What was that she…I can't believe wha…YASH'S TAP-DANCING SHEIST! You're definitely getting the broomstick!"

"You think I care?" Kassi screamed. "No one disrespects Sensei Kelipalo! NO ONE!"

They threw the broomstick down at her feet and yelled their insults while Kassi crossed her arms and glared at each one of them as they stepped forward. Most of them shrunk under her violent gaze, stepping forward timidly, shouting something incoherent, and retreating quickly to the back of the line. Nikola didn't participate. He had taken a seat in the back of the gymnasium and watched the spectacle. Of course, the 800s had that option.

When Muzzey handed Malyra the sonic pulse baton, Kassi snatched it out of her hand with a hard shove while Muzzey was calling the class to attention. Before they knew what was happening, Kassi performed a powerful incantation, a Gelt Hîm her brother, Kairos, had always used as a last resort for his duels and blasted them with a massive sonic pulse that knocked the entire class, including Kassi, off their feet. They flew nearly two meters into the air before crumpling to the gymnasium floor. Muzzey was slow to get back to his feet.

In a daze, Kassi stood, tossed the pulse baton to the ground, and stumbled out into the hallways. The blast had rocked her too, but she didn't regret it for a second.

At lunch, Kassi regrouped with her friends in line, and she relayed what had happened.

"You did, you did what?" Adonis said as his jaw hit the floor.

Fille ran fingers through his hair and said, "You pulsed the entire *P.E.* class!" They almost chuckled, but none of them were ready to laugh just yet.

In *Evéik*, they had a substitute teacher–Professor Zubert. He wrote his name in big cartoonish letters on his holopad and projected it in the air. Shifty-eyed, he skittered around the room for the first half of class asking students to stand up so he could rearrange the desks. In honor of Sensei, Kassi ignored Zubert, put on her HoloGlasses, and dove into her assigned literature. Even if Sensei wasn't around, she still intended to finish it.

After class, Kassi and her friends walked to the docks. Kassi had a lot on her mind. "Don't you think it's odd that as soon as Coach and Sensei confront Farra, they're targeted?" she asked as she balanced behind them on the slidewalks.

"You think Farra had something to do with it?" Savriah asked.

"If she was involved in this one, she was involved in the other ones," Fille said.

"She does enjoy hurting people," Kassi said, examining the scars on her arms. They had mostly faded.

Vi'ella saw them approaching. "Didn' think ya'll would show up today."

"I need, I need to play," Adonis said. "Get my mind off of it."

"Yisû, me too," Fille said. Kassi and Savriah agreed.

"Besides, we can't miss a game or we're out and it was all for nothing," Kassi said.

Kassi changed into her wettie and joined her teammates in

line. When they reached the springboards, Vander gave her a pat on the shoulder before calling to the rest of the team, "Alright chas, let's go win this one for Coach Rockson and Kelipalo!"

Kiowa wasn't there today. They still hadn't seen him since the incident. He was the only one who knew for sure what happened, and Kassi needed to know. It was eating her up inside.

Their first game in the tournament was against the number-one-ranked team–the Red Squalls. Even after losing some of their best players to the Blue Krakens, they managed to keep the top slot in the league.

It was a hard-fought contest–a close first half. Kassi and many of her teammates were slow to get into the rhythm, but they pushed through it and eventually found their calm. They were down by three with only a minute left in the half, but once they focused, they quickly countered with two goals right before the buzzer. By halftime, they were up by a point, 4-3.

When they dove and took their positions for the second half, Kassi saw a familiar face floating on the sidelines. "Kiowa!" Kassi shouted. Everyone turned their heads and swarmed him.

"Sorry I'm late, chas," Kiowa said, his voice hoarse as if from crying all night.

"Any word?" Fille asked, his eyes hopeful.

Kiowa shook his head. "Nothing."

"Nothing? What does that, what does that mean?" Adonis asked.

"It means we still don't know," Kiowa said with a shrug.

"So what should we do?" Kassi asked.

"Compete!" Kiowa said. "Compete as if they're watching from the other side!"

Something about that mindset lit a fire within Kassi. Her mind awakened, her vision of the waterfield cleared. She felt life return to her limbs.

The team took their positions. When the second-half buzzer sounded, Kassi blasted off the line with a fury the Blue Krakens had never seen. She swam circles around everyone, making the Red Squalls look like bottom-ranked amateurs. Anytime one of them got the disc, Kassi was there wreaking havoc and forcing turnovers. When they gave her the disc, she spun and weaved, kicking the disc through the legs of defenders and passing back and forth with her teammates to create one attack after another. Her energy and passion rubbed off. Everyone synced up to her wavelength and performed their best game.

By the end of it, Blue Krakens had won 11-6. Kassi had scored six points on her own, reaching a record-high score for the season. The Red Squalls' captain and a few of his teammates came up to them and congratulated them, offering a low bow of respect before heading back to the docks–high class until the end. The rest of the team stared daggers at Vander and the other former Red Squalls. This loss meant they were eliminated from the tournament and all those who didn't age out would have to wait until next season for another chance to qualify.

On Tuesday, Kassi and her friends routinely grabbed their food at lunch and made their way to Sensei's classroom, even though he wasn't there. They stepped foot into his old room, saw the substitute sitting at his desk, turned on their heels, and retreated down the corridor as Fille said, "Guess we can't eat there today."

The school had an auditorium that had been flooded and abandoned. Rows of seats faced a stage in complete disarray. Many of the seats had been ripped out of the floor. A giant pile of rotting wood from what looked like a hundred-year-old production set cluttered the stage. The bottom half of the auditorium sat under a few centimeters of water while the top rows were still high and dry. This is where Kassi and her friends parked, claiming the most comfortable of the broken, cushioned seats.

They had a day off in between matches. On Wednesday afternoon, they arrived on the docks to find out they were going up against the Black Hydras–the Chinpoke Squad–currently ranked second in the league. The last time Kassi played against them,

Nikola had broken her leg. The thought of it made a wave of fury rise in her with a thirst for retaliation.

"Let's make this one count," Kassi said to her team. "These chas deserve to get pummeled to krill!"

"Kassi's right," Fille said. "These cacafuegos don't score a single yashing point! Got it?" The team grunted in agreement.

Vander added, "Singing small doesn't serve the worlds!"

"Sing it with sháloor!" They chanted in unison and lined up for the kickoff.

Kiowa arrived right after kickoff. He had missed their pre-game training and now watched silently from the sidelines.

Just as Kassi expected, right from the start, the Black Hydras played rough, hoping to cheapshot Kassi again. Malyra relentlessly badgered Kassi, likely wanting revenge for their fight in the gym. Rather than focus on the game, Kassi welcomed the attacks, countering with her own.

When Malyra came for the sideswipe or the kick to the head, Kassi dodged and struck back. She managed to ram full speed into Malyra on two separate occasions. The last one caused Malyra to wince in pain. With Kassi so focused on enacting her own revenge, she had missed easy passes and lost possession of the disc for her team on numerous occasions.

By halftime, the game was scoreless. Adonis and the defense had held their end of the bargain. They hadn't allowed a single point. But the offense hadn't responded, and Kassi had ruined many golden opportunities.

"You with us, Kassi?" Vi'ella asked when they surfaced for halftime.

"Huh?" Kassi perked up. "Yisû. Why?"

"You seem very focused on getting back at these chas," Vi'ella said.

Fille walked over to Kassi, and asked, "Kassi, you with us?"

Before she could answer, Kiowa surfaced and brought the team together for a huddle. He had trimmed off his burst fade mohawk. In its place was a buzz cut with sleek, 360 deep waves.

He was always clean-cut and had the same sparkle in his eye as his dad, but his usual big and bright smile was gone today. "Alright chas, defense is playing an incredible game today. But where's my offense?" He eyed Kassi when he said it. Kassi hung her head and stared at her feet. She knew her focus was off–all she could think about was breaking bones. "You with us, Kassi?"

"Yisû, why does everyone keep asking me that?" Kassi said, annoyed. Of course, she knew exactly why, but she didn't want to admit it.

Kiowa sighed, his demeanor sagging. "Also, chas, I have bad news." Everyone whipped their heads up, attentive. "This is difficult to say, so I'm just gonna say it. Authorities came to my house and said…they're gone."

"Gone? Gone, like what do you mean gone?" Adonis asked. Kiowa just shook his head. They all knew what that meant. Sensei Kelipalo and Coach Rockson were not coming back. The team hung their heads in silence.

Vander spoke up, "There will be a time to grieve, but impossible as it seems, we need to put it aside and win this game."

"Vander's right. They put a lot into you chas–into this team," Kiowa said quietly. "You gotta make it count for something."

Kassi knew they would have been disappointed in her first-half performance. She had lowered herself to Malyra's level. With a long sigh, Kassi dove and took her position on the waterfield, ignoring Malyra's wild-eyed stares.

"Sorry chas," Kassi said. "I stuffed the first half. I'm ready to play now."

"It happens to the best of us," Vander said.

"Glad you're with us!" Vi'ella said.

Black Hydras kicked off the second half, and Kassi was right in the fray. She got a piece of a pass that sent the disc spiraling off course. A Kraken picked it up and began the counter. This time, rather than focusing on collisions and causing pain, Kassi dodged and weaved, slipping through defenders to find openings. With some quick precision passing, they found themselves in scoring position. Kassi faked a shot and crossed it to Vander who had a wide-open goal. He put the first two points on the board.

All game long, the Blue Kraken defense held the line and kept the Black Hydras from scoring. Meanwhile, Kassi facilitated two more scores and scored a ricochet point, leading the team to a 7-0 victory over the Hydras.

The final buzzer sounded, and the Black Hydras scurried back to the docks without any acknowledgment. However, Kassi saw it on their faces as they left. Malyra was ruffled, fuming with frustration. Calandra screamed at her teammates. DeSchuster's fists were balled up, looking for a fight. Nikola was the only one who seemed unphased by the defeat.

As the adrenaline of the game dissipated, Kassi and her teammates sank with the emptiness of losing their heroes–their revered coaches. Rather than celebrating their victory as they advanced to the semi-finals in the tournament for the Miami League title, they sagged. Many, including Kassi, cried and embraced each other.

"They died because of me," Kassi said between sobs.

"Don't say that, Kassi," Fille said.

"If they hadn't come-eh to my defense…," Kassi couldn't finish.

"It was nothing you did," Vander said. "Only the Hel Mafia."

Kiowa swam up to them after the game, "That second half was world class. Dad would'a been proud," he said, his voice shaky and his eyes swollen.

"He's why we're in the semi-finals," Fille said reverently, his eyes downward.

Kiowa nodded. "We're holding a funeral service for both Kelipalo and my dad this Friday."

"We'll all be there," Vander said. "Do you need any help with it?"

"My aunt is taking care of everything," Kiowa said.

Kassi lifted her head. "We should write-eh them a song," she said, thinking out loud.

"I'd like that," Kiowa said with a subtle nod.

Kassi had yet to hear him sing anything other than vocal warmups, but even then his voice sounded like a smooth alto saxophone under the moonlight of an empty street.

"Let's head to Kassi's townhome. We can use the balcony to write," Fille said as he led the way back to the docks.

Out of their wetsuits and back on the slidewalks, Kassi asked Kiowa, "So how are you dealing with everything?"

"I don't know if I am, Kassi. I'm filled with this rage–all the time," Kiowa said as he followed behind. "I just wanna find those responsible and…" He looked off to the side, his fists clenched. He was a whole head taller than Kassi, his broad shoulders wider than the slidewalks.

"We wanna find them, too," Kassi said quietly.

They reached the front door. Moza sat at the kitchen table watching something on his holopad. He didn't look up. Kassi and her friends climbed two flights of stairs to the sun parlor on the top floor. They took their seats on one of the balconies and spent the next couple of hours working on lyrics and melody ideas. Ideas poured out like a steady stream, magically meshing together.

When it was finished, Kiowa said, "This is powerful. People are gonna feel this!"

"I think Sensei and Coach would've loved it," Kassi said, smiling through her tears.

"Thank you for doin' this," Kiowa said as his eyes grew misty. "I'm sure Pop'll be smilin' from the other side."

"Think we'll get in trouble for singing this?" Savriah said. "You know, since it's spiritual?"

"Don't matter," Kiowa said, shaking his head. "Some words are worth the price to say them."

"That's like what Sensei used to say," Fille said. Universalism taught a form of rebirth as the only afterlife scenario that was attainable. They believed human beings died and returned to Earth to inhabit new bodies, having to relive the entire life cycle all over again. The song Kassi and her friends wrote directly contradicted those beliefs.

Friday evening, crowds gathered at the Universalist shrine in downtown Miami, where all funerals were held. The pulpit, made of six miniature golden columns reflected on the smooth, polished flooring surrounding it. Encircling the pulpit stood six larger golden columns propping up brilliant, dazzling lights. At its center, suspended above center stage was a giant golden gong with three eagle heads etched on its face. Filling the gaps from behind the large columns was a floor-lit mosaic depicting a night sky full of starry constellations. Kassi and her 400s friends took their seats toward the back with the other 400s. Vander, Ganna, and the other 800s sat closer to the front. Kiowa sat on the front row, his mother beside him with a black veil covering her face.

Miami's provincial senator, Madame Orsini, stepped to the ornate pulpit and addressed the crowd. She had a teased, edgy bob of salt-and-pepper hair that fell just past her chin. In majestic robes of purple silk tied at the waist with a custom leather belt, Orsini wore two golden necklaces with three pairs of matching earrings and enough bracelets to weigh her arms down–probably more jewelry than was owned by the entire Miami population combined. "We're here to pay our respects to Leisel Kay-li-peh-lo and Touring Rockson." The senator butchered their names.

"Tolin Rockson and Lesley Kelipalo," Fille said louder than he probably intended. Many turned in their seats, including high-ranking members of Miami's Universalism branch, making Fille shrink.

The senator gave a brief, generic eulogy that could have been for anyone. When she concluded, Kiowa stood and stepped forward. "Could I say a few words?"

"What more is there to say?" Senator Orsini asked.

"He was my father," Kiowa said.

The senator looked down her nose at Kiowa, but when she eyed his red 800s armband, she raised her eyebrows and shuffled to the side. "If you must," she said with a dramatic sigh.

Stepping up to the microphone, Kiowa addressed the crowds gathered to honor his father and Sensei Kelipalo. "Many of you know my father as the coach who led more teams to Paradise than any other. What you don't know, is despite his tireless efforts to help so many athletes, he always put his own family first. He was a father before he was a coach, and I wouldn't be here today if it weren't for him.

"Also, Professor Lesley Kelipalo did more for this community than anyone. He gave up his home on Planet Astera just so he could help us Gaians. He taught with passion, he loved his students, and he wanted nothing more than to see us all on Paradise. In honor of my father, Coach Rockson, and our professor, Sensei Kelipalo, my friends and I wrote this song."

Kiowa launched right into it before Senator Orsini could object. All Blue Krakens hummed along. When the second verse rolled around, Kassi stepped forward and joined Kiowa on the stage, her friends close behind.

SEE YOU ON THE OTHER SIDE

Your words are like an echo
More than just a memory
Telling me to let go of my rage
When it's here to give me company

How do I go back to
Tryin' to rise above this
Now that I'm without you to get on my case
Is it really all up to me?

I'm living in the shadows
Ever since your light went out

See you on the other side
See you on the other side
You're gonna be back in my life
See you on the other side

You got me through the hard times
Always had the answers
But now I feel so lost, I am so confused
Drifting like a boat without a sail

I feel like this is my fault
Though you would never blame me
I'm the one who brought all of this on you
No matter what I do, I always fail

We're living in the shadows
Ever since your light went out

See you on the other side
See you on the other side
You're gonna be back in my life
See you on the other side

How do I go back to
Tryin' to find a rescue
Now that I'm without you to guide me home
Is it really all up to me?

See You on the other side

IN EVÉIK

Bud síl în ekobé tuví logosóat
Mas sé în dakiraat
Zélé shi fen pí van nayalí luté mwaat

Máti ik bud famé shi yiv azendûjang mwaat

Kwam bébulak píd nayat shi
Upar rînyûfa shi arugíd ramat
Anish bud kimun tuvé shi prapíd dar nayalí fumébé
    nayat
Tino bud amni nak shi mwabé famat?

Vib lev li tînóbé nayat
Ferna kwan mun píba tuví orûat

Tazíd dar li ali ladobé tuvat
Tazíd dar li ali ladobé tuvat
Bébulak kudad budíd lev nayalí vibé tuvat
Tazíd dar li ali ladobé tuvat

Prapa mwabé méso li sabu agitójang tuvat
Méshû mita li ripostosóat
Da anish hûn perdoba rasana, bud hûn balir nayat
Ándesh síl în karababé kimun în velang

Rasa síl ramé bud nayalí gresté nayat
Víka nukwam olisíd vinatíd mwabé tuvat
Ranaba amni van ramé dar tuvang nayat
Dai ne ankîn tébé nayat, méshû zalósách nayat

Vib lev li tînóbé bizat
Ferna kwan mun píba tuví orûat

Tazíd dar li ali ladobé tuvat
Tazíd dar li ali ladobé tuvat
Bébulak kudad budíd lev nayalí vibé tuvat
Tazíd dar li ali ladobé tuvat

Kwam daid nayat bébulak píd shi

Rînyûsách shi patasách în pastibé
Anish kimun tuvat bud nayat shi vadíd hémé mwaat
Tino bud amni nak shi mwabé famat?

THE FIRST THREE rows were filled with government officials and those with political aspirations. Throughout the song, they made outward displays of shock and disgust in response to the lyrics. A provincial assembly member jumped to his feet and searched the crowds. Spotting a mediation officer, he snapped his fingers and pointed at Kiowa and Kassi as if demanding they respond. The crowds, however, stepped forward and linked arms, surrounding all the singers and keeping authorities out. By the final chorus, many from the crowd had joined in, teary-eyed. Statuses had always divided them, but today, everyone came together to mourn, and it was a beautiful and fitting send-off for Sensei Kelipalo and Coach Rockson.

As soon as the tribute concluded, mediation officers broke through the crowds and took Kiowa, Kassi, and all of the Blue Krakens, binding them and escorting them toward a nearby U.N.O.E. patrol yacht. The crowds shouted and screamed in protest, but as soon as officers threatened to cart them away as well, they dispersed.

Just like the last time, Kassi was shoved into the cabin of a black U.N.O.E. yacht where she endured a severe whipping at the hands of an officer with a sonic pulse baton, her own rage building with each blow. When it was finally over, she was tossed onto the docks of a waterbus station next to her friends. They groaned in pain as they struggled to their feet.

Kiowa was the first to speak, clutching his side. He spat in the direction of the retreating yacht before looking each of them in the eye and said, "Worth it." The rest of them looked at each other and knew this had only strengthened their resolve.

After a short bus ride back to Miami Beach, they each limped away to their houses, shouting, "Ride the tide!"

The next day, after another Saturday at school, they reached the docks and met up with the rest of their team. Everyone shuffled in pain from their recent sonic beatings. Still, they were determined to win today's game and advance to the final round. With only four teams remaining in the Miami League, the docks were almost completely empty.

They faced off against the Tinsel Tiamats. Their last game against the Tiamats proved a major turning point for the Krakens. Besides earning them much-deserved respect from other teams, it was the game that got the attention of Vi'ella and Vander.

Despite their bruised and battered condition, the Krakens synced up and played with heart. It was a close match, and the Tiamats almost came out on top. But in the end, Krakens sealed the deal with Vi'ella's goal off of a penalty kick that advanced them to the finals.

After their win, Joshi shouted, "Chas! Do you realize we're only one match away from qualifying for the Siren Games?"

"Power it down, Joshi," Fille said.

"Yisû, don't jinx it!" Catelyn shouted back.

"If only Sensei K and Coach were here to see it," Fille said.

"I believe-eh they are," Kassi said quietly. Fille locked eyes with Kassi, a questioning look on his face, before he nodded.

That night, Kassi reflected on her father's words in the holovid about plotting a rescue. When she came to Earth three months ago, it was all she could think about. She couldn't have imagined being forced to stay this long. But now, as much as she longed for home, she couldn't leave without her friends. If her family came to rescue her now, she'd lose her chance to help her team win the Siren Games.

On Tuesday afternoon, they had their final match of the tournament. Kassi expected the final game to be more challenging. Instead, they soundly defeated their opponents, the Purple

Piranhas, and solidified their place as the Miami League title holder. Kiowa cheered them on from the sidelines.

"Chas, we did it! We did it!" Adonis exclaimed.

"We're going to the Siren Games!" many of her teammates shouted.

As soon as they reached the docks, they whipped their helmets off and began to chant:

Awaken, awaken, awaken the kraken
Awaken, awaken, awaken the kraken
If I'm not mistaken, we no longer lackin'
I said awaken, awaken, awaken the kraken

KASSI, Kiowa, and her friends all joined in, jumping into a circle and chanting with their team. If Sensei and Coach were there, they would have danced and chanted right along with them.

The next afternoon, the Krakens gathered on an empty dock. "Alright, chas, first of all, no practice today," Fille said to everyone's applause. "And I have some more good news." He pulled out his hologlasses and read aloud. "The Blue Krakens, now to be referred to as Team Miami, have officially entered the Siren Games. Your first match will take place on Friday, July 4th in the Exuma Arena. Your opponent will be Team Rio de Janeiro. We would also like to cordially invite you to attend a Grand Ball in honor of your victory. The Ball will be held on Sunday, June 29th in Toronto, and attendees are recommended to wear formal attire, no armbands required."

"A Grand Ball? What's that?" Joshi asked.

"Dance, it's a dance," Adonis said.

"We're supposed to travel to Toronto for a dance?" Murrey raised his eyebrows.

"Sounds romantic," Ganna said as she hugged Vander's arm.

Of course, you think it's romantic, Kassi wanted to say. *You have someone to go with!*

"And lastly, one more thing," Fille shouted. "Miami Province has provided every one of us with new siren wetsuits fit for champions." The team cheered even louder at this news. All this time, the 400s and 500s had been competing with oxygen tanks and ripped, inferior suits. They would finally have real wetsuits to compete in.

Vander stepped forward after Fille concluded. "We'll resume practice tomorrow with Kiowa here to whip us into shape and make sure we're ready. For now, you're all invited to my place to celebrate!"

Thirty-Four

Once they were on Vander's balcony, Kassi vented, "What's the point of going to an elegant dance-eh in three weeks when I don't have a dress." Her eyes instinctively found Ganna flirting with Vander on the other balcony. "Or a date-eh."

"You gotta, you gotta come, Kassi! When are you ever going to get this chance again?" Adonis had a point.

"What am I supposed to wear?" Kassi said, her hands in the large pockets of her school uniform jumpsuit. "I can't just show up in my school uniform!"

"We can find something in the Market Abyss," Savriah said.

"And pay with what?" Kassi asked.

"Moza won't give you anything?" Fille asked.

"Never in a million years," Kassi said.

"My cousins, my cousins might have a job," Adonis said. "Down at the Market Abyss."

"What kind of job?" Kassi asked.

"Selling contraband holovids," he said.

"Mirific!" Kassi sighed.

With the AquaSphera season over and summer arriving, school let out for three weeks for a brief holiday. Kassi and her team took advantage of the extra time to hit the water and train with Kiowa. Meanwhile, with no other option to buy a dress, Kassi took Adonis up on his offer to work for his cousins. He made the introductions.

After hearing so much about the Market Abyss, Kassi was curious to finally go there. With Adonis' two cousins, Scarlette and Saúl, they took an unmarked ferry to an abandoned cargo ship floating roughly a kilometer offshore. Similar to the bazaars she'd read about, the Market Abyss had overstocked kiosks lining the deck with peddlers selling everything from faux meat and fruit to vinyl records and paperback books. No one wore armbands–Kassi couldn't believe it. It had been so long since she had seen regular civilians without armbands.

A hand-painted sign that read "deep abyss" pointed to a lower deck. "What's down there?" Kassi asked them.

"You don't wanna go down there," Saúl said. His wavy black hair was just like Adonis', but he was at least ten years older, scruffy, and walked with a limp.

"It's where everyone looking for trouble finds it," Scarlette said. She was thin and wiry like Adonis, with thick dark hair that extended to her waist. Kassi was jealous. She reached up and lightly patted her own short braids.

The weeks flew by with training every morning and her Market Abyss job with Saúl and Scarlette the rest of the day. It was an exhausting schedule, but it was nice to have a break from her professors' inane punishments, the constant bullying from the Chinpoke Squad, and the reminder of her inferior status. After three weeks, she had barely enough for the most basic dress on the market.

Collecting her last payment from Scarlette, she walked to the other end of the cargo ship where she had seen a clothing kiosk with dresses her size. As she slipped through crowds of people, a man with a mutton chops beard and top hat jostled her with his elbows.

"Ow, watch where you're going!" Kassi shouted.

The man quickly apologized before disappearing into the crowd. When she reached the dress kiosk, Kassi fumbled through her pockets for the U-Coins she had saved up.

"What? Where is it?" She frantically searched from pocket to pocket, finding nothing–not even the money they had just paid her minutes ago.

Kassi retraced her steps, hoping the money had simply fallen to the ground. Checking her pockets again and again, she came up empty. Scanning the masses, she spotted the bearded man in the top hat and pushed through the crowd.

"Give it back!" she shouted.

"Give what back?" he asked, a bead of sweat dripping down his face. He wore a loose, white button-down with white flat-front shorts.

"The U-Coins you stole-eh!"

"How dare you accuse me of stealing!" he said, whirling on her. "Who do you think you are?" He lifted his shirt just enough to reveal a sheathed knife clipped to his belt. Without a siren suit, Kassi wouldn't be able to defend herself in a knife fight. She slumped and dragged herself back to Adonis' cousins.

Returning to Scarlette and Saúl, she said, "They stole it!"

"Stole what?" Saúl asked.

"The U-Coins I'd been saving up!" Kassi said.

Saúl and Scarlette exchanged glances. "People lose their money here all the time," Saúl said. "Thieves are everywhere."

Scarlette placed a hand on Kassi's shoulder, "I'm sorry, Kassi. It's happened to all of us!"

Kassi didn't want to believe it. The whole point of this job was to buy a dress. Now, she was out of money, out of time, and still without a dress. "I almost had it! I was this close-eh!" Kassi groaned, holding her fingers up. "Why? Why can't I get one break? Zhust one break!"

The day came to leave for Toronto, Kassi sank heavily on her lumpy, smart-less mattress and thought about how her friends were likely on their way to catch a hovertrain from Miami to

Toronto without her. Even though they wanted her to join them, Kassi couldn't help but feel left out.

A knock came at the door. Opening it, she found a curious box wrapped in brown paper on her doorstep. The only packages they ever received were the weekly government rations dropped off every Monday morning. Oddly, this package was addressed to her.

Kassi picked up the box and examined it, trying to guess its contents. It was heavier than it looked. Glancing suspiciously in all directions, she saw only the usual pedestrian foot traffic bustling through the streets. Ducking inside, she closed the front door and ripped it open. Inside, neatly folded, was a breathtaking dress. She held it up and gasped. Running to her room, she shut the door and threw it on, admiring her reflection in the mirror. Even a scratched old mirror couldn't hide its iridescent beauty. A delicate, yet strong material like pearly seashells wrapped and flowed around her like unpredictable ocean currents. The contouring neckline and shape of the dress blended so perfectly with her skin, it was as if it were a part of her body. It was ethereal as if she had somehow stepped into her favorite dream. The dress was obviously the work of her favorite Nemalís designer, Raymare–she'd recognize his work anywhere.

How is this possible?

She searched the box for a note and found a small emerald-cut holodrive like the one that had been slipped into her pocket during the first round of the Siren Games. Excited, she linked it to her hologlasses and opened the holovid.

A holographic projection of her older brother, Caesar, filled the room. He spoke in the calming and familiar Evéik, *"Hi Kassi, we heard you qualified for the Siren Games. We couldn't be prouder!"* Caesar had bags under his bloodshot eyes. *"I know how much you'd love to attend the Grand Ball with your friends and wouldn't have a way of getting your hands on appropriate attire. I had a friend of mine sneak this through the portal. I just hope this gets to you in time!"*

Kassi hugged the dress as tears welled up in her eyes. She wanted to reach through her glasses and hug her brother. He was always thinking of her.

"It won't be much longer. Keep winning games, but if everything goes right, you'll be back home before you know it," Caesar smiled. *"Ashkana tuv, Kassi!"*

The message ended. Kassi wiped her eyes and stood up to admire her new dress. In the mirror, Kassi could see glimpses of her old self. Raymare had worked his magic once again. She wondered how much the dress would sell for on the Market Abyss, and what that money could mean for her Gaian friends.

No time to think about that! I have a spectacular dress, and just in time!

Kassi changed into her siren suit, carefully folded her new dress into the waterproof bag it came in, slid it into the small pouch of her sonopack, and ran out the door. She hurried to Savriah's house to see if they had already left for the train station.

"They left just over an hour ago," Savriah's dad said after answering the door. She could see the striking resemblance. Same bushy red hair and freckles. "Fille and Adonis snagged her to hop a train to Toronto."

"Maybe I can still catch 'em. Thanks!" Kassi threw on her helmet. For a moment, she thought about chancing it and taking flight into the wide-open skies above. Then she eyed the cameras on every corner and knew she would never get away with it. She dove.

Lighting all four bulbs in the flooded streets of Miami Beach, she weaved through taxis and waterbuses, sending ripples and waves in her wake. Reaching the open water, she swam for the Miami River and took it all the way to the train station. Jetting out of the water, she landed in front of a large group of startled pedestrians, accidentally dousing them with water. They shrugged it off–likely assuming Kassi was an 800 with her upgraded wetsuit.

"Sorry," Kassi shouted as she removed her helmet. In the distance, she spotted her friends boarding the train. Heaving gulps of air, she sprinted the final stretch and jumped onto the train just as the doors were closing.

I almost missed it! It took her a moment to catch her breath. Walking down the aisle, she passed a few rows of seats before locating them.

"Kassi? Where'd you come from?" Fille said, jumping to his feet.

"You swam here?" Savriah noticed her dripping wetsuit.

"I thought, I thought you didn't wanna come," Adonis said.

"I got a dress!" Kassi retrieved her bag from her sonopack.

"Bosst!" Fille shouted. Savriah slid over so Kassi could sit down.

"Where'd you get it?" Savriah asked.

"My brother," Kassi said in between breaths. She was still huffing from the sprint. "He somehow snuck it through the portal."

"It's from, it's from…?" Adonis' eyes went wide.

"Yisû," Kassi answered before he could finish.

"Bosst!"

"Can't wait to see it," Savriah said.

"It's gorgeous!" Kassi said, her knees bouncing with excitement.

"Good thing we took the last train," Fille said. "A few of our teammates are scattered throughout the cabins, except for the 800s. They all took a hoverjet, of course."

"We're on the, we're on the same yashing team and they still won't let us fly with the 800s," Adonis grumbled. Kassi didn't mind taking the train. It was a new adventure for her; and besides, she wouldn't have to see Ganna hanging all over Vander for the next three hours.

After catching her breath, she stared out the window at the passing scenery. Traveling at over 600 kilometers an hour, it all looked like a slummy brown blur. It was so…otherworldly to think of traveling as something that took hours. On Nemal, they had over sixty InterPorts that allowed you to travel across the planet in an instant, and with siren suits, you could fly or swim to your destination in minutes.

Eventually, she grew bored of the same view and leaned back in her seat. The low hum and rocking motion of the train put her to sleep. By the time she woke up, they were already arriving in Toronto.

"Wow, I slept through the whole-eh thing." She saw her friends playing card games on the small table between their benches.

"Yisû, you were snoring," Adonis said, imitating her snoring.

"I was?"

"Glad you got some rest," Fille said.

They came to a stop and deboarded the train. Toronto wasn't flooded like Miami Beach. They had dry sidewalks and streets, making it much easier to get around on foot.

"Look at this, look at this," Adonis said of the sidewalks as he danced around a running advertisement for the U.N.O.E. at his feet. In addition to floating holoscreens between buildings, Toronto's sidewalks and streets were covered with video displays. "So this is how the other half lives."

"Have any of you ever been to a dry province?" Kassi asked.

"We've never been outside of Miami," Fille said.

"400s aren't usually allowed to travel," Savriah said.

"So where's, where's the hotel?" Adonis asked.

Kassi put her hologlasses back on. "My directions say to go north until we turn right on King Street."

"That doesn't, that doesn't make sense. North is whatever direction you're facing, just like right is always this way, and left is always that way." Adonis said as he spun and pointed.

"Uh, what?" Kassi furrowed her eyebrows, unsure she heard him correctly.

"If I'm facing this way, then that's north." He turned around. "If I'm facing that way, then that's north."

Fille stopped focusing on the sidewalk ads. "Let me guess. One of your genius cousins told you this?"

"What? I'm telling you, north is whatever direction you're facing!"

"North is north! It's that way," Fille said, pointing northward, "and it's always that way. It's a direction. A constant direction."

"No, I'm telling you…"

"…And," Fille continued, "it's only the direction you're facing when you happen to be facing NORTH!"

"You know, if you stood directly on the South Pole, you'd be correct," Savriah added.

"See? You see? Savvy agrees with me!" Adonis pointed eagerly at Savriah.

"You're not standing on the South Pole!" Fille threw his arms outward.

They ran straight to their hotel where they were provided rooms by the Siren Games Foundation. The hotel wasn't exactly up to Nemalís standards, but it was more luxurious than anything the 400s had ever seen. Each room had two real beds, carpeted floors, fresh pillows and blankets, non-broken furniture, and its own holoscreen that played a small selection of U.N.O.E.-approved TV shows and movies.

"Hey patas, look at this!" Adonis exclaimed as he turned on the holoscreen in his room. Their other teammates had adjacent rooms down the hall. As soon as they settled in, they opened all the doors.

"It's a party!" Joshi shouted as he crossed into their room. Kassi couldn't believe she almost missed out on all of this.

"Power it down, Joshi," Fille said before entering the bathroom. A moment later, he shouted, "Chas–the showers! We've got hot water!"

"We've got, we've got hot water?" Adonis sprinted to the bathroom.

"The bed is super soft," Savriah said, bouncing on it. "Is this what it's like on Nemal?"

"Nemal is even better," Kassi smiled. "Zhust wait, you'll see."

"We should all get changed," Tallie called out. "The ball starts in an hour." She and Adonis held hands as he walked her back to her room. He glanced back at Kassi and the others, a big goofy grin on his face. Kassi was happy for him. They made a really cute couple.

Kassi threw on her new dress and stared at her reflection in the floor-to-ceiling mirror–the dress was otherworldly, but her hair, ordinary.

Ganna poked her head in. "Sorry to pop in. I love doing hair and just wanted to see…" She caught sight of Kassi's dress and gasped. "That is the most majestic dress I've ever seen! No way you found that in the Market Abyss."

"My brother," Kassi said. "It was a gift from my brother. He somehow snuck it through the portal."

"You have to let me do your hair!" Ganna said with both hands on her cheeks. "With a dress like that!"

Before Kassi could say no, Ganna stepped right up to Kassi's hair, inspecting it from all sides. Her hair used to be a great source of confidence for Kassi, but now it was mostly a reminder of her traumatic experiences with Farra. Even though it had started to grow, it would take years to get her full length back, so there wasn't nearly as much hair for Ganna to style.

"My sisters and I always practice doing each others' hair," Ganna said as she started pulling Kassi's hair into braids.

"Ah, so that's why your hair always looks so perfect," Kassi said.

"You're so nice to say that!" Ganna said. "My little sister is the most bosst hairstylist. I keep telling her she'll be a famous stylist on Paradise, one day! She and Verona."

"Who's Verona?" Kassi asked.

"Vandy's little sister. They're best friends," Ganna said as she combed through Kassi's hair. "Vandy and I love talking about what we'll do when we live on Paradise."

"I see." Kassi didn't like where this conversation was going.

"His family and mine will find neighboring houses," she said as if answering a question Kassi didn't ask.

"Neighboring houses," Kassi echoed.

"And after we get married, we'll move down the street to our own house so everyone is close by!"

Kassi straightened in her seat, her shoulders tense. "You and Vandy…uh, Vander talk about that?"

"All the time," Ganna smiled. "What's it like on Paradise? I bet it's majestic!"

Kassi half-heartedly filled her in, struggling to think past the two of them getting married and starting a life together.

When Ganna finished, Savriah hopped over to examine it. "Wow, Ganna, this is bosst!"

Kassi got a good look in the mirror, turning to see all sides. Curled, curtain bangs splashed down both sides of her face while the back was loosely pulled into a low, braided bun. As disheartened as she felt over their conversation, Kassi couldn't help but admire Ganna's work. She said, forcing a smile, "She's right, Ganna. Beautifully done!"

"Thank you," Ganna bowed gracefully. "Now, let's go show everyone!"

Near the elevators, everyone gathered, ready to go. Kassi looked over her teammates. "Wow, you chas look like-eh royalty today!" she said.

"That dress!" Tallie gawked. "Where in the worlds did you find that?"

"My brother got it for me," Kassi said. When Vander looked her up and down with approval, her cheeks flushed beet red.

"When it comes to hair, Ganna's got the magic touch," Vander said. "She's got a fairy wand in her back pocket." He threw his arm around Ganna and kissed the crown of her head before turning his attention back to Kassi. "And that dress is quite the spectacle! You may not have come with a date, but my U-Coin says you'll leave with one." Kassi wished he was referring to himself, but after everything Ganna said, she knew that was nothing more than a smoke dream.

"Well, should we go?" Savriah asked.

"Let's flake off!" Fille said.

"We outie like a bellybutton," Adonis added, slapping Fille's arm.

Fille didn't cut him off this time. "Just this once."

When they arrived at the ballroom, Kassi paused just below the entrance to take it all in. While it wasn't one of the grand halls of Nemal, the ballroom featured an exquisite soaring, oil-painted ceiling and softly-lit crystal chandeliers, elegant arch-ways, and private balconies. U.N.O.E.-approved instrumental music filled the room as siren athletes from all over the world gathered to celebrate, all without armbands. They would soon be aggressive competitors forced to compete in a deadly quadrathlon to earn a better life for their family, but for tonight, they were comrades. Not even star scores would segregate them tonight.

Kassi took a step forward into the light. The second she did, heads turned. Conversations fizzled into silence. The entire room watched her descend the grand staircase. All her life, she had attended upscale events with her family, and she often partici-pated in grand entrances, but it was always in the shadow of her parents. Now, she was in the spotlight all by herself, and it was both intimidating and exhilarating at the same time.

Sirens lined up to ask her for a dance. She gracefully accepted a request from a boy named Levett. He was a siren athlete from Los Angeles of the San Jose province. He had short-cropped hair and chocolate-brown eyes, and he seemed intent on dancing with her all night long. However, as soon as the song ended, Kassi politely thanked him and returned to her friends. He reluc-tantly let her go.

As she walked across the ballroom, her eyes swept across a sea of new faces. She thought she saw Nikola in a well-tailored tuxedo. She did a double take.

What is he doing here? His team didn't qualify!

Weaving through the crowd to where she thought she spotted Nikola, she instead found his brother, Enzo. They looked so much alike. Enzo held a dark-haired girl close to him as they danced, swaying to the romantic music. A waltz played overhead as a heart-wrenching piano glided over an enchanting symphony. She missed listening to music. If she closed her eyes, the music might have taken her back to Nemal, but then she looked more closely at the girl Enzo was dancing with.

Amára? Kassi couldn't believe it hadn't dawned on her that Amára would likely be attending. She wanted to squeal and run to her best friend, but she didn't want to ruin their moment.

Their dance was much more than a cordial waltz among friends. Amára was nestled in Enzo's arms, resting her head on his chest. They were so cute together. At least life on Earth wasn't all bad for Amára. That made Kassi feel a little better, and just a tiny bit jealous.

The song ended and Kassi couldn't contain her excitement any longer. Running as best she could in her heels, she rushed to her best friend. Amára caught sight of her and was just as surprised to see her. They hugged, bouncing up and down, and giggled.

"You're here, too?" Amára said. "We almost didn't even make it!"

"I know, I was this close-eh to staying home-eh." Kassi held up her pinched fingers. "If Caesar hadn't sent me this dress…"

"Is that a Raymare?" Amára said, wide-eyed.

"Who else?"

"We bought mine from the Market Abyss," Amára said, smoothing the front of her dress. "I like it, but it's nothing like a Raymare!"

"I love it!" Kassi said. "You look stunning!"

Amára swooped around, admiring it from all angles. "You look like a fairytale princess, Kassi! But," Amára gasped, her hands to her mouth, "what happened to all your hair!"

Kassi sighed. "I had a grip who…she was just evil! I'll tell you later."

"Let's go outside and chat," Enzo suggested, scanning the crowd suspiciously.

Once they were outside on the balcony, Enzo searched the area to see if he could spot any camera panels. They shifted until he felt they had reached a small blind spot. "We should be good here, but talk softly," he said.

"How have you been since I last saw you?" Kassi asked.

"Well, our team qualified, obviously," Amára said, waving her hand around the room, "so at least there's that. But otherwise-eh, not very good." Amára paused before switching to Evéik, tears welling up in her eyes, *"During the last attack, the Hel Mafia killed our coach, Kassi!"* she said. *"My coach was like family to me."*

"I'm so sorry, Ama!" Kassi reached out, rubbing her friend's arms. The thought of Coach Rockson and Sensei brought out her own waterworks.

Amára read her mind, like always. *"Did you lose someone, too?"*

Kassi nodded, her eyes downward. *"My coach and my mentor were both killed in that same attack,"* she said quietly. *"They were like family to me, too."*

Amára put her arm around Kassi. *"Were they also in Dubai?"*

"They were in the stands."

"I'm so sorry, Kassi," Amára said. *"Everything on Earth is just so ludicray. It's awful! Who would do something like this?"*

"I might know who," Kassi said, lifting her head.

"Not here," Enzo said in English, shaking his head. He glanced around and stroked his chin, "You know since you're both here, I wonder."

"What?"

"I need to check on something," he said. "Give me an hour. Stay here 'til I get back."

"Where are you going?" Amára asked.

"I'll tell you later," he said, hopping forward to plant a kiss on Amára's lips before briskly disappearing around the corner.

With Enzo gone, Kassi and Amára switched back to Evéik and spent the next hour on the balcony catching up on the past few months. So much had happened since they had last seen each other, and Kassi needed to know every detail about Amára's new romance–an hour wasn't enough time.

Enzo returned too soon. He interrupted them and whispered, "Looks like Operation Ruby Slippers is still on."

"You still haven't told me what that is." Amára put her hands on her hips.

Ruby Slippers? Kassi recognized the reference from one of Sensei's assigned readings.

"I can't yet." Enzo's eyes darted back and forth. "Did you bring your wetsuits?"

"Always," Kassi and Amára both said.

"Good, run back to your rooms and change into them, then meet me in the lobby."

Kassi looked between Amára and Enzo. "Are we coming back before-eh the ball's over?"

Enzo gave the slightest shake of his head. Kassi turned and searched the crowded ballroom for her friends. She couldn't leave without saying anything. Amára followed her as they pushed through the crowds. Fille's loud voice carried over the noise.

"There you are!" Fille said. Savriah and Fille were chatting with Adonis and Tallie. Their eyes drifted to Amára, standing next to Kassi.

"Who's this?" Fille asked, a little too eagerly. He seemed immediately taken by Amára. She always had that effect.

"This is Amára," Kassi said.

Savriah's eyes widened. "So this is Amára! Kassi has told us a lot about you. I'm Savvy."

"Kassi, Kassi always talks about you," Adonis said. "But she forgot to mention how stunning you are." Tallie swatted his arm. "What? I can't compliment her?"

"I'm Fille." Fille bowed a little too low.

"Adonis, Adonis Roma." Adonis added his bow.

"Chas, we've-eh got something," Kassi said.

"You forgot something?" Savriah asked, misunderstanding Kassi's accent.

"No, uh…" Kassi realized she had no idea how to explain what they were doing. "Ama and I need to go for a swim and catch up."

"This late?" Fille raised his eyebrows.

"I know. It's hard to explain," Kassi said, shouting over the music. "I'll tell you all about it tomorrow." Fille nodded with a half-shrug while Adonis just scratched his head. Savriah looked disappointed. Kassi waved. "Have fun without me!"

"Ride the tide," Fille shouted. "And be safe!"

"Tide!" Kassi said with a nod.

They ran up to their rooms–Kassi on the third floor and Amára on the fourth. Once in their siren suits, they joined Enzo in the lobby. It wasn't uncommon to see regular people walking in siren wetsuits, so they didn't attract any more attention than usual. Of course, Amára still turned heads wherever she went, so they weren't exactly invisible.

"Next train for Miami leaves in ten minutes," Enzo said. "Let's go."

"Train? A train?" Kassi asked. "I thought we were-eh going for a swim."

"Don't worry, I'll explain everything," Enzo said as he jogged down the street. Amára and Kassi followed close behind.

Once on the train, Kassi asked, "So what's this all about?"

They squished together on a two-seater bench with Enzo in the middle. He whipped out a small whiteboard and an erasable marker, scribbling, *Don't say anything here. Cameras.*

He held the whiteboard at a certain angle to avoid the

cameras pointing at them from the back corner. He erased the message and wrote: *Laugh like I just drew something funny.*

They both giggled on command. He continued erasing and writing. *I need to remove suit trackers. Kick your bag to me. Draw something funny on here.* Kassi and Amára both did as he asked. He then handed Amára the whiteboard and said, "Now your turn." Amára took the hint and tried drawing an elephant. It looked like a lopsided loaf of bread with eyes.

As Kassi and Amára passed the board back and forth, she couldn't help wondering why he was removing their trackers. That's when she remembered where she read about ruby slippers. It was from a story about a girl who was trying to get home. Kassi straightened in her seat.

No! This is a rescue!

If only they had taken the time to discuss this before leaving, she would have stayed behind with her friends at the ball. For now, she played along with his game and waited until they were in the clear to speak freely. Amára and Kassi went back and forth with the whiteboard while Enzo pretended to pay attention while his hands were below the table, fiddling with their helmets.

Should I write it on the whiteboard? Her hand hovered above the board as she thought of how to say it. At the last second, she drew a silly picture and thought better of trying to hold a complicated conversation over a whiteboard.

After a few more minutes with their helmets, Enzo brought his hands back up and took a turn with the whiteboard. Leaning back again to angle the whiteboard just out of view of the camera, he wrote: *Suit trackers now attached to bags. Amára and I exit in Charleston. Kassi in Miami. Laugh.* They reacted as if he were drawing something absurd. He erased it and continued: *Leave bag at home. Meet at Alice Town Training Pools, Sector 7 at 01:30.* He erased it and placed it back on the table as he drew an image of a squirrel.

If they're leaving the train before me, when will I get a chance to tell them? She decided to write on the board, *Can we discuss this?*

Enzo quickly erased what she wrote and shook his head, writing: *Not here. In the water.*

She heaved a resigned sigh and slumped in her seat. After riding in silence for a few minutes, Kassi let out a gargantic yawn.

As if in response, Enzo said. "Let's get some rest. We got another couple hours on this train."

Enzo slipped over to the other side of the table and leaned back. Kassi leaned on Amára's shoulder as the low hum of the train lulled her to sleep once again. She dreamed a beautiful dream of home. Peaceful sleep was soon interrupted as she felt someone poking her side. Opening her eyes, she found Amára sitting next to her on the train. *"Wake up, sleepybutt!"*

It took a moment for Kassi to remember they were on a train bound for Miami Beach.

"This is our stop," Amára said in Evéik. *"Make sure you don't sleep through yours."*

"I'll try to stay awake," Kassi said with a stretch and a roaring yawn.

"You'd better," Amára smiled. *"Ashkana tuv!"*

"Ashkana tuv, ashte!"

It was another thirty minutes before she arrived in Miami. As tired as she was, she managed to keep herself awake by thinking about their current situation. Enzo planned to rescue them–to give Kassi the break she had been asking for since she arrived on Earth. Reflecting back on her dream of home, her mind wandered to her former life. Growing up in a palace with a solid family support group, lots of friends, the best mentors, all the gourmet food she could ever eat, three beautiful planets to explore, a peaceful life and existence, Kassi realized just how many breaks she had had in life. She had it all and never realized it. Everyone had taken it for granted–it wasn't just Kassi. What else did they know? Their life on Paradise was the life all

Paradisers had. Now, living as the Gaians did, Kassi finally understood just how privileged her life had been.

Exiting the train station, she walked back to her townhome. The lights were out. It was already well-past midnight. Doors were locked–Moza was likely in bed, and Kassi didn't have a key. Since she would be returning right after she explained everything to Enzo and Amára, she decided to just leave her bag on the porch.

When I get back, I'll wake up Moza to let me in. I just need to talk to Enzo and Amára first. As much as she used to wish every day for a rescue, she couldn't leave now. She hoped they would understand.

With her helmet sealed on tight, she dipped quietly into the floodwater and swam through the streets until she reached the open ocean. Powering up her sonopack, she blasted toward the Alice Town training pools.

Thirty-Five

Arriving with a few minutes to spare, she turned off the jets and lazily drifted to Sector 7. The ocean was empty, lifeless. On Nemal, even at this shallow depth, Kassi would have seen a myriad of bioluminescent marine life lighting up the ocean. Instead, only dozens of vacant, neutrally lit waterfields illuminated the darkness–like hovering pill-shaped ghosts.

As she floated in the water, Kassi rehearsed what she was going to say to Amára and Enzo. They zoomed into view, and Enzo held out his wrist to Kassi's until they linked frequencies. "This way," he said, waving her to follow.

"Wait, before-eh we go…," Kassi tried to say, but Enzo and Amára had already blasted off.

She caught up and they torpedoed through the water at top speeds until coming to an abrupt halt in the middle of the ocean. In the pitch black, only their glowing suit patterns were visible until they flipped on their suits' floodlights.

Enzo pushed himself this way and that, as if positioning himself into a specific location. After a moment of this, he stopped and stared vacantly into the open ocean.

"What are you doing?" Amára asked. Enzo held up a hand for silence as if straining to hear something.

After a few beats, he turned his gaze back to them and explained, "Underwater sonic focusing." Kassi and Amára shared puzzled looks. He continued, "We've established a communication network across the globe using thermal channels. You have to be floating in precise coordinates for the message to become coherent. Otherwise, it's just warbled noise."

"Yisû, that's all very interesting, but WHO are you messazhing?" Amára asked the obvious question.

"Oh right. It's a rescue. We're taking you back home!" Enzo said.

"Really? You found a way to contact the others?" Amára asked.

"That's what this is for," Enzo circled his hands about his head. "This network is from all the other operatives around the globe. Everyone is accounted for. I've been given a rendezvous point. At supersonic speed, it'll be quite the swim, but we can make it there in about 12 hours if we're careful."

"12 hours!" Kassi exclaimed.

"No InterPorts, remember?" Amára said with a shrug.

"We just need to make one quick stop first," Enzo said.

"Yash, I can't believe it! We're finally going home-eh!" Amára said, swimming up to Enzo and throwing her arms around him.

Kassi stared in the general direction of Miami Beach, "But… what about my friends?"

"I'm sorry about your friends, Kassi, but it'll be hard enough getting the captives through the portal. Our window is now—we have to go!" Enzo said. Kassi couldn't accept that.

"C'mon, Kassi," Amára said. "It's time to go home-eh."

"*I can't just leave them,*" Kassi said, switching to Evéik as she spoke with her best friend.

"*Maybe we can come back for them,*" Amára said, resting a hand on Kassi's shoulder.

"*How?*" Kassi shook her head.

"Let's talk about it on the way down," she said. Then in English, she said, "Come-eh. Everyone back home is waiting for us."

Kassi reluctantly followed Amára and Enzo south. They reached supersonic speeds in less than ten seconds and held that pace until they reached a small island. Almost half of the island was submerged below the rising tides with only a thin strip of land poking out above the ocean.

"What is this place-eh?" Amára asked as she removed her helmet, her razored brunette comb-over bob gently flapping in the breeze. After three months on Earth, her hair hadn't lost its shape.

"It used to be called Half Moon Cay. It was a tourist spot for years before the floods. Now, it's just a refilling station for sirens in the Caribbean," Enzo said.

The station was nothing more than a shanty with a few oxygen pumping stations and two small kiosks reselling government rations and water from a few spigots. Enzo purchased protein biscuits and melon energy chews for each of them. They stashed what they could fit into the side pockets of their sonopacks. He also paid for access to Spigot #2 to refill the water in their hydro-casks. After they were all packed and ready to go, Enzo and Amára drank a large glass of muck juice and chomped down as many biscuits as they could stomach before the journey. Kassi couldn't eat at a time like this–not when there was a possibility of abandoning her Gaian friends.

"Don't you have-eh teammates who are depending on you?" Kassi asked.

"They'll still be a strong contender without us," Enzo said in between bites.

"Their families are here-eh, Kassi. They weren't kidnapped," Amára said. "They don't have to live-eh with abusive grips like you did."

"But they live in the Trench," Kassi said. "Their lives are the worst! We need to help them, Ama."

"But what if we don't win the Games?" Amára asked. "Who are we helping then?"

"They're my friends. I can't just abandon them!" Kassi said, her voice strained. "They won't even know why I left or if I'm going to come back for them!"

"Yisû, but if you stay, who knows if there will ever be another rescue. And then, you'll be abandoning me–your best friend," Amára said, switching to Evéik as if to make sure Kassi understood every word. *"Remember, I'm only here because you insisted we disobey your parents and sneak to the GDC. I wanted to go back!"*

Kassi inhaled sharply as if sonic-punched in the gut. *"I didn't know Ravana would be there! And besides, you followed me!"*

"I couldn't let you go by yourself! What if you got hurt?" Amára said. *"Your mother was right. You do sometimes convince me to do dangerous things."*

Despite the calm and familiar language, Amára's words hit Kassi like a tidal wave and she started to choke up with tears. *"I don't mean to..."*

"I know you don't," Amára said, placing a soft hand on Kassi's arm. *"I'm not mad. I just...just do this for me. Please? Help me get back home."*

Kassi sat quietly, taking a moment to process everything. She eventually said, *"If I'm such a horrible friend, why are you even friends with me?"*

"No, Kassi! Don't say that," Amára said, wrapping an arm around Kassi's shoulder. *"You're not a horrible friend, you're my best friend in all the worlds! I love you! Just because you get me into trouble sometimes doesn't change that. And yisû, coming to Earth was absolutely horrible, but if we hadn't come, I would have never met Enzo."* She pointed to Enzo who sat quietly on her other side, taking his hand. *"I don't regret any of the things we've done together. Not one!"* She looked Kassi in the eye as if to make sure Kassi heard every word. With a sigh, she turned back toward the open ocean and continued, *"I just want us to go home now. Can we go home?"*

Kassi hugged her knees and stared at the sand and gave a subtle nod. *"Yisû."* Tears filled her eyes, almost blinding her as her thoughts bounced back and forth between Amára's words and her Gaian friends. Fille, Adonis, Savriah, Vander, Vi'ella, Kiowa, Sensei K, Coach Rockson, and the Blue Krakens—they had all done so much to help Kassi over the past few months. But Amára wouldn't even be in this hellish situation if it hadn't been for Kassi. And she couldn't suggest Amára go home without her. They were always an inseparable pair–Amára would never leave without her. If Kassi refused to go home, she'd be choosing to abandon her best friend and likely prevent both of them from returning home.

But how can I desert my friends here? No matter what she decided, it would hurt the people she loved. Kassi was pulled in two directions, like entering a riptide while desperately trying to stroke to shore.

Enzo received a message on his wrist, jumped up, and ran to the blue, polypropylene floating docks. He stood still and scanned the water. Kassi and Amára caught up with him.

"What is it?" Amára asked in English.

Before he could answer, two figures swam below them, their siren wetsuits and sonopacks fully lit. A pair of hulking figures emerged on the adjacent beach, trudged out of the water onto the sand, and removed their helmets. Kassi double blinked–she couldn't believe her eyes.

"SENSEI! COACH!" Kassi shouted and broke into a full sprint.

Turning their heads in unison at the sound of her voice, they ran up to meet her. Kassi threw her arms around Sensei Kelipalo and Coach Rockson, tears streaming down her cheeks with the relief of seeing them alive.

After the realization set in, she took a step back and asked, "But how are you here?"

"We'll fill you in on the journey down," Sensei said. "For

now, we need to hit the water if we're going to rendezvous with the others in time."

"But…wait, you're involved in…,"

"Operation Ruby Slippers," Coach said with a nod.

"So you approve of me leaving my friends? What about the team?" Kassi asked.

"It wasn't an easy decision," Sensei said.

"Your friends can still win the Games," Coach said. "We saw you already qualified. I've coached hundreds of teams. Even without you, the Blue Krakens have a real shot–I'll make sure of it. They'll meet you there!"

"Listen, Kassi," Sensei said. "We've been working on this for months. With how complicated it's been to arrange, you can't risk not going. It may be years before there's another opportunity like this."

"Your friends will understand," Coach added.

Kassi wasn't so sure. She hated leaving them without any explanation. For now, she nodded and followed them into the water. With helmets on, they dove and resumed their journey south.

Their song playbook for the journey consisted mostly of rhythmic, repetitive chants to allow them short, intermittent breaks. They would exhaust all energy generated from the sonoluminescence bulbs before commencing a new incantation. It required a large amount of stamina to last for twelve long hours.

ALL THE DAY LONG

Dive in the ocean - cut through the water
Go with the motion that's taking you there
Channel your voices to ride out the distance
Turn up the noise that will drown the fear

Speed is the answer to all the hard questions
Doubt is the cancer that slows it all down

Our hands are stretched and are feet are ready
To blast us faster than the speed of sound

With the shaloor we can sing it out
We sing as one til we feel the power
With our pain we reshape each song
We sing, we dance and we can do this all the day long

A ton of emotion comes with every anthem
This flood of devotion is turning the tide
Our sound is on fire it feels like the remedy
To every sickness that could break my stride

With the shaloor we can sing it out
We sing as one til we feel the power
With our pain we reshape each song
We sing, we dance and we can do this all the day long

We're king of the ocean and queen of the water
The blue has given us a place to be heard
Our lungs are full and our voice is ready
To blast our melodies around the world

With the shaloor we can sing it out
We sing as one til we feel the power
With our pain we reshape each song
We know the music is never wrong

We get fire from within our bones
We're giving life into every tone
We find all weakness and make it strong
We sing, we dance and we can do this all the day long

IN EVÉIK

Jet lev li þalasabé – rîþ méso li akwûbé
Pí kin li gludé sîm bud lénûsách ebi tuvat
Tînyavo vodí zishóbé shi unasomo mun li riketat
Val nak li shumé sîm mukid li tîmoribé

Bud li ripostibé shi amni li sabu swalitó doorat
Bud li rog sîm ta fam amni fichi shabasat
Bud tiriba bizí shohotót, i bud muhan bizí gormót
Shi putikichi káshlu sé li doora van fuig bizat

Édash fam dan kin li sháloor bizat
Édabi áz zot shi sîmetibi li kuasibé bizat
La'morfibibi kin bizí doleré oni hîmat
Édabi bizat, parelibi bizat, i daish ramé amni li tag nubri
    bizat

Jup kin taji mezoré în yako van sinetit
Valách li aliké ram hansup van booktit
Bud dar vier bizí fuigat; rasa síl li ilaché famat
Shi taji beshû sîm harijosh nayalí dabut

Édash fam dan kin li sháloor bizat
Édabi áz zot shi sîmetibi li kuasibé bizat
La'morfibibi kin bizí doleré oni hîmat
Édabi bizat, parelibi bizat, i daish ramé amni li tag nubri
    bizat

Budibi li savrîn van li þalasabé i bôri van li akwûbé bizat
Mita yiva bizé în wahijang shi budíd flitud li blét
Budibi mûng bizí sakoshóbé, i budibi muhan bizí gormót
Shi putikichi hôlû li kazmosé bizí porot

Édash fam dan kin li sháloor bizat
Édabi áz zot shi sîmetibi li kuasibé bizat
La'morfibibi kin bizí doleré oni hîmat

Sápéré bizat bud nukwam falat li porot

Prapibi vieré dari kilev bizí sumukójang bizat
Bud yivách vibé leta taji sian bizat
Patabi amni kamoré bizat, i hulid koahan famat
Édabi bizat, parelibi bizat, i daish ramé amni li tag nubri
   bizat

As they swam, Kassi kept glancing over at Sensei K and Coach. She couldn't wait until everyone else knew! They will be so excited to find out.

And I won't be there to see it, the thought struck Kassi and again, she felt the guilt welling up inside her at leaving her friends behind.

Halfway through the journey, they desperately needed a breather. *Long-distance travel without InterPorts is just ludicray!* Kassi found herself mumbling the songs and falling asleep, her thrusters sputtering. Apparently, she wasn't the only one. Enzo signaled for them to surface. They had crossed the Panama Canal and had been swimming parallel to the Western coastline for the past few hours.

Based on the GPS in her suit, they were somewhere in the Lima Province. Once on the beach, they removed their helmets and sank heavily onto the sand. It was early morning, and the sun had already come up, but the beaches were still empty.

"We're making good time," Enzo said as he and Amára withdrew biscuits and energy chews from their packs. Kassi felt her stomach rumble. Equally hungry and tired, she couldn't decide whether to lie down and rest or sit up and eat. It was quite the dilemma. Ultimately, her stomach won.

When Sensei and Coach sat next to her, she asked around a mouthful of melon energy chew, "So what happened?"

"We were in the middle of convincing Coach Woodross to

stop training his teams to play dirty when I got an urgent message on the holophone," Coach said.

"I got the same," Sensei said. "Said a few of our players had been seriously injured."

"We jumped out of our seats and ran to check on them," Coach said. "Next thing we knew, a bomb had gone off."

"Right where we were sitting," Sensei finished. "The bomb was directly under my seat the whole time!"

"Turns out our players were fine," Coach said. "No injuries."

"Someone tipped us off," Sensei said. "We don't know who."

"But we owe them our lives, whoever they are," Coach said.

Kassi nodded, immensely grateful to whoever had sent the tip while equally horrified that someone would set a bomb under Sensei's seat. One question jumped to mind that Kassi had to ask, "So why then didn't you come-eh back?"

"If the Hel Mafia still wants us dead," Coach said.

"We can't risk putting those around us in danger," Sensei said.

"Well that, and," Coach said with a deep chuckle, "we also don't wanna die!"

"I think it's Farra," Kassi said. "I think she's Hel Mafia."

"That's our thinking, too," Sensei said.

Kassi stared out over the ocean. A cool breeze swept over them. "They're all gonna be so happy to see you."

"Well, it might be a while," Sensei said with a sigh. "As long as we're targets, we can't go home."

"What about Kiowa?" Kassi asked. "He's really been angry and hurt over this. He needs to know!"

"There might be a way to reach my boy," Coach said, his eyes glistening a little. "I'm working on it."

With that, Kassi nodded and lay back on the sand with a ferocious yawn. The crashing waves started to lull her to sleep.

"No, don't you dare-eh fall asleep." Amára knew her all too well. "Sit up!" Kassi didn't budge, so Amára got behind her, hooked her arms under Kassi's armpits and lifted her into a sitting position. Taking a seat next to her, they both stared at the horizon for a moment. Kassi still felt bad from their previous conversation. Amára must have sensed it because she said in soft Evéik, *"Don't feel bad about what I said earlier, Kassi. I wasn't trying to blame you or make you feel guilty. I just need you with me on this. We can't miss our chance to finally go home."* Kassi just nodded. Amára sighed. *"We'll be home soon and everything will be back the way it was."* She threw a comforting arm around Kassi and said, *"Ashkana tuv!"*

Kassi appreciated Amára's words. It felt good to be with her best friend again. But she knew that nothing would ever be back the way it was. Whatever Ravana had done, she had at least shown Kassi how terrible life was for the poor Gaians. Kassi would never stop trying to help them.

Enzo jumped up and dusted the sand off his suit. "We need to get a move on. Let's dive!"

Kassi's body already ached from the swim. Standing on the sand, she did a few stretches and popped both her hips.

"Whoa, that was louder than the waves," Amára said.

"I needed that!" Kassi said as she sealed her helmet and followed the others into the water, resuming their long journey southward.

As they swam south, the ocean water gradually got colder. They reached the rendezvous point, surfaced, and climbed a rocky beach to an abandoned island. It was lined with houses capped with colorful rooftops of bright red, pink, green, and more. Something about it looked vaguely familiar. They sloshed through the flooded streets in search of the others. The sun broke through the clouds, but gave little warmth.

As they jogged down the road, they came across a red-bricked, rundown church. Kassi recognized it immediately. It was nighttime when they were here last, but she would always remember the church they were brought to when they were first taken.

"I know this place-eh," Kassi said, dragging to a stop.

"Me too." Amára shuddered. They both decided not to say more, as if speaking the memory might bring Macks' lifeless body to the surface.

"Why did you bring us back here-eh?" Kassi asked Enzo.

"It's under the radar and on the way to Antarctica," he said.

"I should keep my helmet on." Kassi shivered and said, "It's freezing!"

They spotted a larger group coming out of the water, shuffling toward them. As they drew closer, Kassi saw faces she hadn't seen since leaving this island. Even though Kassi had never really been close with the others back home, they all shared an emotional bond after all they had been through. She and Amára embraced them one by one, with a mixture of laughter and tears as they reunited.

Despite what Farra had said about those that had tried to escape, all the paradisers who had been taken from home were now here—everyone, of course, except for Macks.

Each of the captives had an escort or two with them, like Kassi and Amára had Enzo, Coach, and Sensei. One of them cleared his throat and said, "My name's Ranford, and I'll be taking lead from this point. We only have a short window, so we must move quickly." With short cropped hair and a square jaw, he was a head taller than most, with only Sensei and Coach on his level. Each member of their rescue party had double-mounted sonic cannons as well as hip holsters equipped with sonic rifles. To her surprise, Enzo, Coach and Sensei had them too. "It's a straight shot to Esperanza Base where Earth's GDC is located. Reinforcements are waiting for us there. Let's move!"

They dove into the cold South Atlantic, formed a V formation, and swam south. As the water temperatures dropped, Kassi had to expend extra energy to heat her suit to keep her from freezing. Her helmet display read temperatures of 10 degrees Celsius, making the water nearly unswimmable without a siren wetsuit.

A few minutes into the journey, a flash of movement caught

Kassi's eye—too quick to be marine life. Squinting, she spotted two people zooming straight for them. One of them had hateful eyes and a wicked smile Kassi would recognize from any distance.

Farra! Next to her was the same square-headed man who had attempted to drown her.

Trying to scream a warning to the group, Kassi's voice caught in her throat. Farra and the man torpedoed directly in front of them, circling around as they positioned to strike.

Fortunately, Ranford spotted them. He immediately shouted, "SHIELD WALL!" The team kicked their legs forward and came to a stop.

A small metallic cylinder with peculiar carvings blinked in the water directly in front of them. Sensei noticed it too. He pushed forward with urgency–the rest of the operatives were distracted.

"What is that?" Kassi asked.

Sensei snatched the device and held it close to his body. He huddled around it just as an ear-splitting explosion sent out a shock wave that struck Kassi with such force, she barely stayed conscious. All air had been knocked out of her lungs.

With a violent gasp, Kassi inhaled as she peeled her eyes open. The rest of the squad lay motionless, drifting aimlessly like floating whale carcasses.

Farra and the man next to her took aim, flashing her familiar, thin-lipped smile. Kassi struggled to move. "No, I can't let you…," Kassi tried to say. Her voice was hoarse–she was in no condition to perform a shield incantation. Based on the resonating grunts of pain in her headphones, no one in her party was.

Just as Kassi was about to lose all hope, Farra's expression changed to one of terror. Someone came out of the blue and launched straight at her.

Stretching both arms forward, he blasted Farra and her ugly sidekick with a high-frequency sonic strike, sending both of them reeling backwards, incapacitated. He spun around and returned, aiming his thrusters at the two assailants, his face now visible.

"Nikola!" Enzo shouted. Enzo and the others had finally snapped back to life, stiff and slow as if the ocean had thickened into syrup.

"And just in time from the looks of it," Nikola said, not taking his eyes off of his victims.

Ranford heaved a deep breath as he swam forward, "Thank you! We owe you…"

"I didn't do it for you!" Nikola said, cutting him off. He whirled on Enzo, "What were you thinking, taking them to the GDC?"

As the pain in her chest subsided, Kassi's eyes swept over the rest of them, her mind replaying the explosion. "Wait, where's Sensei?" Everyone twisted in the water, whipping their heads in all directions.

"LESLEY!" Coach shouted, his voice wavering. In the middle of the group, Sensei floated, his eyes closed. The detonated grenade was still clutched in his hands. Coach swam to his friend and checked his vital signs. "DON'T YOU DARE DIE ON ME!" He grabbed Sensei by the shoulders, shaking him. Kassi's breathing quickened, her jagged heartbeat speeding up. She had just barely gotten him back.

Ranford swam to Sensei and checked the reading on his wrist. Placing a sympathetic hand on Coach's shoulder, he said, "I'm sorry my friend!"

Coach hung his head as he pulled his friend close. Cradling Sensei in his arms, Coach Rockson bawled.

Just when she had gotten Sensei back, he was gone again, another bomb. Kassi felt numb with shock. Then she saw Farra cough, slowly opening her eyes. Shock turned to an overwhelming, fortissimo rage. Kassi powered up her suit and closed the distance. "You did this!" Kassi kicked Farra as she screamed, "YOU DID THIS, YOU SADISTIC, EVIL SHEIST!" Again and again, Kassi kicked her former abuser until Amára pulled her off. Farra barely responded, clearly still dazed from Nikola's attack.

"I hate to do this, but we need to go," Ranford said. "They know we're here now. Our window is closing."

"What about Sensei?" Kassi asked.

Ranford just shook his head.

"I'll stay," Coach said. "I'll take care of him." Kassi wanted to stay, too.

Ranford gave a somber nod. "Everyone else, we should move!"

"Come with us," Enzo said to his brother.

"You're not thinking straight, Enzo," Nikola eyed Amára. He lit up his suit and blasted northward. "Don't throw your life away for a 'diser!"

Enzo slumped, looking defeated before joining the other operatives and resuming their journey south. Kassi lingered behind.

Coach lifted his head, locking eyes with Kassi, and spoke quietly, "I got this, Kassi. Just stick to the plan. It's what he would've wanted."

Reluctantly turning, Kassi swam toward Amára who patiently waited. Together, they lit up their sonopacks and swam toward the rest of the group.

An hour later, they reached the rocky coast of Antarctica, floating roughly 100 meters below the surface. "Hold here," Ranford said as he and a few others pushed off into the deep.

While they waited, Kassi took a moment to think about Sensei Kelipalo. He had sacrificed his own life to save all of them, without hesitation. That sonic grenade would have killed them all, just like it had killed so many in the Hel Mafia attacks. Tears rolled down her cheeks as she reflected on all the kindness Sensei had shown her and all she had lost with him gone again.

Ranford and the others returned. "It's dismantled. We should be clear to surface."

"Are there snipers?" Enzo asked.

"Two towers, two snipers each," Ranford said with a nod. "Elena, Mackerel, Kane, and Anker, we've got one shot at this. Make it count!"

Four operatives swam ahead, splitting into two parties before slowly emerging from the water. Their arms recoiled slightly a few times before they returned. "Four snipers neutralized," one of them said.

Everyone swam to shore and surfaced, keeping their helmets fastened to shield from the cold. Patches of snow and ice dotted the landscape. Looming up ahead, behind a security welded fence, was a military fortress. Built into the side of a mountain, its metal exterior had been painted in white camouflage to blend with its snowy surroundings. Empty guard towers separated sections of the fence. A giant bay door opened and two heavily armored vehicles exited the base, driving straight for their party.

"Are they friendlies?" one of the operatives asked.

"Negative. Prepare the EMPs," Ranford said.

Most of them took cover behind a two-story, bright red and yellow building, while a few operatives used their sonopacks to fly and take positions on the rooftops. Since sono-flight had been illegal on Earth, it had been months since Kassi had seen a siren in the sky.

With silent electric engines, only the sound of tires crunching on gravel gave away the position of the approaching vehicles. Two from the rescue party whipped around the wall and slid small metal discs into the road. Ranford flipped a switch to magnetize them both. They clipped onto the undercarriage of each vehicle and set off a short range EMP wave, shutting them off immediately. U.N.O.E. soldiers jumped out and took cover, exchanging fire with Kassi's rescuers. Enemy projectiles nibbled into the wall, showering Kassi and the others with splintered debris.

"Now!" Ranford shouted into their helmets. Behind the remains of the wall, they formed an arched line and performed a high-frequency sonic pulse. A wave rippled through the walls of the abandoned building and struck the enemy soldiers on the other side with a powerful burst of sound that knocked them to their feet. The brief disruption allowed the rescue squad to surround them and demand their surrender. The U.N.O.E. troops dropped their weapons, raising their hands in the air.

Ranford and his team tied them up and left them in an abandoned building with a beacon set to light a call for rescue in five minutes. Kassi thought that was unusually considerate treatment of enemy soldiers.

"We take to the sky," Ranford shouted, leading the way.

Everyone followed, keeping pace as they used their thrusters to push off the ground and fly to the giant bay doors, now closed shut. Even though it had been a while, Kassi maintained a steady flight pattern with ease. A few of their agents raised hand thrusters and sniped cameras with precision, high frequency strikes as they approached the fortress.

Within minutes, they had reached the entrance and landed, hiding within the mountain terrain. The rescue beacon Ranford had attached to the U.N.O.E. soldiers sounded, and the bay doors opened as more armored vehicles rushed to provide reinforcements.

Ah, so that's why he set the beacon!

"You're up, Jericho!" Ranford shouted with a firm hand signal. Jericho dashed into the large hangar with all reckless abandon. "Shield!" Ranford said.

Operatives performed a shield incantation as Jericho leapt high into the air and landed, blasting a massive, low frequency sonic pulse. All U.N.O.E. personnel who had remained behind to secure the fortress were caught off guard. The blast rippled in all directions and sent everyone, including Jericho, crashing into the exterior walls.

With speedy precision, Ranford and his team split off in all directions to bind all enemy troops before they could counter. One of them heaved a stunned Jericho over his shoulder and carried him to cover. They had bound nearly half of the enemy soldiers before those remaining regrouped.

Powering up turret cannons and positioning themselves behind many of the armored vehicles, U.N.O.E. soldiers fired a mix of sonic pulses and explosive projectiles at Kassi's rescue squad. Ranford and his task force took cover and performed shield incantations to minimize any sonic attacks.

"What now?" Enzo shouted.

"Now we see if our inside woman gets the portal open. We have reinforcements on the other side," Ranford said.

"And if she doesn't?" Enzo asked. Ranford just shook his head.

Seeing his response, Kassi realized just how much their rescuers were risking to get them back home.

The walls and armored vehicles took a beating. Their cover wouldn't last much longer. Debris continued to rain down as rapid fire weapons relentlessly blasted. Even with her helmet on, Kassi's ears rang from the incessant, explosive noise. Amára and the other captives waited with fear-stricken faces.

Ranford, Enzo, and the other agents continued performing shield incantations to protect them from sonic blasts. Meanwhile, explosive projectiles bombarded their position and would soon break through. Kassi thought she could see a trace of concern in their eyes.

After a few more volleys of enemy fire, commotion erupted from the back of the room. U.N.O.E. soldiers turned to face a new threat.

"We're in!" Ranford shouted. "Let's move!" They ran and surrounded the U.N.O.E. soldiers, forcing a surrender. Once the enemy was subdued, he ordered his team to close the bay doors before the armored vehicles could return from the beach. When they did, Kassi removed her helmet, cold air filling her lungs.

"Is the enemy contained?" a Nemalís Royal Guard asked Ranford. Seeing the Royal Nemalís Guard almost felt like waking up from a very long nightmare.

"Not yet! We've got two minutes before they get those doors back open," Ranford said.

The Royal Guard ushered everyone up a small flight of grated metal stairs and onto a platform that led to a thick steel door. One of them hauled a cuffed enemy soldier over his shoulder. Fortunately, even soldiers on Earth were skinny, making this one easier to carry. They positioned his face in front of the scanner, and unlocked the door. Everyone filed through the doorway and into a tunnel barely wide enough for two to walk abreast. Lights automatically flickered to life. They were walking on a grated flooring with solid metal railings on both sides that came up to Kassi's waist. On the other side and down below, she saw pitch black emptiness that extended downward indefinitely.

"How far does that go?" Kassi asked no one in particular.

A Nemalís woman marching in front of her answered, "Much deeper than any of us want to find out."

They continued forward through the tunnel until they reached a second thick, steel door. Using the same soldier's face, they opened it. Marching through, they entered a well-lit clearing. A few steps descended to reach the ground floor of the mountain side with a large rock wall up ahead. The air was humid and water dripped in the distance. It smelled earthy and damp, like some of the caves she, Amára, and Caesar would explore back on Nemal.

Directly in front of the portal were six members of the Royal Guard. The clearing was flanked by two high walls where soldiers would have the perfect vantage point to attack any intruders. Four turret cannons hung from the ceiling. Apparently, and not surprisingly, it only took six of their Nemalís elites to take out Earth's GDC defenses.

In the middle of the rock wall ahead of them was the gravity drive center's portal that opened the way for the Rosenbridge. It was a perfectly symmetrical circle approximately five meters in diameter, rimmed with giant cables and machinery. On the other side of it was Nemal–home. Kassi could see it. She was only a few short steps away from Paradise.

Awaiting them on the other side of the portal, Kassi noticed an army of Nemalís Guard with her father at the helm.

"Dad!" Kassi shouted. "Mom, Caesar!"

Leontari Rivernova stood at the ready to receive them. Caesar stood next to him with Vidara and Uncle Sydney not far behind. She couldn't believe her eyes. After months without them, her family was here! Everything was finally over. They reached their arms out to welcome her, tears of joy in their eyes as soon as they spotted her.

At the sight of her family, all her altruistic thoughts of staying for her team washed away as Kassi dropped her helmet and broke into a mad dash for the portal, her arms outstretched. Amára and the others were close behind. With only two steps to go, the portal went dark. Instead of gliding into the beautiful warmth of Paradise and her family's welcoming embrace, Kassi slammed into the dark rock wall of the mountain and crumpled to the ground.

The Guard and their rescuers whipped around, weapons at the ready as they faced a new battalion of U.N.O.E. soldiers and the four turret guns now spinning to life. Soldiers lined both flanks from the upper vantage point, weapons drawn. The entire rescue party was directly in the middle of the kill box.

"We've got you surrounded!" came a shout from behind the front line of enemy soldiers. "Drop your weapons!" His voice was familiar–Griffonage Li. Which meant...

Ravana emerged, stepping forward.

"Weapons down," Ranford shouted, hysteria edging his voice. He shot fearful glances at the other members of his squad. Kassi's eyes swept over the army and spotted her grip, Moza. In his hand, he held up her bag–the one she had left on the porch. Kassi had completely forgotten about it. He likely found it and reported her missing to Ravana.

They're here because of me, Kassi swallowed hard.

Ravana's voice filled the room like a pipe organ in a cathedral. "So after all you've seen, you would just leave the Gaians to starve and struggle on Earth? Without a second thought, you would abandon them and return to Paradise?"

Kassi knew Ravana was right. The guilt formed a pit in her stomach, heavy as a stone. As much as she initially opposed the rescue, she let herself get talked into it. She ran for her family without the slightest hesitation.

I really am a horrible friend!

"You see, this," Ravana addressed her soldiers, "this is why we have measures in place to keep them from leaving. This is why simply showing them the despair and hardships of Earth isn't enough for them to return and convince the council to change. Their parents must see how difficult it is for Gaians to win our place on Paradise by witnessing their own children experience it firsthand." There were a lot more soldiers here than the first time they had been taken, many from the U.N.O.E. Had Ravana been recruiting them to swell her own ranks? Or did the U.N.O.E. send them to support her? Either way, they were all pointing sonic cannons and Kassi, her friends, and their rescue squad, so it really didn't matter where they came from. In unison, the soldiers grunted and stomped in a rumbling chorus of approval.

Troops parted to allow another familiar face through–Nikola. He had returned, this time with Farra and the square-headed man in tow. The sight of Farra made anger roar inside Kassi, completely eclipsing the fear that had gripped her. Bound, they were shoved down the stairs to the ground, Farra's face bloodied from the fall.

"Farra and Volkov," Ravana said with an edge to her voice, anger flickering across her eyes. "You've made a real mess of things, killing Gaians at will." Many from Ravana's ranks spat on Farra and Volkov, showing their disgust.

So Farra is Hel Mafia! Kassi had been right about her. At least now, Kassi knew for sure that Paradisers hadn't been behind the attacks like the U.N.O.E. had claimed.

"I even gave you a second chance," Ravana said, shaking her head with disappointment. "What am I to do with you?"

"I know what I'd do with her," Kassi mumbled under her breath. Her voice carried farther than she intended.

"And what's that Miss Rivernova?" Ravana turned to face her with eyebrows raised. Kassi's eyes darted side to side, too nervous to respond in front of such a large crowd. "Maybe you'd like to duel Farra. After all she did to you, you're certainly entitled."

Give me a sonic rifle and I'll rip her apart after what she did to Sensei! As her mind raced with interest in a duel, she found herself nodding without realizing it. Ravana took it as consent.

"It's settled then. We have ourselves a duel!" Soldiers stomped once again with approval.

Amára quickly stepped forward, "Wait, no let me! I'll duel for Kassi."

Kassi placed a hand on her best friend's shoulder. "No." Amára whipped her head back, pleading with her eyes. Kassi shook her head. "I need to do this."

Soldiers yanked Farra to her feet and handed her a standard sonic rifle, cutting her loose.

"Let Kassiana use mine." Ravana offered her own customized rifle as a soldier retrieved it along with Kassi's discarded helmet and brought it to Kassi.

Anger could have consumed Kassi in that moment. After all Farra had done, Kassi had every reason to fight with all reckless abandon. But as she glared venomously at her opponent, Sensei's voice came into her mind, *Accept the apology you were never given. Forgiveness is what liberates us from the heavy weight of hate.* As much as she wanted to kill Farra, Sensei's words struck her with force. She knew she had to let go of her hate. Taking a deep breath, she found her calm.

Watching Farra sneer in her direction, Kassi remembered

Sensei also told her to stand up to bullies. Accepting an unspoken apology liberated Kassi from her hate, but she also knew that letting an abuser go unpunished was unacceptable. So she took a dueling stance.

"BEGIN!" Ravana shouted.

Farra scoffed at Kassi. "You think you can touch me, little penchode! I can see the fear…"

Kassi didn't let her finish. She burst into a Gelt Hîm and fired at Farra, who took the hit in the shoulder. She screamed and retaliated, but Kassi was ready with her shield incantation. As soon as Farra ran out of breath, Kassi fired again. Her high frequency sonic strike cut through Farra's defenses, fracturing a bone in her wrist.

Rather than drop the sonic rifle, Farra switched hands and countered. Her assault was shaky, as if from undisciplined rage. With full control of her core muscles, Kassi deflected the attack and quickly switched gears. Drawing energy from another Gelt Hîm, Kassi aimed directly above the clavicle and fired.

Farra dropped her sonic rifle and clutched her throat, dropping to her knees. With a panicked look in her eyes, she gasped for air. Kassi knew the feeling. In fact, she knew exactly what Farra was experiencing in that instant.

Kassi had ruptured Farra's vocal cords.

Thirty-Six

Farra lay on the stony, frozen ground, eyes closed and slowly breathing. Soldiers retrieved both sonic rifles. The duel was over. Farra was yanked to her feet with fresh bindings on her wrists. Kassi's elation at defeating her former tormentor was muted as she remembered she and the rest of her group were still in Ravana's power. They were escorted back through the tunnel, into the hangar. Outside, two twin-engine, tandem rotor helicopters were waiting for them.

Lining them up on the tarmac, Ravana said, "And now we address your futile escape attempt. While you took out the GDC's exterior cameras, all the interior cameras still caught your actions and reported you directly to the U.N.O.E. authorities. According to their laws, anyone making a run for the GDC is a terrorist."

"Terrorist?" Ranford protested. "So helping children return home is terrorism?"

"I don't make the laws," Ravana said. "As for all you runaways, you deserters who were so quick to abandon your friends, I'd expect all of you will be dealt with by the mediation officers. How long they keep you, I can't say. But when you return, know that you will be handed back to your grips with a much tighter leash. We've been far too lenient."

Soldiers flanked Kassi and the other captive teenagers, shoving all of them into one of the helicopters, while their rescuers were forced onto the other chopper.

Outside on the tarmac, Nikola was pleading his brother's case. "Let me deal with my brother," Nikola said. "He was just lovestruck. He wasn't thinking straight!"

"I'm sorry, Nikola, there's nothing I can do for your brother," Ravana said. "You'll have to take your objections up with U.N.O.E. authorities. They've given me permission to manage the children, but all major infractions still must go through the proper channels. I can't keep them from punishing anyone who has broken their laws."

The door shut before Kassi could hear the rest of their conversation. Taking their seats, her hands couldn't stop shaking as she tried to buckle herself in. Amára took the seat next to her, her cheeks tear-stained.

"I'm sorry, Ama. It's all my fault," Kassi whispered. "I left my backpack…"

"No, Kassi." Amára interrupted. She slowly turned to face Kassi, revealing puffy red eyes. "This time, it's mine-eh. We never should have left Toronto."

As the helicopter pulled away, Kassi leaned against the window and stared out at the vast ocean. She was too tired and numb to process everything that had happened over the past two days.

They made a number of stops. Each time they landed, one of the kids was removed and handed over to mediation officers who were expecting them. Kassi would soon be next. Seeing her family, she realized how much she ached for home. Thoughts of almost making it home mixed with the fear for her pending mediation session drained every last drop of hope in her body. She went limp.

They reached Miami, and Kassi was yanked out the doors and onto the helipad. Two officers firmly escorted her away. When she twisted to see her friend one last time, the doors were already closed and the aircraft was lifting off.

"Yashing 'diser!" U.N.O.E. mediation officers shouted as they threw Kassi into the extended cabin of a dark yacht floating on the water. Once again, she was forced to endure a barrage of sonic punches from a fully-padded officer and his sonic rifle. After all she had been through over the past two days, it was more pain than her body could take and she fainted.

Kassi drifted in and out of consciousness until she finally awoke. The sun was just coming up. She found herself lying on the lumpy, mildewy mattress of her old bedroom, still in her siren suit. Her body hated her. Every gram of her was stiff as though she'd been frozen for a hundred years. Her head pounded and her muscles throbbed, unknotting themselves. Bruises covered her skin. When she tried to sit up, her body screamed at her.

She was right back where she started. Four and a half months ago, she had woken up in this exact same spot, but now, everything was different. Back then, all she wanted to do was escape. As the memories started surfacing, tears welled in her eyes and streamed down the sides of her face. There were tears of pain for the state her body was in. There were tears of loss as she remembered watching Sensei die right in front of her. There were tears of regret, as she knew she had let everyone down. It was her bag that tipped Moza off and ruined the rescue. There were tears of loneliness as they separated her from Amára once again. There were tears of homesickness at the thought of being ripped from her family, again. Despite all of that, she also cried tears of relief. She had agonized about leaving her Gaian friends behind, and now she could stay and help them.

The first time she woke up in this room–four and a half months ago!—she only thought of leaving. Kassi had no intention of meeting Gaians or understanding their situation–she just wanted to go home. Now, Kassi had friends–close, important friends. They needed her. Even though everything hurt, Kassi carefully rose to her feet and headed for the door. With great effort, she hobbled to the stairs. There was a team waiting for her, and they all had a long way to go and a lot left to do.

Epilogue

"**S**et your coordinates for Exuma and your sights on the palladium medal," Vander shouted. "It's time to make it all count. Singing small doesn't serve the worlds!"

"Let's sing it with sháloor!" Kassi chanted with her team as they powered up their sonopacks and blasted into the blue.

When Kassi had returned to school after being out for two days, she found out that Coach had relayed all that had happened, including the failed escape attempt and Kassi's resistance to the whole idea of leaving. To Kassi's surprise and relief, no one had held it against her for the decision to go along with Sensei and Coach. It had been strange being back at school. Everything was mostly the same as before—bad food rations, and no extras now that Sensei was gone, inane homework assignments, rude professors, including the new Evéik teacher. Without Nikola, the school bullies had become paper thin. Malyra and Calandra made futile attempts at harassment. DeSchuster walked around like a neanderthal without his club, occasionally grunting and flexing at Kassi. When they realized they couldn't get to her, they had eventually given up. Kassi was different. She accepted all the unpleasant parts of her life.

Her focus had shifted now to her team and winning the Siren Games.

Exuma's water arena was one of eight spread out across the planet, Kassi learned. Each Siren Games, they rotated. This season, Exuma would host the first round. Over the next four days, sixty-four teams would face off in the first bracket of the AquaSphera Tournament, the first round of the Siren Games. Teams that won the first game would advance to the next bracket, while those that lost would face off against each other to determine which sixteen teams would be eliminated and sent home.

Athletes were housed in nearby living quarters throughout the duration of their tournament. A match schedule was displayed on a giant holoscreen. Kassi scanned the board to find their team. Joshi spotted it first and said, "Looks like we play tomorrow!"

"Tomorrow's the day," Vander said, patting a few random teammates on the back. "Let's find our rooms and get settled and meet back here at 13:00."

Since they had a couple hours to kill before practice, they decided to huddle in Adonis' and Fille's room to watch the first AquaSphera match on their holoscreen. It was Helsinki vs Charleston–Amára's team.

Charleston played well, and Amára scored a few goals, but it wasn't enough to claim victory. Helsinki won, 11-9. Charleston would enter the elimination round and have one more chance to stay in the Games.

If Ama lost, what chance do we *have?*

That night, like every night since their failed rescue, Kassi tossed and turned, her mind plagued with thoughts of Coach Rockson holding Sensei in his arms and her family at the portal reaching for her. After hours of this, sleep finally overtook her.

Next morning, they stepped onto the open-air elevators that lifted them to the diving platforms of the AquaSphera water arenas. The massive waterfield tank stood above ground at two thousand meters in length and one thousand meters in diameter. It sat in the center of a large stadium filled with hundreds of thousands of people cheering wildly in anticipation. The sounds and smells brought her back to her games and performances back home. She had desperately missed playing in front of a crowd.

Kassi overheard the commentators over the noise of the cheering crowds, "...*the last time we saw a team of 400s make it to the Siren Games was over ten years ago!*"

"*And this year, we not only have one team, but two...*"

Sealing their helmets on, Team Miami dove, and the game soon began. Kassi played well throughout, as did her teammates, but it wasn't good enough. Their opponents simply outmatched them, maintaining possession for the majority of the game and taking more shots on goal. Team Miami lost, 9-8.

The defeat crushed them. They had come all this way, only to fail. In a few days, they would be given one more chance to stay in the games–the sudden elimination game.

If only Sensei were here to help us. He always had the answers.

The day before their match, schedules were posted. Everyone gathered around the screen in Fille's and Adonis' room to see who they would be playing against. Searching through the list of matches, they found Miami. Kassi's heart sank.

Miami vs Charleston.

"Of course they pair us against the only other team of 400s!" Joshi shouted.

Her teammates whipped their heads toward Kassi the second they saw who they were playing against. Vander asked her, "You with us, Kassi?"

Kassi opened her mouth as if to answer, but nothing came out. She stared at the screen. Eventually, her teammates left, some of them patting her shoulder as they passed.

Back in her room, Savriah cast her a worried look before lying down on her bed for the night. Kassi sat on the edge of her bed, her head hung low. Someone knocked on their door. Padding to the peephole, she saw Amára standing in the doorway.

"Ama?" Kassi opened the door. Amára forced a smile and waved for her to join her in the hallway.

"*I saw your match,*" Amára said in Evéik, her voice hoarse. She looked tired.

Kassi let the door close behind her as she sighed and slid against the wall to the floor. "*These teams are so much better than the ones we're used to playing.*"

Amára plopped down next to Kassi on the floor. "*They're the best in all the worlds. During my game, all I could think about was Enzo. I don't think I can do this without him.*" She groaned, "*If only I had listened to you and called off the rescue!*"

"*You can't do that to yourself,*" Kassi said, staring at the floor. "*How could you know Ravana was waiting for us?*"

Amára ran fingers through her hair to pull it up into a loose bun. After a few beats, she said. "*Tomorrow, we have to play against each other.*"

Kassi pressed her back to the wall with a sigh. "*I just wish we could be on the same team like before.*"

"*Me too,*" Amára said. "*But just remember, we're family! As long as one of us wins, we'll both be allowed Paradise passports. Right?*"

"*They'll allow it?*"

"*They have to, don't they?*" Amára said. "*It's the rules!*"

"*But if you win, and my team loses, that would mean once again leaving my friends behind,*" Kassi said, massaging her temples.

"*I guess you better win, then,*" Amára said. Kassi perked up, studying Amára. As if reading her mind, Amára said, "*And no, I'm not going easy on you tomorrow. I want my team to win, too.*"

The door opened and Savriah peeked her head out. "You should probably get some sleep, Kassi. Big game tomorrow!"

"I'll be right there-eh," Kassi said in English, standing up.

Amára stood and gave Kassi a hug. *"Good luck tomorrow. Ashkana tuv!"*

"You, too. Ashkana tuv, ashté!"

Kassi closed the door and slumped to the floor. Savriah was already fast asleep and snoring. Kassi took a moment before returning to bed. Amára was right. The only way back to Paradise with all the people she loved was by winning the Siren Games herself. She had to defeat Amára tomorrow.

Kassi stood and silently paced the room to the rhythm of Savriah's loud breathing. *Winning against Amára means believing it first.* She heard Coach Rockson's voice in her mind, *You have to see it in your mind, first. Believe it will happen. Enter the field as victors who are just realizing the inevitable.*

Their team saying popped into her head. *Singing small doesn't serve the worlds.* She served no one by holding back. After a beat, she retired to bed and fell right asleep.

The team met for breakfast the next morning. Vander asked, "How'd everyone sleep last night? You chas ready to sing it?"

"I slept like a baby last night," Savriah said with a yawn.

"So you peed the bed twice and woke up screaming?" Fille asked, eyeing her.

"I slept, I slept like a cat," Adonis said.

"Now that's more like it," Fille said, cuffing Adonis on the shoulder.

"Kassi, what about you? You with us today?" Vi'ella asked.

"I'm ready to sing it!" Kassi said.

After breakfast, they found themselves standing on the springboards directly above the waterfield. It was a windy day and the water looked cold and unsettled. Rehearsing a meditation exercise to restore her calm, Kassi closed her eyes, found the tension in her body, and released it one by one. By the time she opened her eyes, she was alone. Her team was already in the water. With one final deep breath, Kassi dove. She lapped the perimeter a few times, looking out over the crowds and feeding off their energy.

Sweeping her eyes over the faces in the stands, Kassi didn't see her father in his usual spot. He had always been there for every game, recital, tournament, and performance. His cheers carried over the crowd–Kassi could always pick his voice out. While he wasn't there in person today, Kassi knew he would be watching from home–all her family would be.

During her final lap, Kassi spotted a familiar face in the stands. *Nikola?* "What's he doing here?" Kassi thought out loud.

"Who? Who's here?" Adonis asked.

"Nothing, never mind."

"Kassi," Coach Rockson's voice rang in her helmet. "Today, I want you to focus on your strengths. Amára knows your old weaknesses, and she'll try to expose those as much as possible. But you've turned many of those old weaknesses into your best strengths. Use that. Blast it out the gate with what you're best at. Don't second guess yourself, and don't you dare get down on yourself! This is your moment!"

Charleston won the kickoff. Their end gate lit up a brilliant purple, while Miami maintained their robin-egg blue as their team color. Team Miami huddled for final notes.

"Vander, do you mind if I pick the first song?" Kassi asked.

"You feelin' a vibe?" Vander asked.

"Yisû!"

"Let's run with it!" Vander said with a nod.

"What song you got?" Vi'ella asked.

"Army of Queens and Kings," Kassi said.

"One of my favorites," Vi'ella said with an approving nod.

Vander shouted, "Alright chas. You heard her. Singing small doesn't serve the worlds!"

"Sing it with sháloor!" They recited.

ARMY OF QUEENS AND KINGS

If only one moment

Can put the wheels in motion
And all it takes
Is a little faith
Could I become the master
The one with all the answers
To save us all
From an endless fall
To win this
And be the one to end this
I'll build a thousand bridges
To start the greatest Army of Queens and Kings

If I win this battle
But lose the greater struggle
What do I gain
From a meaningless pain
One heroic action
Is not enough to last when
Everything fades
So with every day
I'll win this
And be the one to end this
I'll build a thousand bridges
To start the greatest army of queens and kings
Army of queens and kings

If I can believe in
All I'm meant to be then
Couldn't you too
And I could rise with you
To win this
And be the ones to end this
We'll build a thousand bridges
To start the greatest army of queens and kings

Me believe it the only thing in front of me is
Me not seeing the only thing in front of me is

IN EVÉIK

Lô hanyaþi zoshukanat
Buvi moda li kolóbé lev gludat
I amni lénû famat
Bud în toba trovat
Téad gorûd li þéné nayat
Li zo kin amni li ripostóat
Shi zînaríd amni bizat
Dari în ikirîm káthiat
Shi ris ramat
I bud li zobé shi ikir ramat
Kudad moshaníd în alf adiróbé nayat
Shi dimaríd li itorlu sebuté van bôritóat i savrînóat

Lô risíd ram bátelé nayat
Da perdod li itoród luité
Té dai huth nayat
Dari în sîmínáchîm dolerat
Zo hérosét sookiat
Bud néz káfibé shi mishar, máti
Píthar tashéat
Hûn kin taji tag
Kudad ikird ramé nayat
Kudad risíd ramat nayat
I bud li zobé shi ikir ramat
Shi dimaríd li itorlu sebuté van bôritóat i savrînóat
Sebuté van bôritóat i savrînóat

Lô buvid truvîníd lev nayat
Amni buda sîmínor nayabé, tum
Téam tuv gam

I téad arugíd kin tuvé nayat
Shi ikird ramat
Tílena sobri bézûat
Shi ris ramat
I bud li zobé shi ikir ramat

Truvîn famé mwa, bud li hanyaþi shéané lev traþ van
    mwaat
Néz tazách mwabé, bud li hanyaþi shéané lev traþ van
    mwaat

Her teammates took their positions. Today, Kassi would be playing midfield since she was the only one fast enough to guard Amára. After the kickoff, Charleston cleared the center quickly, taking Kassi's team by surprise. The center gate lit up bright purple.

Amára caught a pass down field and Kassi was on her. Before Amára could get a pass off, Kassi got a hand on the disc and sent it spiraling out of bounds into the glass.

Charleston still retained possession. They passed it in and sent a cross directly down the middle. Miami defenders deflected the first shot. Amára caught the rebound behind her and kicked it on the swivel as Kassi dove the wrong direction. It was a bullet shot into the outer rim of the goal, past both goalies. Adonis and Catelyn swarmed the far end and prevented the ricochet. 2-0. Kassi cursed under her breath.

"It's alright, Kassi," Coach Rockson said. "Bounce right back!"

Miami kicked off with a series of passes near midfield. Kassi caught a pass and flipped it back to Adonis who sent it barreling forward through the center gate toward Ganna on the other side. Amára was there to intercept, catching it on her foot and flicking it back through the center to one of their gaters. Once again, the gate lit up purple.

They charged down the field with Amára passing it through

defenders. Kassi pushed the limits of her speed, trying to swim in front. Amára was still too fast. Rather than give up, Kassi caught Amára's tailwind and propelled herself forward just in time to block a pass. Murrey snagged the deflection and made a quick counter. They cleared the center as Vander caught it on the other end and charged down field. Kassi blasted toward goal with Amára matching her speed. Vander and Vi'ella threaded the defense waiting for support.

"Cross it!" Kassi shouted.

Vi'ella sent a well-timed disc directly in front of Kassi. Kassi plowed forward, flipping at the very last second to swing her foot forward and tap the disc right between the two goalies–GOAL! Cheers erupted from the stands. Vander wrestled forward to knock in the ricochet point, but the disc grazed his fingertips and sailed out of bounds. 2-2. Amára nodded with approval at her cousin.

Charleston kicked off and sent a quick one-two pass through the center gate. It flared purple behind them as Amára slipped through three defenders before dumping the disc off to another forward. She faked right, then rocketed down field. Before Kassi could pivot, Amára was wide open for a through pass down the middle. With a graceful backflip shot and immaculate precision, she scored again. This time, her teammate rebounded it back through the end gate for the extra point. 5-2.

Kassi took a pass and faked right of the center gate before sending a heel pass to Savriah who shot the disc through the center to Vi'ella. Before defenders could respond, she slotted the disc through two of them right to Vander who made a run for it. He took a shot. One of the goalies got a hand on the disc. Kassi managed to snag the rebound before Amára could swipe it. Crossing it back through the middle, Vander hooked it through both goalies for another goal. Defenders retrieved the disc, preventing a ricochet. 5-4.

For Amára's kickoff, instead of the usual pass, she sent the disc sailing through the center gate from the start. None of the gaters were ready for it. It brushed off of a Miami gater's arm before a Charleston forward scooped it up and claimed it, clearing the center. It was a bold move that paid off. Miami scrambled to regroup but Amára and her well-coordinated offense had all the momentum.

Kassi swam as she sang with all her core strength, keeping four bulbs lit as she torpedoed to intercept. She wasn't fast enough. Amára faked a side-bicycle shot, spinning full circle and popping it to one of her forwards who had a wide open shot–goal, no ricochet point. 7-4.

Miami kicked off and Amára predicted the pass, stealing the disc and making a quick counter. Kassi moved to defend. Amára cleared the center for Charleston, sending the disc downfield to a forward who had made a run behind the defense. He caught the goalies off guard and took a shot. Tallie managed to get a finger on it, but it wasn't enough. The disc went through for an additional two points–no ricochet point. 9-4. Charleston was pulling ahead. Kassi had to do something.

Miami kicked off and Kassi took the pass. Joshi was conspicuously open–likely one of Amara's tricks. Kassi faked a pass to him and sent it to Savriah instead. Amára had already bolted for Joshi and was thrown off. Savriah passed it right back to Kassi who flew through four defenders. Vander read the play and provided a pass option, drawing two defenders. It was enough to give Kassi an open shot, and she took it. The goalies scrambled, but couldn't block it in time. Vander swung around back and knocked in the ricochet point. 9-7. It wasn't over yet.

The halftime whistle blew. For the entire first half, both teams had been in rare form, exhaustion lining their faces. Their very lives depended on winning this game, and it showed.

After a short breather, the brutal contest continued. Back and forth it went, both teams demonstrating exceptional skill. Still, between Kassi and Amára, Amára had proven to be the better player, and Charleston held the lead because of it. It was 14-11 with four minutes left on the clock.

Charleston kicked off after the most recent goal. Miami had to force a turnover. Kassi couldn't allow Amára's team to score again. Amára sent the disc through the center to one of her gaters. Savriah got a hand in the way and sent the disc wobbling right into Catelyn's hands. She quickly responded by sending it back through the center. Gaters on the other end scrambled to retrieve it. A Charleston gater eventually gained control of it and sent it right back through. It was a tussle back and forth until Johnes from Miami bounced a pass that Kassi barely snagged with her fingertips. It wasn't pretty, but it worked.

Kassi kicked it back to Nida on defense who shot a bullet pass down the line to Vander. He made a break for it. Fille was there for support and Kassi swam forward to assist. Vander took a shot on goal, but one of the goalies caught it and sent it back toward the center.

Another scuffle ensued as Charleston pressed to reclaim the center gate. It was one blocked pass after another until Oake, now a gater, took possession and sent it back to their defenders. The center gate remained blue.

Kassi swam back to take a short pass from her defense. She thrusted directly toward Amára who was ready for her. Amára kept her from passing the midway line as Kassi scrambled up and down, side to side, looking for an opening. Amára almost stole the disc a few times, but Kassi managed to keep it away.

Finally, she timed it perfectly, throwing off Amára just enough to find an opening. She launched forward. Defenders rushed her. She sent a through pass to Vander who had made a run toward the center. With a sneaky heel pass, he flicked it right back to Kassi. Amára was positioned to intercept, her hand stretched to snag the disc.

Reach!

Kassi managed to pull forward and snatch the disc just before Amára could swipe it. She sent it wide left to Vi'ella a split second before Amára reached a foot out to block. Vi'ella caught it and Kassi pushed downfield.

She and Amára raced toward goal as Vi'ella sent in a beautiful cross. They blasted forward, wrestling with each other, both with four bulbs lit and extended hands. Amára spiraled to the inside and looked like she might beat Kassi to the disc. Kassi timed her boost and propelled herself just as Amára caught the disc, stealing it right out of her hands. Rolling outward as Amára fought to reclaim the disc, Kassi turtle kicked the disc toward goal. It didn't have enough heat on it, but Fille swooped in and caught it, kicked on the swivel and redirected the shot through the goalies. 14-13.

Once again, Kassi and Amára grappled as they clamored for the disc on the other end of the gate.

C'mon Kassi! Reach!

Kassi flexed, every muscle in her body cooperating, as she sang with all the power she could muster. Lighting the fifth bulb, her center thruster propelled her forward as Kassi, for the first time in her life, out swam her best friend. It was enough for her to catch the shot and send it back through for the extra point, tying the game. 14-14. The crowds went ludicray with riotous applause.

They floated for a beat to catch their breath. Kassi gulped air and could see Amára huffing from the exertion. She shot Kassi a look of surprise, holding up the number five with her hand. Kassi smiled with a shrug.

Charleston kicked off for the final minute of the game. Kassi did her best to calm her breathing and focus. They couldn't let it go into overtime.

Kassi and Amára struggled after the disc, neither of them managing to out swim the other. They were constantly grasping and reaching, getting in each other's way and preventing any passes or shots. Charleston continued trying to get the disc to Amára, but Kassi was there every time, swatting away at it. Whenever Miami got the disc, they would try getting it to Kassi. Amára was right there blocking those passes, as well. No one had cleared the center and time was running out.

Savriah intercepted a pass and shuffled it to Vander. He plowed forward as the gate lit bright blue. Amára shot forward to intercept, freeing up Kassi. He kicked a magnificent, perfectly-timed pass right to Kassi. Amára realized her mistake and tried to correct it, rushing Kassi. It was too late. Kassi launched a bullet of a shot from distance, rocketing between both goalies to score two points with only seven seconds left on the clock. Vi'ella dove for the extra point, barely missing. 14-16. For the first time in the game, Miami had taken the lead.

With seven seconds left, Amára kicked off and sent the disc straight forward to the center gate once again. They didn't have time for anything else. It was a long shot. Gaters fumbled for the disc back and forth until Savriah dove on the disc, wrapped both arms around it and held on for dear life. The buzzer rang. Game over.

Miami had won.

Kassi's teammates burst into wild celebrations, eventually coming together and locking arms. Many swam in a giant circle, throwing their heads back with ear-to-ear grins. More of her teammates joined the victory circle, roping Kassi in. Kassi had played the greatest game of her life. Not only had she swam faster than her best friend, but by the end of the game, she had also outplayed her.

Amára swam to her. They touched helmets.

"I've never seen you play like that," Amára said in Evéik, gulping air and sips of water between words.

"I've had really good teachers," Kassi said, still trying to catch her breath as beads of sweat poured down the side of her face.

"Well, now you'll have to win it for the both of us!" Amára placed both hands on Kassi's shoulders. *"I can't believe you swam faster than me. You lit the fifth bulb and went supernova!"*

"I wish you could join us," Kassi lowered her eyes.

"I will join you. After you win," Amára said with a smile.

They both floated in silence for a moment. Kassi noticed movement around them. Glancing up, she saw both teams locking arms in a moment of unified deference to honor all the 400s who made it to the Games. Many from Team Charleston had tear-streaked cheeks as they knew this defeat meant elimination. It meant returning to the Trench. Despite this, they gave a low bow to Team Miami, their fellow 400s. Amára quickly swam up to join them. Kassi joined Team Miami as they followed suit and bowed in return.

"I'll be with you, Kassi!" Amára said, now surrounded by her teammates. *"Ashkana tuv!"*

"You always have been, Ama. Ashkana tuv, méshû," Kassi cried, which being translated, means "I love you, always."

END

www.ingramcontent.com/pod-product-compliance
Lightning Source LLC
Chambersburg PA
CBHW060604300726
48975CB00005B/1436